AMERICAN *fugue*

To Alan
with my love

Alexis
10/8/2008

AMERICAN *fugue*

a novel by
ALEXIS STAMATIS

translated by **DIANE THIEL**
and **CONSTANTINE HADJILAMBRINOS**

etruscan press

Etruscan Press
Wilkes University
84 West South Street
Wilkes-Barre, PA 18702

www.etruscanpress.org

Printed in the United States of America

Publishers Cataloging-in-Publication
(Provided by Quality Books, Inc.)

Stamatis, Alexis.
    [Amerikanike phounka. English]
    American fugue / by Alexis Stamatis; translated by
Diane Thiel and Constantine Hadjilambrinos.
    p. cm.
    ISBN-13: 978-0-9797450-2-7
    ISBN-10: 0-9797450-2-0

    1. Identity (Psychology)—Fiction. 2. Emigration and
immigration—Fiction. 3. United States—Emigration and
immigration—Fiction. 4. Middle West—Fiction.
5. Greek fiction, Modern. 6. Psychological fiction.
I. Thiel, Diane, 1967— II. Hadjilambrinos, Constantine.
III. Title.

PA5630.T285A8313 2008   889'.334
            QBI08-600127

Designed by Nicole DePolo

The Etruscan Press translation and publication of the present edition of *American Fugue* has been made possible by a grant from the National Endowment for the Arts and the National Book Center of Greece.

NATIONAL
ENDOWMENT
FOR THE ARTS
A great nation
deserves great art.

Etruscan Press is committed to preserving ancient forests and natural resources. We elected to print this title on 30% post consumer recycled paper, processed chlorine free. As a result, for this printing, we have saved:

6 Trees (40' tall and 6-8" diameter)
2,108 Gallons of Wastewater
4 million BTU's of Total Energy
271 Pounds of Solid Waste
508 Pounds of Greenhouse Gases

Etruscan Press made this paper choice because our printer, Thomson-Shore, Inc., is a member of Green Press Initiative, a nonprofit program dedicated to supporting authors, publishers, and suppliers in their efforts to reduce their use of fiber obtained from endangered forests.

For more information, visit www.greenpressinitiative.org

Environmental impact estimates were made using the Environmental Defense Paper Calculator. For more information visit: www.papercalculator.org.

Etruscan Press is a 501(c)(3) nonprofit organization.
Contributions to are tax deductible as allowed under applicable law.
For more information, a perspectus, or to order one of our titles,
contact us at etruscanpress@gmail.com

TABLE OF CONTENTS

PART ONE
THE CANARY IN THE MINE

PART TWO
IN THE BELLY OF THE WHALE

A. LAURA

B. CHICAGO

C. LANDYLAND

PART THREE
NEW YORK

Acknowledgments

A major portion of this book was written at the "Residence for European Writers," at the "Villa Mont Noir" in France, where my residency was funded by a fellowship from the "Conseil General du Nord," and another at the "House of Literature," at Lefkes, Paros Island, where my residency was sponsored by EKEMEL.

The idea for this book came to me while I was visiting the U.S. as a participant of the International Writing Program of the University of Iowa. My participation at the IWP was sponsored by a Fulbright Artist Grant from the Fulbright Foundation in Greece. I want to thank the staff of the IWP, and especially its director Christopher Merrill, and the staff of the Fulbright Foundation, in particular Artemis Zenetou.

For their invaluable help, I thank Loula Anagnostaki, Sofia Nikolaidou, Stefanos Dandolos, Nicole Lafazani, Dimitris Liberopoulos, Dimitris Sotakis, Stratis Haviaras, and Thanassis Cheimonas.

Translators' Preface

ALEXIS STAMATIS BELONGS TO A NEW GENERATION of Greek writers—
a generation that is in some ways similar but in many important ways different from those that preceded it. From the eighteenth century through
the last decade of the twentieth century (a period that includes the struggle for liberation from Ottoman rule; the establishment of the modern
Greek state and expansion to its current borders, 1830 to 1922; two world
wars; and several periods of military dictatorship), generations of Greek
writers tended to focus on elaborating on the Greek experience-from
exploring the historical and cultural connections of ancient Greece and
Byzantium with modern Greece to delving into the contemporary or
recent history of the nation. To consider just a few illustrative examples,
the works of the writers best known in the U.S.—Elytis, Kavafy,
Kazantzakis, and Seferis—have as major themes the relevance to their
personal as well as national experience of the Classical, Hellenistic, and
Byzantine history, the effects of the disastrous war in Asia Minor (1918-
1922), and the Second World War and the Axis occupation. The subse-
quent generation, which also includes names that are not unfamiliar to
American audiences such as Tachtsis, Tsirkas, and Vasilikos, continued
the tradition of focusing on Greek history as their works dealt with the
experiences of the occupation, the civil war that followed, and the military dictatorship of 1967-1974. In effect, for most of Modern Greek history, the works of Greek writers served to present the nation's experience
to the world.

The latest generation of writers—often referred to as the post-Polytechnic generation-whose works began to appear in the last decade of the twentieth century is so diverse as to resist classification into a single homogeneous group. Nevertheless, in this generation writers such as Amanda Michalopoulou, Soti Triantafillou, and of course Alexis Stamatis do share a significant quality: they possess a more cosmopolitan outlook in terms of the focus of their work. Contemporary Greek writers are far more likely to write books that are set outside Greece. Having grown up with the universal constants of rock and roll (as well as other international music), international cinema and television, and now the Internet, this generation is often driven by the need to explore the multiple and complex dimensions of being "citizens of the world" (the fundamental meaning of the Greek word "cosmopolitan").

American Fugue is a prime example of this important type of contemporary Greek novel—not only taking place in but also moving comfortably through an international landscape. This novel continues to examine the basic themes that are persistent in all of Stamatis,s fiction works: an all-consuming but apparently changeable past, the flight to escape one's personal demons, and most importantly, the search for personal identity that is ultimately revealed only through what is unknown to the self. The treatment of these themes is also characteristic of the author's other novels-travel narrative on the surface, mystery or thriller with an existential dimension at another level, but ultimately a quest for self-discovery and personal redemption. *American Fugue* is not only representative of Stamatis's body of fiction; it is his strongest novel to date. Here the author approaches his basic themes with a higher level of intensity, including even the hero's attempt to literally change his own identity. This raises fundamentally important questions. Can people change the course of their lives in a truly basic way? Can one's personality be changed at will? Is it possible to re-write one's own life narrative? And, ultimately, what constitutes being a "writer"—what is the nature of creative writing?

American Fugue is a literary novel that utilizes effectively the style of fast-paced intrigue characteristic of popular fiction and is stylistically emblematic of Stamatis's work. As Nicholas Papandreou says, "Alexis Stamatis always starts his books smoothly, seductively so, but one chapter in you find yourself rushing the pages, intrigued, amazed, surprised. Born with the story-DNA in his genes, his fast-paced novels, unlike so many others, maintain a high literary sensibility." Stamatis's style captivates the reader, but the true power of *American Fugue* is that it continues to reverberate after the reading is done. By treating the universal theme of self-discovery both by what is said and what is left unsaid, and by raising, but not fully answering, important questions, Stamatis has created a book that is different for each reader—even different for each reading.

Alexis Stamatis has been hailed as "one of the most gifted writers of his generation" (Françoise Noiville, *Le Monde*) in both Greece and Europe. In addition to ten books of fiction, Stamatis has also published six collections of poetry. That he is first and foremost a poet is made apparent by his approach to prose writing. His language is rich in vivid imagery, metaphor, simile, and other poetic devices.

The poetic character of Stamatis's prose, along with the theme of the book, made *American Fugue* an irresistible choice for us to translate. While the richness of the language made the work especially appealing to a fellow poet, it presented some significant translation challenges. In many ways, translating *American Fugue* was more akin to translating a long poem than a novel. The book is full of instances where words, sentences, and even entire passages have layered meaning. This complicated significantly our task of rendering Stamatis's work.

For one example of many, on page 151, the sentence beginning "we imagine a face" presented several levels of difficulty. The literal translation is "we prepare a face, and then we meet it." In Greek, person and face are the same word, so the duality of meaning in this choice of a Greek word could not be conveyed in English with a single word. We had to offer a poetic alternative to capture the two concepts: "we imagine a face, we conjure a person, and then we meet her."

Similarly, in the paragraph on page 287 that begins, "an icy feeling permeated him down to the bones," the short sentence that follows contains layers of difficulty in translation. One might first be inclined to translate it literally: "the weather had changed permanently." This, however, doesn't make much sense in English. Another possible translation might be "the weather had changed drastically." But given the previous paragraph's focus on the character's desire to be an "exile from time," it is clear that Stamatis was playing on the duality of the Greek word, Καιρος, which can mean both "weather" and "time." The word όριοτικα means "permanently." The real intention of the author was that the "time had changed permanently." In this articulation, however, the more visceral sense of the weather is lost. Thus, we decided to translate the sentence as "There was a permanent shift in temperature" in order to more closely convey both layers of meaning.

A peculiar difficulty—one that might also be attributed to the writer being a poet at heart—was that the name of the novel's main character is never revealed. This means that the hero is always referred to as "he" (note that in poems written in the third person the name of the character is rarely revealed). In Greek, this does not pose a serious problem as there are two forms of the pronoun "he": αυτός (this one) and εκεινός (that one). In fact, there are two forms for all of the third person personal pronouns in Greek. The two forms can be used to make it possible to easily distinguish actions by two persons without having to refer to them by name. This, however, becomes problematic when translating into English where only a single pronoun "he" is available to refer to each character. Ultimately, we addressed the problem by minimizing the instances where we would have to use the personal pronoun, by changing the syntax, or by substituting where we could the names of the other characters for the pronoun.

Despite or perhaps because of the challenging nature of the work, the translation of *American Fugue* was a deeply satisfying experience. There is something profoundly gratifying in being able to present to a new audience a book with the depth and poetic complexity of this novel that is simultaneously a thrilling narrative. We hope that you will enjoy it as much as we have.

Many thanks to the National Endowment for the Arts and to the Greek Embassy for granting the 2007 International Literature Award that funded our translation and the publication of this book in the U.S. Thanks to our extended family, with special gratitude to our brother, John Thiel, who offered a keen reading of the work in progress during his visit with us in New Mexico while on his own journey across the country. Thanks to our three young children over whose infant and toddler heads their parents discussed many difficult translation points. We appreciate their remarkable patience and are inspired daily by their startling and poetic translations of the world. We dedicate this translation, our first book project together, to our children:

For Christabel, For Aria, For Alexander

Diane Thiel
Constantine Hadjilambrinos

Per me si va nella citta dolente,
Per me si va nell' eterno dolore,
Per me si va tra la Perduta Gente.*

DANTE,
Inferno, III, 1-3

Through me pass into the painful city,
Through me pass into eternal grief,
Through me pass among the Lost People.

PART ONE

THE CANARY IN THE MINE

Εγό

IF, AS THE SAYING GOES, the past is a foreign country, then he had been exiled to its territory for many years now. A foreigner, alone in his own country. He had to leave, to place at least an ocean in between the past and the present. That's why he was going across to the New World. To a country in which the pursuit of happiness is enshrined in the Constitution. He was not going in order to explore a new country, but in order to abandon himself to her liberating power. For the possibility that she could put out this second heart whose beat measured the past constantly inside him.

The light fell vertically—he was possibly the only one with it on. He opened his wallet. There, in the coin compartment, the last melatonin pill. He swallowed it with saliva. He looked around, one hundred and eighty degrees. Window, aisle, emergency exit.

In the net on the back of the seat, a magazine with a canary on its cover. On the small screen a Hollywood movie—old, black and white. A scene inside a mine. He watched for a while. Suddenly a spark. The mine. The canary. The canary in the mine. Old-time coal miners who, before entering the tunnels, would lower a canary to check if it was safe. If there was not enough oxygen the bird was a first indicator—it would die.

Sleep refused to come. He opened the newspaper. To find out what was going on. For the dispatches he would have to send back. "The 'Swift Boat Veterans' cast doubts on Kerry's record during the Vietnam War." Photo of Kerry. Tall, stiff back, dry. Further down: "Hurricane Ivan will hit Florida." *The Midwest is not anywhere near Florida*, he thought. *About as far as Poland from Greece.* He was not heading to a country but to a continent. In a few hours, everything would be ten thousand kilometers behind him. He was sending himself to the biggest mine in the world. Like a canary. To check if there was oxygen.

He was not yet forty years old and his parents were dead. That is, his mother was dead. His father was dead only to *him*. They had not spoken to each other in eleven years. Nothing. Silence. His wife had left him: "I don't feel we are a plural any more," she'd said. "What plural?" he had asked. "'I' is singular, 'we' plural." They had not made love in the ten months before their separation. He could not—not any more.

He had no kids. Almost no friends. He lived only for himself. How is it to live for yourself? Like there is no God, no universe, no humankind, no life on earth, no heaven, no hell. Everything a dream—an endless, dark, stupid dream.

He took out his pen. He wrote a single word: Εγώ (I). He scribbled it out immediately and rewrote it. This time with an omicron. Εγό. Εγό: the word with its closed letter, the omicron a cage full of blood and memory. As he wrote, the light, in synch with the small bumps of the plane, repeatedly cast shadow and light upon his face, as if an invisible pen were drawing lines and roads directly on his skin.

He was a writer. In other words, the window, the aisle, and the emergency exit all at once.

Forget! Remember!

THE THIRD FLIGHT WAS THE SHORTEST. Chicago to Cedar Rapids. Iowa City, despite proudly carrying the name of the entire state, did not even have an airport. After twenty-two hours in the bellies of airplanes and the bowels of airports, he was at last reaching his destination. He looked down, at the landscape. An infinite flat expanse. Antonioni's *Zabriskie Point* jumped into his mind.

Through the earphones, Dylan:

> I'm walkin' through streets that are dead
> Walkin', walkin' with you in my head
> My feet are so tired
> My brain is so wired
> And the clouds are weepin'.

The clouds are weeping. He looked at the last faint traces being cut up by the wing. The clouds were dissolving, retreating into the sky. And the ground was beginning. "Ladies and gentlemen, we will be landing in a few minutes. Our captain, Marshall Fugelman, and the crew wish you a pleasant stay in Iowa." He turned again to the window. He was unable to focus his attention anywhere other than the aluminum crosses in the windows of the dispersed houses below. Like crosses of martyrdom, washed clean of blood. Something cold, human, old. Geraniou Street. Number six. Polar cold. Snow on the ground. February. His winter coat on, alone, shivering beneath. The house blinking like a Christmas tree. She is inside. He outside, in the cold, watching. What? Nothing in particular. He just watched. Ever since he was a child he was the one watching, listening, observing, daydreaming. He turned up the volume of the music, to dispel the memory. Impossible. *When we were browsing each other's faces...* he remembered one of her letters.

This is the price of being a writer: being pursued by the past. Mercilessly. If he were a mechanic, it would have been difficult for memory to affect him so strongly. There are cures for people of action. Things are more difficult for those who live inside their heads.

By the time he got back to the small apartment he was renting, he had already caught a nasty cold. But it was not the cold that held him, for the next four months, first in the hospital and then bedridden. Body and soul were now living two different lives. He was Prometheus in reverse. He had chosen his own punishment. The vulture ate not his liver but his heart. He lived chained to an alien creature: his body. So many small deaths, was it important which one would be the final?

And truly, he had come close to death. But he lived. And there, in the hospital, at home, he went over everything in his mind. Some acquaintances came to visit him—mostly because they felt obligated—and on the third day, she came as well. And in the half hour she stayed, she cried nearly the whole time. For him, it felt like the weeping of a mother or a sister. An older sister. It was the last time he would see her.

When the doctors allowed him to get up, he spent the first two weeks in front of the TV. He watched six movies per day. His favorite directors. Alphabetically. In reverse. He began with Hitchcock and *Psycho* and ended with Antonioni—who else?—and

Profession: reporter.

At some point in time, someone, it seems, remembered him. He was asked to give an interview. "The subject will be white" they told him. "White as in blank paper?" he asked. "White in general—if to you, as a writer, it evokes blank paper, then you can talk about blank paper." He said various brave things: that it had never happened to him, that rather the opposite—he was always too full of ideas to pursue them all. Lies. For the last six years, long before his illness, he had been struggling to finish a novel. He would sit in front of his keyboard, like an angler with his fishing pole over the water. Nothing would bite. The screen would remain blank.

Slowly, he began to go out: first the corner store, then a walk in the nearby grove, later to the city center. But he was no longer the same person. He seemed to have lost all ability to participate in life. Nothing affected him. He observed the world around him like a naturalist on field research. Totally disinterested in things that he used to care about deeply, he had found a little corner of the universe in which to exist. Certain events in his immediate family—the few family members that were left—did not even touch him in any way. He lived silently, not writing, observing. At some point, however, this superimposed zen began to crack. His old self started to squeeze in through the fissures.

And then came the phone call. An invitation out of nowhere. Three months at a university in the U.S. Based in Iowa City, a small college town. All costs covered. He wondered why he was chosen. Maybe it was his next to last book that had been translated into English and was published in the U.K.; perhaps it was his excellent English—the result of many years of study but also of practice with his best friend, an American from San Francisco. What was most important was that the invitation came at the right moment. Also invited were about thirty-five other writers from around the world. Most were authors of thrillers and detective novels. The obligations were few. Peace and quiet. He'd have time to write. And what he wanted most of all was to write. Again. Something.

He wrote mostly thrillers. Not the detective kind—existential thrillers. Novels in which a lonely hero would get drawn into intrigues, with his life in danger, usually because he had inadvertently entered some kind of a danger zone. There, the hero would struggle to overcome the hurdles with his only assets—his imagination and alertness. However, the fast-paced action was a vehicle. The real themes of his books were lodged beneath the layer of intrigue.

He used to enter a room like a lion, looking for his prey. He used to be able to find it everywhere: in the silences, the crisp creases of pants, the quick glances, the gestures. Everything was material that he would grasp with his jaws and take to his lair. And there he would tear into it—sometimes violently, sometimes slowly, sensually. But for the last six years the lion had been captive, in a cage, fed by the zoo-keepers.

He wanted that sensation again. To write literature again, a novel, something other than a newspaper article. Not that he would not write that as well. Writing for the newspaper was his main source of income. "You are going to be there during the national election campaign season; we want you to send us regular dispatches," the newsroom editor had told him. Bush vs. Kerry. The cowboy and the professor.

He looked down again; now he could see details clearly. A boy—shorts, baseball cap—was pitching rocks at a trash can. In front, on the street, a car was moving slowly—the triangular sign of a driving school on its roof. In a field, five large cows with black patches were grazing peacefully. And in the forefront, hazy, reflected by the plexiglass of the plane's window, his own image. The long face with sunken eyes, the thin eyebrows, the slightly hooked nose, the strong jaw, the full lips with the two curved wrinkles like framing parentheses.

Suddenly the plane banked and everything—boy, car, cows, reflection—disappeared. A few minutes later he felt the thump of landing.

Like nothing

"NOT POKER," said the well-built young man, as he stepped on the brakes at the first red light they encountered since leaving the airport. On the CD, Eminem, in low volume. "Our game is Texas Hold 'em".

"Which is… ?"

"Like two in the hand and five down. You are dealt the two first. Then three are turned face up, down. And the last two, like, one at a time".

"Why do you keep saying 'like'?" he asked.

"What do you mean?"

"Why did you say *like* one at a time? Don't the cards get turned up one at a time?"

"Ah, 'like' is a national epidemic. Wait till you hear the girls talking."

"Yes, so it doesn't really have a meaning—you are not using it in a simile."

"No, don't say that. It gets in everywhere. A cherry on top," said the young man.

"Like a cherry on top?"

"Ha! Just cherry on top…"

"Anyway, how do you play the game?"

"The basic difference is that only one player can win. Like whoever's left at the end."

"That's why it's called 'Texas Hold 'em', eh? Shootout…"

"Shootout… Here in the US, second place is like nothing."

"Like nothing, eh?"

"Like nothing."

They did not talk for a while.

"Are you in the creative writing program?" he asked finally.

"Yes. I volunteered to drive the van for the international program. I've driven all of the foreign writers into town. You are the last one. The Greek, the last. And you speak the best English. Like an American. Perfect pronunciation."

"Thank you. Are you a fiction writer?"

"Yes, mostly short stories."

"Ah… On what subjects?"

"Nothing, like subjects from life, you know… And you?"

"The same," he said.

"Such as?"

"Such as love, death, power. These are the subjects."

"Like sex and money, eh?"

"No. Love, death, and power, as I just said."

"Ah, I get you… I get you…"

Long pause.

"What author do you like?" the young man asked.

"In general?"

"Ours, contemporary."

"Mailer, DeLillo, Pynchon…"

"All old men."

"Well, Banks, Oates…"

"And I like the Beatles."

"Are you pulling my leg?"

"It seems to me you don't read what's current."

"OK, I've read Douglas Coupland."

"I mean the literature of today, like now, that speaks about America."

"It's not easy to fit a country in a book."

"Well, yeah… The landscape is too big. In which case metaphors, like, make sense," said the young man, pleased with his comeback.

"In other words, let's say, a grain of sand as a metaphor for the earth?"

"Or, like, a drop of water as metaphor for the ocean."

"Or the whale as metaphor for the ancestor. And there you can have everything, no? Life, death, history, even unrequited love."

"OK, my friend, I've read *Moby Dick,* and it didn't explain to me anything I want to know about America. Moby, the musician— he gets it. He is Melville's great-grandson you know," said the young man.

"I know. And how do you think America can be explained?"

"It can't be explained."

Shorter pause.

"Wonderful! And may I ask, is the whole landscape like this?" he asked.

"Like what?"

"Like this, wheat fields…"

"Ha! It's not wheat, it's corn fields."

"Anyway, is the whole place the same?"

"The same, like a carpet. The Turk asked the same thing."

"Did you drive the Turkish writer?"

"Yeah, him and a Korean woman, very beautiful. You're lucky," said the young man.

"Do you think?"

"If you play your cards right."

"I don't gamble any more."

"Not gambling at all is like not being alive."

"That's right."

"So you agree then?"

"I'm saying your use of 'like' is right."

"Ah, like, right."

"Like, right."

A very long pause. The minivan cruised down the highway. The landscape remained unchanged. Endless cornfields on either side.

"Oh, I never introduced myself. My name is Nick," said the young man.

"Yes."

Pause. Nick waited, in vain. When he gave up he asked, "Why did you come? To write?"

"Yes, but not only for that."

"For what else then?"

"To get away."

"To get away? Like, from what?"

"Are you holding the wheel tight?"

"Yes."

"Then look behind you for a moment."

Nick turned and looked back. As the van sped forward, the road sped backward while, right and left, tall corn stalks seemed to close in behind them.

"Turn back now so we don't get killed."

"I don't understand. You came, like, to get away from corn?" the young man asked.

He laughed. "Let it go. It doesn't matter."

Nick turned the music up. They did not talk again for quite a while.

Out there

IT WAS ONE OF THOSE HOUSES you see in films like *The Truman Show*. It looked like a prefab one but it was not. It fit perfectly into the neat, pretty little town, as he had observed it from inside the car. Low, wooden houses, wide, empty streets—like Academias Street in Athens in the month of August, when the entire population of the city, it seems, is away on summer vacations—tall trees, freshly mowed lawns. He even exclaimed to Nick: "It's like they're artificial."

"You see, you've already been infected with 'like,'" answered the young man laughing.

The party was taking place in the back yard. It had gotten dark, and tired from the awfully long intercontinental trip, he could hardly stand on his legs. Nick led him directly to James Frost, the host and director of the program, a likeable man with a small brown beard and spectacles; beside him stood Mel Hepburn, his tall, skinny aide. He had arrived late, and they were all, some sixty people, in the happy mood that comes after the first couple of drinks. He slowly began to make out the other foreign authors. Harim, the Turk, was a red-faced man with long curly hair fixed in a bun and round glasses. It didn't take long to identify the Korean girl: an elegant figure and a face like a figurine; her name was Tan. Gradually, he met all of them. Some of them impressed him. Eki, from Chile, a short man with a well-groomed three-day beard, well known in Latin America, and Aaron, slim, with delicate movements, an author of detective stories from Israel, and finally Martin.

Martin Shawnessey was an Irish poet who, in order to make a living, wrote thrillers under a pseudonym. Already in the first ten minutes of their meeting, he managed—with mellifluous speech, full of symbols, aphorisms and wordplay—to paint, not only a detailed family portrait, but also a whole world, full of images, references to books and theatrical plays. An impressionist of words, with a funny straw hat and braces, he was a professor in Lugano, where he had taken refuge after his second divorce from his Jamaican wife. The rest of the guests were university professors and students of the creative writing program.

Frost was discussing politics with the Turk, the Chilean, and the Israeli. "There is a disease of language in America, an amputation. Anything can be justified by the use of distorted, counterfeit forms. For example, 'compassionate conservatism' was Bush's slogan at the Republican convention. The image, however, that he is foisting is exactly the contrary. It isn't accidental that he made Schwarzenegger call the Democrats 'girly-men.' It's as if he's saying: 'Look, the enemy is so dangerous that there is no place for talking, only action, machismo.' And the scenario has been set up: The Republicans present themselves with a claim to power, while the Democrats appear just interested in obtaining it. It is no coincidence that in Bush's speech there was not one metaphor. Only facts."

He approached them.

"Not 'like,'" he said.

Frost looked at him and smiled.

"Oh, no, with Bush there is no 'like,' there's 'as.' 'As I want.' But how does he manage to sell a rhetoric based on the obvious distortion of reality? By taking advantage of the herd mentality that has its roots in the birth of the American nation. Don't go by what you see here. This is a university town, an island in the ocean. Out there, things are totally different."

"It's that 'out there' that I want to see," he said. He did not, however, mean America.

He returned to the hotel around midnight. His first night. Big room, TV set, high-speed internet. Above the bed there was a poster of Vermeer's painting *A View of Delft*. A marvelous, somewhat cloudy sky, dawn. The air had just cleared up after a sudden shower. Below the clouds and the blue sky, the lively contour of the city of Delft. He felt safe, having such an image above his head. *Better than a cross,* he thought. He fell asleep right away. He woke up at four in the morning because of the jet lag. Melatonin: useless. Not to mention the fact that the room did not have any curtains and that he felt he was sleeping like a camper—he'd wake up with the first light of dawn. He tried to get back to sleep. Impossible. Countless thoughts, mixed up, random. The heart of the problem was slipping away from him. Or rather, he did not allow it to beat. But that was how it was. Naturally, he was not the only one who, within himself, resisted the ferocity of the cannibalistic nature of the human condition. He, like everyone else, perfumed it, redefined it, seasoned it. He was, however, one of the few who knew that the hair in the soup, the dirt under the carpet was not someone else's but his own, his very own. And that was something that hurt, hurt terribly.

Quiet (?) Days in Iowa City

FOR SEVERAL DAYS HE DID NOT SLEEP WELL. Jet lag had knocked him off his rhythm. He spent most of his time in his room, mostly reading and downloading music from the internet—something that amused him somewhat. The rest of the time he spent walking around the small town. He had already come to know every corner of it—it wasn't all that hard. A series of vertical and horizontal streets arrayed in a classic grid pattern. In between, houses, university buildings, fraternities and sororities with the characteristic Greek letters displayed in front: Alpha, Ypsilon, Delta-Phi, Beta, Kappa.

During his wanderings, he tried to keep his mind blank, which, all things considered, he managed to do. But there were times when, behind the street covered with plane tree leaves, in the absolute silence of Java Café (the student coffee shop where everyone read in an almost religious silence) or in the hurried step of some blond co-ed (who—dressed in the "uniform" of the college student: shorts, too-large T-shirt with the university logo, and running shoes—would be walking holding a paper coffee cup like a baton that she needed to pass on to someone somewhere, but to whom and where?) or even in the eyes of Herky the Hawk (the town was full of various statues of the anthropomorphic bird, the mascot of the local University), he would see something irrevocable, something so eternal and immovable, that he would feel the air being sucked away from his lungs and his arteries being filled with images. Old images, painful, sharp, that would circulate inside him, puncturing him like pins. Fortunately, there was the moon that allowed him to forget, an archetypal moon the likes of which he had never seen anywhere else. The way it lit the quiet plain, it looked like a brilliant hole drilled in the sky.

The events of the program were few. During the first week, he did a reading that was broadcast live by the local radio station. With him was Tan, inaccessible in her alabaster beauty, and a Japanese writer, Shimata, who, after reading excerpts from his book *Recollections of a Mummy*, closed explaining that his name means "elegant thinker in the isle of plains."

When it was his turn, he read the first chapter of his last novel, which he had written six years before and now had come to almost hate. Totally distanced, he read as if from a book that someone else had written.

One day he went with Martin to Walmart to buy curtains. In the checkout line, the Irish writer recited Shelley to the trashy blond freckled cashier. On the way back, Martin confided in him that he was in the early stages of a painful and ultimately fatal disease— multiple sclerosis—and began a conversation about life and death. "Death," Shawnessey said almost sweetly, "is the purpose of life. Ceasing to exist fulfills one's existence. Death does not negate being, just as empty space does not negate a solid. Each is a necessary condition for the realization of the other."

The curtains gave him two extra hours of sleep. The following day, he made the great decision and started writing. He made up his mind that the principal character would be a writer, and he moved the action to a university town. *A mystery novel set on a college campus had never been written in Greec*e, he thought. He wrote five thousand words within a week. He introduced the hero by setting him loose in a dreamy situation and then tried to follow the outline. From the first pages, he already had moved away from the subject. He started to transpose phrases and paragraphs back and forth, as if he were playing a game and ignoring the rules. At the end of the week, he printed what he had written, read it out loud, and without a second thought, threw the pages into the garbage and the word processing files in the computer's recycle bin.

At the same time, he wrote articles for the newspaper in Greece. Most of them dealt with the American elections. That was when DVDs with the hostages' beheadings were being sold in the markets of Baghdad for one dollar, when President Bush strongly maintained that Saddam Hussein was behind the September 11 attack, and when the electoral battle was being played in flashback in the marshes of Vietnam, with discussions about what Kerry did—or did not do—in that war.

"Why is it that this all-powerful country operates in such a self-destructive way?" he wrote in the last days of September. "What is it that drives it into a series of fitful, erratic actions? To understand this it's necessary to examine the nation's historical roots. America is a country built by the Europeans, who were trying to escape, and therefore forget, the European nightmare of poverty, persecution, and conflict. It is a country where democracy was based on outstanding humanistic documents. From the beginning, however, something was missing from the basic structure of this 'constructed' motherland. And that was the adhesive material: memory, tradition, historical reference. *Tabula rasa* is a very cruel thing. Even if the best of us are left alone on an almost vacant planet, we will make a mess of it in the first three hundred years. America reminds one today of an adolescent who may have great talents and incredible possibilities but whose body is in upheaval: hormones are playing ping-pong, the libido is crashing automobiles, chaos..."

One Saturday, a local association invited the writers to a picnic in a small park. The hosts were extremely hospitable and had brought along homemade food. Everyone sat on oblong benches, and Mel, Frost's assistant, sat opposite him. Tall, slim, with an aquiline profile, Mel had been itching to talk politics since the early morning. Beside him sat a rather plump man with a gray beard, who gave Mel the cue: "Today, on the radio, a Native American said that war in the world is taking place between two evils: Bin Laden and Bush. He said he was very happy that the one is striking the other. And when the anchor asked him about September 11, he answered that Native Americans have had September 11 for four hundred years." Mel shook his head and said that, statistically, September 11 was not much; we are talking about two high-rise buildings and just 2,500 dead. The man with the beard commented, "For two high-rise buildings we occupied two countries."

After that, the discussion turned, strangely enough, to American football, and Mel laid down his theory, based on the fact that the specific game is a reflection of the American way of life. "Before the Civil War, the game was played on the ground only. After the First World War, the first forward pass was made. That was for America a great symbolic moment. For its moral substance."

At this point, he could not stand it any more. "It's after that, that America started to attack other people," he said, and the two men turned to him at the same time.

"Nah, there was the Mexican War in the 19th century before that," said the man with the beard.

"It all starts with the crusade syndrome. Against the witches of Salem, against the foreigners, against the communists, and now against the Muslims," said Mel. "Against the Other," he added.

"Against the Other," echoed the man with the beard. "We can't exist without an enemy. We create him, we fall in love with him, and we incorporate him in our culture. Like Ahab in *Moby Dick*."

The whale. Again.

"No," said Mel, "in *Moby-Dick* the whale is not the Other, it's Christendom. It isn't accidental that, finally, the pagan of the crew,

Queequeg, harpoons it.

"The whale is Melville himself; the whale is the author," he commented in an undertone. He knew, of course, deep inside himself, that the whale was something entirely different.

Two days later he gave a lecture. The subject: "Why do I write what I write." He was asked what it means to be a Greek author at the beginning of the twenty-first century. "Nothing and everything," he answered. "The real writer is my conscience. *It* records what is happening around me. The setting, the place, might be as likely a courtyard in provincial Greece or an apartment in Prague."

"And what is your identity as an author?"

"My identity is the Other," he answered. "Through him, I understand myself." He partly was telling the truth, despite the fact that inside himself, the "Εγώ" was teetering between the omicron and the omega.

At that moment, he suddenly felt dizzy, the color drained from his face, and he stopped talking. The audience froze. A young woman and a professor jumped up to the stage immediately. They wiped his brow with a wet towel and moved him to the adjoining room. Some ten minutes later, he began to feel like himself again.

He stayed in bed watching TV for two days straight. Watching everything indiscriminately. Political discussions, the Howard Stern show (even the episode about the beauty contest of the mutilated women), *Extreme Makeover* (a reality show for women who decided to change everything about themselves, including their bodies), the History Channel, baseball, the Texas Hold 'em tournament, some crappy movies, everything. In the meantime, he tried not to think, not to remember. He did not always manage to do it. For a few days, life was derailed from its chronological order by a series of flashbacks. How ironic that his convalescence was plunging him into the angst of lost time.

The squirrel

DINA WAS A STUDENT in the poetry section. He met her at a lecture, after he had completely recovered. The next day, they went to a cafe and after that took a stroll along the city's river bank. Her dark blond hair was flowing like "wind-blown wheat fields"—he remembered Hemingway. The pale skin, the slightly protruding chin, and the strong cheek bones made her look a little like Vanessa Redgrave in *Blow Up*. Dina had a seven-year-long relationship with a man from Mexico and was learning Spanish in order to be able to communicate with her in-laws after the upcoming wedding. They stopped at the bank of the Iowa River. It was a small river with dark water that crossed the city. They lay down on the grass—he, leaning on the ground on his elbows, she, on her back.

At a certain moment, as he was saying "in my opinion," she brought her face close to his, and before he could even continue with "in America, space is being dissolved," she leaned over and kissed him. He accepted her kiss as if he were expecting it; the contact of her lips, however, and the nearness of her face surprised him. It had been quite a long while since he had felt another face so close to his. With a shiver, he felt like he was floating out of his body. Almost mechanically, he took her in his arms. There was no one else near them. He started to caress her but when his hand started moving toward her breast, he felt hers grabbing it. "Don't!" she said. They both turned on their backs, and for a while neither said anything. He focused his gaze on a small tree at the river bank. Its shape looked like a human profile. After some time, he felt a dark shape moving to his right. He turned his head and came face-to-face with a squirrel. It had stopped less than ten feet away from him, had stood on its hind legs, and was looking at him straight in the eyes. The little animal's eyes were strangely deep and moist. The squirrel moved its head slightly to the right, as if it were pointing in the direction of the flow of the river. Then it lowered its front legs, stood for a few more seconds looking him in the eyes, and with a few short jumps, disappeared behind the root of a tree.

He sat up. The sun was burning hot, but a cooling light breeze was blowing, making the trees murmur. Seemingly out of nowhere, he felt a strange, sudden wave of happiness. Almost in the same instant, however, the pleasure turned into a shudder. His past had attacked. He tried to push it back at once, awkwardly. The battle raged on, and inevitably, it was not long before he was decisively defeated. There was nothing he could do. He mentally cursed the squirrel's eyes. Another pair of eyes had burned itself in his memory, a penetrating gaze of some ten years ago, on Mount Lycabettus, in Athens. *When we were browsing each other's faces...* He tried to erase it. Impossible. But it was not only *her* eyes. It was others' and others', and others', all of them. Even his own eyes, in the way they were reflected into all those that had once really looked at him. He had been expecting this attack of gazes. Why, however, had it come in that precise moment?

Suddenly, he thought he was facing something big, something totally different. In another gaze, from another time. Not from the past, from a *different* time. He looked in front of him, at the river. Then, all around him. There was nobody. He turned then to Dina, who was lying down with her eyes closed. As if feeling his gaze, her eyelids opened. "Are you alright?" she asked.

"Yes."

The young woman propped herself up on her elbows and looked at him. "I hope that you don't..."

"No, it's alright."

"It's like… like everything all at once."

"Yes, I understand," he said, and without another word, stood up, turned away, and started walking towards the riverbank. The small tree seemed different to him. He wondered if this sensation was due to the different angle or to the *way* he saw it now. Was it a matter of place or of time? The river was flowing slowly. He bent down, took some water in his hands, and splashed his face. Then, he brought the palm of his hand to his face and sniffed it. There was *something* in the scent of this water. He looked up at the sun, at the sky was like a huge bright smile, then back at Dina, who had again lain down and closed her eyes, and turned to the right, following the flow of the river in the direction that the squirrel had "pointed."

He walked along the river bank, following something that was totally unknown to him. The clouds were casting their shadows into the river, creating intricate shapes like rafts crossing the waters. Everything was radiant. The scenery looked familiar, but he did not remember whether it was something he had seen or something he had written. A cord connected the two possibilities, pulling them first in the one and then the other direction. He walked on for about twenty minutes until he reached a point where the river took a sudden turn. Here, there was a clearing and a bench close to the river bank. And there he saw him.

He was about sixty. He was wearing a black jacket, black pants, and a white shirt. He had an oval face, with sharp curved eyebrows, droopy eyelids, large brown eyes, and a short moustache above a refined, voluptuous mouth. They looked at each other. The stranger did not lower his glance, instead made a movement as if inviting him.

He approached and stood before him. From that close, he seemed to be wearing a bit of make-up, with a little shadow around the eyes and imperceptible rouge on the cheeks.

"Sit down." The man motioned to a spot beside him.

He hesitated a bit, but did so.

"Nice, huh?" said the stranger, indicating the river.

"Yes."

"How I would have liked to be seeing it through your eyes," the man said looking at him.

For a moment, he regretted his decision to accept the invitation. He did not have any desire for conversation.

"I think that we are like sealed gondolas crossing the river. How wonderful it would be if we could open up and see things as others see them!"

"I'm sorry," he said, "but I'm not in that kind of mood."

"And in what kind of a mood are you?"

"I don't know."

"But that's what I mean. Nothing helps our mood more than sharing it. To be looking through someone else's eyes," said the stranger slowly and again looked at him intensely.

He felt strange. A subtle threat. Although inside him an impulse was pushing him to talk—and he had so many things to say about everything he had heard—he was afraid. He stood up and, avoiding his eyes, mumbled a confused "Thank you, but I must go," and started walking again, back the way he had come.

"Other eyes. Don't look for other landscapes—look for other eyes," he heard the man's voice behind him.

Back to the future

THE AMPHITHEATER WAS FULL OF STUDENTS. A seminar: International Literature Today. It was his turn to present. The students had already read the first chapter of his book in translation. He asked: "Does anyone know Greek?" No answer. "We'll see about that," he said and started reading slowly:

"It is Zeus' anathema on our epoch for the dynamism of our economies and the heresy of our economic methods and policies that we should agonize between the Scylla of numismatic plethora and the Charybdis of economic anemia." He went on for two or three minutes, reading the paper before him, to conclude: "In my epilogue, I emphasize my eulogy to the philoxenous autochthons of this cosmopolitan metropolis and my encomium to you, kyrie, and the stenographers."

He lifted his head up and looked at the audience. "Did you understand it?"

"Yes," was heard from most of them.

"It is an economic analysis by the former Prime Minister of Greece, Xenophon Zolotas, written in English. However, all the words, except the articles and the prepositions, have a Greek root."

Some brief chuckles—the audience did not seem impressed. He went on with a brief presentation of Greek literature. Solomos, Kavafy, Kazantzakis, Elytis, Seferis.

After that, the students asked him questions: "Do you think that *My Big Fat Greek Wedding* is representative of Greek culture?" "Why do Greeks have such close relationships with their families?" "Your book starts with an intensely sexual scene. I believe that two things in life cannot be described: sex and pain." A slim girl with freckles spoke in the end: "Do books with sex sell a lot in Greece?"

To the last question, he responded, slightly annoyed: "My book has nothing to do with sex. There is a scene in the beginning and another fleeting description in a total of four hundred pages."

"Bravo, Colossus!" said Martin, congratulating him at the end.

The Irishman had started to call him "Colossus," in honor of Henry Miller. He collected his papers, and as he was stepping out in the crisp air, something within him was telling him that he would not be doing another talk in America again.

He did nothing but read during the next few days. The books of a writer, Walker Percy, who had been totally unknown to him. Percy's heroes—isolated, solitary, wandering about as if lost, with no aim, almost lethargic, like shadows—carried him away. He almost never went out. He did not want to see anybody. He also ate less—once a day, some frozen TV-dinners that he heated in the microwave. He read and tried not to think of the past. "We are pilgrims, wayfarers on a trip, neither pigs nor angels," Percy wrote. Nevertheless, he *wanted* to cross from the angelic to the animal, from everyday life to the unforeseen, from repetition to change. But, mainly, from memory to amnesia.

At the student center, which was immediately next to his hotel, there was a theater playing European films. One evening, he went with Tan and Eki to watch *Last Tango in Paris*. A film that he, aware of the subject, had purposefully avoided watching each time the opportunity to do so presented itself. He went this time, hoping the distraction would help him. However, somewhere inside himself, he knew it was almost masochistic. He left ill. He went up to his room and tried to drive away all thoughts. But he could not get the image from his mind: a man and a woman, in an apartment, dressed, approaching one another, looking for a long time into each other's eyes. They suddenly embrace, frantically assaulting one another's bodies, making love, rolling on the floor, screaming and climaxing together in a frenzy, as if a grenade were exploding inside them.

This, however, was not even the most disturbing image. Because there was also the scene with the woman committing suicide and Brando's monologue next to her corpse. She'd stabbed herself. His own dead woman was beautiful, too, with all those flowers in her hair, her chest, her hands, all those multi-colored little bouquets of flowers surrounding her. A flowery sea. They had also applied make-up, but not as heavy as in the film. Although he had not liked this at all, he had not wiped off the dye with the towel, nor had he spoken to her as if she were alive. He had only looked at her, looked at her eyes for a long time, there, at those big eyes that—how ironic!—although wide open, had closed forever of their own will. Perhaps inside himself, he, like Brando, wanted to swear at her, to kiss her, to shake her, to ask her why—why had she done it? But he had remained silent, perhaps because he imagined that the people who bring us into this world, having carried out their mission, have the right to leave it when they choose. Moreover, as they say, suicide is the only true philosophical question that exists. He had, therefore, done nothing. Before leaving, he had simply touched his mother's cold hand for an instant.

In the film, Brando had felt guilty for his wife's suicide. A wife is one thing, but a mother is another; nonetheless, he also had felt guilty, because he had not done anything to prevent it. The courtroom inside him was in session for years, the verdict condemning him every time. The sentence was heavy—he had not proved to be enough of a man, he had not saved her—but the guilt was shared. The main culprit, in his very soul, was the next closest person in his life: his father. And the penalty was exile. He had driven him away from his life. Ever since. Eleven years ago. Eleven years of silence.

He could not get any sleep. He got up and went to write. He could not. The hotel was perfectly quiet. Everyone was long since asleep. He turned on the TV, watched for a little while, and turned it off. Suddenly, he felt something powerful. An impulse? A temptation? It was more like a desire for return, a return to a lost bright landscape, a place from where he had been driven away in the past. A place that, precisely because he had been forced to abandon it, had in some magical way, during the long time of his absence, come to exist independently of himself. But, the strangest thing was that he felt, that in order to return there, he had to get away from everything. Forever. Almost absurd, but that is exactly what he wanted: to keep the absurd alive.

He stayed awake all night. At a certain point, he went to the laptop and started writing an article for the Greek newspaper. It was about the elections, and just as he was reaching the climax—"an inner anger is overflowing..."—he suddenly stopped. He let the phrase hang in the air. He then sent the article by e-mail, like that, unfinished. At dawn he took a shower, drank two cups of coffee, took all his money with him, and went out. The sun in Iowa City on this Saturday morning was still very low, but it was poised for a magnificent vertical ascent.

Lost road

THE CITY HAD JUST WOKEN UP. A few students were walking in the streets, and here and there a few cars were driving by. Peace and quiet. He walked up to the main road, Washington Street. He then turned left, onto Market Street, and walked up about six blocks. Next to the big Post Office building, there was an *Avis* rent-a-car office. It was a single-level construction with a large area on the right side, where the rental cars were. A capital "A" towered above the central entrance, which was closed. He looked at the sign; it would be opening in half an hour. He sat on the ground, next to another statue of Herky the Hawk—Herky as a policeman—and waited. When the manager arrived to open the office, he asked about renting a car.

"For how many days?" the manager asked him.

"How much is it per week?"

"A compact, let's say, $129."

He paid cash in advance and gave his driver's license. The manager made a photocopy, and they went outside to the parking lot. He chose a silver Ford, took along a complimentary map of the state, and drove away.

It did not take him long to get out of town. He drove east, without knowing where he was going. Before long he was crossing end-less cornfields. The sky was pure blue, and the sun that gradually rose made the landscape shimmer. The American countryside was bathed in light, a brilliantly illuminated golden plain. Everything glimmering brightly, as if polished. During the drive, he paid atten-tion to the billboards: "Marvelous Pizza," "The Best Cranberries," "Rancho Motel," "Western World Development," as though he were expecting some sign. The upper part of the windshield was of a greenish color—it acted as a filter against the sun and created a very nice effect, the way it filtered the fields that covered the land-scape all the way to the horizon. When he got tired of watching the yellow-green gradations of color, he centered his attention on the electricity poles, trying to detect a regular pattern in their distances. He had driven for two hours. He was thirsty. For quite a distance , there hadn't been a good place to stop. Finally, he saw a big build-ing on the right side of the road. There was a large sign on top: "Kalona Sales Barn."

He parked the car in front and got out. The sun had climbed a third of the way up the sky's arch. It was already quite hot and everything indicated that it would get even hotter. As he entered the building, he found himself walking along a long corridor, which led to an area shaped like an amphitheater. It was full of people. In the center was an area covered with dirt, like an arena. Opposite the entrance to the arena, behind a high bench, like a judge, sat a bald man with a microphone before him, and next to him a young woman taking notes. In the middle of the arena, a guy with a long beard and a cowboy hat from time to time opened a gate from which would exit sheep, goats, pigs, and small horses. These he would guide solemnly back and forth across the arena. The bald man was speaking constantly at a machine-gun pace, with numbers being the only intelligible part of his speech, while to his right and left, statistical data appeared on two large screens. He realized that he had found himself at a livestock auction. In one of the corners was a counter selling coffee. He ordered a cup, drank it down in almost a single gulp, drank two glasses of water, and went to the toilet. On the inside of the men's restroom door, were stuck two bumper stickers: "Give war a chance: peace through missile superiority" and lower down, "'We are working hard to bring food to your family.' George Bush."

He returned to the amphitheater, watched the auction for a while, and when he got bored with it, walked around the seats, towards the backstage. Down a narrow corridor, he found himself in a raised up area: a huge barn. Underneath, packed in small pens, dozens of sheep, goats, and pigs waited their turn to parade before the potential buyers. Confined in such small spaces, the animals exhibited high anxiety and were constantly moving. Each pen looked like a huge body with multiple flailing limbs. An old man with a straw hat and boots entered the pen with the pigs and started hitting them with a stick.

He turned around and, without looking behind him, went out of the building and climbed in the Ford. He started the engine and sped away.

He drove for another hour on the main road. Sometime later, he found himself at a crossroads. A narrow road was leading to the left. On this side of the main road there was an uprooted signpost. The sign at its end was pointing towards the sky. A strange thing was written on it: "Vieu Gift[1]." Without knowing why, he turned the wheel to the left. After half an hour or so, the road narrowed even further, while the landscape changed dramatically. The cornfields gave way to barren land, and the soil seemed to become drier. About fifteen miles later, the paved road gave way to a dirt road and the cultivated farmland to a desert, with only a few scattered bushes breaking the monotony of the bare earth. The idea of turning back never crossed his mind. Not even when the surface of the road deteriorated further, with plenty of rocks strewn about, nor when all signs of civilization disappeared. The only visible feature of the landscape was hundreds of miles away: a pale mountain range. The sun was by now approaching the top of its arch, and the heat had become unbearable. He rolled up the windows and put on the air conditioning.

He had spent one more hour driving into the unknown, when suddenly he heard a noise from the front of the car, something like a small explosion. The Ford rolled on for a few yards and stopped with a shudder. He got out and opened the hood; smoke was coming out. He checked the antifreeze tank. It was empty. There was a hole on the bottom of the radiator. All the coolant had drained out. He looked around. There was nothing except a low bush on the left side of the road. In front of it, someone had placed a rough cross made from two reddish-brown pieces of wood nailed together. By this time, the sun had reached its zenith and was reflected by the white stones. He sat for a while cross-legged on the ground. From high up came a flapping sound: a swarm of birds. He waited for some time in case a car might come by. Half an hour went by, then one hour. Nothing. He was lost in the middle of nowhere. He stood up, took the rental papers, the money, and the keys from the car, and managed, with difficulty, to push it to the side of the road, beside the cross. He locked it and started to walk straight ahead, to the east. It was a bit windy, and this made the heat more bearable. When he had walked about a mile, he turned and looked back. By now the Ford was nothing more than a black spot in the landscape.

For the next two hours, he walked non-stop. There was no sign of life on the road. The only things he came upon were scattered bones of dead animals, tin boxes thrown away, and two disintegrating condoms, strange findings for such a remote place. He stopped to rest for a while; his throat was getting parched, his joints ached, he was dizzy. The wind had become stronger. For the next hour, the only living thing he came across was a low-flying eagle. The desiccated land started to engulf him; he gradually felt he was becoming one with the dirt, the stones, the air. With every movement, he felt the sun embracing him, pressing him, plunging him into a deep intoxication that started numbing his limbs.

Within this fog, certain images started suddenly to emerge, like swords springing up vertically from the ground. A stone house with red door frames, a room with a green carpet, a cast iron table with a loaf of bread in the middle, a middle-aged woman—beautiful—on a rocking chair, knitting, a man with glazed eyes in front of a glass of wine. He shook his head trying to drive them away. He could not.

Suddenly, almost of their own accord, he felt his feet moving faster. He had started to run in the desert. A crazy run, into nothingness. As though he wanted to reach his destination, into the void, to the end, as soon as possible. But what sort of an end would that be? Voluntary? Like hers? Maybe. Maybe that was the solution.

He ran for quite some time, as much as his strength allowed. Finally, he became exhausted and fell down. He had no idea how long he stayed this way, lying on the ground in the middle of nowhere.

One sign: the sun. A brilliant rain of rays was falling from above making the landscape glimmer. Second sign: the wind. The wind, which constantly began a melody, but always shifted to another too soon, while at the same time, in the background, it was as if there was another wind repeating the first in a different tone. One wind chased another, and then another came, and another, and another. One after the other. Escape. Movement. Change. Ancient, these things, eternal.

His breathing was becoming irregular. He felt as if his last moment had come. The sun, the sun and the wind, would finish him. He did not care any more. Really. Maybe he even liked that he would be lost right there, in the light and the wind. Maybe that was what he had always wanted. To be gone, not violently, but to get lost, to melt down, to evaporate. Suddenly, he stood up as if somebody had ordered him to do so. He lifted his hands to the sky and shouted loudly, "Whatever the future brings!"

And then, suddenly, as if coming out of the wind's melody, another instrument emerged. A wind instrument also, but heavier, with a strong hum. For a moment, he thought he was hearing bubbling, something impossible since there, in this bleak landscape, there could not possibly be any flowing water. Nevertheless, a watery image spread inside him. A freshness of mind—strange. He stood up, turned back, and saw it far in the distance, surrounded by a cloud of dust. It was black like a hearse, its aluminum parts glistening in the vertical rays of the sun, and it was coming straight at him to change his life.

Marcelo

THE CAR WAS APPROACHING, leaving clouds of dust behind it, like a horse galloping in the desert. He was standing in the middle of the road, motionless. When the black Mustang came to a distance of fifty yards, its driver abruptly slammed on the brakes. The car came to a screeching stop, while the cloud of dust wrapped around it in a gray halo. For a few seconds, all he could see was a gray whirl, but as the dust settled down, he saw a tall darkly tanned man, around forty, opening the driver's-side door and stepping out of the car. He was wearing black pants, brown boots, a red checked shirt, and a necklace with small beads. He had long hair and fine features; he was unshaven and looked as if he had not had a good night's sleep for several days. The driver came closer, patting the dust from his hands, his breath reeking of booze.

"Hi, I'm Marcelo. Marcelo Emerson Diaz," he said, holding out his right hand.

His voice was incredibly hoarse, as if coming from the bottom of a well, with a slight Spanish accent. "Sorry about the voice, I have a little knot on my vocal cords. I was shouting a lot recently. Really, I'm not supposed to speak at all for three months."

"Hi," he answered, exhausted.

Marcelo seemed to be waiting for a name, but did not insist. "You look awful, you got lost, huh?" he asked.

"Yes, my car broke down a few miles back."

"A silver Ford?" Marcelo asked.

"Yes."

"I saw it. And you walked this far? Tough! You're lucky I came by; I'm taking a shortcut this way. I'm going to Missouri—Hannibal—and this way I'm saving eighty miles. Sure, there's a lot more of this fucking dirt road. But East is always East. And the straight road is the shortest. Ha! What am I telling you now... You're falling apart... Where are you going?"

"I don't know."

"Is anybody looking for you?"

"No."

"No, huh? That's fortunate. Because I don't even have a cell phone for you to use, in case you'd want to call somebody. I threw it away, the fucking thing, along with my watch. I only kept the laptop... Though that's dangerous too. If they trace it..." Marcelo added in a low voice.

He made a feeble gesture as if asking "who?"

Marcelo kicked a rock with his right boot.

"Screw it, my friend, seize the day, live for the moment—there are no ancestors, nor any... descendants. All the fuckers that came before have been forgotten, all those who will come... As if I've ever seen them? I have no idea—not the slightest!" His breathing was fast, as if he'd been rushing to catch up to something. "Screw it... Now, can I give you a lift, big guy?"

"The only thing I want is to sit down somewhere, drink some water, and get back."

"Yeah, but I am not going back that way, I am going to Hannibal. It's the other way. Just past this wasteland," Marcelo said and pointed ahead.

He looked at the void that spread before him. Then, at the void behind him.

"Whichever way you're going. Thanks," he gasped.

"Come on, get in. I have water for you to drink and wash your face."

They went to the Mustang. Marcelo got in the car and gave him a bottle of water. He splashed some on his face and drank insatiably. Then he went around to the passenger side, but there was a black box on the seat. Marcelo took it, got out of the car, opened the trunk and put it inside. He glanced at the back seat: a big red suitcase was on the right and a baby seat on the left, with a laptop case sitting in it. A book was on the floor. He managed to see the title. *The Sound and the Fury*, William Faulkner. Marcelo got back in the driver's seat, started the engine and drove away, raising another cloud of dust.

They talked for the next half hour. Or, rather, Marcelo did all the talking. He chain-smoked the whole time. He talked non-stop. He talked about almost everything: the weather, the West Coast, the elections, nature, the necklace he was wearing—"It was given to me by an Indian. It symbolizes harmony, something like that," he said. He was obviously drunk, but could still drive. Jazz was pouring out of the car's stereo speakers.

"Now, this is music!" he said. "Miles is today's Beethoven."

At one point, he reached over, took out a flat bottle of whiskey from the glove compartment and took a generous gulp. He had started his trip in Los Angeles and had now driven through half of the US. He was going to Hannibal where a woman whom he had met on the web was waiting for him.

"Laura. I don't even know what she looks like. She hasn't sent a photo."

He figured he should at least ask something. "So, she's waiting for you?"

"Let's say she has given me a sign." Marcelo took his eyes off the road and looked at him. "You know how many e-mails we've exchanged, big guy? A thousand! Five hundred each. A thousand e-mails in nine months... They are all in there," he said and pointed behind him, at the laptop case. "She's a wonderful person, a tormented girl but with a great soul. That's what I want. A great soul. Back there, they are all... fucked, that's it. I'm risking it, I'm risking everything... It couldn't go on like that any more. I had to do it."

"Do what?"

"Just forget it."

Marcelo did not speak for some time. Suddenly, he seemed agitated. He opened the glove compartment and took another gulp. His hands started to tremble slightly. Suddenly he veered to the side, almost losing control of the car.

Having recovered from his ordeal, he decided to try to help Marcelo keep his eyes on the road.

"You like Faulkner?" he asked, motioning toward the back seat.

"Oh that, I found it at a gas station. I liked the first chapter, where an idiot is talking," said Marcelo. "After that, I got mixed up..."

A tale, told by an idiot, full of sound and fury, signifying nothing, he thought, but was too tired to articulate it. In any case, it wouldn't be useful in keeping Marcelo focused. It'd be better to change the subject. He remembered the baby seat, behind them.

"Do you have a kid?"

"My wife has him," Marcelo answered. "My ex. We aren't divorced, but we don't talk to each other any more. I really fucked things up... She won't even take any money from me... In the end, the children belong to the woman... She's a nurse, she's better qualified. I've kept the seat like that, since then."

The car hit a stone and bounced. He saw Marcelo looking behind, a bit worried. The trunk, he thought.

"And that box you put back there, what is it?"

"That? Gravity, suspension, centrifugal power, angular momentum, everything..."

"Are you a physicist?"

"No, no..." he said and burst out laughing.

The CD ended and Marcelo put on another immediately.

"Miles' requiem... Ha! Now he plays for the angels... She also likes him... She wrote me that she does."

"Who likes whom?"

"Laura likes Miles."

"Which means she's a perfect match..."

"Yeah, we have a lot in common. She is also a loner. She likes dogs and Miles Davis and doesn't go out much. Her father is a pastor, just like mine. Garcia Emerson Diaz. Reverend Diaz. I lost him the year before last. My mother, I lost a while ago. I have no one any more. No friends, no wife, no kid."

"I'm sorry."

"Reverend Garcia Emerson Diaz. He was a very hard-hearted man. A man of God but hard-hearted."

Then Marcelo began asking him what he was doing in the US. He answered vaguely, indicating that he didn't want to talk about his personal life. Marcelo had no problem going on talking himself.

"Me, you see, I know too much... That's why I left L.A. I had a good job, but the company... But if this works out... If this works out... I'm playing them all, big guy..."

"What are you talking about? What do you mean, 'playing them all'?"

Marcelo went on in the same vein, ignoring the questions.

"It was lucky I found Laura. I only want a simple life, my friend. A simple fucking life. You know, the straight and narrow, no games. This woman... I have imagined her, you know... Like a bright star that will come and wrap itself around me. You know, stars are nothing but cosmic dust, right?"

They drove through the same unchanging, desolate landscape until finally, the first signs of vegetation appeared. Some red-green bushes, a few scattered trees. Marcelo kept on drinking out of the whiskey bottle at regular intervals. After a turn in the road, a light-blue streak appeared far away on the horizon.

"Look," Marcelo said. "Water."

When they got closer, they realized it was a small lake. Marcelo stopped the car and they got out. They cleaned up a little and lay down in the sun. They didn't talk. The wind had become stronger and the sun had sunk a bit lower.

"I'm coming," Marcelo said suddenly and got up.

He remained lying, with his eyes closed, trying not to think. It wasn't easy. The silence made things bigger. He wondered what he would have done if the Mustang hadn't come by. He would have melted in the sun. He would have let himself liquefy and spread out, dissolve into the ground, get lost. Some time passed. He heard a noise near his ear, and just caught a glimpse of a little lizard disappearing in the small lake. He propped himself up on his elbows and heard, at that moment, a choked sound, like a human cry. He looked in Marcelo's direction. The sound came from a small tree to the right, at the edge of the lake. He jumped up quickly and ran there. Behind the tree, Marcelo was lying face down on the ground, motionless.

Other eyes

HE BENT DOWN AND TURNED HIM OVER. Marcelo's eyes were open and had a surprised expression. He took one of the man's wrists in his hand. There was no pulse. He started to massage Marcelo's chest. Nothing. He pushed more vigorously, with all his strength. He gave him mouth to mouth, as well as he knew how. Nothing. Marcelo was dead.

He looked around. He was in a small oasis, in the middle of a desolate landscape, alone, with a virtual stranger lying dead beside him. By this time, the wind had gotten so strong it started to blow dust up from the ground. A feeling of recognition came over him. He was able to finally identify an old vague sensation. It was the feeling of living on the edge, being in a situation that is overwhelming, all the while following himself experiencing all of its tragic dimensions as if everything was happening to someone else. Living inside out. As always in his life.

Like that time. Or not? No, no, this had nothing to do with that time. The wind was not blowing then. It was raining, and it did not happen in the open—it was inside the house, in the room with the mauve wall paper, and he could hear the raindrops falling from the garden's orange trees, and he knew that this sudden shower would make them more beautiful and that his mother, who was watching them from the nearby window, would fix her eyes on their wet leaves and would stare at them until they became dry. And that this glance, her staring at the orange trees, would be the last image he would have of her eyes because the next time he would see her— in the evening, when he would be back—his mother's eyes, although open, would not be seeing anything at all. She had shut her own eyes, leaving them wide open.

Maybe, however, it was more like the time when—some years later—he had come out on the small balcony of his house and was watching her leave. Yes, that time the wind was blowing and made the tent flutter, while she, not his mother this time, *she*, was walking down the slope toward her car, parked at the cross street. He was holding in his hands a piece of paper shaped somewhat like a seashell, with a black 9.4-millimeter speck. Sixteen hours later, the speck would exist no more. It would never become a 185 centimeter body—he had always wanted a boy—and she would leave him, exterminating inside herself even this last sign of his, which should have been his most intimate element, an authentic part of himself.

He knelt down in front of the dead man and looked at him. Marcelo's face was long, his nose curved, his upper lip somewhat larger than the lower. Strong cheek bones. Worry lines on the forehead, curved black eyebrows, the same color as his wavy hair. Dark circles under the eyes. He leaned closer trying to make out their color. They were light brown. He bent down even lower and studied the dead man's profile. His eyes followed the line that began at the forehead, traced out a small elegant curve and then gradually rose up only to drop down abruptly, beginning this tiny embrace between the nostril and the upper lip, making a three-quarter turn downward, and with a clear cut stroke, finally resting on the small wrinkle at the throat.

He stood up and walked to the small lake. He bent and, taking a little water in the palms of his hands, once more splashed his face.

As he did this, he noticed the concentric circles moving away from the spot where his hands had entered the water. Each circle chased the previous one, and, by the time that one subsided, a new one formed and then another, and another—a constant cycle of birth and annihilation, a constant chase. When the water calmed, the only thing that remained was the reflection of his face on the water's surface. His own face. He looked at himself for a long time. He then turned his head sideways and, with the corner of his eye, examined his profile.

The wind had become even stronger. Even with his exhaustion, he felt a burst of energy, an intense drive, as though he was being compelled to carry out a prescribed series of actions. The first was to go to the car. He searched it thoroughly, including the trunk. There were some clothes, first aid items, and two or three paperback mystery novels in the red suitcase, along with a small book of quotes by American authors. Besides the suitcase, he also found a set of tools, a blanket, the laptop in its case, and the black box. Marcelo's papers were in the small compartment between the front seats. Passport, social security card, driver's license. Marcelo Emerson Diaz: born August 30, 1965, Los Angeles, California. Occupation: Data processing. Married. Name of spouse: Candice Dolores. Her maiden name: Durincova. The passport photo was an old one, showing a twenty-five-year-old man with long hair and a beard. There was a piece of paper folded inside, where his life insurance number, his Internet connection password, and two doctors' phone numbers were written. Deep inside the storage compartment, he found three pill boxes. He read the labels: "Pravachol," "Prinivil," "Pensordil"—heart medications all three.

Then he took out the laptop. He opened it—the battery was charged. He searched—the only things he found on the hard drive were a folder containing photos and another two with text data. One of these contained, copied in chronological order, the e-mails exchanged between Marcelo and Laura. He read some at random, until he reached the last one.

Dear Laura,
I can't stay here any more. I've made the
decision. I hope your invitation regarding
Hannibal is still valid. So I'm leaving by
car. I reckon Saturday or Sunday I'll be
there. I have your address: Laura Chance, 16
Rock Street, right? Maybe it would have been
better if I had called you, but a deal is a
deal. No phone calls, as we had agreed from
the beginning. I'm a little afraid, but as
Dennis Hopper says in a movie by a German guy:
"There is nothing to fear but fear itself." I
didn't like the movie much—it was slow and
dense, but I liked that line from Hopper.
xxx
Marcelo

The answer was brief.

OK. The address is correct. I'll be waiting
for you.

Laura

He opened the photo folder. There were not many photos: a
sweet child of about three, with a red balloon in his hands; Marcelo
with short hair, clean shaven, wearing a suit and tie; an elderly man
with a clerical collar and a stern look; two tall dogs; some New
York pictures; and another, very blurry, showing a man naked to the
waist looking away from the camera, while in the center of the
frame there was milky streak, as if the film had been exposed to
light. He stared at it for some time. Suddenly, he closed the laptop
with a snap.

He got out and went to where Marcelo was lying. He took hold of the dead man by the shoulders and pulled him with great difficulty up into the car. He laid him down on the rear seat and covered him with a blanket. Then he got in the driver's seat and started the engine. For a few moments, he didn't move. He turned back and glanced behind. An endless dry expanse. He turned and looked ahead again. In the direction of the lake. Finally, he took Marcelo's passport and studied the photo. For a long time.

The idea had been there from the beginning, from the first moment, even before the tragic event. There are times when the idea exists before the conditions that would make it possible have come to pass. The appearance of the conditions simply confirms the alignment of circumstances set up by the secret processes of time, which arrange and suddenly reveal everything as if saying: "Here, take this and do with it what you wish." But while he was studying the dark, mysterious look of Marcelo in his passport photo, it was as if somebody suddenly drew a curtain shut inside his mind and everything immediately turned black, pitch black. And it was he, himself, the same unknown hand, who wrote on that inner blackboard a word in chalk: Fear.

Annoyed, he threw Marcelo's passport on the passenger seat. He put his foot on the gas pedal and floored it. The car lurched forward—East.

He had driven for maybe an hour, when he spotted a dark form in the distance. Drawing nearer, he realized it was a gas station with a convenience store. The sign read: "Robertson's Gas Station." When he got there, he told the attendant to fill the tank. He paid and went into the shop. To the right side of the entrance, there was a pay phone. He lifted the receiver. He knew the number for emergencies. He dialed the first two numbers. When he reached the third, he hesitated. His eye was drawn to a sticker pasted on the phone. It had the image of a squirrel at the center, while abstract acorns bearing the prices of various spa and cosmetic treatments were falling around it. At the upper part of the logo, there was the phrase "Change me: Squirrel Spa Treatment." And in that instant, without exactly knowing why, *the idea* came back, stronger than before. The curtain opened up again, an invisible sponge wiped out the word from the blackboard, and dozens of colors poured into the darkness, took *the idea* and brought it back before him, splendidly illuminated. He took a deep breath, put down the phone, went to the back of the store, bought water, two big turkey sandwiches, coffee, and asked the attendant for a rag. He also bought a gasoline can, which he filled at the pump outside. Back in the car, he started the engine and made a hundred-and-eighty degree turn—back west, from where he had come.

By the time he reached the place where he had left the Ford, it had started to get dark. The sky was glowing—it looked like it had been filled with red glittering streaks. The car was exactly where he had left it. There was not a soul around. Dead silence. He stopped the Mustang close to the Ford, got out, opened the rental car's driver's side door, cautiously lifted Marcelo's body out of the Mustang and moved it to the other car's driver's seat. As he was setting him down, he noticed the necklace with the small stones on the dead man's neck. An elongated humanlike figure was carved on the stone at the center, holding four strings in its two hands. He carefully took it off and put it around his neck. He returned to the Mustang, took out the gas can and splashed the rental car thoroughly with it, inside and out. Then he took the rag and dipped it in the remaining gas.

He stood in front of the Ford for a few moments. The barren landscape was glowing in the evening light. He felt excited, warm inside. A wave of memory detached an image from the recesses of his mind and propelled it to that place, the purgatory of vision, where memories jostle before being launched into consciousness. It was the image of a woman, or rather several women, overlaid one upon the other like Photoshop layers.

With a sudden move, he lit the rag with Marcelo's cigarette lighter and threw it into the Ford. Almost at a run, he jumped into the Mustang, started the engine, and pressed the gas pedal to the floor. Three hundred yards away, he stopped. He turned back and saw the Ford engulfed in flames. A few moments later, he heard a violent explosion. The car was now an inferno. He stepped on the pedal violently and drove again towards the East. *Other eyes*, he heard a voice inside himself. *Other eyes*.

PART TWO

IN THE BELLY OF THE WHALE

A. LAURA

Hannibal's Veil

WHEN HE GOT BACK to the gas station again, it was already dark. He asked the attendant for directions to Hannibal. The man told him to continue straight ahead to Highway 61, follow it up to where it met Highway 36, and then turn right at the first exit. It was about a hundred miles away.

When he got on the highway, he tested how fast the Mustang could go. The car was flying. Driving, he caught a glimpse of his reflection in the mirror. Tired, with black circles around his eyes, unshaven. A bizarre amulet was hanging from the rear view mirror. A foot.... As if Marcelo had put it there on purpose. For a month since his father was hit in the accident, he had been constantly dreaming the same dream: a human foot on the ground. He would fall on it, and the foot would suddenly spring back to life and start chasing him. He would run outside the house to save himself, cross the road, zigzag in the narrow side-streets, and the foot would be always there, behind him, not letting him take a breath. Until, finally, it would reach him and start kicking him hard until he would wake up. When his father returned home, he could not, for a long time, look at the bandaged foot even when his father himself would lift it up and say, "The family's foundation is swollen," bursting into laughter. Dad had a unique sense of humor. At least.

He was getting thirsty again; he'd finished the water he had bought. Just before reaching the intersection, he saw a light on the right hand side of the road. He moved the car to the side of the road and stopped. It was a small canteen, a run-down structure that looked out of place in the middle of the highway. The sign said: "Hannibal's Veil—Jack Beckley." There was a bronze doorbell beside the closed door. He rang. He waited for a while until a man appeared and opened it to let him in. He was fat, about fifty years old, and he had a hard time walking. Disheveled, as if he had just gotten out of bed, with a cigar hanging from his mouth. His pale blue eyes were kind of cross-eyed. The man motioned him in, led him to one of the three small tables inside, and fixed him a cup of coffee. The place was a cross between a small cafe, a convenience store, and a stuffed animal head exhibition. There were deer, wolves, even a bear. The smell of stale smoke and cheap booze filled the room. A poster of the Republican party with the elephant logo was hanging next to the refrigerator. On an ancient TV set, George Bush was addressing prospective voters in Ohio, chanting "Freedom will prevail" with that characteristic half-smile of his. Beckley took a chair and sat beside him.

"Beautiful night."

"Beautiful night."

"Heading to Hannibal?"

"Yes."

"Why?"

"I want to stay there for a while."

"Why there?"

"I've heard it's a nice place."

"Where are you from?"

"From L.A."

"You don't sound like you're from L.A."

"I'm Latino."

"*Esta ciudad puede tragarte*²," uttered Beckley, looking him over.

"What?"

"Don't you speak Spanish?"

"No."

"Why? Didn't your parents teach you?"

"They died when I was young."

"I'm sorry... "

"Could you recommend a hotel in town?"

Beckley went behind the bar counter and returned with a business card.

He drank his coffee, paid, and before leaving asked, "Do you know a Laura Chance?"

The man turned quickly around. "The Red?"

"What do you mean 'the Red?'"

Beckley didn't answer. He took out a lighter and lit his cigar. Then, he stared into the eyes of a mounted deer head as if he were seeing it for the first time. "You like it?"

"I don't like dead animals."

Beckley took a good sip of his coffee and went on with the questions.

"Have you ever been stung by a dead bee?"

"No. So, what did you mean by 'the Red?'"

"They sting just like the live ones."

"I've never been stung by a live one either. So?"

The man shook the ashes from his cigar and, with his eyes still fixed on the deer head, said, "Do you believe that a person's actions in an ordinary situation, in which they have no stake, reveal everything about this person's life?"

"Yes."

"Now did you answer that way because you know it's what I want to hear?"

"No, I said it because I believe it."

"What do you believe?"

"That a person's actions in an ordinary situation, in which they have no stake, may reveal some things about this person's life."

"I didn't say 'may.'"

"That's why I didn't say 'everything' either, I said 'some things.'"

Beckley looked him over from head to toe.

"*Eres muy listo. Vas a tener problemas*[3]."

"No problem," he answered and saluting the man, opened the door.

Travelodge

HE TOOK HIGHWAY 36 and turned to the right at the first round-about. At exit 157, where it merged with Highway 69, he saw a sign: To Downtown Hannibal. Taking the ramp, he got on to Mark Twain Avenue, passed a big yellow-red sign announcing: "Welcome to Hannibal, Mark Twain, Tom Sawyer, and Huckleberry Finn's hometown." Following the buildings' address-es, he came to number 500, where "Travelodge Hannibal" was located, the hotel on Beckley's card, a four-story building, the tallest in the area. The streets were wide and the houses low, some-what like Iowa City, but the twenty-first century did not seem to have knocked on Hannibal's door. Had there not been neon signs, power cables, and cars, one could have argued that he had come back to the time of the author of Tom Sawyer. As he rolled down the car's window, he felt in the crisp air a tinge of humidity—*the Mississippi*, he thought. Then, down a cross-street to the left, he saw the river flowing in the distance behind the railroad tracks.

It was late and there was no one on the streets. He parked the Mustang, got out, and knocked on the door. There was no answer. He pushed the door and went in. A bell rang when the door opened. Within seconds, a tall, slim man appeared, wearing a black vest, white shirt, and black pants. His thinning hair was combed with a neat part. He looked like a butler, walking with a ramrod-straight back.

"My name is Morris Kuntz, how may I help you?" he asked with a slight stutter.

"Is there a room available?"

"Of course, for how many nights?"

"I don't know yet."

"Okay. Do you have any luggage?"

He motioned in the direction of the parking lot. They went out together, and Morris helped with the luggage. They came back to the reception desk where he gave Marcelo's ID and took the key to room 4B on the fourth floor. Forty dollars a night. Walking up the first flight—Morris offered to help him, but he politely refused— he heard a child's voice behind him. Turning back, he saw a red-haired, well-endowed woman chasing a little boy wearing a base-ball cap.

"Achilles, come here! Now!"

A little girl, younger than the boy, was close behind the woman. Morris said from behind the desk:

"My wife Maya. Our kids Achilles and Athena. This is Mr. Diaz, our new guest."

"Welcome to Hannibal, Mr. Diaz. I don't know, of course, what a gentleman like you is doing in a place like this," said Maya with a bright smile. Her style was as if she had copied it from some low-budget soap opera.

He smiled, remembering the image of his face in the rearview mirror.

"Maya..." Morris began.

"I'm happy to be here," he interrupted, looking at Mrs. Kuntz. He imagined that her favorite food was peanut butter and jelly sandwiches. She would be eating them watching Oprah Winfrey, commenting on the show out loud.

"Diaz, Diaz, *buenos dias*," shouted the boy.

Behind him, a dog was jumping and wagging its tail. It ran up to him and started licking his shoes. He got nervous, as he always did when dogs got close to him, ever since the time when, as a young boy, he had been attacked by a German Shepherd. He'd had three rabies shots. He quickly picked up his suitcase and went up to his room.

It was a small room with a bed, a desk, a TV set, and a mini fridge. The window looked out on a big fake palm-tree, neon green, that almost hid the bar across the street, a traditional two-story building like an old saloon. Fortunately, the window was covered by two heavy blue curtains. The walls were covered by a cheap green wallpaper with pictures of plants, mostly lilies. Upkeep and cleanliness were not Travelodge's forte, a fact that made the suggestion "Simplify, Simplify," which in big red letters dominated the only picture in the room, seem rather ironic. At the bottom, the author of the quote was revealed: Henry David Thoreau. When he went to put some water into the kettle to make some tea, he was surprised to find two strands of hair on the spout, and when he opened the book with information about the city, he discovered a half-smoked joint in it.

He drank the tea, plugged Marcelo's laptop to re-charge, and went to bed. He immediately fell into a heavy sleep. When he woke up it was already after noon the next day. He was awakened by a knock on the door—housekeeping, coming to clean the room. The woman, an overweight forty-year-old African-American with short curly hair and disapproving droopy lips, looked at him suspiciously. He told her to leave the curtains drawn.

Alone, in the foreign womb, he didn't want any light. Let it come gradually. Come out gradually. In the way one's skin changes, waiting for the cells to reproduce themselves. He felt oddly numb. His new world was following a new set of rules. Time took the place of space. Things emptied themselves of space and became filled with time. Fresh, renewed time. Ahab reborn in the belly of the whale, self-sufficient, refreshed, a new person. He took a deep breath. No matter what may happen, he would still be a writer. Or wouldn't he? The aisle had led him to the window, and the fire exit was a leap from the window-sill.

He did not open the curtains. He drank a strong cup of coffee, opened the laptop, and started reading the e-mails exchanged between Marcelo and Laura, while taking notes on a piece of paper. When he had finished, it was past one in the morning. He took the paper and read what he had written:

> Nine months ago, Marcelo enters an internet dating site as "Rider from Heaven." He finds Laura's e-mail (he learns her real name later), who has entered with the username "Lonely Planet." In her profile on the site in the category "Women looking for men for friendship and, possibly, a relationship," she writes: "SWF, 34, alone by choice, who believes life is an optical illusion, waiting to meet that mysterious being that is developing inside her like a butterfly in its cocoon." He sends her an introductory e-mail, trying to get a photo. She positively refuses: "No photographs. Only words." In the first ten e-mails, we have a Marcelo trying to break the ice and even challenging: "What you have written is contradic-tory. How can you want to be intentionally alone and also waiting to get to know somebody? How can this person possibly be already within you? You write as if you are attempting to get to know yourself." And a Laura who is trying to muddy the waters: "Maybe I want to get to know myself through another person. Maybe I am the other person." "Why did you enter the site?" she asks him. "Because, I'm alone" he answers. Laura writes in a

very simple way, so much so that Marcelo wonders: "Did you write your profile yourself?"

The correspondence continues with Marcelo playing the role of the hunter and Laura leaving behind her indiscernible tracks. At a certain point, however, the woman recognizes that they have something in common. Marcelo writes to her about his dog that got sick, and then her manner changes—she becomes more gentle, starts asking him for details, treatments, etc. From that point on, we have a different Laura. A Laura who gives advice, who is even interested in Marcelo's health, suggesting to him a healthy diet, even making jokes. The new Laura reveals another part of herself: she is an active citizen, is interested in public affairs, is a member of Greenpeace, has taken part in demonstrations. She speaks passionately about the "Rainbow Warrior" and the events surrounding its sinking in New Zealand in 1985. She is emphatic about what a catastrophe for the country Bush's re-election will be. Marcelo, however, seems not to be particularly interested in politics. He gives the impression of having a well-established life: he mentions a company, an office, working hours, colleagues. But there is something that worries him. "My greatest flaw is that I trust people. It's best to do your work quietly and not get involved in anything." Laura reveals Hannibal as her home, and her professional occupation: working as a cashier at the Mark Twain Museum. She loves music very much and plays the piano. Lives alone in Hannibal, her parents come from Oklahoma. He asks her about them, but she doesn't answer. Every now and then she mentions God—she seems to have a contradictory relationship with religion. "When I lost my faith" slips out at some point.

The relationship evolves. Marcelo starts talking about

more personal things. He is divorced. His wife, a nurse on early retirement, left him and took their kid. Laura wants to know why. "Irreconcilable differences," Marcelo puts forth. "And your kid? Don't you get to see him?" On this issue, he becomes somewhat inconsistent, saying that according to the court decision he has no right to see his kid whenever he wants, but then he adds that both ex-wife and child have moved to Florida, that she is in a relationship with someone else, and that by now he knows that he will never see his kid again. "Things are very bad with Candice—my ex-wife has a lot of problems, she suffers from depression—our life together was hell. It was my fault, too, of course, I got very frustrated, I couldn't bear it," he finishes. "I am, however," says Marcelo about himself, "a man with deep emotions. I want to find out that other half of me that must be somewhere out there—my sister soul." It is significant that he makes no mention at all of parents or relatives. As if he has no one else in the world. She still keeps some distance and does not reveal too much of herself. "If all those things hidden deep inside us come to light, who could bear such illumination?" she writes somewhere—her beloved verse, as she says.

In one e-mail, she peppers him with questions. Beginning with what position he sleeps in, what his favorite food is, even what kind of wine he likes, since Marcelo has already told her that he enjoys a glass of wine now and then. He jumps at the opportunity and suggests: "Anything you don't like, I'll change. Something tells me that the two of us will be a great match." It seems, however, that he overdid it, since a whole week of silence follows until Laura writes back with the question: "What kind of person do you think I am? Do you think I'm some nut looking for a man on the web?" Marcelo retreats, puts all the blame on himself, asks her to forgive him. Then, he explains what he does. His job is data collection at a high-speed communications company. She does not understand. "I collect and analyze material from the web and other networks and organize it for various uses. I record communications. I break codes. I organize and store everything in digital archives. I take care of words as if they were babies." "For what uses?" "That's none of my business." "Is it legal?" asks Laura anxiously. "It is a perfectly legal company. It even works for the government. Information nowadays is the most crucial thing, even more important than weapons." Laura comes out of left field: "This country kills people with information."

He realizes that it is not to his advantage to continue discussing his job and changes the subject. They start conversing about the world in general, nature—Laura exalts the beauty of her part of the country—and there a cutting remark slips: "...here, where I live now, because Oklahoma..." "Isn't Oklahoma nice?"—Marcelo thinks he got a break. "Yes, it's a nice place, but I was talking about something else, about how it was growing up there," and in the next e-mail she unexpectedly confesses: "My parents were from the South, Baptists. You know, everything we learn from the Bible, all this mythology, with miracles and prophets... For them all this is real, namely that there is a Hell with fires blazing and all the rest, and all the sinners are cast down there and suffer for all eternity. And, if you can imagine, my father was a gang member when he was a kid. He was a drug addict and a dealer; he was going to Hell for sure. One day, as he was riding his motorcycle, he lost control, crashed through a store window, and landed inside, almost at the feet of a pretty woman, shocked, who

worked as a model with the local advertising agency. He
didn't get hurt, but my mother was riddled with shards of
glass. He took care of her, they grew fond of each other,
started to date, and the romance led to marriage. From
the moment they met, they both changed a hundred and
eighty degrees. Born-again Christians. My father
became a pastor, and my mother helped him with his
ministry and took care of the house. They raised me
according to the laws of the Church. For years, I
believed that the soul was cursed because of original sin.
When I was about seventeen years old, everything
changed." She stops there. Marcelo pressures to learn
more; she clams up. Sometime later, she writes: "I once
read that man deserves man. Some philosopher wrote it.
And then it happened to me. Everything became crystal
clear and I saw that God couldn't possibly exist; no God
would allow such things to happen in the world. Man is
an animal, a brute with a mind well suited to wreaking
destruction and perpetrating crimes. Until then I hadn't
seen anything of the world—at college I didn't make any
friends, didn't take part in any sorority, didn't have any
boyfriends, didn't go out in the evenings. And that was
when I left home and never laid eyes on them again."

After pointing out the coincidence that his father was
also a pastor, Marcelo, who understandably does not
seem to believe that the switch is deeply felt, wonders,
"What happened that affected you so much?" Laura
doesn't answer, doesn't say anything specific, but offers
a hint: "You give him everything and he is silent. And
not only is he silent, but he thrusts you into the worst sin.
After that, you are the only one left." And with that, she
cuts off discussion on this topic. In the following e-
mails, she talks about the various jobs she had at different times: waitress in diners, usher in multiplex movie

theaters, nanny—"and some that were even worse," she adds.

In one e-mail, Marcelo asks her to describe herself. She refuses and answers with a short diatribe about external appearance ending up with: "I am against beauty." It seems that this affects Marcelo, since for some time he doesn't write at all. Then Laura sends him an electronic postcard for his birthday; there is still, however, no reply from Marcelo.

By this point I have read through about half of the e-mails between them.

Laura sends three e-mails that remain unanswered. When Marcelo returns, he seems to be in a state of intense crisis. He only gives one-word answers. One e-mail is even encrypted and is totally unintelligible; it might perhaps have been meant for somebody else. Laura is worried, she does not understand. Finally, Marcelo sends an e-mail from a hotmail address and not from the one he was sending from until then (marcelo@min.com); apparently the company he worked with was called MIN. "Don't send anything to the old address. You can't be too careful these days."

The situation calms down somehow, and the e-mails become personal again. "How do you imagine me to be?" asks Marcelo. Laura replies, "I don't know. All I know is what you have told me about yourself. When we speak to other people about ourselves, we are not sincere. Whatever we say depends on what we believe they like in another person." Marcelo gets in another kind of crisis; he seems to be writing in a hurry, under some stress, because he makes a lot of spelling mistakes. "Fucking country," he says, "they attack us, they say, because they hate our democracy and our freedom. As if we are God's chosen people. I can't stand America any more. It's chewing me up..." "The point is what are you doing so that your country might become better?" answers Laura, and then they start a discussion about Clinton. Marcelo manages to turn the discussion to Monica—he probably wants to interject a little sex into the conversation. Laura doesn't bite. "Sex is a very personal matter. You can't judge it. Neither can you write about it."

I am getting close to the end of the e-mails and Marcelo is getting antsy about his situation in L.A.: "I can't stand it here any more. I have to go" and there he tosses in the first hook: "How is it in Hannibal?" Laura takes the hint with delight and goes into an exposé of small-town life. She talks about the people of the city; someone named Lester makes frequent appearances. After a number of e-mails, it is she who finally makes the proposal: "It looks like you need a change of scene. I would be happy to put you up for a while." Marcelo doesn't reply for a few days. And then he sends her the last e-mail. That's it. I find it interesting that Marcelo does not mention anything about the bad state of his health, which is evident from the pills in his car and, of course, from his tragic end. Understandable from a certain perspective.

I summarize: A lonely woman, formerly religious (with a dark past), but with an interesting philosophical view of life, comes into contact with a nervous, impulsive, contradictory, distrustful employee of a communications company, who has some sort of trouble developing at his job. He has been exposed in some way, somebody is after him (?), he is possibly in danger. The employee comes to a dead end and finds refuge with the woman as a possible solution. What does one expect from the other? The employee imagines a double

refuge—shelter from danger and a woman's embrace
(?)—while the woman is looking for something that will
get her out of her routine without, however, seeming to
be ready to surrender herself. How would Marcelo
approach Laura on his arrival in Hannibal?

If I, let's say, were to write this as a chapter, how
would I describe him? He is supposedly under a great
deal of stress, has come here in order to escape (from
whom?), puts his trust in someone he doesn't, after all,
really know. So, he'd be ambivalent, would be trying to
exercise self-restraint. He'd be feeling some shame (sub-
consciously), overflowing angst, would have a sense of
a certain bond, and certainly an impulse to flirt, probably
ineffectually.

He read what he'd written again. It was as if he had two strong
characters quite ready, with impressive résumés. If things were different, he would have buckled down and started writing. But he was
already too much entrapped in the story he was describing, as much
as the story itself was entrapped within him.

A "quiet" town

THE FOLLOWING DAY HE WOKE UP EARLY. He took a long shower, drank two cups of coffee and opened Marcelo's suitcase. The late Marcelo's aesthetic was "mix and don't match": from multi-colored checkered pullovers to shirts with polka dots, and from conservative jackets to oversized Bermuda shorts. The wide selection of clothes for all occasions suggested that where he was going he intended to stay for a while. In a pocket of the suitcase he found a day planner—almost blank. The only thing Marcelo had written in it was Laura's address, but on the November 1 page a series of numbers was written: 1614180207. Underneath there was a note: "time limit." He copied the numbers on a piece of paper and put it in the dead man's wallet, by now his own wallet.

He tried on a pair of corduroy pants; as he had thought, they were a perfect fit. The blue striped shirt also fit. As he closed the suitcase, his eyes fell on the black box he had taken with him from Marcelo's car. He took it in his hands. It was a long rectangular box, six by six by four inches, rather light, locked with a small golden combination lock with ten cylinders with numbers on them. He had an idea. He took out the piece of paper and counted the figures. There were also ten. He tried them on the lock, but the box didn't open. He shook it; it made no noise. He pried a nail out of the wall and poked at the lock with it. Nothing. Finally, he took the box and placed it in the small safe inside the closet. He entered a four-digit code and closed the door of the safe. He took his wallet out, put Marcelo's driver's license in it and went down to the lobby. Maya was sitting on the couch watching TV. As soon as she saw him, she got up, smiling. She was wearing tight pants and a shirt tied at the waist, showing off her belly button.

"Ah, Mr. Diaz!"

"You can call me Marcelo."

"Marcelo! What have you been doing, Marcelo, stuck in your room two whole days? The weather has been so nice!"

"I was resting. It was a hard trip."

Maya toyed absently with the cheap necklace she was wearing. "Do you mind my asking—why did you come here?"

"No particular reason. Just to get some rest."

"You sure picked the right place! Especially now..." Maya sighed dramatically.

"Why now? What's been happening?"

"Oh, you won't believe it! A few days ago there was a murder... The first murder in Hannibal in twenty-three years!"

"Oh really?" he said, acting disinterested. Maya, however, seemed to be dying to tell the story. She made him sit on the couch, fixed him a cup of coffee, and started talking in a rapid-fire rhythm. A twenty-three year old woman, Mary Lou Dobson, had been found dead in her home by her husband Tom and his friend Jack Macy. She was gagged, with hands and feet tied to a chair, with a pool of blood underneath. Her arms had slashes all over them. She was sitting in front of a video camera. The first theory, based on what had been found at the crime scene, was that the perpetrator, having tied up the girl on the chair and slashed her arms with a sharp instrument, had taped the whole time until the girl bled to death. The

State District Attorney had come to town, but the murder hadn't been solved. It was, of course, the only subject of conversation in Hannibal for the last three days. Maya went on barraging him with details about the various rumors circulating—that the woman's own husband Tom had first been considered the main suspect, and had even been held by the police for a whole twenty-four hours, before being let go for lack of evidence, while many people in town thought that Jack Macy, who had had a conviction for assault, had done it.

He waited patiently for her to finish her story, and when Maya stood up to fix another cup of coffee, he took advantage of the interruption and waved, "Bye now! I have to get to the bank," and escaped into high noon Hannibal.

The town was quiet; there weren't many people in the streets. He went up Mark Twain Avenue until he reached Hill Street. To the left of the railroad tracks he noticed a bronze statue of two boys. When he walked up to it, he realized he was looking at Mark Twain's two most well known heroes. Tom Sawyer with the bag on his shoulder seemed to be looking ambitiously toward the future, while at his side, Huckleberry Finn with a stick in his hand was more light-hearted about the matter. In Tom's shirt pocket was a slingshot, while a bulge in Huck's back pocket hinted at a long thin pipe. Tom was better dressed than Huck; although they both had patches on their clothes, Tom's patches looked as if they had been stitched by a more capable hand.

He went on to the right, and going up a small embankment, he found himself on the tracks. In front of him, the Mississippi spread in all its huge width and splendor. A bit further up there was a long bridge connecting the two banks. He had never seen such a wide river. River. The word had a particular significance, had been, in fact, a kind of code within his family. When his mother would say: "When the 'river' was alive," she meant her mother, his grandmother. This grandmother had been with the guerillas in the mountains during the Greek Civil War. Her alias had taken on new meaning in the most tragic way when, after a battle, she had drowned in a river in Thessaly. At the time, his mother was not even four years old. She was raised in the village by her aunt, the "river's" sister. A hard woman she was, who kept his mother under strict discipline. But only until his mother turned seventeen and his father came along— at that time he was a traveling salesman, with a moustache and large sideburns—and stole her away. Literally.

He went down to the bank of the river and, when he reached the water's edge, bent down, took some water in his palms, and splashed his face. Turning to go, he noticed a half-broken pillar in front of him. Flowers had grown on it, and a little lizard had climbed to the top. It had an odd beauty, like an ancient ruin. As he looked at it, it seemed to become quite complete, but where could it have come from? Maybe it was part of an old house, a column that had supported a place where some people had once lived and loved each other. Now it stood broken, solitary and eternal. He too was alone, lonely, unknown, far from anything familiar.

There was no home, not even the memory of a home, to carry with him. He was far away. Away from the eyes he had once loved. Eyes that for him had now closed forever, had been lost. A half-broken column.

A haziness had spread in the sky. He looked across, at the other bank. An old wood shed stood there. *Good hiding place*, he thought instinctively, feeling a vague sense of guilt.

He was hungry. On the road to the center of the town, he stopped at the Mark Twain family restaurant. At that hour, there were no other customers in the place. He sat at a table in the center and ordered a steak with potatoes and a Coke. Shortly after, two men in their mid-thirties came in. One was tall, skinny, black, with a handsome face, who looked a bit like Denzel Washington, and the other was shorter, white, with long straight hair and a flat nose, and was noticeably chewing gum. He had a tattoo on his right arm with the Marine

Corps eagle. They ordered hamburgers and sat close to him, at the next table. They were talking loudly, so he could hear every word of their conversation, which revolved around the subject with which the whole town was apparently obsessed: Mary Lou Dobson's murder. From their conversation, he understood that the white man, Roy, was a friend of a certain guy, Paul, who lived in the house next to the one where the girl was found dead. The black man, Lester, was peppering him with questions. Roy was talkative: "Yeah, I gave statements to the sheriff and to that guy, Rather, the District Attorney. Paul was at home the whole day but didn't hear a thing. It's those double-paned windows he has; I never understood why. I went to his house at noon to have a cup of coffee with him. I left at about 3:00 p.m. Tom found the body at 4:30 p.m. What can I say? Anything is possible."

The waiter who brought the beers weighed in: "She could seduce a saint." Then Lester argued that it was absolutely impossible for Tom, her husband, to have done it. "He loved her too much," he said emphatically.

But Roy interrupted, saying that anybody could have done it: "Even the guy next to us," pointing at him.

He pretended not to hear.

"Hey, man, I don't suppose you like splatter videotapes?" Roy said louder.

"I'm sorry, I don't understand what you're talking about."

"Come on, Roy, leave him alone. He's not from around here," said Lester.

"What's your name?" asked Roy.

"Marcelo."

"What are you doing here?"

They started talking, and it came out that Roy Gamba was an electrician, born and raised in Hannibal, while Lester Dietrich had come to town five years ago from Saint Louis. Lester was a saxophone player, but earned a living mainly making handicrafts he sold to tourists. "We are a very touristy town; half a million people come here every year," he commented.

Something had intrigued him from the moment he had heard the black man's name. Suddenly it dawned on him! Lester Dietrich, yes, he was the guy that Laura mentioned in the e-mails, the one she jammed with now and then—of course, it was the sax! Her only friend in Hannibal—"He's very respectful, a real gentleman." He thought of asking him about Laura, but checked himself. When he finished eating, he paid the bill and said goodbye to the two men.

He went out on Hill Street and turned uphill, away from the river. The street was lined with mostly one-story wooden buildings of varying styles with a few two-story buildings interspersed. On one corner, a two-story structure displayed the sign "Jack Clemens—Attorney-at-Law." It was the building that used to house the office of Mark Twain's father. He opened the front door and found himself in an area shaped like a courtroom, where Jack Clemens had tried cases and had taken depositions. A bit further up the street, there was another two-story wooden construction with a plaque mentioning that Mark Twain was brought up in this house. He asked a woman about the museum—it was a couple of blocks away, on Main Street.

Entering the Mark Twain Museum, he found himself inside an exhibit based on scenes from the author's books, staged like a *tableau vivant*. He passed Tom Sawyer's fence, the cemetery where Tom and Huck Finn saw the murder, Indian Joe's treasure, the cave where Tom and Becky Thatcher were lost when their candle went out, Huck Finn's raft tied to a make-believe dock. The Museum was full of visitors, mostly children. At the back of the exhibit, behind the cave, there was a souvenir shop. And there, behind the counter, stood a woman of about thirty, thirty-five.

Her blond, almost golden hair was cut very short, like a boy's. From where he stood, he could only see her from the waist up. She was wearing a light blue v-neck sweater. Her thin face with pronounced cheekbones looked fresh and vibrant; she was wearing absolutely no make-up. Her eyes were light-colored and set somewhat wide apart. Full lips, with the upper lip thinner than the lower one. Her hands slim, with long, delicate fingers. Her appearance troubled him—it was one of those faces that one could not read right away. A face full of promise but at the same time missing a certain element, a key to open it. At that moment, the woman turned around to the shelves behind the counter in order to get something. The image he faced took him by surprise. Like a playing card turned over to reveal an unexpected symbol.

Below the line of the short-cut hair, vertically, along the whole length of the back of the neck, appeared a tattoo. Not a common tattoo. It consisted of two masterly drawn ideograms descending down to the third vertebra of her spine:

恐

惧

He felt an urge to speak to her immediately, but held himself back. He wasn't ready yet. He pretended to look at the exhibits while, out of the corner of his eye, he watched her wrapping up a large bowl purchased by a fat woman wearing jeans that were too tight. He stayed there for a while and then left for the hotel without a backward glance.

Crossing the hotel lobby, he noticed the little boy, Achilles, absorbed with a video game. The boy was wearing a T-shirt with a picture of Brad Pitt in the role of his namesake from the film "Troy." As he approached the reception desk, his eyes fell on a red campaign button on the desk: "Vote Bush, liberty marches on!" Next to it there was a poster with the image of Jesus looking toward the heavens, waiting for something that did not seem to come.

When he went up to the room, he did something he had been

thinking about for some time. He connected Marcelo's laptop with the telephone line. He logged on to the Web and googled his name and Iowa City. The first link took him to the local newspaper's site, to an article with the title: "Greek author probable victim of accident." The report mentioned that the car, evidently rented by the author in Iowa City, was found smoldering on a deserted road. Inside the metal hull destroyed by the fire, a body was found that had been reduced to ashes, which is presumed to be that of the Greek author. It also mentioned that a gold wedding ring, engraved with the name Candice and a date, was found at the place of the accident. This was strange since the author was divorced from his Greek wife. "The police investigation is on-going." A short biographical note of his followed, which he found rather flattering. Then, he typed into the search engine the name of Marcelo's company: "MIN, Los Angeles." This search brought up no results.

On the laptop's tool bar he saw a little envelope flashing, which meant that there were some new e-mails in the "Yahoo" account. He logged in. There were two messages. The most recent had been sent two days ago. The sender had the address cod-america@aol.com.

> Your terms are accepted.
> Of course, we also want the instructions...

The other had an earlier date. Four days ago. The sender was in this case smada@aol.com. He opened it. There was only one phrase:

> Open the attachment.

He double-clicked on the paperclip and immediately entered Windows media. It was a video. He pressed PLAY.

It was a short film, about twenty-five seconds long. It had been filmed by a hand-held camera. A door opened and the camera entered an apartment. First into a small entrance hall toward a wall decorated by a painting—an idyllic landscape with a river—then turned to the right, into a brightly lit living room with a loveseat, a small coffee table and a TV set. The wall opposite was taken up by sliding glass doors with half-shut vertical blinds that did not prevent the light from penetrating. One could see through the blinds the roofs of the tall buildings opposite—an indication that the apartment was located even higher. On the wall to the right there was a painting depicting a shark. The camera turned a little more to the right and revealed a thin folding screen hiding the back part of the sitting room. Then it turned around and, passing again through the entrance hall, captured a fleeting shot of a small kitchen with white tiles, and another shot to the left through a half-open door of a bathroom. It continued straight ahead and entered a sparsely decorated bedroom: a double bed, a bookcase, a desk with a laptop, and a small piano. The camera turned to the bookcase and slowly zoomed to the gray spine of a book, sandwiched between two classic novels of American literature: *Uncle Tom's Cabin* by Harriet Beecher-Stowe and *The Great Gatsby* by F. Scott Fitzgerald. The screen was then filled by the vertical title: *The Catcher in the Rye* by J. D. Salinger. On the lower part of the spine, there was a penguin inscribed in an oval with an orange background, the label of Penguin Books. He was well acquainted with this book, one of his favorites.

He watched the video several times, and then sent a reply to smada@aol.com.

More details are needed.

The e-mail router returned the e-mail almost instantly.

User unknown.

He shut down the laptop and lay down. He had a headache. He tried to relax but couldn't. He got up, took a hot shower, and returned to bed. His eyes fell on the picture opposite him with the slogan "Simplify." He smiled to himself, turned the other way, and after a while managed to fall asleep.

He is running like crazy. They are after him. He doesn't know who, doesn't know why. They are breathing down his neck. A turn onto a narrow road increases his lead, and he suddenly finds himself in front of a car and gets inside. The engine is running. He doesn't know how to drive. From the back seat, a male voice gives him instructions: "move the gear lever to first, ease up on the clutch pedal..." He is off. In the rearview mirror, he sees that it is his father who is in the back seat, covered with bandages. After a while, he realizes that he has escaped his pursuers. At a traffic light, his father hands him an envelope. Suddenly, something hits the windshield—probably a stone—and shatters it into a thousand pieces. At this moment it starts to rain. The rain falls into the car, and he is soaked through. He drives a little further. As he enters an empty avenue, he looks at the mirror to check the back seat of the car. But there is no one there. A hand touches his. He turns to the seat beside him: his mother is there. "Don't be afraid," she says, "I will show you the way." They reach a bridge spanning a river. The pavement is slippery. Suddenly, he loses control, and the car falls into the river. He is drowning. A hand grabs him and brings him to the surface. Lying down, he sees, leaning over him, the man who pulled him out. It's Marcelo, but he is also pale, like a corpse. The envelope has fallen beside him. Marcelo opens it and shows him the contents: a blank page. He feels that life is draining out of him. A meadow is visible in the background. At its center a flame rises into the sky.

Suddenly, a scream. Since arriving in America, he had been flooded with dreams. As if the thoughts and anguishes of a lifetime had detached themselves from the bottom and were floating in his sleep. He woke up at once, went into the bathroom and stood under the shower for an hour. When he felt like himself again, he went back to the laptop and entered the websites of Greek newspapers. He searched for some time but finally found it. The story of his disappearance and of the discovery of the burnt car and the body took up a single column. There was no mention of the ring. The article seemed to have some reservations about what exactly had happened, but the style was generally mournful. This article also ended with a short biographical note listing his works and a short analysis of his literary production. A small photograph from an old event at an Athens bookstore was underneath. He remembered that day. And that time. A time when everything he did was done fast. He lived fast, thought fast, walked fast, wrote fast.

"Life here has a crazy pace. How can anyone enjoy anything?" Tan, back in Iowa City, at a little bar one evening. Mel was with them—he had an obsession about the Civil War period.

"Back then, in the South, people lived by the seasons of the year, the movement of sun, while in the North they had discovered the clock. As you can imagine, the power that won the war was the time-table."

"But today, the South is even more conservative. All those fanatical Christian fundamentalists are from there. Nevertheless, everything has its silver lining: George Bush, the authentic child of Texas, has a direct connection with the spiritual plane. Oh, George, please tell us, what do you see behind this curtain?" commented Martin, gulping down his third gin-and-tonic.

"Christians, my foot. None of them is a Christian; the last Christian died on the cross."

Mel also had an obsession with Nietzsche.

"In the end, this country is like a broken high-tech toy," he had said earlier.

"Nah, it's just stupid. Like a big stupid dog with sharp teeth,"

Martin had replied, putting an end to the discussion. Iowa City's climate was very conducive to simile.

It was time—early evening. He opened Marcelo's suitcase again and chose the best clothes he could find: a white shirt with a pointed collar, black well-pressed pants, black shoes with rounded toes. He checked himself out in the mirror. He didn't like what he saw. He went to the bathroom, shaved, combed his hair, and finally got out of the room. This time Morris was in the lobby. He was watching TV, the Fox Channel. He turned around as soon as he saw him.

"Mr. Diaz, how are you? Everything O.K.?"

"Everything's fine."

"Bill O'Reilly," he said, and showed him the commentator. "The best journalist on TV. They are trying to bump him off. This woman Mackris has sued him for sexual harassment."

"Who?"

"Andrea Mackris. She used to work for him. Now she's saying that he sexually harassed her—all made up. If you'd seen her, you'd say she was asking for it. And she's a compatriot of my mother-in-law. Greek."

"Oh, that's why the children..."

"Yes, we gave them Greek names. We adore Greece. Homer, the ancient times. The Greeks were the first to discover democracy. A professor once told me that, if you read about Greece in the history books, you'll be learning everything about America. Read the history of Ancient Greece, continue from where the Romans came in, and nothing will surprise you again. You will understand what America is. I think that our President has been influenced by Greece. Don't you agree?"

"I wouldn't say so," he said. "Have a good day now."

"Going out for a walk?"

"Yes."

"Have fun," said Morris and went back to the TV.

As he walked away, he could hear O'Reilly saying:

In this age of terrorism, we should have correct and objective information. Since we now have a war in Iraq, we expect every American to support our troops. If you cannot do this, simply don't say anything. Those Americans, but also foreign allies, who actively are opposed to our army while there is a war, I'll consider enemies of the state.

The gun and the piano

ROCK STREET WAS TWO BLOCKS NORTH OF HILL STREET—a ten-minute walk from the hotel. Number sixteen was a typical small wooden single-family house, with a well-tended garden facing the street. The lights inside the house were on. The outline of a sitting room was visible through the thin curtains of the large front window. The garden gate was unlocked. He opened it, and the moment he entered the garden, he saw a small brown dog running straight at him. He froze. He tried to stay calm. He let the dog sniff him, and when it started to wag its tail, he did something that, in his case, took a lot of courage: he petted it and calmly walked toward the front door. A wind chime hung above the door, playing a sweet melody as it swayed in the light evening breeze. He rang the doorbell. He waited some time but no one answered. He rang again. Nothing. When he tried knocking on the door itself, to his great surprise, it swung open.

The door opened to a simply decorated living room. He could hear water running somewhere in the back of the house, as if somebody was taking a shower. Without thinking about it, he took a couple of steps inside. He immediately tripped over something sitting on the floor—a woven basket full of balls made of cloth—and fell flat on his face. As he fell, he knocked over a small table with a little glass vase that crashed to the floor and shattered. The sound of water stopped abruptly. He heard quick steps approaching, and in matter of seconds a woman appeared at the other end of the living room—stark naked. She was slim, with breasts that were somewhat large for her body and smooth pale skin. He recognized her immediately. She was the woman from the museum. The dog also came in and started barking, but did not attack. When she saw the stranger on her living room floor, Laura screamed and ran to a desk on the right. She opened the top drawer, took out a gun, and holding it tight with both hands, pointed it at him while words came pouring out.

"Who are you? What are you doing here? Don't move! Don't get up or I'll shoot! I swear I will! Don't you dare get up!"

Taken completely by surprise, he stammered:

"I'm sorry, I'm sorry, calm down! I've been knocking at the door for a while and it was open. I don't mean any harm, I only wanted to talk to you."

It was the first time someone had threatened his life with a gun, not to mention a naked woman he'd never met, in a foreign country—a woman who did not know who he was, not even who he was pretending to be.

"To talk to me?" screamed the woman, gripping the gun with both trembling hands. "Don't move!"

The dog had been barking the whole time, and it looked more scared than its mistress.

In an instant the future flashed in front of his eyes. He could see the bullet exiting the dark muzzle of the gun and, like in a Tarantino movie, traveling through the air in slow motion, while he, all during the fatal flight, would know that the final destination of the little metal tip's trajectory will be his body—his belly, his chest, or his head—and that this small, dense piece of metal that would spring from the tiny dark hole of the muzzle of the gun would have only one mission: to open within him a hole of the same diameter. And that imaginary line that the woman was preparing to create, pressing the trigger with her finger ever so slightly, that line which had as its object to unite the two holes—the smooth, factory-made one of the gun muzzle and the gaping, bloody one in his body—would tear the last image he would ever see in his life straight down the middle. A slight pressure of one muscle in the woman's index finger would bind them for life. Executioner and victim. For a brief instant in time he thought that, whatever happened, it would not be he who would die since he was already dead, in fact twice over. The next thing that crossed his mind was to do exactly whatever would make Laura connect the two holes, but what finally happened was something else. He said, or rather he felt a few words escape him as though someone had dictated them to him:

"I'm Marcelo."

For a few moments Laura stood still with the gun pointed at him. Then, she reached with her left hand and grabbed a robe that was draped over the desk's chair. Always pointing the gun at him, she tried to work the robe over herself and cover her nakedness.

"Marcelo? Marcelo who?"

"Marcelo Diaz, the one you've been e-mailing all this time. Almost every day."

"And how do I know that you are who you say you are?"

"Ask me something. Ask me something that only I would know. Something from the e-mails. But, for Heaven's sake, stop pointing that thing at me."

"What are my parents' names?" she asked nervously, keeping the gun pointed at him.

"Anthony and Vera."

"My dog's name?"

"Moxy."

"Why?"

"Because your father called you that when you were a kid."

"What kind of job did my mother have before she was married?"

"A model in advertising."

"What company was she doing advertisements for?"

"Some soap. Ivory soap."

"Ivory soap is not 'some soap.' It's an American icon."

"'So pure it floats.' Wasn't that the motto?"

Laura slowly lowered the gun and wrapped the robe around herself. Both of them stayed still for a few moments, she with the gun hanging from her hand and he sprawled on the floor. The woman spoke first.

"I didn't expect us to meet this way. You can get up now."

He got up slowly and stood there awkwardly, in obvious embarrassment. Laura pointed at the sofa.

"Please, sit down."

"OK."

"Give me a minute to get dressed."

Before too long Laura was back, dressed in simple jeans and a white T-shirt. Neither of them could find the courage to break the silence.

"I didn't think you'd show up in the end," she said.

"But as you can see, I'm here."

"I wasn't even sure you existed. That your name is really Marcelo."

"I can show you my passport..."

"You have a strange accent," Laura interrupted.

"Really?"

"Yes, I can't pin it down. You're Hispanic, but... Anyway... I'm sorry for everything. Things aren't normal in this town. We are all afraid after what happened. Right here, in Hannibal, the other day..."

"Yes, I know. But then, why did you leave your door open?"

"I'm totally dumb, stupid. I'd just come in and the phone rang, I was distracted and forgot all about it, and then I went to take a shower."

An embarrassed silence followed.

"Your dog doesn't seem to be much of a guardian."

Laura looked at him disapprovingly. "It's not Moxi's job to be my guardian."

"When he heard his name spoken by Laura, Moxi sprang towards him. He automatically leaned back.

"What, are you afraid of him? Didn't you write me that you had a dog yourself?"

"Yes. It's just that I'm a little..."

"I know. It's crazy. Let's sit down and relax a little. Let's talk about something else. So, when did you get here?"

He talked to her about his trip, making up a five-day odyssey across the country. She listened silently, watching him studiously. When he finished, he asked her out to dinner. She wasn't in the mood for that but suggested she cook something for him at home instead. He offered to help. Laura cleaned up the broken pieces of glass from the living room floor, and then they went to the kitchen and prepared pasta and a salad. He cooked the sauce. They did not talk much. The only thing Laura kept repeating was how bad she felt that she had welcomed him that way.

"I can imagine how ridiculous the whole thing seemed," she said.

"Ridiculous? No, it was anything but ridiculous," he answered.

"Scary?"

"Not that either."

She toyed a little with her hands. "How's L.A.? I've never been there."

"Big."

"And disjointed, no? Urban sprawl."

"Yes, it has 17 million people. If it were a country, it would be the fifth largest economy in the world. But nobody knows each other. Too impersonal."

Stolen words. Spoken by Tom Cruise in *Collateral*. He had seen it recently in Iowa City.

"All those cars... The ozone layer will be a sieve in a few years."

"You think so?"

"Some day the sun will rise, and the sun's rays will go through the Earth like X-rays."

Now he thought that she too had stolen her words from somewhere, but he couldn't remember from where.

When they sat at the table, Laura tried to fill his glass with wine. He refused, but when he caught her surprised look, he remembered Marcelo's relationship with alcohol and gave the excuse that he didn't feel like it at the moment.

At the end of the dinner that dragged on in general awkwardness, Laura said almost in a whisper, "The other day, someone came around asking about you."

"Where? Here?"

"At work. He asked me whether I knew a Marcelo Diaz," she said, stressing each word.

"What did you tell him?"

"I told him 'no.' Was that the right thing to say?"

They looked at each other. She seemed to be one of those women who look people straight in the eye. Hers were light blue, big, intelligent, soft and absorbing like blotting paper. Her face had begun to gradually reveal its secrets to him. It was exceptionally well-shaped. The lines of her cheekbones were strong but graceful, curving slightly and continuing until they joined together into a slim, delicate chin.

"What did he look like?"

"He was about thirty, slender, with straight blond hair, wearing a gray suit. His face had acne marks and he was wearing round glasses. He looked like a high-level business executive. He said he knew you. I asked him why he'd come to me. He said: 'We have information.' 'And who are you with your information?' I asked.

He didn't answer, but instead he gave me his card and asked me to call him if I saw you. 'It's very important for you,' he said."

Laura stood up, went to the desk and took something out of a drawer. She gave it to him. On the card was printed: "Thomas Jefferson—Imports" and below it was a cell phone number.

"Thomas Jefferson," he echoed, "like the president."

"You know him?"

"No. So, will you call him?"

"What do you think?" Laura answered, finishing her drink.

Another wave of silence came over them.

"It's hard face-to-face, isn't it?" This time it was he who broke the ice.

She looked at him but didn't answer. Then she got up and went to the other end of the living room, where there was a piano. She sat at the keyboard.

"I'm not the artsy type. I've written all this to you. The only thing I know is how to play the piano. And piano isn't culture. It's a bunch of white and black little strips that, if you touch lovingly, produce melodies. So here it is, my favorite piece of music: Bach's Fugue in G sharp minor."

She was very good. Her hands danced on the keys, producing notes that seemed to be chasing one another. A theme would start and run non-stop from one tone to another. The tones would return like waves, giving the impression that one was hearing many voices together. He was not an expert when it came to classical music, but the feeling that this piece evoked in him was like being in a theater, with different groups of dancers performing the same choreography, but in a different way, one after another. A continuous chase. The way she played was such that you felt that harmony was not the objective but the result of the movements of all those different tones. It was a dialogue between pieces of the same whole, chasing one another. A continuous melodic flight.

When she finished, she remained still for a while, with her head bent over the keys. He clapped.

"Bravo, it was wonderful!"

"A fugue," she said, "is like playing chess blindfolded," and raised her head slowly.

He noticed a black speck on her right nostril, probably a remnant of a nose piercing. Looking at her face more closely he saw a similar mark on her upper lip, another on the lower, and one below the right eyebrow. He remembered the ideograms on the back of her neck. Laura was a piercing veteran. She read his thoughts and explained.

"Ancient history."

"How ancient?"

"Quite."

She closed the piano's cover and turned toward him.

"What's that you are wearing around your neck?"

"A talisman," he said. "Native American."

"It's nice."

"Yes."

Another awkward silence fell over the living room, which Laura interrupted suddenly.

"Why did you come here?"

"I had to leave."

"Why?"

"I couldn't go on the same way."

"And why here?"

"Something brought me out here—luck, destiny, I don't know."

"Who is after you, Marcelo?"

He instinctively turned and looked behind him. His eyes fell on a little zinc doll standing on a sideboard. It was a chubby female form wearing a hat decorated with flowers, and it had wings on its back. He smiled.

"Whatever is after all of us."

"This guy looked like he was after something specific."

"I don't know him."

Another interval of awkward silence.

"After what happened with Mary Lou, and with this man asking about you, I don't know... I'm having second thoughts about it..." said Laura.

"About what?"

"About your staying here."

"Don't worry. I have already checked in at the Travelodge."

Laura seemed to be impressed. "Oh, yes?"

"I didn't want you to think that I..."

"To think what? What are you talking about?"

"That I want..."

"But who do you think I am? Do you think I'm looking for a man on the internet? I'm not looking for a man! I'm not looking for anything!"

Her tone had started to rise. Trying to calm down, she took a deep breath.

"Look, I liked what you wrote me. And from close up you seem to be a nice guy, though there is something strange in your story that I can't explain. You must have realized that I've been through a lot of shit. I can't, I don't have the luxury to waste myself. I don't even know what I wanted to get out of our correspondence. These last few months I'd been feeling very down. The net was a way out, but now I don't know if it was such a good idea."

"Maybe I should leave..."

"I almost shot you a little while back. OK, you've booked at the Travelodge, but now that I think about it, the least I owe you is to put you up for one night. There is a room available."

"I wouldn't want you to do it for that reason."

"Alright then."

He stood up, and with him, Moxi, tail wagging. But there was something he wanted to know.

"And you... why did you invite me to come?" He asked.

Laura stretched, arching her back. Her bosom heaved up. He couldn't keep from staring.

"Because of something you wrote in one of your last e-mails," she said.

"What was it?"

"We have the duty to get out there and face life not as something that has been given to us everlasting, but as something incomplete..."

He interrupted her and continued the sentence.

"...because our destiny is to extend it, to explore that which changes every day before our eyes."

"You remember it..."

"I remember, but it isn't mine. It's Norman Mailer's."

It seemed that Marcelo had been trawling in books for material.

"You didn't mention that in your e-mail."

"I don't know how much of what I've written to you is really mine."

Laura lit a cigarette. She drew the smoke in quickly, nervously.

"Was it borrowed? Did you copy other people's feelings?"

"I think that everything I wrote reflected my feelings."

"You think?"

"I think."

She smiled.

"What do you want from me, Marcelo?"

"I don't know exactly. The only thing I want is to get to know each other from up close, as real people."

"Some good start we made..." said Laura.

She rose from the piano and sat on the sofa. He moved closer.

"Which only means we can't do any worse... So, let's look at the bright side," he said, sitting next to her.

He looked into her eyes. Silence. He moved his hand behind her back. He entered his role—the way he thought Marcelo would act. The way he would have Marcelo act if he had been a character in one of his books. This sort of thing helped him. He would never have moved that fast.

"That's what it's all about? You've come so many miles, all the way here, for that?"

He didn't answer. He touched her shoulder. She turned her eyes toward him, challenging him. "It's almost a year since I've been with a man."

He drew her slowly closer to him. He caressed her hair.

"Won't you ask me why?"

He brought his face as close as possible to hers. Clear eyes, moist, tormented, beautiful.

"I don't..."

Before she could continue, he bent down and kissed her. She smelled wonderful, a perfume reminding him of laurel. She accepted him softly, as though she had been waiting for him. And then, suddenly, she pulled back and looked at him strangely, as if seeing him for the first time.

"I think it would be best if you go now."

"As you wish," he said, and stood up.

He didn't look behind him, but that didn't mean anything. He would be back tomorrow.

Aisée

THERE WAS A TRIPLE KNOCK AT THE DOOR, professional. It was
nothing like the knock that announced housekeeping. He glanced at
the clock. 9:43 a.m. He'd been awake just about an hour and was
watching TV, a re-run of the second Bush-Kerry debate, which had
taken place two days before. The knock came right at the moment
that Kerry mentioned the shares Bush owned in a timber company.
George Bush, Jr. had shot to the podium—the debate was more
relaxed than the first one, with each candidate being able to move
around on the stage—had taken the microphone and with a puzzled
grimace, twisting his mouth to the left and pointing his chin forward, had retorted, "I own a timber company? That's news to me!
Need some wood?"

He opened the door. At the doorstep was a tall forty-year-old
man with buzz-cut hair and freckles. He was wearing all too well
ironed blue jeans, a red shirt with ivory buttons, tall boots, and a
brown Stetson hat with a star in the middle.

"Mr. Diaz?"

"Yes, that's me."

"John Walzlager, I'm the sheriff here. May I come in?"

"What's the matter?"

"Nothing," said the sheriff and, without waiting for permission, entered the room and walked around checking things out. Then he sat on the only armchair, which was facing the TV.

"Good comeback, no? Don't shoot your mouth when you don't have proof." The sheriff took off his hat and laid it on his knees. "Now Mr. Diaz, do you like Hannibal?"

"Yes."

"It's a very nice town. And we have our history: Mark Twain, the river. There are so many tourists visiting us every year. But not many of them drive all the way from the other side of the country..." he said and stopped, waiting for an answer.

"Do I have to say something now?" he responded, annoyed by the attitude of his uninvited visitor.

"No, I'm only happy that someone like you is willing to drive thousands of miles in order to honor us... What is your profession, Mr. Diaz?"

"I work for an IT company. Data collection."

"Oh, yes? And what sort of data did you come to collect in Hannibal?"

"Nothing, I came to rest."

Bush was speaking on the TV about the threat of terrorism. The sheriff turned his eyes to the screen.

"America is a tolerant country, Mr. Diaz. Everybody fits here. Everybody that is, except certain people. You know who?"

"Who?"

"Those who don't appreciate the freedom that it offers them. You think it's easy to appreciate freedom, Mr. Diaz?" he said turning to face him.

"If you don't take it for granted, yes."

"Hah! Smart, eh? Bravo! Tell me, how do you know Laura Chance?"

"Do I have to answer?"

"No, no, you do not have to do anything, Mr. Diaz. You are free. Could you just do me a favor?"

"What?"

"Stop for a moment and think."

"Alright then, I'm thinking."

"No. You aren't thinking. You're wasting your time being a smart-ass. Now I want you to stop being a smart-ass and think for a moment."

"What are you getting at? What's the matter?"

"Let's just say there's a problem."

"What problem?"

"I know that some people are looking for you. Your name's been discussed around town. Whatever you're mixed up in, that, of course, is your problem. What I want from you is to sit down and think if you should stay here. You know what's happened here, Mr. Diaz?"

"I know."

"That's what I want you to think about. Since you just want to rest, think whether you've come to the right place at the right time. We'll talk again. Ah!" he said and pointed at the TV that was showing a close-up shot of Kerry. "And finally, you know, it's our guy who's going to win. Not this one, he's a know-it-all. The other one, he's one of us. Now I've got to go, I have something urgent to take care of. I'm sure you understand. Good day, Mr. Diaz."

The debate was coming to an end. Kerry was gesturing to emphasize his words. He switched to another channel. A minister was yelling: "Where's the cavalry? Where are the spaceships? Nowhere! Only Jesus will be there when the end comes." On the next channel, a gray-haired skinny man with a funny little mustache was answering the questions of an NBC anchorman. He was the president of a multinational corporation. "I am breaking in through open doors," the reporter was saying, "but they say that your company has the power to intervene decisively into the country's political life. Your grandfather and Kennedy..." The man interrupted: "I know what you're getting at, John. That we are making and breaking governments. Yes, you can also talk about my great-grandfather, talk about Hoover, Truman, talk about whatever you want... It's your job to make up interesting stories. Our job is doing business. The politician's job is to govern. We support the globalized economy that will bring jobs and prosperity to the American people. We don't play favorites. We work for consensus, John—Walter Lippmann's[4] words—he was a colleague of yours."

He turned the TV off and went to the laptop. He felt the urge to write but didn't know what. He didn't know anything any more. He tried to get his thoughts in order. He had met Laura. She was more or less as he had imagined her, but there was something else that he couldn't get a handle on. He read some of Marcelo's e-mails again and noted the borrowed phrases he could recognize. Most of them were Norman Mailer's, but there were lines from songs, as well as from movies. He then made two columns, one with his own name and one with Marcelo's. As soon as he finished writing his name, he tapped backspace repeatedly and deleted it as fast as he could. In its place he typed several dashes. In the column below he typed a description of himself, or at least of what his idea of himself was.

    Egocentric, over-sentimental, swings between
    extremes of fantasy and reality, has need of
    emotional anchor, needs a sense of mission in
    life, sense of incompleteness, need of con-
    stant   stimulation,   deepest   loneliness.
    Constant self-doubt, sense of rejection,
    unclear sense of self, loss of sense of self
    when emotionally weak, absorption by the other
    person, idealizes women.

In Marcelo's column he wrote:

    Troubled mind, stress, confusion, lack of
    self-awareness, unresolved conflicts caused by

tension between duty and desire, need of emo-
tional anchor, impudence, ability to
change(?), irresponsibility, naiveté, immatu-
rity. In regards to women: fear along with
admiration, prone to acting impulsively (does
kissing Laura fit the role?).

He read them. They meant nothing to him. Under the two paragraphs he wrote:

There is nothing more real than that which is
described properly. The description of a
flower in a book can be more real than a blos-
som you come upon by chance in a garden. Man,
however, is indescribable; there are only
embellishments. So then, I simply state: Me: a
fugitive. Marcelo: a dead man. That's the
truth. Therefore, I as Marcelo: Hubris?

He sat for a while looking at the paragraph he had just written.
Then, he got on the Web and played again the short video clip of
the interior of the apartment. He played it again in slow motion. In
the room next to the laptop there was a chessboard. He froze the
picture. All the pieces were in their place except for the black
knight, which was in the middle of the board. What did that mean?
What did all of it mean? What if he looked at everything as ele-
ments of the plot? But what kind of plot would it be? What sort of
conceit did it serve? And who might be the author? His head was
spinning. He went into the bathroom, took a cold shower, got
dressed and went out.

At the restaurant, Lester was alone this time. They sat together. He
got an update on the latest developments in the investigation. The

news was that Paul, Roy's friend, the one who lived in the house next to the one where the murder took place, had disappeared. "Strange guy, we'd never seen him with a girl. We knew he went with prostitutes, but with a regular girl, never." Roy had been questioned again and could confirm his friend's alibi for certain hours. Then, moved by a song of the group "Violent Femmes" that was playing on the jukebox, they talked about music, until, as their dessert arrived, Lester mentioned Laura. "I know you were there yesterday." He couldn't deny that. Lester talked to him about her at great length. For as long as Laura had lived in Hannibal, she had not made any friends. He was the only person to whom she had opened up. Lester confirmed what Laura had told him about her parents, her religious upbringing, her sense of guilt. It seems that after leaving home, Laura went through a very wild phase—she was way out there. Drugs, sex, poverty, loneliness. "Of course, she hasn't told me any details. Only that, had sugar been illegal, she would have sniffed that too." She went through very rough times, and when she managed to kick her drug addiction, she found refuge in Hannibal.

Leaving the restaurant, he turned towards the river. He wanted to clear his head a little. He saw a riverboat going by. A tourist boat, some people on the deck were waving Panama hats. How strange! It made him remember his grandfather. His father's father. He too had a Panama hat. He wore it in Aegina—he and his parents used to stay with him on the island during the summer months. Grandpa had been a great storyteller. He was born January 1, 1900. He was the first baby of the century. Terrible stories. Most of them were about Asia Minor, the disastrous year 1922, when hundreds of thousands of Greeks were driven away from their ancestral homes, after the Greek army had been defeated by the Turks.

The most memorable story jumped into his mind. Grandpa was in the army, and his company had been stationed for a couple of weeks in a wooded area. At night he would hear a distant cry, it sounded like a woman weeping. He was the only one who heard it, nobody else did. Each time he'd get up and go searching in the dark foliage that surrounded them. For three nights in a row he couldn't find anything. But on the fourth night, he saw her. It was a young girl who'd hidden in a ditch and had piled up some shrubs over herself so that she would not be seen. She had a broken leg. She was a Turk, but spoke a little Greek. She was extraordinarily beautiful. Grandpa got in also, in the hole, and they… got together there. Then, he carried her two kilometers back, to the Turkish frontline, putting himself in danger. Aisée was her name and she had some eyes—oh God, her eyes! He would ask Grandpa to tell him the story again and again, each time with more details. One time he'd talk about her eyebrows, another about her breasts, another about her arms. His grandfather! How he wished that *he* had been his father instead! He had based a short story of his on this story, with a few changes, set in Yugoslavia during the civil war, with the characters a Croat man and a Serb woman. And he superimposed his father's face on the Croat. The writer. The con man. He dressed his father in his grandfather's clothes. Grandfather, the father's father. The past of the past. A present that was gone, twice.

The smell of dried seaweed. A sparkle of light flashed on the surface of the water. A small bird took wing. The moments rained down like drizzle, even though there was not a cloud in the sky. He felt a headache coming on.

He sat near the bank and watched the riverboat disappearing around the bend of the river. Then he decided to turn back. While he was walking along the tracks, he saw a short man with a chubby face, well-dressed in black clothes, coming towards him. When they got close to each other, the stranger stopped in front of him. His skin was very pale, his eyes round, his eyebrows arched, his lips delicate.

"Don't I know you from somewhere?" the stranger asked in a deep voice.

"I don't think so, I just got into town."

"No, we've met somewhere else, a different place."

"Where?"

"Out West."

"I don't think so, I don't remember you."

"That's strange."

"That I don't remember you?"

"Yes, usually people remember me," said the short man and came a step closer to him.

"Well, is there something you need?" he asked.

The man fixed his eyes on his face.

"I think you know what I need," he said slowly.

"I have no idea. I don't know you," he said and went on his way.

He spent the entire afternoon in his room at the Travelodge, reading the e-mails and trying to understand Marcelo Diaz as best he could. His first impressions were correct. Marcelo seemed to be very stressed out. He might even have been suffering from a persecution complex. The words "We must be careful" came up frequently, as well as "They are everywhere." It made him think of the mathematician John Nash in the film *A Beautiful Mind*, who saw communist agents everywhere. Marcelo, however, did not give any names. He conveyed an aura of a vague threat, as if some people coveted something in his possession. Combining this with the sheriff's visit, with what Laura had told him, with his recent meeting with the strange man, and moreover with everything the late Marcelo had managed to tell him before his death, it became obvious: someone was after Marcelo. That is to say, someone was after *him*.

For a brief moment, something went through his mind. The opposite of *the idea*. That he'd had enough. No more. It was the first time since he had seen Marcelo dead that he realized the full extent of what he had done. Hubris. He had wanted to disconnect himself from the past. That was fine. But could it be that at precisely the moment when you renounce it, your past becomes your destiny? Maybe there was still a way out. Maybe it wasn't too late for him to turn back. He would get in the Mustang, drive back to Iowa City, leave the car hidden someplace and present himself to Frost. "It was just some crisis I went through; I needed some time alone. I rented a car to get away for a couple of days." And the burnt car with the dead body in it? "Somebody stopped me on the road; he had a gun. I managed to escape. He took my car. I don't know what happened afterwards. I was in shock. It took me a few days to recover."

He thought it over. It was not believable. It was worse than a third-rate mystery novel. In any case, this missed the point. The heart of the matter was that he did not want to go back. He had made up his mind—first at the lake and then at the telephone booth. He was now in the game. Events now followed their own momentum. He had left; he had flown away, down, into the depths of the mine. Into the deepest tunnel. And this canary had strong lungs.

Back to Marcelo. Back to his pursuers. Back to the sheriff. What was his role? If those people had gotten in touch with the sheriff, why did they not approach him as well? Why didn't the sheriff tell them where he was staying? Or was it Walzlager who sent him the man at the railroad tracks? What was it the man wanted in any case? What could Marcelo have that was so valuable? What was this MIN company that did not exist on the Net? His work brought him into contact with a lot of data; could it be that some of it was classified? Was that how Marcelo had come into contact with something that was outside his purview? Could it be perhaps that the black box contained all the answers? Despite having the proper training, he couldn't get the answers to these difficult questions. He went to the closet and took the box out of the safe. Although he knew it was useless, he started playing with the combination lock, trying different numbers. Ten minutes later, he'd had enough.

He went to the bathroom, undressed, and looked at himself naked in the mirror. He thought he looked thinner than before. He went back into the room, opened the suitcase, and this time chose a pair of blue jeans and a thin blue sweater. As he was putting on the jeans he felt something in the front right pocket. He took it out—a notepad. He started looking through the pages. They were blank. Close to the middle was a photograph of a woman in her thirties, glued on the paper. She had blond curly hair, a full face, strong cheek-bones, slim nose, penetrating eyes. She was holding a child in her arms, about two years old, dressed in blue overalls. It was the same child as the one in the photo he had found in the Mustang. She was probably Candice, Marcelo's wife. He looked through the rest of the pages. They were all blank except for the last one. There was a phrase written there in blue ink that seemed to be the deceased's motto: "There is nothing to fear but fear itself."

A statement that had a lot of truth in it. He continued along this line of thought. Fear takes revenge on those who feel it. You transmit onto others every fear you have ever experienced. The level of personal development of every human being is reflected in the way he transmits his fear—from where and to whom. His own wife would have quite a few things to say about this, his mother too. But this time it was somebody else, an unknown American of Hispanic origin he had accidentally met in the wilderness, who had transmitted to him *his* own fear.

He had decided to go out, but now felt too exhausted. He lay on the bed still dressed. He fell asleep almost immediately, but not for long because, perhaps ten minutes later, he was jolted awake by a knock on the door. He got up, went to the door and asked who it was.

"It's me, Laura," a woman's voice answered.

"Just a moment," he said. He went to the laptop and turned it off. Then he opened the door.

Laura was standing in front of him, beautiful, almost a different woman. Her hair, backlit by the hallway lights, looked as if it had caught on fire, and her lips were a shadow framed with red flowers. The hallway had been suddenly transformed into a small beautiful corner of the world.

"May I come in?"

"Yes, of course, come in."

She entered the room, walking slowly. She stood in the middle and turned to face him. It was obvious she wanted to speak, but something prevented her. She seemed to have come with a planned speech, now totally forgotten.

"I wanted to see you," she said after a few seconds, and he understood immediately. He had understood right away, from the moment he looked into her eyes when he opened the door. But he was not prepared for the little earthquake that her words unleashed inside him. And this was something that did not fit in with the role he was playing.

He walked to her and took her in his arms. Their bodies bound themselves together. The laurel scent enveloped him. He looked at her. There was a certain glance, an intimate smile. He bent down and kissed her on the back of her neck, right above the ideogram.

"The man who wrote the e-mails"

DANCING ON A TIGHT ROPE. That about described it. There was a feeling of wholeness within the fragmentation, something familiar inside the unknown. When he looked into her eyes a bit later, the old familiar heavy feeling had returned: the cold loneliness of a lost paradise that even being in love cannot restore. Or else, the memory of a primordial, long-lost joy that the joining together with another person only makes more painful. In short, the feeling of the eternally exiled. But within a moment she did something—small, barely perceptible, a slight opening of the mouth along with a turn of her head to the side—that was nonetheless enough to insert in this new life of his a feeling he had never felt before: *this exile was not his alone.* He shivered and entered her with all the force of a hope unexpectedly bubbling up. And for the first time in a very long time his body responded to him again.

Together in bed. She was smoking while he stroked her belly. When she finished the cigarette, she started talking without looking at him. Her monologue took a whole hour, maybe even more. He did not interrupt her once. Laura started hesitantly, saying how awful she felt about the way she had received him—"Surely, at some point it became funny," she added. "Coming from the other end of the country to see a naked woman pointing a gun at you..." Then, how different she found him up close, how less nervous, less stressed than the man who wrote her the e-mails. She said it exactly like that: "than the man who wrote me the e-mails," which disturbed him but he didn't let it show. After a brief pause, she said that she had never done anything like this before, coming to a man uninvited like that. "Something happened when you came to my home, something nice." She repeated that he seemed a little strange to her, that she felt there was something dark in his life and that she was ready to hear everything.

"I'm not a person who gets easily shocked. You can trust me. I've been through all sorts of things, and I know there's often a lot beneath the surface."

She stopped there, looked at him, saw that he was not going to interrupt her and continued, starting to explain what the "all sorts of things" were. It was the continuation of the family story from the point where she had left it in the e-mails. First, she repeated everything about her father: about how, after meeting her mother, he found God, repented, and changed from a petty criminal to a religious fanatic, about the extreme religious upbringing she received at home, until her story took an unexpected turn when she suddenly said:

"And who could imagine that a child like me, who believed that everything the Holy Bible said was literally true, that Hell and Heaven exist exactly as described, with the fire and the brimstone, the gardens and the trees, that Adam and Eve were real people, that such a child would suddenly, at the age of twelve, wake up one night and see the same person who had raised her according to these moral principles, the person whom she trusted as the only man in her life, the personification of honor and protection, her own father, lying next to her in her bed, beneath an emaciated crucified Christ, gaunt as a concentration camp victim—and taking her in his arms."

What followed was even more painful. She talked about how, for a long time, she would feel his breath, his hands on her, caressing her gently, not forcefully, even with tenderness. And that this would become the usual thing, and each time, every night, under the eyes of the dying God, the caress would advance some infinitesimal space on her skin, to the point that she would not even know the difference and couldn't tell whether this was fatherly tenderness or something else. But even if it were something else, she would not have been able to distinguish it, to name it, since everything she knew, everything she learned, came from him. The man of her life, her father. Later, when she was older—fourteen, fifteen, sixteen years old—and was having nightmares every night that kept her from sleeping, her parents would take her in their bed every evening between the two of them, and she would sleep with her father on her right and her mother on her left. And her mother would turn away from her, and her father would caress her, always softly, without ever descending exactly where she was afraid of, but almost touching her nipples, rubbing with his finger the top of her pubis. The way he did it, she was always left with a feeling of being unsatisfied, to the point that she thought: *Oh God, let him go further down.* But to do what? She did not really know. The only thing she knew was that some kind of act had begun, a situation that, on the one hand, was dirty, horrible, wrong, but on the other, the slow, routine way of its progression, instilled within her a level of acceptance which liquefied her, robbed her of words with which to understand it, and so, in a way, absolved her. And this act remained always unfinished; in order to understand its horror, she would have to live it in full, to taste it, so that she might someday be able to put it behind her. Her mother, in the meantime, made not the slightest comment, as if all this was perfectly normal. And even for Laura, it had by now become something expected.

And one night when she was alone in the house with him, she came out of the bathroom naked, almost provocatively—"It's something I seem to do, coming naked out of the bathroom when I'm not expected!" she laughed at herself. Her father was watching TV in the living room, when he suddenly saw his daughter coming out of the bathroom with only a skimpy towel wrapped around herself and that night what was bound to happen happened. "I don't know exactly what—I have wiped it out of my memory—in any case *something* happened that was different than what had been going on," she said. She did not run away immediately. The situation continued for some months and this "something" happened four or five more times. Her father would plunge into the Bible each time after the "act," and she was slowly melting away. She ate almost nothing at all: her weight dropped below one hundred pounds. Then, one night, he saw her on the street corner by the house, kissing a boy. It was the first boyfriend she'd had in her life, a sensitive boy who fell in love with her, in part because he felt sorry for her. Laura's father beat her mercilessly—her mother was in the other room. At daybreak Laura packed her things and left.

It was then that she had the ideograms done. She wanted to have a phrase on her body, a word that, her whole life, would remind her of what had happened. And this phrase, this word, she wanted to be understood by as few people as possible. That was why she had chosen the ideograms. They had been done by a local tattoo artist. They cost her almost half her savings. No, she would never erase them, but she had sworn that some day, when all this was firmly in the past, she would let her hair grow long to hide them.

He asked her what the phrase on her neck meant. She didn't answer and went on with her story. When she left home, she wandered many places, until finally she ended up in Saint Louis. She worked there as a waitress, a baby-sitter, and was also involved in other things she could not talk about. "I don't want to remember it any more, you understand?" "Drugs?" he asked. She wouldn't give a straight answer. "I hated my body. I took revenge on it in all possible ways. I did things that were quite extreme."

However, a few years later her "guardian angel" appeared—a

musician, very well known. She met him one evening at a bar by chance. He invited her to his table and heard her story. He talked to her the whole night, and she would never forget what he said. "He's the wisest man I've ever met," she said. He helped her financially as well—"Don't think anything bad, he didn't want anything in return"—and she managed to get back on her feet. "I owe him everything. He opened my mind. He told me something that might sound simple but that I will never forget: "Life is hard, but compared with what?" He asked her who the man was, but Laura didn't answer and went on with her story.

Two years ago, she moved to Hannibal. She didn't make any friends, lived alone. The only person who got close to her was Lester. They talked about politics—he was also a member of Greenpeace. When a scandal broke about genetically engineered foods, she tried to organize a protest, but nobody wanted to take part—"People are ultra-conservative here." Lester wanted to get closer. "Very subtly I indicated to him I just wanted to be friends."

"And the musician?" he asked again.

"We don't see each other. He's become something of a recluse and now lives on a farm, but we talk on the phone two or three times a year."

The Treasure Room

HE TOOK HER IN HIS ARMS. They held each other for a long time. Then he began to tell her about himself. It wasn't easy. He had to remember what he'd read in Marcelo's e-mails and avoid any contradictions and inconsistencies. He took what Marcelo—who had never referred to his parents—had written to Laura, and combined it with an elliptic account of his own life. He talked mainly, without going into too much detail, of his mother's suicide: "I found her. I was twenty-seven years old. I'd been knocking on the door for a long while. I knew she was in there. Finally, I broke down the door. She was face down in the bathroom. The pills had spilled all over the floor tiles. She had taken them by the handful, a huge amount." To Laura's understandable confusion as to why he had not mentioned something so important in his e-mails, he answered that it was something he had not talked about with anyone for many years—and he was telling the truth about that. He went on to talk about the conflict with his father: "It was his fault. He destroyed her. He was a loser, someone who'd never achieved anything substantial in his life, the ultimate egotist. He hit her, he humiliated her in front of other people, had affairs. Finally she couldn't take it any more and gave him a taste of his own poison. From then on, it was pure hell. He insulted her all the time. Me too. Not only did he never encourage me in anything, but he underestimated me. He never understood what I found in books—'You are a coward,' he'd say. 'You hide behind your books.'"

He realized his mistake the moment the words had left his mouth. "What do you mean with books?" asked Laura confused. "I mean studying. Math... and everything I was reading in college," he covered his fumble. He continued with his relationship disaster: "I married her so I wouldn't lose her, and the prison I'd built, I discovered much too late." He concluded conveying a sense of complete, overwhelming loneliness. He was speaking about himself, but everything he was saying was through the filter of an American corporate employee from Los Angeles, who had been abandoned by his wife and child. When speaking of Candice, he was talking about his own wife, and when speaking about his child, he had in mind the seashell-shaped piece of paper with the 9.4 mm speck. Before coming to America, he had realized he would never become a father. He would only remain the angry son of an angry father.

"Finally, I decided to change completely, to get reborn," he concluded.

"'Man must be reborn'—the words of Christ to Nicodemus," said Laura.

"Yes?"

"And Nicodemus asks him: 'How can a man be born when he is old? Can he inhabit a second time his mother's womb, and be born?' And Jesus answers: 'Man must be reborn through water and the spirit'—this was his favorite passage from the Bible."

"Whose?"

"His."

It seemed that on that day she had already used the word "father" too many times.

Just before three, Laura left—"I don't want them to see me in the morning, it's bad enough Maya saw me coming up."

She was not wrong, since the next day, while he was having

breakfast in the lobby, Maya started gossiping about Laura. "Be careful," she said, "that woman is dangerous." They say she's a witch. No one has ever seen her at church. I'm telling you for your own good: stay away from her."

He smiled and, changing the subject, asked Maya whether she knew what her name meant in Greek. "Of course! My mother was from Greece, from Lamia. Her name was Calliope Georgiou." Maya started talking to him about her family's history, until the phone rang and she had to go inside.

He took advantage of the opportunity to escape and went back to his room. He opened the laptop and got on the Web. He typed his name in the search engine and found some new information. A major Athens newspaper had an article. Some writers from Iowa City were interviewed. Frost said that he was shocked, Harim that he did not believe he had been killed, and Martin, with his characteristic stolidity, said something that would be incomprehensible to most: "'To be born again,' sang Gibreel Farista tumbling from the heavens, 'first you have to die.'"[5] Between the lines of Martin's statement, he perceived an echo of a two-hour-long conversation they'd had, which dovetailed perfectly with the conversation he'd just had with Laura. In any case, it seemed that in Greece they really considered him dead. Moreover, a literary evening dedicated to his memory had been announced to take place at his publishing firm's offices.

Then he did something that had been on his mind from the moment he had arrived in Hannibal but that scared him. He logged on to his Internet Service Provider in Athens and opened his own Greek e-mail. There were twelve new messages. Three from the newspaper—the editor-in-chief writing him that only half of the report had arrived, then again that he was still waiting for the rest and finally, that he was wondering whether it had been lost. Another message was from an old friend of his, a translator—her impressions from her trip to Israel, going into details about her visits to the Wall of Tears and to a kibbutz (how is it that she had remembered him?). There were four spam e-mails, three invitations to literary events and, finally, the twelfth came from her, from his wife. A year and a half later. He moved the cursor on the little envelope and touched her name. He held his finger over the button and let it hang like that for quite a while. Her messages. He had once printed them all and put them together in a volume, had bound it with red cardboard and had given it as a present to her. It was on the island of Hydra in the summer, on their anniversary. He clicked on the message, moved the cursor to delete and sent it to the Recycling Bin without reading it. He did not stop there, however. He accessed his Internet Service Provider, typed in his password— the one he knew by heart—and changed it. In its place he typed something at random, without looking at the keyboard. He copied the random password to the confirmation request, and saved it knowing that now, even if he wanted to, he could not have access to his e-mails any more.

At that moment he heard a sound coming from the street. It was faint at first, but was constantly growing in volume. After a couple of minutes he could clearly hear: "Missouri Senator Jim Talent will be speaking to the young people of Hannibal at two in the afternoon, at the Ronald Fine Art Center on the campus of Hannibal La Grange College." A glance at his watch—one o'clock. He'd intended to go out anyway. He stayed in the room for a little longer, recording on the laptop what Laura had told him the other day, and worked a little more on Marcelo's profile. He understood him better now. He also copied and put together in one file some representative excerpts from his e-mails to Laura.

```
What can I tell you, my past is for me like a
stone wall that I'm always pushing hard against,
and sometimes something shifts slightly and I
can take a look through some crack. My life is
```

passing me by. I'm trying to make do, but it's
very difficult, especially when it comes to
time. Things have become even harder lately,
ever since something new entered my daily routine.

What this "something new" was, Marcelo did not elaborate on.
Laura asked a few times but never got an answer. At ten to two, he
turned off the laptop and went out.

"Our strategy is a success! Four years ago, Afghanistan was the
stronghold of Al Qaeda, Pakistan a transit corridor for terrorist
groups, Saudi Arabia a fertile ground for financing terrorists, Libya
a center of production of secret nuclear weapons, Iraq a constantly
growing threat, while Al-Qaeda could attack wherever it wanted,
without fear. Today, the government of a free Afghanistan is fighting terrorism, Pakistan is arresting the leaders of terrorist organizations, Saudi Arabia is also doing the same. Libya has dismantled its
nuclear weapons program, the army of a free Iraq is fighting for
that nation's freedom from terrorism and more than three quarters
of the most important members of Al-Qaeda have been arrested or
killed. Under the leadership of President Bush, we have taken the
lead, shown the way. Many other countries are following us and
now the world, America, Missouri, Hannibal and each and every
one of you are much safer!"

He was a man of about forty-five, with reddish-brown hair, a
youthful face and slim eyeglasses, wearing a tight blue jacket. With
each point he made, he hit the podium with his right fist. When he
finished, the whole amphitheater rose and cheered him for a full
five minutes, shouting: "Bush for liberty" and "Talent is power."
The people seemed happy, were waving little red flags and signs
with the face of the President from Texas. After playing the
National Anthem again—it had been played at the beginning of the
event—the public left in an orderly manner. He had reached the exit

of the Center, when he felt a hand touch him. Someone had slipped something into his coat pocket. He just managed to catch sight of him before he disappeared into the crowd. He was a thin young man, unshaven, with a blue cap covering his hair. Just before he was gone, he turned back and gave him a meaningful look.

He put his hand in his pocket. He pulled out a piece of paper and read the note:

> About the subject of our mutual interest, meet me at the Mark Twain Cave, in the Treasure Room, tomorrow, at one o'clock sharp. Doc sent me.

The plot thickens, he thought. And the actors are appearing one at a time. First, the short man on the tracks, then, the young one here. Since he had no idea what it was all about, he'd have to follow their leads.

Back at the Travelodge, the scene with Laura pointing the gun at him jumped into his mind for no apparent reason. Why this image? Maybe because he had reached the point where he did not know whether he was himself the gunman, the target or the bullet.

He spent another day with Laura, at her house. They talked about various things. He answered her questions playing the role of Marcelo perfectly, based on what he'd learned from the e-mails. She talked about her life, adding details to what she had already told him. But mainly they made love. When she fell asleep, he lay quietly looking at her, wondering how things would have been if Marcelo were here in bed with her instead of him. Taking Marcelo's place he had made a bargain. But one does not make deals with the dead. With whom, then, had he made this bargain? Who was *his* Mephistopheles? And what would be the price he was bound to pay?

The Mark Twain Cave was a little ways outside Hannibal, below a hill. Arriving at the stone entrance, he read on the brightly lit display case outside that this area had been bought in 1840 by a certain Dr. McDowell, who had sealed it and used it to conduct experiments and research on human corpses. The character of Indian Joe who stole bodies from the cemetery is said to have been based on this same doctor. The outlaw Jesse James had also used it as a hiding place in 1879 for a while. The cave, however, became famous mainly from Twain's book, since the underground labyrinth of its passages inspired the author to make it the place where Tom Sawyer and Becky Thatcher get lost. It had been an important tourist attraction since 1886.

He bought a ticket and went in. He was carrying a backpack with the laptop and the box inside, in case this proved to be Marcelo's important meeting. He would wait, though, to find out first what the dead man's role was in this story.

It was a complicated route through the cave, with its arched ceilings and twisting passages that often crossed each other. The cave was really impressive. There were not more than two or three tourists in it. He walked for quite a while, following the signs marking each area. He went by the Five Points, Aladdin's Palace, the Spring, and the Grand Avenue, where a bat supposedly blew out Tom and Becky's candle. The route continued through the Parlor, a natural underground room—the place where Tom swore to Becky that he would find a way for them to get out—until he finally reached the Treasure Room.

The light was dim, but it wasn't hard to recognize the young man's silhouette holding a gray bag in his arms. He approached him. The young man glanced quickly around to make sure no one was watching, and when he was sure they were alone, said to him in low tones, "Sorry for the trouble, but this seemed to be the safest way."

"Okay."

"Doc sent me, you understand?"

"Yes."

"The *interested party* is ready," said the young man and looked at him.

He had no other choice. "Who is ready?"

"I'm speaking about the *interested* party, you understand? Right?"

"Yes."

"The total offer has been increased to one and a half million. And you are going to work it out with Doc. Okay?"

The guy is obviously only a messenger, he thought. He probably shouldn't show his cards now.

"Yes."

"Doc said that you'll have everything ready."

"Yes. Will you be taking care of the deal?" he risked it again.

The young man looked at him strangely.

"Of course not. I'll tell you where you need to go."

"Where, then?" he asked, realizing that it would have been a big mistake if the guy had seen the box.

"The meeting will take place in Chicago. In the bag is the down payment in cash, the date and the address. As for the rest, you know, right?" he said and moving a little to the side, pointed at the backpack. "That looks pretty heavy."

"Yeah, I'm going on a little hike after this."

"Good. I'll leave first; I'll walk around the cave. You stay another five minutes and then leave," said the young man. He gave him the handbag and with slow steps walked away to the back of the cave.

He waited for the five minutes to pass and then headed towards the exit. When he got out in the fresh air, he looked around. Not a soul. He opened the gray bag and looked inside. It was full of stacks of hundred dollar bills. A folded piece of paper was placed in the front pocket. He unfolded it.

Joshua Patterson, 7th floor, Room No. 15, 46 Quincy Street, Chicago. Tuesday, October 19, 1:00 p.m. Don't knock. Entrance code: 190760.

He clasped the handbag to his chest and started walking towards the town.

When he opened the door of his room, he found himself in front of a shocking sight. It was as if a tornado had passed through. There was total chaos: his suitcase upside down and its contents thrown about, the sheets torn off the bed, the closets open, socks, shirts, underwear, even his razor on the floor, the TV upside down in a corner. He looked around the room quickly to see whether something was missing. No. Whoever had done this had not found what he was looking for. In any case, Marcelo's inheritance held nothing of interest, except the box and the laptop. It had been a very good idea to take them along to his meeting after all.

He went down to the reception desk and got Morris. When the hotel manager saw the situation, he was shocked. He said he had not seen anyone suspicious going upstairs—the hotel was practically empty at that time, and he knew all the guests by sight. Morris claimed that he'd been at the front desk the entire time Marcelo was away, except for about twenty minutes that he'd gone down to the basement to do some maintenance work. His embarrassment seemed real.

Morris began to call housekeeping in order to clean up the room. He stopped the manager and asked him to call the sheriff instead. Morris made the call but the sheriff, dealing with a rush of calls, sent a young boy wearing oversize pants and running shoes, who, after asking some standard questions, took two or three photos with a cheap-looking camera and left.

When he was alone in the room again, he remembered that he was still holding in his arms the bag full of money that he hadn't even counted. He locked the door and opened the bag. He counted a hundred and ten thousand dollars. He put the money back in and wondered what Marcelo would be paid "a total of one and a half million" for. It had to be the contents of the black box. Did it have anything to do with the book he had seen in the video clip in Marcelo's e-mail? What could a home movie of the interior of an apartment, ending with a close-up shot of a book by Salinger mean? What kind of shady deal was Marcelo involved in? Money laundering? A drug deal? And who, then, was this "interested party?" And what did "*a total* of one and a half million" mean?

Suddenly, he started laughing. It was funny, but the whole situation reminded him of one of his first books. There too, an unsuspecting hero had gotten involved in a similar situation, when he had come upon a cross that had been thrown away in a small grove. In his book, the cross played a role similar to that of the ear that the hero in David Lynch's *Blue Velvet* finds, an accidental finding that embroils him in an incredible adventure. At one point, the guy's house is broken into, and things are rifled through. The cross is what everyone is after; it is being claimed by two rival factions. If the future held any more things in common with his book, at least there would be a happy ending. His hero survives the terrifying ordeal, and having been shaken out of a state of chronic lethargy, starts a new life.

His eyes fell on the lilies that filled the wallpaper. Then at the bag with the money. He couldn't stay there any longer. He packed his clothes, took the black box, wrapped it in a plastic bag and put it in the gray bag with the money, which he then placed at the bottom of the suitcase. He came down with his things, settled the hotel bill with Morris, and got into the car. At a hardware store downtown, he bought a strong lock that he used to secure the bag with the money and the black box, before returning it to the bottom of the suitcase, wrapped in Marcelo's coat. He put the key to the bag on the key chain with the car keys. He drove first to Laura's workplace, but the museum was closed, so he drove on to her house. He could see her silhouette in the window. She opened the door looking quite surprised, since he was holding the suitcase in one hand and the laptop in the other. For a moment, he was afraid he had made a big mistake.

The next few minutes showed him that Laura had just been startled. He asked her if he could stay at her house for the night. He did not say anything about the break-in at the hotel.

"I'll be leaving tomorrow."

"Why? Did something happen?"

"No, nothing in particular."

"Is it because of the way... that I made the first..."

"No, no..."

Laura looked hard into his eyes. "You're afraid?"

"It's not what you think... I simply want a change of scene, to go somewhere else."

"And where are you planning to go?"

"To Chicago, probably."

"Marcelo..."

"What?"

"Nothing," she said, took him by the hand and led him to the bedroom.

They made love until it got dark. Then they had dinner, talked for a while, and lay down again. She fell asleep immediately. He, on the other hand, was wide awake. After a while he got up, took the suitcase, and put it underneath the bed on his side, feeling he needed to have it as close to him as possible. Then he went to the kitchen, drank some water, and ate a piece of cake. Laura had stuck some photographs with little magnets on the fridge. She was in the largest one, with long hair, looking very beautiful. In another one, smaller and somewhat fuzzy and faded, there was a couple: a gray-haired man with a determined face and strong cheekbones, and a thin woman with brown hair, with traces of fading beauty. The picture was scratched, as if someone had crumpled it up. The rest of the things on the fridge related to Laura's activism. A little magnet-button of Greenpeace, a picture of the Earth with the slogan: "Help us to address global warming," and a small poster depicting a huge mushroom cloud, underneath which, handwritten with a marker in what looked like her handwriting, was the following:

Citizens of Hannibal
You live within the fallout zone of the Callaway nuclear reactor. It is a 1,143 megawatt pressurized water reactor, which was constructed by Westinghouse Electric and belongs to American Corp. A serious accident at Callaway would cause up to 11,500 immediate deaths and another 9,600 deaths from cancer for the exposed population.

Moxi was in the living room, looking at him and wagging his tail. He approached and almost unconsciously petted him, something he never imagined he could have done. He sat on the sofa for a while with the dog in his arms. He couldn't relax. He thought drinking some wine might help. He hadn't had any alcohol for many years, but—he thought and smiled—Marcelo really liked his booze, and Laura had already shown her surprise when he had refused a drink. He found an unopened bottle in the fridge and looked around for a corkscrew. He looked in a couple of drawers. Nothing. Opening the third, he froze, shocked by what he saw. In it there were no knives, forks, or napkins. There was only a female doll, made of cardboard and cloth, with a wooden stake going through it from top to bottom and three needles pinned to her body. He quickly closed the drawer and went back to the bedroom. As he got into bed, Laura, in her sleep, pulled him into her arms. Shaken, he let her hold him tight.

Exit

WHEN HE WOKE UP, breakfast was waiting for him in bed. Laura was snuggled next to him, naked. Her face looked fresh, relaxed.

"I have a proposal for you," she said.

"Yes?"

"Wait two or three days and then let's leave together."

"What do you mean, 'leave together'?"

"I'm thinking of coming with you. I'm fed up with this place. I need a change, too. There's nothing to keep me in Hannibal. Besides, the place is too conservative for me. The people are like zombies; they believe whatever the Fox Channel tells them. So, would you like me to?" she asked again.

He looked at her. She was the same naked woman who, when they first met, had been pointing a gun at him, but now she seemed different. He answered without a moment's pause, even last night's image of the doll having been pushed right out of his mind.

"Yes."

He turned to her and took her in his arms. They made love, slowly, with a different intensity. There was a new intimacy between them—surprising, considering the short time since they'd met. And this intimacy was the difficulty, not the sex.

When they got up, Laura told him that this would be her last day at work. She would submit her resignation to the manager that morning, would take care of a few things, and then they could leave. He immediately agreed. For a moment he thought he had played his role better than Marcelo's wildest dreams. But the word "role" made him uneasy for a moment. Then he asked her to put his suitcase and laptop in a safe place until they left. Laura looked at him suspiciously, but without saying anything, put them in a cupboard, locked it and went into the bathroom to get ready. He was sitting in the living room, drinking his coffee and waiting for her when there was on knock on the front door. Laura, from inside the bathroom, asked him to answer it.

He opened the door to find the sheriff standing on the doorstep, who, the instant he saw him, grew pale, but then an ironic smile crossed his face.

"Mr. Diaz, what a surprise..."

You're here to see Laura?" he asked abruptly.

"This time, yes. Don't worry though. I wouldn't mind talking to you also. It will be good for you to hear what I have to tell her."

Soon, the three of them were seated in the living room. The case of Mary Lou Dobson's murder had taken an unexpected turn. The forensic exam had revealed some bite marks on the victim's neck. A specialist with many years of experience investigating murders like this one had come to Hannibal. Through an elaborate process of formal reasoning and analysis, he had come to the conclusion that the murderer was most likely a neighbor—someone who, in the initial stages of the investigation, had probably helped the police. Paul, the man living next door, had been found in a motel in a neighboring city. Interrogation revealed inconsistencies in his account—the sheriff did not get into details. Moreover, Paul had failed a lie-detector test. The police soon realized, however, that although Paul was hiding something, he wasn't the murderer. When they went to his friend Roy Gamba's house—the man he had met at the restaurant—nobody answered. Roy had skipped town, too. A first search of the house had produced nothing incriminating, except that Roy's bookcase was full of books on black magic—on hearing this he felt a shudder run through him—a fact that proved that Roy was not your run-of-the-mill electrician. Upon closer examination, however, they had found a hair belonging to the victim on one of Roy's shirts. Gamba must have been a very bad driver, since only a day later he was arrested in a nearby town for causing an accident. He'd been immediately moved to the Hannibal jail. Roy's teeth matched the bite marks on Mary Lou's neck. Just the day before, Roy Gamba had been charged with murder, and Paul James with obstructing justice. Not only that, but the sheriff was now investigating the possibility of Gamba having committed other unsolved murders in the area.

Hearing all this, he recalled his meeting with Roy. He would have sworn the guy looked entirely ordinary.

"But why are you here, Mr. Walzlager?" Laura asked. Looking at her, he noticed she had grown a little pale.

The sheriff paused and looked around. "How well did you know Roy Gamba, Laura?"

"Almost not at all. He was in my house once, just to do some electrical repairs."

"Electrical repairs? Just that?" said the sheriff with a wry smile.

Laura looked at the sheriff angrily.

"What are you implying?"

"We found two pictures of you in Roy's house."

"So what?"

"Here, take a look."

The sheriff took out an envelope from his bag and opened it. There was a black-and-white portrait photo of Laura. He turned it over. On the back was written: "To you with love."

"Is this your handwriting?"

"Of course. But this had nothing to do with Roy Gamba. This

note was for someone very close to me. He must have stolen it when he was in my house."

"And why would he have done something like that?"

"I don't know. What do you want from me, Sheriff?"

"To come to the police station to give a statement. And to be careful about who you let into your house."

"What's the matter? Am I in danger?"

"I don't know. The young man here can tell us."

"Tell you what?"

"What kind of...*business* have you gotten this girl involved in?"

"He hasn't gotten me involved in anything," Laura said.

The sheriff burst out laughing.

"Did someone visit you lately, Mr. Diaz? It seems you're a very popular guy. Quite a few people want to get to know you."

"I don't know what you mean. And I don't really care. Anyway, I am leaving today or tomorrow."

The sheriff smiled.

"Aw, how come? Don't you like our town?"

"Too Republican for me."

The sheriff glanced at Laura.

"Has she recruited you? 'Red Laura' we call her here."

He managed to answer first, before Laura could say anything. "I have my own opinions, sheriff."

"And what opinion do you have about serial killers?"

"What are you getting at?"

"Let me tell you," the sheriff said. "The serial killer is like someone trimming his nails. Before he starts, he's bored, but once he gets started, he wants to keep cutting deeper, faster, until his hands get bloody. When he's done with his hands, he starts on his feet, and when he's done with those, he can hardly wait for his nails to grow again."

He raised his hands and showed the sheriff his nails that had obviously not been clipped for quite a while. "So what you're saying is that it's about time for me to strike again" he said calmly.

After a while, Walzlager left with Laura for the police station.

He stayed at the house for another half hour but grew bored and decided to go out. He walked down to the river trying to collect his thoughts: the evidence against Roy Gamba and at the same time Laura's decision to come with him, the young man and the money, the rendezvous in Chicago... so many things. He was somehow managing to stay calm. His new self surprised him. Something deep inside told him that his chosen course—that is, letting events unfold on their own—was the right one. For the first time in ages—something very odd, given everything that was going on—he felt a sense of freedom. It was an exhilarating feeling, almost a longing for something he couldn't put his finger on. He didn't know where it came from. For a moment, he felt it was the memory of something lost or, possibly, something that had been missing, that struggled to reach the surface of his consciousness. It was an amorphous feeling, however, since he couldn't connect it to some old experience. One thing was certain: never in his life had he felt or acted this way, gone with the flow. And now that there was a flow to go with, albeit a borrowed one, the threats that were appearing on the horizon did not seem to be able to stop it. What threats? There was the threat from Marcelo's dark past that pursued him, but also the threat from Laura—the unexpected vulnerability this woman caused in him. This threat was magnified by two things he didn't really understand about her: the voodoo doll in her kitchen and her relationship with Roy. Notwithstanding the dark corners, an area was left open, strangely free, unknown and intriguing. An area for action. He would talk to her, yes. He would ask. But not yet.

He heard the far off horn of the riverboat. He turned around and suddenly saw a human form in the distance. Whoever it was turned quickly to the right and disappeared behind some trees. He got back into town and walked to the Mark Twain Restaurant. He ordered pasta and a beer. Before paying, he went to the men's room. As he began washing his hands, he felt a touch on his back. He turned around. It was the young man with the cap who had given him the gray bag. His face looked awful, as though he'd been beaten up very recently.

"They are here. You have to get out right now."

"Who hit you?"

"It doesn't matter. My cover's blown now. Doc said you should go as soon as you can."

"To Chicago?"

"To make the delivery. You hear me? The way things are going, the 'interested party' needs it as soon as possible. Forget October 19. It has to come out at least three weeks before."

"Three weeks before what?"

The young man looked at him incredulously.

"Before the elections. Three weeks before the elections. The meeting has now been arranged for October 11. Same place. This coming Monday, 10:00 a.m. Understand?"

"Yes. But why before the elections?" he risked it.

"Doc's orders. Since we've decided to push up November 1, we need to get it done now. Let's get going. You go first. I'll go after five."

"Okay," he said and opened the door.

When he got out in the street he felt uncomfortable, as if he had all of a sudden become the center of interest for everyone in Hannibal. Any casual glance at him by a passer-by made him feel as if he had a sign hanging around his neck with the word "guilty" emblazoned on it. He crossed the main street briskly and scurried into an alley. Some children were playing with a bicycle wheel. A pickup truck went by on the main street carrying a huge poster of Bush. High in the air, a flock of birds filled the narrow strip of sky that was visible between the buildings. He felt dizzy and stopped to take a breath. The kids ran by in front of him. He turned to the right into what turned out to be a dead end—it was a narrow lane between two fences. Not a soul in sight. He leaned with his back against one of them and slowly slid down until he was sitting on the ground. He took a deep breath and stayed like that for a while, trying to clear his thoughts. Impossible. The only thing he really wanted at that moment was to see her. As he rose, he saw a shadow on the wall to his right. The sun was behind him. He turned around. The main street was obscured by a large black car with a white hood, blocking the entire lane before him from one side to the other. Two tall, well-dressed men were standing in front of the two doors, one blond with straight hair, round glasses, and acne scars on his face, and one with a shaved head and a moustache. Between them, in front of the car, stood the short man with the chubby face who had stopped him at the river. The man took a few steps forward.

"Well, well! We meet again," he said.

He quickly assessed the situation. As things stood, the only escape route was to jump over one of the fences.

"This time you're not going to tell me you don't know what I want from you, right, Marcelo?"

"I don't know you, sir," he said.

The man laughed.

"Then, I'll introduce myself to you again. My name's Jimmy. We've talked before—I'm sure you remember. So, what are you going to do about it?"

He realized he had to play ball after all. But he needed to stall for time.

"Look. It can't be done now. In the afternoon."

"So, your memory has come back?" said Jimmy. "In the afternoon? No way, man, we want it now. The claimants are in a hurry. Maybe some things have changed, but everything else is ready, and they are waiting for you as was arranged."

New information—apart from the interested party there were also the "claimants." There was no time left. He had to improvise. He thought quickly.

"I have to go see the sheriff. He's waiting for me."

"The sheriff? You're kidding!"

"I have to go give a statement about the murder case."

"What have you got to do with it?"

"It's about the woman I've been staying with. If I don't go she'll be in trouble. You're welcome to follow me if you don't believe me. When I'm done at the police station, we'll go together and I'll get it for you."

Jimmy glanced at the others and then turned back to him.

"We'll be following you the whole time. Be careful what you do. You realize there is no point informing the sheriff about this. The sheriff won't do anything to help you. I'm sure you understand..."

He gestured to his men, and they all got into the car, which backed out of the lane and cleared the way for him to leave. He walked out of the dead end and turned towards the center of town, his mind racing. A plan for getting out of this had already started forming. He smiled to himself—the lion was out of the cage.

The car with the short man was following him at a safe distance. The police station was not far from the museum. At the entrance, he asked to see Sheriff Walzlager. On the wall, next to the front desk, there was a floor plan of the building. A gift from God. He surveyed it quickly and found what he was looking for.

The sheriff was drinking a cup of coffee in his office. He looked surprised to see him.

"What's up? Have you decided to turn yourself in?" he laughed out loud.

"Where is Laura?"

"How should I know? We finished and she left. If I were you I'd leave her alone."

"Do you have her phone number at work?"

"Great boyfriend! He has the house keys, but not the phone number!"

That said, the sheriff reluctantly gave him the museum's num-

ber. He went to the pay phone in the hallway, found the label with
its phone number, and called her. He spoke in a low voice.

"It's me."

"Where are you?"

"At the police station. Now listen... Did you really mean what
you said?"

"What?"

"That you wanted to come with me?"

"Yes. Why? Did you change your mind?"

"No. Quite the opposite. We have to move things up. We have
to leave right away."

"Right away? Why?"

"I don't have time to explain now. I'll tell you on the way." He
told her to go home, pack as quickly as she could everything she
would need, and put the bags in the Mustang. "We have to leave
now. We're going to Chicago. Take my suitcase with the laptop and
also that pretty thing you were holding in your hands when I first
met you." Laura got worried at the mention of the gun, but he interrupted her. "Please bring it with you. Then come to the street
behind the police station. Be careful not to drive in front of the station. Do you have a cell phone?"

"Yes."

"When you're ready, call me at 272-5673. If anyone else
answers the phone, ask for me. It should only take me a couple of
minutes to come out the back of the building, so keep the engine
running. We'll need to take off right away."

He went back to the sheriff's office. Walzlager was in a cheery
mood and started to talk about this and that and to poke some fun
at him. On his end, he kept prodding the sheriff and thus managed
to keep the conversation going for about half an hour, until an officer knocked and put his head in the door.

"There's a call for Mr. Diaz on the pay phone. That's you,

right?"

"Mr. Diaz! At the police station! You're so popular in Hannibal you should run for mayor!" the sheriff said.

He left the office and went to telephone booth.

"I'm outside," said Laura.

"Yes, great, I understand. I'll be at the meeting on time. Thank you," he said and hung up.

Then he asked the officer for the restroom. He went toward the stairs as he'd been directed. But, instead of going past them, he went down to the ground floor. He crossed a dark hallway and reached a storage area. There was an exit there, as he had seen on the floor plan of the building. He opened the door. It led to a loading dock and the back street. To the right, he spotted Marcelo's Mustang and Laura at the wheel. He ran and opened the door to the passenger seat. On the back seat Moxi was wagging his tail.

"I'll get down so they won't see me. Pull out nice and easy, and keep an eye out for anyone following us. When you reach the end of town, floor it. Let's go!"

Laura gave him a perplexed look. For a moment, everything felt unreal. But when he heard her say: "OK, let's go" and saw her pressing the gas pedal, the reality of everything that had happened filled him with a feeling of dread.

B. CHICAGO

Sentimental education

LAURA DROVE STRAIGHT TOWARDS BROADWAY and then turned left onto Highway 36. Moxi was curled up on the back seat. No one seemed to have followed them.

"Do you know how to get to Chicago?" he asked.

"Yes, I've gone there several times."

Before long they were on I-72 heading towards Springfield. They did not talk. He felt a constant humming within him. Everything was vibrating. Even the flow of air, the way it was hitting his face through the open window, seemed to be pulsating in a menacing frequency, almost unbearable. The new land, the new way of life, and this unexpected development that his new life had taken, sharpened his senses to the point they had become raw. However, now that the adrenalin rush had subsided, he found it hard to focus. The unexpected self-control he had exercised during these last few hours, the escape plan he had so calmly organized, the ability to navigate with absolute composure the uncharted shoals that had surfaced in his life—his *own* life?—had started to come apart. Now he felt all this breaking up into countless pieces, each of which, however, remained unbearably present: Laura a thousand shards of memories, juices, glances; the road a medley of interwoven, contradictory signals; the landscape an abstract, confused bunch of objects. As if all the components of each incidental image he saw invaded his senses, each independently and forcefully at the same moment. His world had become a network with multiple entry and exit points, a current of constantly shifting frequencies, requiring twenty brains and fifty consciences to process everything and return him to the familiar order.

He was almost in physical pain. He tried to sort out all these contradictory feelings. Impossible! An avalanche of motives and desires, memories and repulsions, images and voids fell on him together and simultaneously. Everything stuck together and at the same time broken into pieces, cut off—a parabolic asymmetrical incision into the world. Surely, this development was not the one he had wanted that moment at the lake, when he looked at the profile of the dead Marcelo.

Suddenly, with the force of those unique, magnificent times, when the words he wrote seemed to be dictated to him from a faraway place by an unknown voice, somewhere out of the depth of his mind a line from a poem popped up. It was one of his favorites: "...symmetrically we danced / symmetrically let us die..."[6] And then a small light lit up within him. This deluge, this chaos was reality. And this new reality was as real as the old one. Or, rather, even more real. It was simply bounded in a different way. Upside down. A reflection on the surface of the lake. His new reality consisted of all the things that the old one left out. What he needed to do now was to put this chaos in order. To structure it. Besides, that was his job as a writer: to edit chaos.

He had started to live his life at last. Even if this life belonged to someone else. When he had arrived in Iowa City, he had decided to erase his memory. To get away from that cemetery of experiences that is housed so persistently in the present. He gradually realized, however, that such a thing was not feasible. Not because the wound cannot be patched up. But because memory, the value of memory, is based on the terrible contradiction that nothing is in the past.

Once you recall it, everything is once again present. His suicidal mother, present. His rejected father, present. His ex-wife, present. Even the dead Marcelo, present. So long as he remembered them, it was like they were present. "Like" they were present? Perhaps what he was really looking for in America was to get lost in a continuous metaphor, to abandon himself to an ongoing simile, same as Nick, as the coeds in Iowa City. Because he could not yet figure out what the thing he was looking for was "like."

"Aren't you going to tell me?" Her voice penetrated his thoughts.

"Tell you what?"

"Why we had to leave so suddenly? What happened?"

"I told you, I had to go."

"To Chicago?"

"To Chicago."

"And the gun, what do you want that for?"

"For protection."

Laura gave a wry smile. "I've done many crazy things in my life, but going away like that, leaving everything behind, with someone I barely know—I've never done that. You told me that you would explain everything."

"Trust me."

"Why? Why should I?"

"Trust in momentum. Life is motion, stillness is death."

"I like the way you think."

He looked to the right. They were passing a small town named Hal.

"Why do you think I'm doing it? Coming with you, I mean," she asked.

"You must have your reasons," he answered.

"Yes. Can you guess what?"

"No."

"I think we're in the same circumstance—you and I. Only something is after you, while I am after it."

"Do you know what this something is?"

"Maybe. What about you?"

"Hold the wheel tight and look behind us."

Laura did.

"So?" he said.

She turned her eyes back to the road. Her answer surprised him.

"Yes," she said quietly. "I saw it."

He watched her as she drove. As if he could follow her thoughts. They leapt between her eyes and her mouth, a dance from security to insecurity and back.

They went through another two cities, Berry and Pittsfield. From time to time he turned back and took a look at the road. No, this look was not anything symbolic. It meant something different, more practical. And she understood that.

"You're still worried that someone is following us?" she asked.

"Everything's OK."

For the next few miles, Laura did not talk—it seemed like something was the matter with her. Finally, she told him she wasn't feeling very well, and he took the wheel. After they passed through Springfield, Laura asked him to stop at the next town. She felt dizzy and wanted to rest for a while. He saw a sign on the road: "Lincoln 5 miles."

"We're about halfway there. Let's stop in Lincoln. We can stay there for the night."

In Lincoln they found a hotel. Clean, cheap, but no pets were allowed in the rooms, so they had to leave Moxi in the car. They took the luggage upstairs. He wanted to have it close by. Laura, exhausted, fell into bed immediately. He still felt stressed and could not relax. He ordered a bottle of wine from room service. In an hour he had drunk almost all of it. It had been a long time since he had drunk that much and it knocked him out.

In his haze, he was thinking that nothing, not nostalgia for the past, not loneliness, not even the most terrible change can really transform a person. The character, the personality, is in the final analysis something incredibly still, immovably silent. Just like history itself. Full of blood, upheaval, tension, but despite all this, imperturbable, almost quiet in its relentless progress.

He lay down next to her and tried to pull her close. Laura, in her exhaustion, rolled over letting him know she was not in the mood. In a few moments, he had also fallen into a deep sleep. And there, in the depths of oblivion, he saw it again. It had been a while since he had last seen it. That same dream—that was not a dream, but reality within sleep—with his father.

Everyone has lived through something that he or she would gladly erase from memory. He had too many of them. The worst among them was the one that for years had become a short film that haunted so many of the nights of his life.

The "edge," as he had named it, was the memory of an actual event. He watched that same event that night in his sleep at the little hotel in Lincoln—the day he saw him hitting her. He watched hiding behind the half-open door of the living room. He watched him beat her brutally until she fainted. His father, so drunk he didn't even realize it, and when his anger was spent, just went to bed and fell asleep. And he, tiptoeing into the living room and shocked at seeing her with blood pouring from her nose, down on the floor, motionless, "like" dead. And he hadn't done anything to stop it. This feeling would haunt him his whole life. That he'd left her alone, helpless, in his hands. So what if he was only ten years old? Guilt has no age limit.

Nonetheless, this memory, in all its gloom, had a surprising positive side, at least a side that was useful to him, that gave him a purpose in his life. This memory coincided with the moment when, still a child, he realized something strange: that "grown-ups can be wrong." And then he had made the decision: his sentimental education would not concern anyone but himself. He would rear himself—all by himself—whatever that would mean. With the naïveté of his age, he started looking for some institution, some vehicle that would undertake this education. He had rejected school for this role. He had a mature insight into everything, very different from all his schoolmates, with the result that he got incredibly bored with lessons. His relationship with teachers was always problematic—he had great difficulty "doing as he was told." So, the solution that finally emerged was those small rectangular objects filled with little black symbols: books.

He decided that everything he would learn in his life, about good or about evil, about what was moral and immoral, would be through books. And from then on, he launched into a marathon of reading that included everything: novels, fairy-tales, essays, plays. Texts, most of which were anything but appropriate for his age. Even so, in the innumerable pages, words, stories, and images, he discovered a new world—a world with a modicum of security, a modicum of structure. A parallel universe that did not exist anywhere other than inside his head, but a universe which, in its complexity, looked much more real than the one he was facing each day. And so the authors and their heroes became his true spiritual family. As for his biological family, it was nothing more than two ghosts, two images, two shadows. When later, as was natural, this childish transposition collapsed under the weight of reality, the two images came back, magnified, reinforced by time and more untamed than ever before. And then, in order to survive, he retreated into the deep recesses of the subconscious where everything is not "matter," but "meaning"—that is to say, everything is terrifying.

For a long time, he lived distanced from the activities of society, studying his own actions, commenting on them, incorporating them into the big celebration that is the world as if they were not exclusively his. He treated himself as if he were some important character in the play of life, someone who "did" something within a "greater common act," within an infinite mural, covering wall-to-wall a museum, which had no end. It was inevitable, therefore, that he would reconstruct the world of his childhood, this time as a writer. And because, like most tormented people, he did not want to express directly what he really wanted to say, he used in his stories an "elevated" reality, with his hero entering a strange, hostile world where he had to apply all of his inventiveness in order to survive. The dangerous new world was nothing other than the unbearable everyday reality, and the attempt to discover himself in it was the only way to survive.

The emperor of dust

HE WOKE UP WITH A CRY, AS ALWAYS. His teeth hurt. He must have been clenching them again in his sleep. His dentist had warned him "You must use a tooth guard if you don't want to have to use dentures in ten years." He unconsciously turned to take her in his arms. He hugged her pillow instead. Laura wasn't there. He got up, still dizzy with sleep, and went to the bathroom. She wasn't there either. He looked around for a note, something. Nothing. Suddenly, he had a crazy thought. "The bag!" he almost shouted. He went to his suitcase. It was the first thing on top of the clothes. This wasn't right, since in Hannibal he had put the bag at the bottom of the suitcase, rolling it up in Marcelo's coat. A curse escaped from his lips. He looked for the keys. They were next to him on the nightstand. He went to unlock it; it wasn't locked. But the money was there. The black box was also there, but the plastic bag was next to it, a sign that someone had unwrapped it. He looked for her suitcase. He was relieved to see that it was at the right side of the bed, in the same place where she had put it down when they had come into the room. He glanced at his watch. It was just after nine. He'd slept for fourteen hours straight!

He wrapped the box in the plastic bag and locked the gray bag.

He took it with him, got out of the room, and hurried to the reception desk. Before he could say anything, the hotel manager informed him that his car had been broken into during the night. It was a junkie, well-known in the area, whom they caught a little later. He had not taken anything apart from some cash he found in the glove compartment, but the dog was gone. "We notified Mrs. Diaz"— those were the manager's words—"and she came down to the lobby. About an hour later she went up again and then left right away."

"Did she say anything? Did she leave a message?"

"No."

He hung the "Do not disturb" sign on the door and went out. Lincoln was a small town, smaller even than Hannibal. To the right of the hotel began a street that seemed to be the town's main. He started walking along it. He went into every coffee shop, bar, store that he passed, and looked around. After forty-five minutes, he had reached the other end of town, and there was no sign of Laura. He continued on the parallel street, then onto the vertical narrow lanes. By noon he had gone through every public area of the town with no result. He went back to the hotel hoping that she might have returned. The receptionist dashed that hope. The room was exactly as he had left it. He didn't know what to do. He remembered that Laura had a cell phone. He looked into her suitcase and did not find it. He thought he should lie down for a while to calm down. He could not. He got up and started pacing around the room like a wild beast in a cage. Then he went out again. He entered the nearest restaurant and ordered a steak. He ate mechanically. He killed some time there watching the crowd and got back to the room after having procured another bottle of wine.

In the room, alone. With a woman before, now without. Just like his home... then. When she left—a haunted house. He kept finding things that belonged to her, all the time. Once an eyeliner pencil under a stack of magazines, once a scribbled note—"Get some bread when you go out. Whole grain. Put splendid bytes into the computer and make them produce beautiful images"—or her photograph, forgotten in the back of a drawer. The good times. Before he'd realized that his wife had a totally different bet going in her life. That, in other words, his wife had a bet on life itself—on living it, not on analyzing it. And that on the canvas of everyday life, he was only placing a few random brush strokes, without ever painting a picture, waiting, with almost masochistic joy, for those minor episodes that would make the old wound bleed.

Haunted house. There was also the folding screen. Two carved wooden panels—she took the one. The other left behind, crippled, dusty, hiding half of what it was meant to. His house, full of dust. He didn't care about order, about his appearance, about anything. Dust. The emperor of dust.

He turned on the TV and began drinking straight from the bottle. He chanced on a *Tonight Show* rerun in which Jay Leno was interviewing John Edwards, the Democratic candidate for the Vice-Presidency. Leno said he wondered what was hidden under the unusual wrinkle on the back of Bush's jacket, in the first debate with Kerry.

"Many said it was a wireless receiver that allowed him to be fed answers through a hidden earphone," the comedian said, twisting his mouth.

"Nah!" answered Edwards seriously. "I think it was his battery."

He went on channel surfing for another hour, trying not to think. The whole American madness paraded on the screen: organizations of Republican students that supported abstinence before marriage and urged people to vote for Bush, an analysis of the New York Mets latest game, a report about a company that discarded toxic waste close to a residential area in Texas—he stayed on that channel for a while—and ended up watching a show with a gray-haired, smiley-faced comedian who was proposing a set of new laws:

> A new law for President Bush: Stop saying that Kerry can run, but he cannot hide. It was exactly what you'd been saying about Osama Bin Laden, who's been able to hide after all. Boy, how good he is at hiding. We can't find him with cruise missiles or with satellites, not even with $25 million dollar rewards. But no one has thought of the obvious: look for him at www.presidentspartner.com...

He turned the TV off. He went to the bathroom and took a shower, shaved, and changed clothes. He went out into the hallway. There was a cigarette vending machine next to the elevator. It had been eight years and some months since his last cigarette. He had given it up on April 10, 1996. He remembered the date. He inserted a five dollar bill and selected a pack of Marlboro Lights. He came back to the room and opened the laptop, lighting the first cigarette. He inhaled the smoke deeply and immediately started coughing. The tenth drag was more relieving. The smoke had begun to find its old familiar lairs.

After half the pack, he had written three pages. He filled another glass of wine and started reading:

> We are creatures of habit. No matter how hard we try, we will not escape our old habits. But who wouldn't want, once in his life, to change skin? It is a crime to camouflage oneself. A war crime. Because life is a war. And as in every conflict, it holds within it all the old wars. I had decided to forget them, to erase all the battles, to surrender, to put an end to the story. What happened to the Ford happened to me, too. I've been wrung dry, ran out of fuel. But the moment I saw Marcelo dead, there was a spark. Along with the Ford, it set memory on fire and destroyed all the old resentments. They were incinerated instantly,

completely. And from their ashes a different reality emerged, more true. Everything is now illuminated from a different source. And here's me, not "like" me. I could take the money and go to the Bahamas, to Hawaii. But it would be treason, I would betray the "idea" itself. New laws, new plan: I follow my new destiny, the destiny of a new skin...

And right then he heard a sound and the door to the room opened. It was Laura.

Memory of the future

SHE CAME IN WALKING CAREFULLY, almost on tiptoes. She stood before him and looked at him. Her features were drawn as if she'd been crying. He lit a cigarette. He was annoyed with her but did not want to show it.

"Won't you ask me where I was?" Laura said, figuring out he wasn't going to say anything.

"It's the third time you asked me this kind of question: whether I am going to ask you something."

"Moxi's lost. A junkie broke into the car last night."

"I know, they told me at the desk."

"I took the keys and drove around town. I looked for him but no luck. When I got back, I locked the car up and left the keys for you."

"I'm sorry about the dog..."

"You don't know what it's like for me. He's been with me for three years..."

"Maybe he'll come back on his own."

"I don't think so. But don't worry about me. I'm used to losing those I love. I can cope with it. But it wasn't only because of Moxi that I left."

"Because of what then? Sit down and let's talk."

Laura remained standing. She looked at him intensely.

"I want you to tell me the truth," she said.

"The truth about what?"

"Who you are and what you are up to."

He took a deep drag.

"Where were you?" he said.

"So, now you want to know? You're a pro at changing the subject. But I asked you a question first. And I think mine is more important than yours."

"Where were you all this time?" he repeated.

"Is this the game you want to play? Well then, I needed some time alone. To think. Okay?"

"To think about what?"

"What I'm doing here with a man who came out of nowhere to find me, who has someone after him, and who has a bag full of money in his suitcase."

"And what did you decide?"

"That's what you want to ask me?"

"That's it."

"I haven't decided anything yet."

Another deep drag. The smoke traveled everywhere inside him and, together with the wine, started to make him dizzy.

"I have to tell you that I don't like it," he said.

"You don't like what?"

"That you went through my stuff."

"I didn't like it either. I've never done it before. I'm sorry. But I had to figure out what's been going on somehow, since you're not telling me anything," she answered, without any sign of being flustered.

"Okay, then, ask me something specific."

"To begin with, where did you get all this money? Is it yours?"

"No, it was offered to me in order to deliver something."

"What?"

"You saw it, since you unwrapped it. The black box in the bag."

"And what's in the black box?"

"It doesn't matter," he improvised, rather unsuccessfully.

"It doesn't matter? You've been given a pile of money for something that doesn't matter?"

"It came into my possession not long ago. Since then, some people, people I've never met in person, contacted me and offered me a lot of money to deliver it somewhere."

"Somewhere in Chicago?"

"Yes. The people who are after me obviously don't want me to make the delivery."

"And you want me to believe that it is something that doesn't matter? What is it? Drugs?"

"No, it's not drugs. Is that good enough for you?"

"No, it's not good enough."

Laura looked angry. He saw that he had to give her a more plausible explanation if he didn't want to lose her. He thought he was lucky, he had the recent channel surfing to fall back on. He made up a story, that in his work, he had come across data from a certain company, showing that they were dumping mercury-laden waste in a drainage ditch close to a residential area in California. The data was encrypted, but he had managed to partially break the code, so he'd figured out what it was all about. What he had been able to read made it clear that the rest was truly incriminating for the company. The people who paid him wanted the matter to be brought to light. The wine had really loosened up his creativity.

"Mercury waste in California. Are you talking about the toxics they brought from Taiwan? It's about the Taiwan Plastics scandal? But that happened back in '99."

He took a deep breath. He had forgotten that Laura had a history as an environmental activist.

"No, I'm talking about another company. I can't say which. The scandal is far-reaching."

"And you are getting paid to cover it up?"

"No, I'm getting paid to uncover it."

"You consider this ethical?"

"The people who paid me understand the risk I'm taking. The data is classified."

"I find it contemptible taking money for something that may save lives."

"The lives will be saved whether I'm paid or not. In any case, I didn't ask for money. It was offered to me. And this is only an advance. I'm going to Chicago to deliver and get the rest. Would you have given it back?"

Laura looked at him almost aggressively.

"I wouldn't have done it for the money."

"I'm not doing it for the money, I told you. I took a huge risk; there are people after me. Obviously, they're willing to do anything to keep this from getting out. The money came after I began trying to find the right people to give the data to. So, are you coming with me to Chicago, to deliver?"

"If you tell me exactly what it is about."

"I've already told you a lot. I'll tell you the rest after I make the drop in Chicago."

"And why should I believe you?" asked Laura.

"Why do I believe you?"

"I don't think I have so many ghosts in my closet."

"Perhaps you have them in your kitchen drawer?"

Laura raised her eyebrows.

"What do you mean?"

"In your kitchen drawer there was a little 'ghost' run through with a needle. Did Roy teach you that?"

Laura stood up. Her face was red.

"You have been going through my things!"

"Who's talking..."

"That is... It's..."

"It's what? I'd like an explanation."

"Explanation about what?"

"About the voodoo setup. About that guy, Roy."

"What? You think I'm a witch or something?"

"Well, you *have* cast a spell on me..." he said, smiling.

"Are you joking now? On top of it all, you're making fun of me? Well, I'll tell you since you're so interested. Yes, something did happen between me and Roy. I was stupid. I'd been alone for such a long time."

"But didn't you tell me..."

"That I hadn't been with a man for over a year. But Roy wasn't a man. He was nothing. A one-night fuckup."

"I can imagine how sex with a psychopathic killer was."

"We were drunk. He didn't even manage to get it up."

"Spare me the details. It's the 'ghost' I'm interested in."

"In the morning I kicked him out. The next day I found that thing at my door."

"And you kept it?"

"In case he did something more, I could go to the police with it. It was proof."

"And the photos?"

"There weren't only two photos, there were three. He stole them from me. In the morning, when we woke up, we had a fight. He refused to leave. He became aggressive, and I was afraid. I locked myself up in the bathroom with my cell phone and told him that if he didn't get out in five minutes, I'd call the police. That's when he must have taken them, they were in plain sight. When I found the little doll, my third picture was pinned on it."

"And what about Lester? Wasn't he supposed to be your friend? I saw him with Roy and it looked like they were pals."

"Nobody knows anything about that night—only Roy and I. Lester is naive. He trusts everybody. Okay now? These are my 'ghosts.' If you remember everything I've told you, I've got more in my closet, worse than these. Is that what you wanted to know? Happy?"

He slowly pressed the cigarette down in the ashtray, putting it out. He'd gotten himself into a very dangerous situation, he knew that by now. Several new links had been added to the chain, and all of them made him nervous. But, for the moment, alcohol had made him invulnerable to fear.

"Ghosts are not always so bad. There are ten of them for every one alive."

He remembered the chair. His mother's old folding chair. He had taken it home after her death. To look at it. To see his personal ghost standing on it.

"What are you talking about now?" she said.

"Since the beginning of the world about a hundred billion people have lived. Today, there are ten billion alive. For every one alive there are ten ghosts."

"If that's true, then there are twelve for me..." she said, obviously implying her parents.

Night, late. Miserable, sick. Picking up the letter opener—a gift from her. And stabbing her with it. Slashes everywhere. The chair ripped to shreds. Then, looking at his work—the ruins—and seeing her eyes. And then, his mother's eyes. Shards. He had to do something. He ran out of the house and walked the streets. Once he thought to go to his father, wake him up, and tell him everything. But death pressed on him in the cold night. He looked up high. The sky was full of stars. He let his eyes wander. To get strength. He heard her speaking to him from above. With the hoarse voice of her last days. "I am dust—stardust." He walked and felt as if he was carrying her on his shoulders, lighter than ever.

He had drifted away, to some other place.

"Where are you?" she asked.

"I'm here... I was thinking that there are also about a hundred billion stars in the universe," he continued.

"What now? You've hit your poetic vein?"

"It's nice to know that for every human being there's a world out there..."

"Yeah, sure... But also a death. Don't forget!" Laura said.

At that moment—he had no idea why—he saw something for the first time. Something like a future. Together with her. Suddenly, a lightning strike. Where? On the retina? No, further back. As if it were the night he saw her for the first time. His wife. In Athens, on Metamorfoseos Street, walking leisurely and gracefully by, alone, beautiful. And his wife taking on Laura's face. We imagine a face, we conjure a person, and then we meet her.

"Laura, something..."

"What?"

"Something like..."

"Like what?"

"Like dripping..."

"What?"

"A memory."

"Memories don't drip," she said and laughed, breaking the tension.

"Don't laugh at something like this."

"But it's funny... Memory..."

"It may sound funny. But it's fierce. It's a memory of the future."

"Are you on something? Maybe it's all the wine you've drunk?" she said pointing at the bottle.

"Something's got into my head, yes."

Laura didn't answer. She paced around the room. Then, she came close to him from the back. She wrapped her arms around his neck.

"You're crazy," she said.

The chase, the well, the reflection

THE SIGN READ: "CHICAGO 166 MILES." He was driving. They did not talk. He had turned on the radio. To the news:

> In a strong speech in Wilkes-Barre, Pennsylvania, President Bush made his strategy for the remaining days of the campaign clear. He emphasized the uncompromising policy of no withdrawal from Iraq and stepped up the intensity of his criticism of John Kerry, focusing on the deficiencies of his Democratic opponent, in both domestic and foreign policy issues. "You can't win a war if you don't believe in fighting," the President forcefully declared. George Bush, listing Senator Kerry's contradictory declarations regarding the war in Iraq, emphasized: "You hear all that and you can understand why somebody would make a face." It was the President's way of explaining the un-photogenic grimaces and annoyed looks that were caught on camera during the first two debates. In his speech, the President avoided any reference to the report by the head of the Iraq WMD Survey Group, Charles Dulfer, which formally concludes that Saddam Hussein did

not possess a chemical weapons arsenal and did not have an on-going nuclear weapons development program. There also was no mention of the growing number of dead American soldiers, a number that now stands at 1,060.

"The idiot!" said Laura. "Six more were killed yesterday in Fallujah. When the time comes to speak about casualties, they play dumb. A thousand dead... A whole small town. In this country they're in love with the word 'war.'"

"No, they're in love with the mythology of war."

"What do you expect from a country that was born out of the worst genocide in history? Even worse than Hitler's."

"And these children, they whip them into patriotic frenzy, promise them honor and glory, and then they bring them secretly back to their families in coffins."

"Have you been in the army?"

He was about to say "yes"—images of the ship, the naval station, the German numbers on the sentry-box of a car cemetery, the mice in the shower, the forced drills in the deadly cold, a wasteland and time lost, flowing through the fingers, dry. Fortunately, he caught himself.

"No."

"My uncle, my father's brother, was in Korea. When he came back he couldn't cope. He drank himself to death."

"I'm sorry..." he said.

"In the end, he found religion... A religious fanatic drunk... What is your relationship with God?"

"Unfortunately, non-existent."

"Could have been worse."

"Is there worse?"

"I don't know... Being a member of some crazy cult?"

"And what do you think religion is? A successful cult."

Laura smiled and changed the subject.

"There is no solution with Bush. If this was the '60's, I'd have joined the Weathermen.[7]

"They were into armed resistance. Would you have been able to shoot a man?"

"When you know the right's on your side, you can do some horrible things."

"I don't know... Of course, it was different back then."

"Yes, fifty percent of the country's population was in its twenties. There was anger, real anger. But they destroyed them—they pushed drugs on them—they swallowed them up and spat them out. Please, change it, I can't listen to him any more."

He scanned the channels. One station had a special on Prince. He stopped there. They didn't speak for a while. This was fortunate, since for the last five minutes he'd been trying to think of how he should react to what he had seen happening behind him.

"No matter what, the idiot will be re-elected," Laura said.

"You think so?"

"Kerry isn't appealing. Bush is selling God. And here we are crazy about God. In Tennessee, I'm told, some people sued their school district so that they'd have to put stickers in biology textbooks stating that the Theory of Evolution has not been proved. That we are not descended from monkeys."

"And from whom do we descend?"

"From Adam and Eve."

"There goes Darwin out the..."

"What Darwin? We are made of clay..." Laura left the phrase hanging. "Look behind us," she said.

"What?"

"That black car with the white hood. I think it's following us."

"I saw it a while back. It's them."

"Who? The ones who don't want you to make the delivery?"

"Yes."

They were driving on I-55. The road was wide. There wasn't much traffic. He saw a sign ahead: "Bloomington 8 miles."

"Hold on to your seat," he said and floored it.

The driver of the car behind seemed taken by surprise, but a few seconds later he managed to catch up with them again. He was driving like crazy, passing every other car. The other drivers, scared, were moving out of the way to let the two cars chasing each other go by. In the rearview mirror he saw Jimmy, the short man with the chubby face, sitting next to the driver.

"Where have you packed the gun?" he asked.

"You're nuts!" she cried. She was hugging the seatbelt as if that could give her more protection.

"Where is it?" he repeated louder.

"In my suitcase, behind us."

"*Gamoto!*"[8] he cried, impulsively, in Greek.

Laura looked at him strangely. For a moment, he felt suspended between the cuss that had escaped him and the black car that occupied the rearview mirror. He stepped on the gas pedal even harder, wanting to drive the image out of the mirror. But the black car was still gaining on them. Before long it got so close its bumper touched theirs. The Mustang lurched. The two cars, almost joined now, were going over ninety miles an hour, while almost everyone else on the road was automatically moving to the side. Up ahead, only a Jeep was still in their lane. As he squeezed past it, he almost grazed it and saw his passenger side mirror smashing into pieces. Strangely, Laura seemed quite cool. His mind was operating with the clarity and speed it now seemed to find every time it had to. Their survival depended on it. Out of the corner of his eye, he saw a dirt road running parallel to the freeway a few hundred feet to the right. He checked ahead. The road seemed to be connected to an exit that was coming up and to lead to a line of gray buildings visible in the distance. He made his decision. He pressed the gas pedal and managed to put some distance between them and their pursuers.

The black car continued to follow them. As soon as he passed the exit, he suddenly turned the steering wheel a bit to the right and hit the breaks. The wheels screeched as the Mustang turned around, sliding into the right lane. A pickup truck, whose driver, having seen the chase, had moved all the way to the right, barely managed to avoid them. The black car, going as fast as it was, passed them on the left. He pulled out of the spin by stepping on the gas again, now moving against the traffic. Two or three cars that had been behind them moved quickly out of the way. Honking the car horn constantly, he drove for a few hundred yards against the flow of oncoming traffic, and when he reached the exit, turned left on it. In the mirror he could see the black car stopped on the freeway, its driver also trying to make a u-turn. But by the time that had happened, he was already on the dirt road and had almost reached the gray buildings. He had lost them.

It was a soap factory. There was a green area like a park behind the buildings; a worn out road led into it. He followed it through all its twists and turns. A short while later, the road came out of the wooded area at the top of a long slope that ended at a crossroads, from where three roads went off. He chose the worst one. It was very bumpy with loose rocks everywhere. The Mustang was struggling over this surface, but he kept on going.

Laura had said nothing the entire time. She had hardly even moved, sitting straight, with her arms crossed over her chest. He kept checking behind them. The landscape was flat, dry. For a long time he did not see anything. No sign of life. They had not just escaped their pursuers. They were lost in the wilderness.

It was hot. Drops of sweat were flowing down his cheeks. He turned on the AC.

"Where are we?" Laura finally asked.

"I have no idea."

"Let's stop somewhere. I can't take it anymore."

He looked ahead. He noticed a dark mass on the horizon.

"Let's get to that and then we can stop."

It was a well made of stone. He stopped the car next to it.

"You're thirsty?" Laura asked ironically.

"There's water in the glove compartment. Let's get out and rest for a while."

They sat next to each other, with their backs against the well. Laura looked exhausted. She had bent her head down and was hugging her legs. He slipped his arm around her shoulders, and they stayed like that for a while, in silence. Finally, he got up, leaned over the edge of the well, and looked down. The well was very old. Flowers had grown on its walls, and the mortar between the stones had cracked. The way the cracks lined the interior, with the sun shining on them from directly overhead, they looked like silver blades shining in the dark. He wiped the sweat from his face. This was the hottest day since he'd come to America. He focused his attention on his image, trembling on the surface of the water. Like not so long ago, when he'd found Marcelo. Only now, the liquid mirror was not the surface of a shimmering little lake but a dark circle of still, dirty water, at least twelve feet down, and his image was little more than a barely discernible blur in the depths. He felt a pang of fear. Unconsciously, he turned his face to the side, as he had done then, looking at the dead Marcelo. Memory struck him once again. This darkness that you can never penetrate, though you know very well what is behind its veil—the terrible treasure that, although now gone, is nevertheless unbearably present, maybe even more present than when it was alive in its own moment.

And so, like in a double exposure, he saw, superimposed on his image, himself as a child. At the courtyard of their house. They had an iron well there, in the middle, crowned by vines. It was before his father had decided to move the family to Athens—he still owned that store at the center of the small town where they lived. He was with one of his friends; he still remembered his name— Andreas. They were playing an improvised basketball game, trying to throw small stones into the well, when he suddenly stopped and looked at the sky. "Look! Unbelievable! The clouds are dancing," he said to Andreas. He never until then had thought that clouds could move—he always drew their pictures like stamps, unmoving. He thought that they were nailed on the firmament, a natural ornament of the sky. Andreas was fascinated by his friend's discovery.

It was something that he too had never imagined. Behind them, his mother, wearing a light floral-print dress, beautiful, happy, with gardening shears in hand—were they gardening shears?—burst out laughing. His father was in the house fixing something, but he could hear everything through the window.

"Of course clouds move. They travel," she said.

"And who moves them?" he asked.

"God, honey."

"What nonsense are you telling the child?" the bass voice was heard from within.

In no time his father was outside.

"Look here, nobody moves the clouds. Nature has made them like that."

"And God?"

"God doesn't exist. Have you ever seen him? He's like Santa Claus. Everybody's talking about him but nobody has seen him. In this family we always tell the truth"—his father said, immense, silhouetted against the sun.

Of course this wasn't the case. He wasn't telling the truth—something that he later felt directly on his hide—but neither was she. His mother was also a liar. This kind of "meteorological" mystery gave him no clue about her secret life. There were no clouds in the sky that day, in his seventeenth year, now in Athens, when on his way home from school, he saw her on a side street, inside a strange car kissing a strange man. The sky was perfectly clear when his mother leaned her head back to offer her neck to the man's kiss, immersing herself in the pleasure, and her glance chanced to move to the right. She saw him. He saw her. In a single moment, life drained of all meaning. He left first, ran away as fast as he could, back home.

He was lost in a ferocious storm. He was furious, his face dark, his soul bleak, everything inside him in an upheaval. She came back and took him aside to talk to him. She was afraid he—still just a boy—might tell on her. He listened to her crying, her begging, her saying that "it's not what you think," as if *he* was the husband she was cheating on.

He let her go on for a long while. Maybe on purpose, as a punishment. Then, he looked at her seriously and said, "Don't worry, I didn't see anything."

His mother, however, was not that lucky afterwards. The next eyewitness was not the son, but the husband who, of course, had never imagined that what he'd been doing all along would some time, even only once, be done to him, and that the beaten down, neglected woman would pay him back in kind.

A sunbeam suddenly fell into the well like a lightning bolt. A cleft in the moment. His image was illuminated. Maybe it was the landscape; maybe the fact that he'd been looking at himself in about the same way as back then, before making the decision to take Marcelo's identity; maybe the heat; maybe his mother's image from many years later, after that painful episode, two days before she'd be lost, gone forever. That day even the clouds were crying, when she had looked at him with those big eyes of hers and had said: "Weak. I'm weak." Maybe it was all these things together that made him tear his eyes away from the water and turn them to Laura.

She was still in the same position, with her back to the wall of the well, exhausted, dead. The words had crowded, were pressing on his tongue, were choking him. They wanted to pour out. To talk to her. Tell her the truth. That he is not Marcelo, that he is not even American, that he is a Greek writer who has come from the other side of the planet to spend some time in a small Midwestern town to write and give lectures. And that, when he came, he was carrying a cross inside himself. And how, instead of delivering him from this unremitting burden, this landscape and this country had pushed the cross even deeper into his heart. And that destiny had given him the chance to shift his unbearable load onto someone else's shoulders. And that no, this other person would not suffer; he would not be haunted by his ghosts, be plunged into his darkness. It was a just, honest transaction, since this other person was already dead. "I'm not Marcelo," he would tell her. "Marcelo is dead."

He came closer and caressed her hair. She held up her tired, drawn face and looked at him. For a moment he felt the ground shifting under his feet. He tried to say something, but his reflection in the well jumped into his mind. And his mother's image as well, at the end, made up with rouge on her cheeks, dead.

"Let's go," he said.

"Where to?"

"Chicago."

Chicago

THEY NEEDED TO GET BACK TO THE FREEWAY. Chicago was probably no more than a couple of hours away. Doing that, of course, was inherently risky. Their pursuers could very well be lying in wait for them. Still, there was no alternative. Before they took off, he asked Laura to get the gun and put it in the glove compartment.

"Do you have a license for it?" he asked her.

"No, a friend gave it to me three years ago. I keep it for security."

He looked at her. She had changed. Her features had found again their natural tranquil beauty, as if inwardly, she had taken a deep breath and made peace with the situation. For a moment, he felt that there was something she liked about this mess. There weren't many women who, after the way things turned out, would stay so cool in the passenger seat.

"Are you afraid?" he asked her.

"About what happened back there? Back there, I had other things on my mind. Also, like I told you in Hannibal, there's not much that can shock me."

They got a little lost on the way back, but they finally managed to get back on the freeway. The black car with the white hood was nowhere to be seen. He tried to turn on the radio, but there was nothing but static. The antenna had been broken off.

A couple of hours later, the skyline of downtown Chicago appeared on the horizon. The Sears Tower—until recently the tallest building in the world—was the first thing they could identify, a glass and steel totem with its 1,451 feet of height thrusting into the sky. They were entering Chicago, the "Windy City." It seemed like the local motorists adhered to Greek driving customs since, from the point where Chicago's suburbs began, there was plenty of dangerous passing, greater reliance on horns than turn signals, and generally chaotic driving conditions.

"Let's stay somewhere close to the center."

"Then, get off on the Michigan Avenue Exit, and turn left," Laura said.

They stopped at the first large hotel they found. It was the Congress Palace Hotel. There was a picket line in front of the hotel's entrance. About ten people were walking up and down holding signs and shouting: "Don't stay here." They found out at the reception desk that the hotel had fired about thirty-five percent of the employees, who, for the past thirteen months(!), had been carrying out the protest outside. Laura then argued against choosing this hotel—"How can we stay at a hotel that fires all these people at will?"—but tired as he was, he said he just couldn't stand having to go look for something else. They booked a room on the tenth floor.

As much as the lobby was luxurious and impeccably decorated, with mosaic tiles and elaborate crystal chandeliers, so neglected and depressing was the room. The frame of the bed was sagging, the sheets were threadbare, the wallpaper peeling, and the curtains had holes and stains. A kitsch velvet print of the Sears Building was on the wall, while the bathroom was paved with tiles so ugly they would have brought eternal shame to any self-respecting interior decorator. Moreover, when he went out to get some cigarettes from the vending machine, he got lost in a maze of deserted, surrealistic hallways, which reminded him of the Coen Brothers' film *Barton Fink*. Ironically, next to the cigarette vending machine there was a plaque with an inscription stating that the hotel was originally designed and built to accommodate visitors to the 1893 World Columbian Exposition and that, at various times in the past, five Presidents of the U.S. had honored it with their presence.

When he got back to the room, Laura was in the bathroom. He took out the laptop and called to her that he was going down to the lobby—"I'll be back in a couple of hours," he added. Although the hotel was clearly going through some hard financial times, there was free wireless Internet access in the lobby. He first searched the Greek web sites. He was looking for some news about himself. Nothing. No new articles, no new references to his name, nowhere. Then he logged onto Marcelo's e-mail. Two new messages had appeared in the account. The first was—once again—the video clip with the apartment. The other had cod-america@aol.com as the sender. The text of the message was:

```
I hope you are coming to Chicago. J is expect-
ing you on the day and time we have agreed upon.
The interested party is anxious to get the
delivery. And, of course, the instructions about
the code number.
```

He thought that the sender must be this "Doc" that the young man in Hannibal had said sent him—cod spelled backwards. He replied immediately, asking where he could find him. He signed the e-mail Marcelo Diaz. He waited for a while and in a couple of minutes the server returned the e-mail as undeliverable—user unknown. And J? He must be this Joshua whom he was supposed to meet on Sunday. It was Friday, he still had two days to go. He made an effort to order things in his mind. The "claimants" were the people after him—Jimmy with the black car—and the "interested party" those to whom he should deliver. Doc, as well as the young man in Hannibal, belonged to the "interested party." They were offering money; the "claimants" were not, at least for the time being. Or maybe they did—who knows what prior communication Marcelo had with them? What everyone wanted was, without a doubt, the black box. Doc was asking him to deliver the code as well, or rather, instructions about it. Did Marcelo know the code? And if so, had he written it down anywhere? It was not the series of numbers in his notebook; he had checked that.

And the video clip? He watched it once again. The skyscrapers in the background indicated that the apartment was in some big city. Especially on the right side of the picture, there was a gray building of ultra-modern architecture that narrowed progressively into a pointed summit. Was this building in Chicago? Who had sent him the video? And what was the meaning of the book *Catcher in the Rye*? Suddenly he had an idea. He turned off the laptop and asked at the reception desk for the nearest bookstore. It was two blocks to the west, on a street perpendicular to Michigan Ave. It was not difficult to find. Of course, they did not have the first edition, but a 1991 edition published by Little Brown and Company.

On the way back to the hotel he walked in front of an art gallery. The title of the exhibit on display made him stop: *Dia de Los Muertos*—The Day of the Dead—a special exhibit of artifacts pertaining to the Mexican feast where the dead are honored and the fleeting nature of the human adventure on Earth is recognized.

He went in and took a look around the exhibits. Altars decorated with flowers, photographs of the dearly departed, candles, skulls made of sugar, paintings on cardboard depicting skeletons dancing and playing banjo and billiards. He stood in front of one of the altars. The deceased was one Eduardo Percegido. There was a photograph of a forty-year-old man with a mustache, with a cigar in his mouth. The altar was surrounded with marigolds while on the floor there was a tequila bottle and cigarettes. Two papier-mâché skeletons were placed in the center: a man and a woman, holding hands, wearing a tuxedo and a wedding gown. A handwritten note lay at their feet: "God pours life on death and death on life, without spilling a single drop." He shuddered, bringing back to his memory the image of a Ford burning in the bleak expanse.

When he got back to the hotel, he sat in the lobby and started reading Salinger's book:

> If you really want to hear about it, the first thing you'll probably want to know is where I was born, and what my lousy childhood was like, and how my parents were occupied and all before they had me, and all that David Copperfield kind of crap, but I don't feel like going into it, if you want to know the truth.

So begins Holden Caulfield, the sixteen year-old hero of the novel, who contests the duplicity of the grown-ups and defends innocence with all his strength, deriding success, marriage, the craze for exercise—all the American clichés of the time, the early 1950s. Holden, who rejects everything counterfeit. Holden, who wants to save children from the hardships of life and stands alone at the edge of the precipice to catch them before they fall. Holden Caulfield. The Catcher in the Rye. The author, Salinger, had become a recluse fifty years ago, after the huge success of his novel that was made a best seller by the same system he was condemning. A persecuted Jew, an author who wanted to escape from the book that glorified him.

But what did all that have to do with Marcelo, Doc, the claimants, the interested party? Was there any relationship between the novel and the black box? That sort of puzzle was not an easy one to solve. He tried to bring his old capabilities to bear on the problem. He let his mind wander among various crazy thoughts so that he wouldn't let any possibility go unconsidered, but he did not manage to make any connections. *It's been too long since I've written anything; my mind is rusty*, he thought.

He looked at the dark red curtains of the lobby. Heavy, creating an almost theatrical atmosphere. They reminded him particularly of that theater where he had the first reading of his work. He couldn't even get himself to speak. He muttered a couple of words: "The book speaks better than the author," and passed the ball to the person introducing him. The public, down there, was looking at him as if he were some exotic fruit.

When he went upstairs, he found a different Laura. She had washed her hair, had changed clothes—she was wearing black low-waist pants with a thin pink shirt—she seemed a different person. They made coffee, talked some about the hotel, and suddenly, she said something unexpected.

"This box... you've got to open it."

He was surprised.

"I can't," he answered automatically.

"Why? Didn't you lock it in the first place?"

He was in a bind. The question was potentially dangerous.

"It's not so simple. I did lock it, but it must not be opened again. The lock is a security one, specially made. It will show if it is opened once it has been secured. My instructions are to deliver it closed."

Laura insisted. He wouldn't back down.

"There are only two days left now. I'll be delivering it Sunday morning and we won't have to worry about it any more."

She tried to push the issue, with no result, and when she figured out that he would not change his mind, she asked about something else.

"What was that word you said when they were chasing us?"

"What?"

"A strange word, "*gamito*" something like that. What is it, Spanish?"

"Oh that! Nothing. I say it when I'm nervous; it doesn't mean anything, just a word I picked up at school."

"'*Gamito*'—it sounds funny!"

It was late. Now it was he who felt completely exhausted. He decided it'd be better to order something to eat from room service. So they ended up trying to eat two tough, overdone steaks with pre-fried potatoes. Afterwards they went straight to bed. Though he felt a suspicion, an itch inside himself about what he imagined was hidden behind her wanting him to open the box, they made passionate love. Because love is not confidence—love is nourished by insecurity, by fear, and by ignorance.

Nighthawks

HE WOKE UP EARLY THE NEXT MORNING. Laura was still asleep. However he may have reacted to her urging him to open the box the night before, she had given him an idea. He took the box and went out. He asked at the reception for some store specializing in welding or construction work. A half hour later, a taxi was dropping him off in front of a metal workshop. He asked the owner to tell him whether he could open the box or break the lock. After carefully studying the box, the man said he could do neither. The material the box was made of, as well as that of its lock, were virtually indestructible; it would take ages, even with a special drill. A blowtorch might be faster, but the heat could very well damage whatever was inside. He returned to the hotel. Laura was still sleeping with her arm around his pillow.

They had a whole day to spend in Chicago until the meeting. They discussed not leaving the hotel at all, probably the safest thing to do. Laura didn't think it was necessary: "This isn't Hannibal. It's a huge city, and they can't be looking for you on every street corner." After a while she managed to convince him. She knew the city well, and she promised to take him to some interesting places. They started walking along Michigan Avenue, going north. Despite the bright sun, a penetrating wind was blowing. Chicago was living up to its nickname. There were a lot of people on the street, a very diverse crowd: yuppies in business suits, kids on skateboards, tourists, eccentric faces. They saw an old woman in front of an old hotel, with her hair half-made-up, walking a huge husky with sad-looking eyes. She looked at them with eyes that were even sadder than those of the dog. A little further away, a skinny guy wearing a Chicago Bulls cap was selling fake name-brand watches out of a cart. To his right, a chubby red-haired woman, wearing a fur coat over a pink running suit, was walking, looking completely lost. There were beggars at almost every corner.

All around him, there was a cacophony of different accents. He was reminded of the words of some great author—that in the distant future the English language, through its intermingling with other languages, is going to become the music of humanity. There was still a long way to go for that theory to be proven right.

After a bit of walking, they found themselves before a beautiful building in the Italian Renaissance style.

"The Art Institute of Chicago," Laura said.

He had heard of it of course; it was one of the most famous museums in America. They went in. Inside, there was unbelievable chaos. It seemed that the city's schools had all selected this day for their fieldtrips to the museum. They waited in line for what seemed to be forever. When they finally got their tickets, he wanted to go directly to the European art wing, while Laura insisted on American art—she wanted to look at something specific. He gave in. In a little while, they were standing in front of Edward Hopper's most famous painting: *Nighthawks*.[9] A night scene in a diner, separated from the rest of the world by a glass wall, with three customers, two men and a woman, lost in their own world. The harsh fluorescent lighting created a dramatic effect in the composition, emphasizing the clients' isolation. The diner radiated an otherworldly bright-ness—a lighthouse on a dark street corner. The four anonymous figures—customers and server—appear cut off, from each other and from the viewer.

"From the time I left home," Laura said, "I've had a reproduction of this painting hanging in every place that I lived in. Look closely, there is no door to the diner. There is no way to get in or to get out."

"I think that the men have come for the woman. In the next scene they are going to talk to her."

"Oh, no. All three of them are like birds. Three birds caged behind the glass. That's how I felt also. A bird in a glass cage, constantly hitting its head against the glass."

They looked quickly at the rest of the exhibits—as best they could, considering the throng of visitors—and then worked their way to the European wing. It was magical. Toulouse-Lautrec, Monet, Manet, Cézanne, all the greats. He stood before a painting by Seurat: *A Sunday on La Grande Jatte.* A pointillist composition, perhaps the best example of this style of painting. The French painter translated light into color. Daily life suddenly opened up into a transcending world. The most banal subject—a stroll in the sun along the banks of the Seine—took on such a metaphysical dimension that you felt you were in a dream.

"Look there," he said and pointed at the painting's right side, noting a couple: a young man and an elegant woman with a pet monkey on a chain.

"How nice!... Now that Moxi's gone, I think I'll get a little monkey," said Laura.

"It's as if time is suspended, no? The opposite of Hopper. All of them are in their own worlds, but they are not alone in their loneliness..."

They looked at all the paintings one by one. They left Van Gogh's self-portrait for last. The crowd had become even more packed, so they had to stand on one side looking at the painting from a distance.

"He must have been influenced by the one before," said Laura, referring to Seurat's painting.

Indeed, the technique was very similar. A deluge of blue and red strokes was floating over a dark green background, producing the image of a man expecting a storm to suck him up.

"He must have been staring into his own eyes for a long time. He painted his own madness. It's frightening," he said.

The painting was one of the most popular in the museum. Dozens of people were packed together in front of it, while a guide was analyzing the painting for a group of Japanese tourists. He had started to feel uneasy since there was almost no room to move. He looked for a way out, and at that moment his eyes fell on a well-dressed middle-aged man with short gray hair and a well-groomed short beard, who was holding a straw hat in his hands. He was instantly bathed in cold sweat. The man, who was looking at the painting so intensely that it seemed like he was trying to get into the canvas, was Martin. Martin Shawnessy, the Irish poet he had met in Iowa City.

Laura was in front of him and did not sense his agitation. He pulled her by her shoulders and tried to move to the left, while keeping an eye on the Irishman. At the same moment, Martin moved to the right, and their eyes met. He stood frozen, while an expression between terror and surprise appeared on Shawnessy's face.

"Colossus..." Martin stammered.

This shook him into action and, turning his face away, he drew Laura abruptly to his side.

"What are you doing? You are hurting me!"

Holding her now tightly by the arm, he pulled her again to the right, whispering, "We need to get out of here right now! I'll explain outside."

Martin was now frozen and looked shocked, as if he had seen a ghost—which was not too far from the truth—as another wave of schoolchildren arrived in front of Van Gogh's painting, compacting the crowd even more. As they were moving as fast as possible toward the exit, he could not resist looking back. Martin, having recovered from the first shock—as much as was possible under the circumstances—had started to move in their direction. Fortunately, the crowd had become almost impenetrable by now. They reached the exit, went running down the steps, and turned into a narrow street leading to the back of the building. At the same time, Martin, much more sluggish, was stuck at the exit.

They ran north, along Michigan Avenue, zigzagging through the people on the sidewalk. Ten or so minutes later they stopped in front of a huge sign that said: "Urbs in Horto[10]—Millennium Park." It was a post-modern park full of monumental sculptures and futuristic glass structures, the most recent architectural treasure of the city. They went in and got lost among the thousands of visitors who, notwithstanding the strong wind, were enjoying the sunny day. They turned right and found themselves in a plaza paved with granite slabs, at the center of which stood two big glass towers, about forty-five feet high, placed at the two ends of a shallow reflecting pool. Water was flowing from the top of each of the towers, while slideshows with everyday images of people played on their surfaces. And there the artist's playfulness revealed itself: the faces were transformed into digital spouts, with water bubbling up from their mouths. A monument to time, as Heraclitus would have designed it, had he lived in present times and had he been an architect.

He stopped to look behind them. He didn't see Martin.

"Is it them?" Laura asked.

"Yes. Let's get out of here," he answered.

Coming out of the plaza, they found themselves in an open area. In its center was a strange, elliptical, stainless steel sculpture with reflecting surfaces. It looked like a huge kidney-bean mirror, a giant amoeba that reflected its environment with its entire body. In a way, it was a hole in space, a non-object. Chicago's skyline, with its skyscrapers, created a dramatic backdrop to the sculpture. Many passers-by would walk around it, studying their reflections on its surface, their images changing with every step they'd take. Standing close to the sculpture, one saw one's reflection almost close-up while, a little further away, one could see a wide-angle image covering a span of almost 180 degrees, with the skyscrapers of the skyline seemingly bending down. They approached and mixed with the crowd. He looked at their reflections on the sculpture. For a moment it seemed to him as if the two of them were hovering somewhere in space, two lonely astronauts swimming in a luminous vacuum, with the buildings behind flowing like celestial bodies into the heavens. However, they were simply a man and a woman, lost in the American landscape, absorbed in this parabolic mirror one afternoon in a park in Chicago.

Suddenly, in the upper part of the gigantic mirror he saw the silhouette with the straw hat approaching. This time he was prepared. He whispered to Laura to walk forward and join a group of German tourists who were leaving. They followed them as they moved on and found themselves at a large structure that looked like an open-air theater. Leaving the group, they turned to the right again and reached a busy street. The name on the sign was Randolf Street. An empty cab had just started moving in their direction from the traffic lights at the intersection. He flagged it down and they got in.

"Tell him someplace to go, someplace you know," he said.

"To Lake Michigan," she said to the driver.

The taxi-driver, a small bald man who had a pin on his shirt with a flag and the words "Sri-Lanka" beneath it, shifted into drive and they took off. Surprisingly, they reached their destination in less than five minutes.

"Lake, lake, here," said the driver in broken English, as if they couldn't see the expanse of water in front of them.

There was a park at the lakefront that seemed to be a continuation of the Millennium Park where they'd just been.

"I forgot, yes, Grant Park is right next to Millennium Park. But, shouldn't we get further away?"

"No, there's no danger any more," he said, thinking that Martin, with all his health problems, couldn't possibly have transformed himself into a trained FBI agent.

They paid and got out. They walked toward the shore of the lake. There was a tall tree there with a thick trunk, a plane tree. They sat at its base with their backs resting against the bark.

"In the end, you were right," she said.

"Yes. But, I didn't really think they would find us here."

"And now, what do we do?"

"We stay here for a little while, and then we get back to the hotel and stay there until my meeting tomorrow. It's probably the safest thing."

He told her where and at what time he was to meet the person to whom he was supposed to make the delivery. She insisted on details—Whom had he seen at the museum? Was he the same person who was after him in Hannibal?—but he did not give in. How could he, in any case? What could he tell her? That it was a colleague of his, a writer with whom, only a few days ago, he'd been taking part in a program in Iowa City?—let alone the degree to which this encounter had shaken him. He was sure that Martin had recognized him. But, how on earth did the Irishman end up in Chicago? But yes, since...

Suddenly, everything made sense. He remembered that Martin had been planning to travel for a while—leaving earlier than the others to take advantage of the program's offer of a free trip and two weeks' stay in a city of the participants' choice, and he had obviously chosen Chicago. How stupid of him, he thought, not to have taken the basic precaution of changing his appearance somehow, even in a small way—letting a beard grow, shaving his head, wearing glasses, something, *anything*. Now the damage was done. Martin would talk about his encounter with the supposedly dead Greek writer and that would create a chain reaction. But was it really such a big problem? There was no proof, everything would be based on the eyewitness testimony of only one person. A rumor would likely spread—that he had been seen alive in Chicago. And would that rumor reach Greece? Supposing that it would, what would be the likely fallout? There'd be some talk, some of the few people who knew him would begin to hope that they'll see him again, and before too long that hope would also fade. That's how it is: each miracle has a three-day shelf life. Inevitably, another possibility crossed his mind: to call Martin. He could easily get his cell phone number by calling the program secretary in a changed voice, pretending that he was a relative of Martin and looking for him— and ask him to not say anything about having seen him in Chicago. Shawnessy was a stand-up guy; maybe he would respect his request. On the other hand, there was a hazard in this idea. The Irishman, notwithstanding his serious health problems, drank, with legendary vigor. And oaths and promises, plus alcohol, make for a particularly volatile cocktail.

While his mind was occupied with these thoughts, with Laura silently sitting next to him looking at the lake, a young black man with faded jeans and a rainbow-colored Jamaican knit cap on his head, approached them. He bent close to his ear and asked him in a conspiratorial way:

"You want some weed, man? I got good stuff. And cheap, man."

A joint! He'd only smoked pot a few times in his life. However, the way he felt at that moment, with the tension that had built up inside him, he thought it might not be such a bad idea for relaxing. He gave Laura a meaningful look, as if asking, "What do you think?"

She, having figured out what the guy wanted right away, made an abrupt gesture of disapproval, so exaggerated that the guy turned around and left, uttering various oaths under his breath.

"What's the matter? It wasn't a big deal, just a little joint," he said.

Laura pointed to her head.

"I want this clear. I'll never fill it with that kind of junk again."

It seemed he had hit a sore spot. Laura instantly forgot all about being chased, and the dangerous predicament in which they had found themselves, and started talking about her relationship with drugs. As though it was something she'd had kept pent up inside for a long time and really needed to get off her chest.

"From the moment I left home, I felt I was nothing. There was an emptiness inside me," she said. "I had to fill the void with something, to become someone. When they approached me, I was drawn in immediately. I saw them as my family—the guys with whom I got high, the dealers, all of them. It made me stop thinking, but at the same time, inside and through the drugs, I had friends. I had love affairs. I believed they were real. We were all into the same shit, in the same boat. What I needed was to stay high, to not feel what was going on around me. And I dumped into my body everything you can imagine: pot, uppers, downers, ecstasy. I even got to the point of snorting coke and heroin. Eventually the group broke up. By that time each of us had to deal with our own shit. So, I was left alone and totally messed up. Until I met my friend, the musician I was telling you about. That was the first reality check. The second was someone else I met. It was after I got to know him that I finally decided to stop. 'How?' you may ask... I fell in love. And when the man I fell in love with realized what was happening, fortunately, he did the right thing. He put a mirror in front of my face. For the first time in a long while, I really saw myself. And I was frightened."

"Who was it?"

"It doesn't really matter. It was several years ago, in Saint Louis, a man older than me. Fifteen years. He'd lost his brother to heroin."

"And what happened with him?"

Laura stopped talking for some time. Then, she said in a low voice:

"He couldn't wait for me any longer. And when he finally left me, I got serious and cleaned myself up."

"How?"

"I didn't want to go to Drug Addicts Anonymous. I just couldn't stomach the religious nature of that program, you know, that story with the twelve steps: '...We came to believe that a Power greater than ourselves could restore us to sanity. We are entirely ready to have God remove all our defects of character. We humbly ask Him to remove our shortcomings. We seek through prayer and meditation to improve our conscious contact with God, praying only for knowledge of His will for us and the power to carry that out...' All that frightened me even more. I had gotten God out of my system. I'd seen first hand what he'd done to my home and to me."

"So how did you mange to stop using? Don't tell me you did it alone?"

"No, I did something that maybe sounds crazy. I committed myself to a psychiatric hospital. For two months I was locked up in a ward with schizophrenics and other mental patients. I told myself: I am sick, my disease may be different than theirs, but it's still a disease. And I got clean. It was the most important thing I've ever done in my life. And from then on I never used again. I haven't smoked even a joint. I don't want any more intermediaries in my life. Since I became a teenager, I never got to have anything that was mine, anything that I could control myself. Not even my body. Or rather, I did have one thing. When the stuff I told you about, with my father, was happening, when it began, I had a small toy that for me symbolized everything I loved, everything that was most important. It was a little fairy—a tiny doll, a cheap one, a trifle really. So, when that stuff happened, I went and buried it in the garden. I buried it so deep that when I looked for it later I couldn't find it. I never did find it again. Somehow with the drugs, in the beginning, I thought that I had found it, that somehow it poked up its head from the dirt, but it wasn't this sweet little face any more, it was a monster. I know what you're going to say and, no, I didn't find it even after I got clean. I got out of the psychiatric hospital having been given a second chance. They say the only second chance one has is to make the same mistake again. But I've managed not to relapse. No, I haven't made any mistakes again, at least not the same ones. I tried to protect that spark of light, the memory of that little lost doll. But I became hard-hearted. I built a wall around me, a wall that stayed there, impenetrable. I don't know why I'm telling you all this..." she said and turned her eyes to the lake. She was in tears.

"I'm sorry, I didn't know..."

"There are many things you don't know."

He took her in his arms. They stayed there holding each other for a while and then walked back to the hotel. They stayed inside for the rest of the day, making love, and eating the awful food brought by room service. Before going to sleep, he asked her again what the two ideograms at the back of her neck meant. She turned around, gave him a penetrating look, and said to him a single word: "Fear."

That night, he dreamt of Martin, dressed up as Laura's lost doll, waving a fish-bone like a magic wand, constantly repeating the same word: "Fear...fear..."

Joshua Patterson

ON MONDAY MORNING, they woke up at about eight-thirty. They had a hearty room-service breakfast—at least the croissants and cereal were tastier than the previous evening's dinner. He had already bought, from one of the stores in the hotel lobby, a plastic tote bag and a map of the city. He put the black box in the bag. He checked the note with the address he kept in his wallet. He looked at the map. Quincy Street was only two blocks west of the hotel— a narrow lane in between Jackson Avenue and Adams Street. They spent some time planning what to do. He suggested that she should wait downstairs while he went up to the seventh floor and delivered the box.

"It may be dangerous, I should come with you."

"No, I think it would be best if we split up."

Laura accepted this, but didn't like it at all when he asked her to give him the gun. He insisted, though, and she reluctantly gave in. At a quarter to one, he put on Marcelo's dark brown jacket and put the gun in an inside pocket. It was the first time in his life he carried a gun. He shivered when he thought about it, as if the gun was pointing at his own heart.

Outside, the temperature had dropped and the wind was even

stronger, but the sun was still shining. Coming out of the hotel, they turned left on Michigan Avenue. A double-decker bus was moving slowly along the street. It had on its side a large photograph of John Kerry with the sign "Kerry: The Real Deal" in bold letters underneath. On the open top deck, a dozen girls with bright, toothpaste-ad smiles were throwing to all passers-by flyers with slogans supporting the senator's candidacy: "Let's make America great again" and "Stronger at home, more respected abroad." They turned left again, on Van Buren Street, and right on State Street. On the corner, there was a butcher shop with plucked birds, skinned rabbits, and slabs of raw meat hanging in the window. Laura turned her face away with a disgusted expression. A few yards past the intersection with Jackson Avenue, he saw the narrow street to the left: Quincy Street. Number forty-three was a tall glass office building.

He told Laura to wait on the corner. He gave her the number of the office and instructed her to come find him if he didn't return in half an hour. He went inside. In the lobby a security guard was sitting behind a metal desk. He approached the desk.

"I'm here to see Mr. Patterson," he said.

"Is he expecting you?"

"Yes."

"May I see your driver's license?"

It hadn't even crossed his mind he'd need identification to get in. "I'm sorry, I don't have it with me."

The security guard pressed a button and raised a telephone receiver to his ear. He waited for a minute. "There's no answer. He had some other visitors just a little while ago. Are you sure he's expecting you?"

"Of course. It's a business meeting. He even gave me the entrance code," he said with a solemn expression.

"Very well. Please sign in," said the guard, pointing at a logbook on the desk.

He signed using a false name: Peter Fowles.

"I need to check your bag, sir."

He gave the guard the tote bag. The guard opened it and pulled out the black box.

"What is this?" he asked.

"It's for Mr. Patterson. I'm delivering it to him."

"What's inside, please?"

"I told you, it's business related, for Mr. Patterson."

"Could you open it please?"

"It's to be delivered unopened."

At that moment the phone on the guard's desk rang. It must have been something very personal because the guard started whispering into the phone, seemingly a bit shaken. He waited, standing in front of the desk.

"Didn't I tell you 'no'? Don't do anything yet, for God's sake!" the guard said, and covering the mouthpiece with his hand, motioned him through.

"OK, Mr. Fowles, you may go up."

He got in the first elevator on the left, while behind him he could hear the guard speaking into the phone, agitated. On the second floor, the elevator stopped and a pretty brunette wearing horn-rimmed glasses and a conservative business suit got in. She pressed the eleventh floor button. Their eyes crossed momentarily, and then as if choreographed, they both turned their eyes to the small display in which the floor numbers flashed one after the other. When the elevator stopped on the seventh floor, he got out into a granite-paved hallway. There was no one around. Office number 15 was at the other end of the hallway. Next to the sign "Joshua Norman Patterson LLC," there was an electronic keypad. He checked his watch. It was 1:07 a.m. He was late. He keyed in the code, 190760, and pressed ENTER. The heavy metal door opened with a slight "click." He stepped inside and closed it behind him.

He was in a room with a large desk, positioned to directly face the entrance. No one was there but what he saw was utter chaos.

Drawers were gaping open, paper was strewn on the floor, as if someone had gone through everything methodically. Impulsively, he put his hand in the inside pocket of the jacket. He felt a little safer when he touched the cold steel of the gun.

Behind the desk was a glass partition. One of the panels was ajar. He went to it. A large room was behind it. The wall to the right was covered with a huge map of the U.S. Here too everything was in shambles—dozens of file folders on the floor, furniture turned upside down, documents thrown about everywhere. In the middle of the room was a desk with a computer and a large flat panel monitor on it. As he moved to the right he saw something that took his breath away. There was a hand visible behind the monitor—seemingly disembodied, sticking straight up. With halting steps he approached the desk. The hand was attached to a body, and this body was lying behind the desk, bloody, apparently lifeless. It was the body of a man, middle-aged, graying hair, somewhat overweight, wearing a white shirt and black, pinstriped pants.

His first impulse was to get out of there as fast as possible. But, as he turned, he heard a choking sound. The man on the floor moved slightly. He was still alive. He knelt and bent over him. The man's eyelids fluttered. His hand fell down from the desk. There were two large round bloodstains on the front of the white shirt.

"Who a-are you?" the man said in a trembling voice.

"Marcelo."

"Did… you bring it?"

"Yes."

"You must de-deliver it…"

"To whom?"

"Talk… talk to Doc."

"How can I get in touch with him?"

"There's… in-inside…"

"Who did this to you?"

"Doc… You must…"

"How can I reach him?"

The man's eyes began to glaze.

"Wil-Wilma…" he exhaled, and his head rolled to the side.

The man was dead. It was the third time in his life that he was looking at a dead person. For a few moments, he stood frozen, not knowing what to do. Through the window, he could see two workers on a platform cleaning the glass of a skyscraper. The workers seemed to be floating at the end of a contraption that looked like a miniature crane. At that moment the phone rang. Startled, he moved towards the door. After four rings, an answering machine picked up: "You have reached the office of Joshua Patterson. Please leave a message at the tone."

A nasal male voice came from the speaker.

"Where are you dammit? I called your cell phone and no answer there either. Did he come? They need it urgently upstairs. Call me ASAP."

The caller hung up. He went back into the office and looked at the display of the phone. It had caller-ID. The call had come from the 212 area code: New York City—Manhattan. He thought fast. He had to do it. He dialed the number. The same voice answered.

"What's going on, man? Have you lost it? Not picking up?"

He masked his voice.

"…I've been busy…"

"Busy? Are you kidding me? What's up, do you have it?"

"…Yes…"

"What's wrong? Why do you sound like this? Are you sick or something?"

"…I have a cold…"

"And with the carrier? Is everything OK, are we done?"

He was silent for a couple of seconds. What did "done" mean?

"…Yes…" he finally answered.

"Did he give us the code?"

"…Yes…"

"All right! You've done great. You must bring it ASAP."

He chanced it.

"...Give me the address again..."

"Are you crazy?" the voice exclaimed. Then silence. It returned after a moment. "All right. I'm going to tell you. So, Rock, tell me who you're speaking with: Paper or Scissors?"

That threw him. What was he supposed to answer now? It was a safe bet that the dead man was "rock," so he had a fifty-fifty chance. He gambled.

"...With Paper..."

Again silence.

"Who are you? Where is Rock?"

"I'm a friend of Marcelo's," he said with his natural voice, and immediately regretted it. If this whole thing was so dangerous, Marcelo wouldn't have been using his real name.

"Bullshit... Who are you? How do you know that name? Is this some kind of a joke? Put Rock on."

The caller had proved him wrong. Marcelo had been using his real name.

"Not possible. He's dead."

He heard an oath and the line abruptly went dead.

He found a pencil and wrote down on a piece of paper the number he had just called. He now had the calmness and sharp focus that he seemed to find every time that real danger presented itself. Life's small unpleasant surprises may still have overwhelmed him, even panicked him, but huge, significant difficulties only strengthened his resolve and composure. It was this composure that led him to wipe his fingerprints from the phone and answering machine. For a moment, he thought there was no need for that, since he was officially dead, but he continued wiping everything he'd touched. When he was done, he wrapped the handkerchief around his hand and did a quick search of the broken-into filing cabinets and strewn-about folders. He picked one up at random. It contained printouts of what appeared to be accounting ledgers. Looking through several others, he gathered that almost all of the documents in the room were of a financial nature: contracts between Joshua Patterson and various clients, financial analyses, budgets, etc. On the floor, near the desk, he finally found something interesting: an address book, filled with names and contact information. He looked through it. His face lit up at one entry. "Doc—Scissors." He looked at the number he had written down on the piece of paper. Doc's telephone number and the number of the man with whom he had talked on the phone were the same. He checked the time: 1:17 p.m. He had to go. He went out, closing the metal door softly behind him.

He took a deep breath as he stepped out of the elevator on the ground floor. The security guard was still talking on the phone in a hushed voice. He walked in front of him, trying to avoid any eye contact. He was happy to feel the cold wind that hit his face the moment he got outside. Laura was waiting for him at the corner. He motioned her to keep quiet, took her by the hand, and started walking at a normal pace. With his peripheral vision, he kept checking everyone around them. Before long, they were back at their hotel room. There, without mentioning that a dead body was now complicating the situation, he told her that the delivery had been a trap, that he'd almost lost his life, and that those who wanted the box were probably not, after all, as honest as he'd thought.

"What have you gotten yourself into? I told you we should open it."

"Laura, please, I thought I'd explained it to you."

Laura paced around the room. Suddenly she uttered the name of God, simply, as if it was something she often did.

"My God," she said. And then, she instinctively brought her hand in front of her mouth.

He looked at her. He noticed the two lines that embraced, like parentheses, her mouth. They had become deeper—she looked exhausted. Every intense experience shared by two people imparts, in its interludes, a strange familiarity. He felt that, at that moment, Laura was almost as tired, as confused, as he. Somewhere, in the recesses of his heart, he liked that feeling.

"So, what are you going to do now?" she asked.

"I don't know. In any case, there's this new consideration. The people to whom I'm supposed to deliver the box are as dangerous as the ones trying to stop me."

"How can that be, if the two groups are opposed to each other? Don't those who want you to make the delivery want the scandal to be revealed?"

Laura's question was helpful. For a while he was lost in his thoughts. Laura continued to look at him, not interrupting, waiting for an answer. Suppose that Joshua, who was obviously one of the "interested party," was eliminated by the "claimants," Jimmy and the rest, who'd been after him. However, if the "interested party" wanted to reveal whatever was inside the box, then why did the man on the phone, Doc, act the way he did? Is it possible that the messenger was to be eliminated? Had Marcelo been sent on a suicide mission? Fleetingly, he thought again of his second book. The cross—in this case the black box—that the main character had found was basically a ticket to Hell. Its discovery had put the hero's life in mortal danger. In the end, after a wild chase into a world of darkness, the hero did survive. But this, what he was now involved in, was not a doppelganger story, like in Poe or Chuck Palaniuk. There was no Marcelo in the action any more.

"Where are you?" he heard Laura ask.

"Nowhere, I was thinking. I don't know, they may be rival groups after all. Maybe they wanted to get rid of the delivery man. I am only a simple intermediary in any case."

"But, how much do you know in the end? Whom are you working for?"

Laura was starting to get suspicious again. He had to find a way out. "Listen to me, please. It's all very complicated, but it only involves me. I have to figure out what to do. And soon. If you can't take it, of course, you are free to go. I've already told you too much—I can't tell you anything else. Believe me, that's the way things are. If you can't accept this, you don't have to come with me."

"So, that's the way it's going to be?"

"That's the way it has to be."

Laura was quiet for a while. There was a struggle going on inside her, he could tell. For a few minutes he felt that these were the last moments they would have together. Her reply took him by surprise.

"Great... So now there's danger from both sides. What are we going to do now?"

"Right now, nothing. We're going to stay here for a little while."

"What? Stuck in this room?"

"That would be best."

"Not me. No way!"

She told him she'd made plans to see a friend of hers, an old girlfriend from St. Louis who now lived in Chicago. He didn't like the idea at all, but she wouldn't give in. "I can't live like a fugitive. Going from one prison to the next. I didn't get out of Hannibal so I'd live in hotel rooms. That's not what I had in mind at all," she said. The exchange got heated, and after a while, Laura left the room.

He was left alone. He didn't know what to do. His eyes chanced on the plastic tote bag with the box and his thoughts jumped to the other bag, the one with the money. The idea he'd rejected as a betrayal of sorts came back to him. He had enough money on hand. He could start a new life, rent a house, buy furniture, get a credit card, find a small town in the middle of nowhere and settle there. Mr. Marcelo Diaz. Alone? With her? Why not? And what would he do "for a living?" He'd get an undemanding job and he'd get by, live day to day. Simply, quietly, "like the neighborhood convenience store clerk," as he used to say to describe that kind of life.

Until? Until what? This wasn't what he had in mind when he acted on *the idea*. No! Not for anything. He wouldn't give up so easily. He pulled out of his pocket the piece of paper with Doc's number and dialed it. The number had been disconnected.

He took the laptop and went down to the lobby. A large conference was beginning that afternoon, and the place was chaotic, with hundreds of guests arriving and trying to register, and many more clustered in groups or moving about the lobby in search of conference information, meeting rooms, etc. He looked for a relatively quiet corner, sat down in a plush deep-red armchair, and turned on the computer. There was nothing new in Marcelo's e-mail, and there was no mention of him at any of the Greek newspaper sites. The major news of the day was about the sparring taking place between the government and the main opposition party. "Conflict to the limit?" queried the most prestigious newspaper. "Will there be limits to the conflict, or will the conflict go to the limits? The Prime Minister declares: 'We must all pull together to resolve the crisis.' 'Make a true commitment to transparency and I will support you,' says the leader of the opposition." The rest of the news included reports about the hunger strike of the imprisoned members of the "November 17" terrorist group, the record world oil price— at $50.50 per barrel, and the death of Christopher Reeve at age fifty-two.

He leaned back and looked around the lobby. At the reception desk, the lines were getting shorter as, one by one, the conference participants got their keys and moved towards the elevators. Suddenly he saw something that turned his heart to ice. Behind a well-dressed businessman with a Samsonite suitcase stood a man he'd seen before. He was tall, well-dressed, with straight blond hair, round glasses, and the tell-tale acne scars on his face. He was one of Jimmy's men, the "claimants"… When it was his turn, the man went up to the reception counter, leaned over, and talked to the hotel employee behind it in a conspiratorial manner. The employee shook his head. They talked for a short while and then the man moved toward the elevators. A line of people and luggage had formed there and the man joined it at the back. It was certain that there wouldn't be enough room in the first couple of elevator cars going up.

He had to think of something, fast. He slid the laptop under the armchair. He located the nearest emergency exit and walked to it. When he was in the stairwell he ran up the stairs as fast as he could. At the tenth floor, he burst out of the stairwell into the hallway, but then slowed down to a brisk walk. As he passed the elevators, he saw someone in a business suit getting out of a car that had just arrived. He peeked inside but the man with the acne scars was not in it. When he got to the room, he stuffed their clothes into the two suitcases as fast as he could. The bag with the money was already in his suitcase, but the black box was in the room safe. He opened it and tossed the box in the suitcase. He collected as many of their toiletries as he could see and tossed them in the suitcases as well, then closed the cases and pulled both of them out of the room. He ran to the nearest emergency exit as fast as he could. He almost killed himself running down the stairs with the two suitcases in tow, all the way to the ground floor. When he got to the lobby, he recovered the laptop, put that too in his suitcase, and left the hotel as quickly as he could manage.

The Mustang was parked three blocks west of the hotel, at a spot that he'd judged to be pretty safe. It didn't take him long to get there wheeling the suitcases behind. He put them in the trunk and started the car. He drove into the downtown area, following side streets, turning this way and that, not really knowing where he was going. When he got to a major street, Halsted St., he stopped at a pay phone and called Laura on her cell phone. Without getting into details, he told her to come, as soon as possible, to where he now was. She resisted at first, but his voice carried such urgency, that even Laura, who wasn't "easily shocked," appeared to be affected by it. She was getting in the car with him within a half hour.

"We're taking off," he told her sharply.

She shook her head, assenting.

"*Gamito*," she said. "At least, with you, there are no boring moments," she added ironically.

He gave her a half smile and explained what had happened. "Double jeopardy, like you said. This time we need to go somewhere where nobody can find us, lie low for a little while, let some time pass. I'll say it again: if you think this is too much, you can stay here."

Laura looked at him intently. "You said that, after you made the delivery, you'd explain everything to me."

"Yes, but I didn't make it. Please, I need some more time. But I understand where you're coming from. You are free to do as you see fit."

Laura didn't say anything for a while, she seemed to be thinking hard about something. "I'd like to come with you, but we need to make a deal."

"What kind of deal?"

"You want to lie low for a while. We'll go someplace I know, where I wanted to go anyway."

"Where?" he asked.

"Ron's place."

"Who's Ron?"

"The musician I told you about. The one who helped me out back in St. Louis. He lives at a farm in Indiana, far away from everything. I haven't talked to him in a long time, but I think he'll be willing to put us up for a while."

"Is he someone we can trust?"

"He's the only person I know for whom I'd take an oath on the Bible—if I still believed in that stuff."

"OK then."

"I'll get out and give him a call," Laura said, pulling out her cell phone.

She was gone for a while, but some fifteen minutes later she was back, holding a small piece of paper in her hand.

"All right. We're welcome to stay as long as we need. I got the directions." She started reading: "It's east of Chicago. We take I-90, and then old US 6. Then we take US 33 East for about ten miles, until we get to Wolflake, a small town in Indiana, near Wawassee Lake. Once in town, we get on Washington Street going West, and about two miles outside the town, we'll see a sign: "To Landyland." There, we get on the unpaved road and…"

He tried to interject something, but Laura kept talking.

"…we go exactly 30 miles—we'll have to make sure we keep track of it on the odometer—and when the road reaches a clearing, we stop and call him on the cell phone. He'll send someone to show us to the farm. It's about three and a half or four hours from here."

"Landyland?" he finally managed to ask. "Is it Ron Landy that we're talking about?"

"Yes."

"*The* Ron Landy?"

"Yes."

"I can't believe it… I've been a great fan of his since I was a teenager." Somehow, despite the difficult situation they were in, this cheered him up.

"Really?"

"I know his early ballads by heart. He's a great poet—incredible songs… Yes, I'd read that he'd withdrawn from public life, he doesn't give any interviews, isn't writing music any more…"

"He left everything behind… Ron is a wise man. Strange but wise. He still writes music, but only for himself. He got sick and tired of the whole music scene. We're very lucky that we're being let in. I'm sure very few people have ever been to his farm. It took me a while on the phone because I had to give a detailed account of who you are."

"So, who am I?"

"You're my boyfriend. I told him it's been a difficult time for me and I'm in desperate need of a quiet place where I can get away from everything for a while."

"And what do I do?"

"I told him you work for an information technology company. But that kind of stuff doesn't interest Ron much. He's only interested in what kind of person you are."

"Have you been to his farm before?"

"No, but I know that he doesn't want any uninvited visitors; that's why he's chosen such an isolated and remote location. I couldn't imagine a safer place for you. And I wanted to see him again. I don't know if you really understand this, but I'd gotten to be very close to him. Even though I was a drug addict when he and I met, he was able to see deep inside me. To tell you the truth, I need to get away from all this for a while. But I need you to do something for me."

"What?"

"Give me back the gun."

He pulled it out of the pocket of Marcelo's jacket and gave it to her. Laura wrapped it in a plastic bag, got out of the car, threw it in a trash bin and got back in the Mustang.

"OK, now we can get out of here."

"OK," he answered and stepped on the gas.

As they got out of Chicago, the wind started to quiet down. As if it was sending them a message.

C. LANDYLAND

The farm

WHEN THEY REACHED THE OUTER SUBURBS of Chicago, they stopped at a large gas station with a store that had everything a motorist might need. There they repaired the broken antenna, replaced the shattered mirror, and got water and sandwiches for the road. Three hours later they were in Wolflake. They stopped for coffee and then took Washington Street towards Ormas, Etna, and Wilmot. Exactly as the directions Laura had gotten called for, two miles outside the town was a red sign with an arrow pointing in the direction of an unpaved road, above which was written in blue letters: To Landyland. The sign was small and easy to miss if someone wasn't looking for it. He turned onto the unpaved road and zeroed the odometer. The place was deserted, and after a while, there were no signs of civilization at all. The weather was nice, with no wind. Several miles down, the road started climbing higher. They were going up a wooded hill. He checked the odometer, which was already at twenty-two miles.

"You didn't tell me it was so high up," he said.

"It must be at the peak," Laura answered, pointing higher.

When they had gone thirty miles, they entered an open plateau where there was a large building like a barn. The road ended there.

"This must be the clearing. Call him on the cell phone," he said.

Laura punched in the number. He heard her answer "yes" repeatedly.

"So, we're going to wait here. I talked to one of his assistants. Landy is working outside all day today. He's sending one of his people to bring us to the farm."

They waited in the car listening to music. He was on his third cigarette when, at the edge of the clearing, a man appeared, about forty, thin, fidgety, with an angular face, long, stringy hair, and an unkempt beard. He was wearing dark glasses and a felt hat, and his red shirt was totally unbuttoned, revealing well-toned muscles.

"Howdy, I'm Sam," he said, extending his hand to shake theirs.

He helped them take the suitcases out of the trunk, opened the garage door, and told them to park the Mustang inside. In the garage, there already were three large SUVs, a small subcompact, and a large silver Cadillac. Then Sam took Laura's suitcase and started heading in the direction from which he'd come.

"Aren't we going to drive there?" he asked.

Sam turned and gave him an examining look.

"There's no road for a fucking car. We have to walk."

"Is it far?"

"A fucking twenty minutes."

"Through the woods?"

"Through the fucking woods, that's right."

It seemed that "fucking" was the same for Sam as "like" was for Nick and the coeds in Iowa City.

They walked across the clearing, the edge of which was marked by a stand of tall cedars, and they entered a lush woods: mature oaks, some nearly one hundred feet tall, walnuts, cypresses, pines, and flowers, wildflowers everywhere, cyclamens, daisies, blue-bells, violets, their colors shining in every sunny spot and small clearing they passed. The fauna was as impressive as the flora. Copper-green frogs hopping along the banks of small streams, small tortoises slowly dragging along their large shells, squirrels, and even deer who seemed unfazed by their presence created an idyllic backdrop that somewhat relieved the burden of the heavy suitcase he was carrying. After ten or so minutes, he asked for a short break. He had a bad back and, normally, shouldn't be lifting any significant weight. He explained this to Sam, who gave him a condescending look, mumbling: "fucking back!" After resting a bit, they started walking again through the dense vegetation. Suddenly, the patch of sky above them was almost entirely covered by the shadow of a huge bird hovering above the trees. It had a dark body and white head and tail. Sam looked up at it.

"The Indiana Bald Eagle. You don't usually see them around here; it seems like this one is coming back from the lakes. Looking for fish, along with the fucking vulture and gold eagle. They're a protected species but some assholes still hunt them."

"The fucking assholes!" he said.

They stopped for another short rest, and a little later came out into another clearing, just below the top of the hill. The air had the musky fragrance of fresh dirt. He was beyond tired, but the view that opened up in front of him made him forget his exhaustion and his back that had been feeling sharp pains. On the hillside there were five buildings with shingle roofs. Four of them looked like typical farmhouses, until one noticed the large windows and the use of modern building materials, such as steel and granite. The second building from the right, the tallest one, was an extraordinary mansion in ranch style, with beautiful finishes decorating its façade. Near the right edge of a fence that surrounded the buildings was a wooden sign with the word: Landyland. Underneath the name were five dark lines, but at that distance, he could not make out what they said. Next to the sign, there were three flagpoles, each flying a flag with a face in a white background. The compound was spread over a large lush green area. Behind it, one could see several large fields surrounded by wooden fences. In one of them, ten or so horses were grazing peacefully.

It was a truly startling image, an imposing estate set in the middle of nowhere. That wasn't all, however. Higher up, almost at the top of the hill, at a spot from which a small stream seemed to spring, there were three colorful triangular shapes. At first he took them for ethnic large-scale sculptures—signs of Landy's eccentric sensibilities. However, when he looked closer, he figured out they were teepees. Indian teepees like those he'd only seen in movies.

"Are there Indians living in this area?" he asked Sam.

Sam turned and gave him an angry look. "This isn't the fucking America you know," he said.

"That's for sure," Laura commented.

When they got closer to the compound, he was able to make out the words on the sign:

> The sun is beginning to shine on me
> But it's not like the sun that used to be
> The party's over, and there's less and less to say
> I got new eyes
> Everything looks far away.

Under the faces in the three flags, names were printed in bold black letters. They were Ralph Waldo Emerson, Henry David Thoreau, and Thomas Jefferson. Under Jefferson's portrait there were three words: Life, Liberty, Property—the three rights proclaimed in the Declaration of Independence. Someone, however, had added with a red marker a large question mark next to the word "Property."

"This way," Sam said and led them to the most remote building on the right.

On the lintel above the entrance, the phrase "E pluribus unum" was carved. He knew it was from Virgil and wondered about it, until he remembered it was also on the Great Seal of the United States of America: it is held in the beak of an eagle. Out of the several states, one nation.

A very tall man with long black straight hair and a muscular build was sitting in a chair by the entrance, carving a piece of wood with a knife. He was wearing jeans and a multi-colored vest over a white shirt. His features were pure Native American. His calm eyes followed their progress to the door.

"Hi, Devdan," Sam said.

The man raised his right palm in reply. Laura and he nodded, somewhat awkwardly, in Devdan's direction.

"This way," Sam said, opening the door.

They entered a large room with walls covered in wood paneling. In its center, there was a curved stairwell, also wooden. The room was furnished in antiques, the large windows were framed with heavy curtains, the floor was covered with intricate carpets, and the walls were decorated with numerous paintings: portraits and landscapes. Sam put Laura's suitcase down and opened the drawer of the umbrella stand that was next to the door, obviously looking for some key. He took the opportunity to look at the paintings more closely. There were portraits of John Adams, Benjamin Franklin, Alexander Hamilton—three of the Republic's founding fathers—as well as of Robert E. Lee, Simon Bolivar, Charles Dickens, Leo Tolstoy, Sitting Bull—the Sioux chief who defeated Custer at Little Big Horn—Miles Davis, Martin Luther King, Jr., Timothy Leary, and even Stanley Kubrick—something very surprising, since the famous director almost never allowed photographs of himself to be taken, let alone sat for a portrait. The landscapes were representative of the nation's many notable sites: the Appalachian mountains, Lake Superior, the Brooklyn Bridge, Yellowstone.

Sam located the key he'd been looking for and motioned them to follow him to the staircase. At the top, it led to a long corridor with six doors on each side. Each door had a sign: "Mayflower Compact," "Evangeline," "Tea Party," "Cherokee," "Pater Patriae." Through an open door, he saw a young man arranging clothes in a closet. The last door on the right had the sign: "Status Quo Ante Bellum." Sam opened it with the key, and they walked into a spacious room with wood-carved ceiling, pine floorboards, a king-sized canopy bed, a large antique armoire, and a huge mirror precisely opposite the bed. The window had an expansive view, all the way to the flat plain, while a small door opened to an unpretentious, neat bathroom.

"Make yourselves comfortable, settle in, and I'll be waiting for you downstairs to show you around the farm. You'll be having dinner with Ron at the big house in the evening," Sam said.

When they were alone, he commented:

"All of this is unreal."

"I wasn't expecting anything like it either. A refuge from the outside world," Laura said.

"He seems passionate about American history."

"Everything evokes the 'Wild West.'"

"Together with the twenty-first century. Quite a combination. He's extraordinary."

"Ron is a very unusual human being."

"In what way?"

"You never know what he'll do. Sometimes he is very quiet, and sometimes he can talk your head off."

"Is he still married? If I remember correctly, he had a very beautiful wife in his glory days."

"Maude... No, they're divorced. I'd say that it's his most vulnerable side. He hasn't told me any of the details, but whenever he referred to her he called her the 'enchanting woman.' They have three boys together."

Sam gave them a tour of the other major buildings of the compound. In the living room of the first, two men in their thirties were sitting, playing guitars. They looked very much alike, except that one had long hair tied in a ponytail, while the other had his head cleanly shaven. They stopped as soon as they saw them. Sam made the introductions, somewhat curtly. Their names were Tom and Jason—two of Ron's three sons. They exchanged a few formalities, stayed to listen to a song, and then went on to continue the tour of the farm.

One of the other buildings was the "big house," Landy's mansion where they were expected that evening, while the other two were housing for the farm workers. In the fields immediately behind the housing compound, there were six smaller auxiliary buildings. Two of these were horse barns. Landy must have been a great horse-lover. Every stall had a sign with the breed of each animal: American Saddle Breed, Pinto, Thoroughbred, Appaloosa, Morgan, Mustang—almost all of the major breeds of the North American continent were present in Landyland. The third building was a storage shed, while the fourth was a kind of two-wheeled vehicle museum, since that's where Landy had stored his collection of classic motorcycles. Each had a small plaque in front of it. There were virtual works of art, such as an 1894 Hildebrand & Wolfmueller and a 1940 Indian Sport Scout "Bob-Job," and classics such as a 1969 Easy Rider Harley-Davidson Chopper and a 1989 Buell RS1200. The next building housed various workshops: a carpentry shop, a small smelter, and a traditional blacksmith with horse-shoeing facilities, where the metal was heated in glowing charcoal. On the west side there was a kiln, built with special bricks.

The last building housed organic agriculture facilities. Behind it, there were fields in which, as Sam explained to them, special "healthy" soils were maintained. This was done through the use of compost that essentially recycled the food, agricultural, and animal waste products of the farm, through the plants that became nutrient-rich fertilizer when they were plowed under the soil, and through a rotation planting system that used legumes such as peas, tare, and lentils, to enrich the soil with nitrogen. Various plants were grown together on each plot to create a hospitable environment for microorganisms, insects, and birds that, in turn, naturally enhanced the productivity of the soil. Landyland produced vegetables, legumes, citrus, and even grapes, from which it bottled its own wine, Landymark.

"It takes you right to heaven," Sam said laughing.

On the other side of the fields were pastures and special pens for cows, sheep, and pigs. All in all, their guide informed them, there were about twenty-five people living and working in Landyland, both men and women, most of them Native Americans. The teepees near the top of the hill were where they lived.

"They don't want to sleep in no fucking houses. They live this way, just like they did a hundred fifty years ago."

When they got back to their room, Laura seemed very impressed with everything they'd seen. "I want to stay here forever," she told him. He smiled. It was crazy, but what he needed at that moment, given the aura of the place, seemed to belong to the realm of science fiction. He was looking for a phone outlet to plug the laptop into. He couldn't find one. He went downstairs and, not finding anyone, went out the front door. He almost collided with a man who was leading a gorgeous light-gray horse by the reins.

"Would you know where Sam might be?" he asked.

"He's gone up," the man said.

"Up where?"

"Into the forest."

"Is there a phone somewhere around here?"

The man smiled ironically. "There are no such things here. The only phone line is in Ron's house."

He took a short walk around the farm before returning to their room. Laura was sleeping, curled up in a fetal position, nude. He laid down next to her and looked at her for a long time. He studied her narrow waist, her shapely legs, her breasts as they rested on the sheets. He noticed her fingernails. They were long, unpainted, some cracked. He wrapped his legs around hers and whispered a Greek phrase in her ear. Laura stretched in her sleep with a contented purr. Outside he could hear the irrigation system's sprinklers, watering the soil.

Without warning and for no obvious reason the images returned.

He did not want to remember. He wanted to forget. But the terrible mechanism through which memories come to life when the surface is scratched cannot be easily defeated. The brain is an infallible psychic computer. It stores an almost perfect archive of life's experiences. The passage of time turns all of us into exiles from our own past. Returning to it can last a lifetime.

Trying to pull itself free from the disturbing invasion of the past, his mind began to wander along strange paths. *What would happen,* he thought, *if I could erase my memory completely? If I were transported to a place of isolation—such as this farm, let's say—where the past wouldn't exist? How would it be if the entire universe were to crystallize into a single moment and humans to be stuck in the present, in a continuously shifting instant? But how?—since we are nothing more than a collage of successive emotions, replacing one-another in a never-ending flow, with a speed that makes it impossible for us to comprehend them. If memory didn't exist, how would it be possible for anyone to maintain some continuity, without roots, without old images? How would a life disconnected from the past be? Certainly horrible.*

He found some consolation in the thought that, if something like this were to happen, the horror of it wouldn't affect him. Because, in that case, he wouldn't even be able to remember the meaning of the word.

He dreamt that he was sitting alone in a room. Seemingly out of nowhere, a man holding a tape-recorder appeared. "I came to help you deal with it," the man said and pressed "play." His mother's voice poured out of the machine, singing an old Manos Hadjidakis song: "Paper Moon." When the song was finished, the man rewound the tape and played it again. This happened again, and again, until he woke up with the melody still in his ears. He got up and went to the bathroom. He looked at himself in the mirror. *A coward, a real coward, is he who is afraid of his memories*, he thought. He went back to bed and fell asleep again—a deep sleep this time, with no dreams.

Ron Landy

THE SUN HAD ALMOST SET WHEN they were woken up by a knock on the door. It was Sam, who told them that Landy was expecting them in twenty minutes at his house for dinner. They dressed quickly and followed him outside.

The weather had deteriorated somewhat. The wind had picked up and the flags by the gate were flapping wildly, distorting the features of the depicted figures. A flock of birds flew high overhead, in a perfect "V" formation.

"Wild Canadian geese," Sam told them. "They're migrating south from fucking Toronto," he added, and started singing with a totally off-key voice:

> *The hunter shot at the flock of geese*
> *As they flew low over the reeds*
> *Two were hit and with fluttering wings*
> *They fell into the shore's dry weeds…*

"My own lyrics," he said. "I've given them to him to set to music." They walked in the direction of the large building, which, in the soft light of the sunset, looked as if it had been pulled straight out of some Victorian painting. On the way, they passed two small Native American children who were playing with a wooden wheel. The youngest turned to Laura and pointed her out to the other child. She nodded a silent greeting to them and smiled. He, on the other hand, had had a strange nervousness setting upon him for a while now and was lost in his own thoughts.

Sam knocked at the heavy wooden door. A tall black woman opened it. She looked around forty, with a full, sensuous body, and quick movements, and had incredibly striking gray eyes. Her hair was pulled back into a braid, and she was wearing a flowing one-piece dress that displayed her curves to full advantage. She was wearing a heavy red bone bracelet on her wrist and a necklace of rough semi-precious stones around her neck.

"Howdy there," the black woman said with a ringing voice. "I'm Carolyn. You must be Laura and you…"

"Marcelo," he replied and extended his hand to her.

"Very happy to meet you. Come on in. Ron is waiting for you upstairs, in the dining room."

The formal living room was full of furniture. Big, small, everywhere, like in a show room. On the walls were hanging dozens of musical instruments: guitars—both electric and acoustic—banjos, harmonicas, even an accordion. *Like trophies*, he thought. In a corner there was an arrangement of photographs of Landy at concerts and various other events. In one, Landy was with Neil Young, in another with Jerry Garcia, and in a third with Jerry Rubin. He knew about the concert with Neil Young. It had been filmed as a documentary by a well-known movie director. He'd seen the documentary during his first trip abroad. Eighteen years old, in London, after he'd crossed half of Europe on his Interail pass.

They climbed the staircase, arriving at a large hallway. Carolyn pulled a sliding door open, and they entered the dining room. In the center, lit by an antique chandelier, was a large oak table. Near the window on the right was a shiny black grand piano, while on the other side, above a stone fireplace, hung two crossed rifles. A green velvet armchair was positioned facing the hearth. The wall behind the table was dominated by a large Chagall painting in which an angel, a couple holding hands, and a cow were flying gracefully over the central square of a town, where a touring burlesque troupe was giving a performance. He instantly thought that if Landy were to have an affinity with any great painter, it would most likely be with Chagall. His greatest songs seemed to have been written from the point of view of someone—whether an angel or a tramp—flying high over the world, and providing a commentary on the magic tricks each of us has to perform in order to survive in a social system in which the only thing one can do is laugh at one's misfortunes.

Suddenly, out of the armchair, the back of which they had been looking at all this time, rose a lean man, about sixty years old, who had until then remained totally hidden from them. His face was full of wrinkles, his skin toughened by the sun, his nose narrow and hooked. He was wearing tight-fitting black pants, a wide white shirt, and a black vest with silver buttons. His wavy graying brown hair was pulled back with a red bandana, beneath which it fell freely to his shoulders. Next to him a cigarette was slowly consuming itself in a turtle-shaped ashtray. *He's gotten old*, he thought, feeling his pulse beating all the way to his fingertips. A transformation that had to have been caused by something even more merciless than time.

Landy came towards them with quick movements. He was relatively short, but despite the marks of time on his face—time, the tamer of everything—his body appeared to be in exceptionally good shape. He wore rings on almost every one of his fingers, just as in the concerts he had seen on television, when the camera had zoomed in to Landy's hand as he was playing his guitar. His eyes were perhaps the most impressive feature of the man. Intense, penetrating, with the pupils moving incredibly quickly up and down, and from side to side, taking in everything around him.

"Hi, I'm Ron," he said with a low, rough voice.

"I'm happy to meet you, Mr. Landy. It's such an honor, sir, to..."

"Come on, get off this formal stuff. I don't want anyone here to call me 'Sir' and 'Mr.' Let's sit down at the table," he said, and, shifting to fast motion again, led the way to the center of the room.

Dinner, which Carolyn served with grace, consisted almost entirely of the farm's produce: vegetables, beans, fruit, "Landymark" wine. Only the whole grain pasta was imported—from Florence—Ron informed them. When she was done serving, Carolyn joined them—Landy's current lover he thought, judging from the way she looked at him. However, on the wall across from the window there hung another painting, a portrait of a dark-haired woman. A refined face with large, violet, almond-shaped eyes, pale complexion, and a look of sweet innocence. He recognized her from the—very few, it's true—photographs of her that had appeared in the press. It was Landy's first wife, Maude Miller. His eyes must have lingered on the portrait for a while because he suddenly became aware of Landy looking at him. A silent exchange seemed to pass between them.

During dinner, Landy talked almost exclusively with Laura. Not being the focus of attention suited him just fine. For one thing, it gave him the opportunity to study closely this extraordinary man, whose social interactions seemed to have some contradictory element, proving Laura's earlier comment to be on the mark. On the one hand, Landy seemed prone to long silences that created a certain awkwardness around the table, while on the other, he could latch onto a word or phrase and use it as a point of departure for a long monologue, which he'd deliver with drawn out, emphatic words, skipping vowels when they, apparently, were not absolutely necessary. Something about him made one think of an old feline who, after having spent most of his life on the savannah, had now settled down with people. The quick but noble movements, the languor of his speech, his eyes: the instincts of a tiger but also the affection of a house cat. A unique feline, an endangered species.

It was strange, but Ron Landy seemed to be fundamentally shy. Especially strange for a man who'd performed in stadiums full of fifty- or sixty-thousand fans, who had been on the cover of *Time* magazine, and whose posters had decorated—thirty or more years ago, of course—countless teenager rooms. The same man now discussing wine-pressing and horse breeding! The same man who, referring to the self-sufficiency of the farm, at some point said:

"Here we enjoy the product of our own work."

He took the opportunity to comment in response, "Emerson, who I noticed is one of the guardians of the gate, used to say: 'The reward for something well-done is having done it.'"

Landy gave him a sideways glance. They were already well into the third bottle. "Emerson was the type who survived strictly on wine. He could not stomach the food on the plates," he said, lighting a cigarette.

"America was founded on great minds like his but now…"

"Oh, don't start now," Landy interrupted. "I don't like discussing politics any more. That country has ceased to exist. It's slipped through our fingers."

"But what can we do to…" Laura started saying, but Landy interrupted again.

"Nothing at this point. Oswald robbed us of our last chance."

"It's true that you can fool some people all the time. It's also true that you can fool all the people some of the time…" Carolyn began.

"…but you can't fool all of the people all of the time. Abraham Lincoln. Great president, but pretty bad lawyer," said Landy.

"But, you used to speak to your audiences about…" he tried to interject.

Landy jumped.

"Me? Speak to audiences? I only spoke to myself. Audiences took my songs and did whatever they wanted with them. What matters is breaking your own path, with your own footprints. Now, I'm sure you'll ask me why I stopped even making the effort to walk.

About five or six years ago, when I didn't live here yet, the media were camped outside my house, asking me that same question."

"Why aren't you writing music any more?" he said in response.

"Yes, and why have I become a recluse? I never would answer them of course. There was no reason to. Music used to be an art form. Now it's a permanent background of noise, present everywhere. Like the human voice, which used to be the most noble of sounds. Now it is just another noise. Speech, music, everything is a manufactured backdrop. After a while, I figured out that I was just adding to the noise, and then I became disgusted with myself. 'The king of the ballad,' 'the king of blues,' 'the king of rock'... They didn't even know which label to fix on me. However, all kings are, in the end, boring little people. I started to figure this out when I began having kids. Every child is a total stranger. And a stranger can teach you a heck of a lot of things. It was like a bomb went off in my head—it sure woke me up. And maybe I've finally found my way." Fixing his eyes on him, he asked: "So, Marcelo, do you have kids?"

He wasn't taken by surprise.

"Yes," he said. "One. He lives with his mom. I don't get to see him enough."

Laura looked at him intensely, while Carolyn refilled the glasses all around. It was a topic that they'd hardly touched on since they'd met.

"That's too bad. Two of mine live here. The third, as in your case, lives with my ex."

"Do you get to see him often?" Laura asked.

Landy took a long swig.

"No," he answered.

Afterwards, the conversation turned to literature. He talked about Hemingway, Dos Pasos, Bellow. Carolyn, who appeared to be very widely read, commented on these writers, while Landy just listened, occasionally nodding. Laura was looking at him with wonder, obviously impressed by the fact that a guy working for an information technology company should be so knowledgeable about American literature.

"Since I was a child, I wanted to be Huck Finn," Ron finally said. "To be free. To travel the country without having to be accountable to anyone. But when it comes to books, the one that has always affected me the most contains the reflections of an ancient Greek philosopher, Zeno. Do you know of him?"

He smiled. "I've heard of him," he said.

"He's extraordinary. He proposed some incredible ideas about motion. At one point he theorizes that motion is not really possible because every moving object must reach the half-way point before reaching the end of its trajectory... The point is illustrated with the story of Achilles and the turtle: in a pursuit, the faster runner can never, logically, pass the slower runner, because the pursuer must always reach the point that the other runner has already passed—which implies that if the slower runner begins with a lead, he will always maintain a lead. What do you think Marcelo? Good point?"

"So, whoever is after us can never actually catch us..."

"Never. Take Laura here. She's always had some real ghosts coming after her. If she could realize that they can never catch her, she could be a happier person."

"They are not after me—they inhabit me," Laura whispered.

"Is something after you, Marcelo?" Landy asked, not having heard her interjection.

"We all have something that's after us," he answered.

"Zeno, my friend. But listen to this now. I've come up with a hole in his theory. There is one scenario in which someone who's after let's say, you, even if we accept Zeno's logic, can reach you no matter what. Can you think..."

He thought about it for a while, but nothing came to him.

"If you die, my friend, your pursuer will catch up with you."

The conversation went on in a very pleasant atmosphere. Carolyn brought another couple of bottles of wine, while the host chain-smoked through the evening. Looking closely at him, he observed the double golden nicotine stains on his index and ring fingers, and their contrast with the gray age stains that had started to colonize Landy's hands. When they had finished with the dessert, Laura told him:

"Why don't you go stand next to Ron and I'll take a picture of you with my cell phone."

Their host instantly objected.

"That is the devil's invention. Anyway, it won't work here."

His right eye had begun to tear up.

"Do you have a problem with technology?" he asked Landy.

"Not when it amplifies my guitar. But all this junk—cell phones, i-pods, chat rooms—it doesn't bring people closer; it isolates them. Even the noise of the day isn't what it used to be any more," he said, elongating the vowel in "day." "Now, you see everywhere people staring at their digital organizers, walking around with those bluetooth earpieces, mumbling constantly, seemingly to themselves, like mental patients on the loose. Entertainment has become an obsession. You think you've personalized everything, you've got your personal photo-lab on your little computer screen, your personal bank in a little plastic card, your personal music in a little box, your whole world in the palm of your hand, but you have no clue that all of this has been predetermined by others, and they've got you in their grip. I too have a music box, but it's very different—come see," Landy said and walked to the other end of the room.

There, on a chest of drawers, was a carved black box. *Like Marcelo's*, he thought. And indeed, the dimensions were about the same. But Landy's box had no combination locks or number puzzles. It opened easily at the press of a button, and from inside it a small porcelain doll with jointed limbs sprang up. It portrayed an elderly black man, sitting on an old chair, holding a guitar. He had white hair and was wearing dark glasses.

"This is Blind Willy McTell. Listen!"

Landy pressed another button, and the doll started rotating

around its axis, moving its head rhythmically and plucking the guitar with its right hand. Music had started coming out of the box, along with a deep voice that was singing:

Tombstones is my pillow, cold grounds is my bed
Tombstones is my pillow, cold grounds is my bed
The blue skies is my blanket, and the moonlight is my spread

Early one morning, death walked into my room
Early one morning, death walked into my room
Oh well it took my dear mother, early one morning soon

She left me moanin' and cryin', moanin' like a turtledove
She left me moanin' and cryin', moanin' like a turtledove
Death walked in and got my dear mother,
  and the only friend I loved

Mmmm..... eehh....
Cryin' Lord have mercy, and she was the only friend I loved

Ever since my mother died and left me all alone
Ever since my mother died and left me all alone
All my friends have forsake me,
  people I haven't even got no home

Mmmm... Feel like moanin' and cryin'
Mmmm... Feel like moanin' and cryin'
Death walked in a got my mother,
  and that was the only dear friend of mine.

When the song was over, the doll lowered its head in a salute.
"Willy was blind. He read and wrote music in Braille." He took another swig and returned to the table. "Alone in his darkness. He became a preacher in his old age." Then, as if this musical interlude

had never happened, he returned to the earlier conversation topic. "Does anyone remember that song: "The Future's so Bright, I Gotta Wear Shades?" I always found it very ironic—it reminded me of something that happened early in my career, when a reporter asked me to bite on the temple of my glasses for a picture. If you change the words of the song a bit, you'll figure it out: 'The future is so dark, you'll need to be blind to see it.' That's Willy McTell. He could truly see." Landy stopped for a moment to take another swig of his wine, and then went on: "These days they overwhelm you with choices. They give you a false sense of free choice, in the most devious ways. For example, you walk into a large department store and you get a call on your cell phone with a message saying: 'Dear Laura, some months ago you bought such and such microwave oven. Would you be interested in this set of microwave-safe china, or, perhaps that set of especially for the microwave baking dishes?' We are fooling ourselves with the statement that we are our choices; we are *their* choices. 'Dear Laura, do this, buy that…' And all the Lauras of the world—I'm sorry my dear, I'm just using you as an example—all the Marcelos of the world, obey. Every child is a prospective consumer. He or she comes into this world ready to inhabit this lie, this hoax. Uneducated for a lifetime, despite having read some books, seen all the movies, and listened to all the great music in mp3. It used to be that the enemy, no matter how terrible—whether it was Hitler, or Stalin, or Nixon—was visible, we knew him, he had a name. So we could react, whether in a bad way or in a good way. Now it looks like there's no enemy, because the enemy has turned into thin air, has become digitized, is broadcast, and so now is everywhere, in every molecule of our atmosphere."

"I wouldn't say that," he commented. "The enemy is still visible today. The problem is that he is so enticing that you just can't resist him."

Everyone around the table fell silent. Landy looked up at the ceiling, as if he was trying to remember something, and then said:

"Let me tell you a story. A while back I had come to know a real estate developer who was known to have leftist leanings. I was still married then. We were on a family vacation somewhere out West, and he had offered to fly us back on his private jet. With us was also a well-known art dealer. At one point during the flight, the developer, looking out of the plane window, pointed to the ground, turned to the art dealer and said, 'Charles, you may collect landscape paintings of the American West, but I am collecting the American West itself. All of that land down there belongs to me.'"

"Everyone laughed, except for me. The next day, the same guy was giving a television interview in which he spoke against Reagan's policies... That's the way it is. In the old days, they kept us shackled with chains around our legs. Now the chains are around our brains."

"But this can't go on forever. At some point things will change. People will act to change things," Laura said.

"'I don't do formulas for little pubs of the future.' Isn't that what the Jew used to say?" Landy responded.

He knew that the remark was referring to Karl Marx. He wasn't surprised by the almost racist use of the word "Jew." Having read fairly widely about Landy's life, he knew that from an early age, the famous musician had rejected his Jewish identity. The name he'd been born with was Ronel Ramstein.

Their host put out his cigarette and continued talking: "During the French Revolution, the British dock workers refused to load the warships that were being sent forth to attack the revolutionaries. There you have a grassroots act of resistance, carried out by ill-organized simple workers. How many people today would refuse to perform some very simple tasks: use a cell phone, give out personal information on-line, have their iris scanned... Who would even stand to wait to hear a song for the first time at a live concert, feel the singer's breath, enter the magic of the moment? There is no melody in the world any more, only sounds broken down into bytes. In this whole place there's only one phone line—the one in this house. It's to be used only to do the work of the farm. And as

I've already told you, cell phones don't work here. So, my dear Laura, you wouldn't have been able to take the picture you wanted in any case. There's a security bubble that covers the entire farm."

"I don't like discussing politics any more," Landy had said earlier, he thought.

And Landy, as if he'd read his thoughts, answered, "It seems strange, doesn't it? I don't like discussing politics but my conversation always ends up on that topic. It's the inherent contradiction of this country. The leader of the free world..." he said ironically.

"At the same time the most apolitical country in the world," Carolyn added.

"Shouldn't be surprising since, ultimately, it's the corporations that govern," he said.

"Of course, it's your employers who govern," Laura interjected.

"The government is the shadow that business throws on the citizens," Landy said. "And as for you, they brainwash you with the idea of harmony in the workplace just so they can keep you from unionizing. 'Unions are anti-American!' They've even invaded the educational system so they can proselytize the generations of prospective workers. Even back when I was in high school, half of the textbooks were 'donated' by corporations. In the name of the free market, freedom and equality. There are no class distinctions in the American system. The word 'class' is a curse-word. We are all equal," he said ironically. "We are all Americans. We all coexist in harmony and freedom, sharing the great American values. Hurray!"

"But there's still some resistance against the government... There are..." he managed to say.

"Resistance against the government?" Laura interrupted him. "But that's exactly what they want. Leave the corporations alone and attack the government. That's America for you."

"America," Landy whispered. "Everything begins with 'A': Alpha, Adam, Abel, America."

Carolyn brought more wine and they all sat around the fireplace. Landy seemed to be in great form. The wine had loosened his tongue, he was unstoppable. He kept on talking about America, first the contemporary nation, but then he went all the way back to Columbus.

"I try to imagine his sailors, when they broke through the horizon of the medieval world. When they sailed out into the endless ocean, I wonder, what did they expect they'd find at the end of their journey? Monsters, mermaids, leviathans, dragons? And what did they find in the end? The poor Indians! The greatest genocide in human history. Our own history begins with a massacre of the innocent: the Pequots, in 1636. Have you heard the joke: Illegal immigration has always been a huge problem for America. Ask any Indian... Even so, in the end we didn't even have the courage to have children with their women... At least then we'd have been a wonderful mixed-race people..." he said and drank some more wine. "But I was talking about Columbus' sailors... Will any human being ever have that same feeling? Of leaving the known world behind? Perhaps when we escape the solar system. But then, wherever we end up, we ourselves will be the Indians... The Indians are the best people. We live here together so beautifully," he went on talking about the tall man they'd met earlier, Devdan. "He is the wisest human being I've ever known. His mind is crystal-clear. He's told me so much about their history, their stories. Oh, the 'Spider Woman' story... You'll have to ask him to tell you. He lives up on the hill. His teepee is the one on the right. He is a Navaho. We took everything from them, too. We even used their language in the Second World War, during some of the worst battles in the Pacific."

"How?" Laura asked.

"In wireless messages encoded in their language, which is not written. Fighter planes were 'Colibris,' depth charges were 'hawks,' submarines 'iron fish.' The Japanese had been able to break almost every code the American forces used, except the one based on the Navaho language. Haven't you ever heard of the 'Code Talkers'?"

"Are all the Indians here Navaho?" he asked.

"Most of them."

"Are they working for you?"

The alcohol had made him brash. "For me!" Landy said almost with disdain. "We don't have this kind of arrangement here. We live together on whatever the farm produces. We are a small commune. I don't manage the finances. We have a committee that does that."

"But you are the boss, right?"

"Next you'll call me an exploiting capitalist! You wanna join them and lead the uprising? Oh, you *have* to get to know Devdan… Look, everyone who's here is here for a reason. They've run away from somewhere, if you catch my drift."

"Like us," Laura said.

"Like me, too," Landy said. "OK. Enough with this. Let's have some fun."

Landy was over-exuberant. He was so drunk that, at one point, he grabbed Laura and started dancing to the tune of some imaginary tango music.

"I want to talk to you," he heard her say to him.

"Tomorrow. Now we're having fun," he said, and after a few more twirls he let her go and asked Carolyn to get his guitar from the other room. It seemed it was his favorite because he caressed its curves as if it were a rare breed of horse, and then he started singing some classic American blues. Carolyn backed him up. She had a divine voice. He could not believe he was getting a private concert from Ron Landy. He too was a bit drunk, and the loss of inhibition enabled him to ask Ron to play one of his own songs. At first Landy gave him an angry look, but then he obliged. Partially. He only sang the refrain from one of his least known songs.

"Have you written any new ones?" he asked when it was over.

The question was almost rude, but Landy answered it: "I've got material for twenty new albums. I'll never release them. In my will, I've given instructions that everything should be destroyed after I die. On the day of my funeral, Carolyn will set the recordings up to play all day long, and when the funeral is done—that is when the cremation is finished—she'll hit the ERASE button."

At that moment, they heard music from the piano. Laura had sat down and was playing a Polonaise by Chopin. He recalled the day they'd first met in Hannibal and, when she was done, asked her to play a fugue.

This time she played one by Brahms. Her face had lit up. Her thoughts seemed to be somewhere far away when she was at the keyboard. He looked at her hands. They were caressing the ivory keys passionately, in the same way they caressed his back, his thighs, his face. When she finished, Landy went to her and kissed her hand.

"I have to reply to this," he said and started playing a fugue on his guitar—one by Bach. "I picked it up from a Segovia recording," he said in the end. "What a piece, what a pursuit, merciless!"

The night went on with even more alcohol. Landy took up classic ballads. Playing "Mr. Bojangles," he was slurring the words so much, it was impossible to understand the lyrics. After a while he got tired. The last chord of "The House of the Rising Sun" sounded like a falling curtain.

"Curtain," Landy said, drinking the last sip of wine remaining in his glass. "Tomorrow will be another day," he continued, putting out his cigarette.

Carolyn was the first to say goodnight and she disappeared through one of the doors to the living room.

Landy escorted them to the front door. The three of them were not too steady on their feet. At the door, he hugged Laura and said to her, "Come over in the morning and we'll talk." And to him: "I'll let Devdan know that you'll go see him tomorrow. Walk up to the teepees. His is the one on the right. You're a good guy, Marcelo. You got depth. You sure don't seem like a West Coast computer geek. To me you seem much more the Chicano intellectual type…" He laughed but immediately turned serious: "Take care of this girl. There are no more like her out there."

As they walked out to the porch, and while Laura had walked a few steps ahead, Landy held him lightly by the arm.

"There's something about you…" His right eye was a bit bloodshot. "There's something…"

They made quick love; he was too drunk for anything more. Just before they turned off the light, Laura asked him how he knew so much about literature.

"It has always been my secret passion. I wanted to tell you about it face-to-face," he replied.

A few minutes later, Laura was asleep and he was looking through the open window at the almost full moon bathing in its light the three teepees at the top of the hill. The scene was immersed in a deathly silence. A fly was walking up the opposite wall. He got up and rested his elbows on the windowsill, enjoying the view. Suddenly, from somewhere far away a sound rose up. It didn't sound human. Whoever or whatever it was, however, must have been music-loving because, slowly, progressively, a melody emerged, which he recognized—how strange!—as an echo of the one his mother had been singing in his dream that afternoon.

He closed the shutters and went back to bed. He leaned over her. She had pulled off the sheet in her sleep. He could see one of her breasts, a thigh, and the delicate curve of her back. A nudity that was natural, innocent, shining like an emerald in the diffuse moonlight. In the remnants of the alcoholic haze still clouding his brain, he thought of everything this body had gone through in the past twenty years and he shuddered. He felt devotion, affection towards the sleeping woman. Love. And immediately guilt. Because now, the way things had turned out, first thing tomorrow he needed to tell her the truth. Not only that he wasn't Marcelo, but everything. The whole truth. For the first time in his life, he felt the need to confess all those things he'd never told another human being. He leaned over her further. Their faces were almost touching now. He focused on her lips. They had a sensuous expression, which nevertheless contained something painful within it. Suddenly, a small twitch in her sleep. He knew that twitch, second nature to him. And he thought right away that no, she was too much like him for him to reveal everything to her now. Now they had to survive. Afterward. He crawled inside the covers and took her in his arms.

Somewhere inside himself he could hear Marcelo's lament. And it is hubris to be able to hear the lament of a dead man.

Spider Woman

WHEN HE WOKE UP LAURA WAS ALREADY GONE. His head was still buzzing from the previous night's indulgences. There was a note next to him:

I've gone to Ron's house. Good morning, mystery man.

He took a quick shower and went outside. It was a sunny day, but cool. The fresh air felt invigorating as he breathed it in deeply. He looked towards the barns and fields. A great number of people were working there. Most were Native American, but he could also make out some middle-aged white women and several young men with long hair and tattoos glistening in the sun. Everyone seemed happy, apparently enjoying thoroughly whatever they were doing.

He started walking up toward the teepees. The treetops created a green wave in the horizon. A world full of color, peaceful, pure. The heads of wildflowers, poking out of the dense vegetation, seemed to be swimming in the light breeze, which joined its melody to the sounds of insects. A blue-and-yellow butterfly followed him for a brief moment and then settled on a large flower, ready to collect its nectar.

When he reached the top of the hill, he walked to the teepee to the right. The sides of the tent were painted with various symbols. Outside it there was a flagpole with a flag flapping in the breeze. In the center of the flag, there was a copper-colored shape that looked like a map of one of the states. Inside it, there was a similar shape, dark brown. In the four corners there were four mountains, while a semi-circular rainbow arched over the field.

He heard a rustling sound behind him. He turned; it was Devdan. He was taken aback. How was it that he hadn't seen him as he approached the teepee? Before he could say anything, Devdan spoke. His voice was rough and his English did not betray any accent.

"Do you know what you're looking at?"

"No."

"These are the four Sacred Mountains. The outer map shows the present boundary of the Navaho nation, which covers parts of Arizona, New Mexico, and Utah."

"And the inner map, the brown one?"

"The area that was given to us in the treaty of 1868. The rainbow symbolizes our sovereignty."

"What does that mean?" he asked, pointing at a circular symbol on the teepee, flagged by two corn stalks.

"The sun. And these," Devdan said, touching with his fingers three animals in the center of the circle, "our economy."

Next to these, there were also drawings of an octagonal building, a modern-looking house, and an oil drilling-rig tower.

"And these are the future?" he commented.

"They represent the wealth of our lands. That is where our various settlements are."

"How is it that you don't live there?"

"That's the reason," Devdan replied, pointing at the drilling-rig tower.

"I understand…" he said.

He looked at Devdan closely. His eyes were deep-set. Dark. Jet-black, like his hair. Their expression seemed to proceed from a great depth, from the hidden recesses of his body—as if it had emerged from the smallest possible particle of matter, passing through the quark, the proton, the nucleus, the atom, the electron, the DNA molecule, the lymph cell, the blood vessel, the vitreous humor, the lens, the iris, and, finally, the cornea, reflecting its entire voyage. Devdan gazed, with the full meaning of the word.

"Come, let's go for a walk. Ron told me about you in the morning," the Indian said.

They walked downhill for a short distance and entered the forest. Devdan walked as if he was dancing on the grass, like a god of the forest. He was asking him various questions. The Indian would answer him laconically. When he finally stopped asking questions, he understood why. Devdan had something specific he wanted to talk to him about—he had an agenda. Perhaps Landy had asked him to give him an overview of Navaho tradition. In the beginning, Devdan described to him the Navaho story of creation—the four worlds. The First, the Black World, was occupied by spirit beings, and that was where the First Man and First Woman were created. They escaped, through a small hole into the Second, the Blue World.

"In the Blue World," he said, "there lived beings that were in eternal conflict, so they decided to leave that world as well. First Man made a wand that transported them to the Third, the Yellow World. This world was traversed by many wide rivers. One day, Coyote..."

"Coyote?"

"Yes, it's a sacred animal. Coyote stole First Baby from the riverbank and caused a great flood. First Man ordered everyone to climb up the reeds in order to save themselves. The reeds led them to the Fourth World, the White one. There, First Man and First Woman built the four Sacred Mountains with sacred earth they had carried from the First World."

All of this reminded him of Dante. He tried to talk to Devdan about the *Divine Comedy*, but Devdan gave it a different interpretation.

"The gods are not a comedy," Devdan said. "These stories explain what happens inside ourselves. When I recall that I am a continuation of this story, I feel liberated, as if I've been baptized in an irresistible force."

They were now a good distance from the farm and were walking on a narrow trail that ran through a grove of silver birch trees. The setting was magnificent, so alive it seemed to possess a soul. The clarity of its sounds was its language, the multitude of color of its flora its harmony, the movement of its leaves its melody. After a while they entered a clearing where a small waterfall emptied into a small pond that was surrounded by rocks.

Devdan stopped in front of the falling water, and without uttering a word, he started to take off his clothes, one by one. He had a perfectly chiseled body. When he was totally naked, he turned and looked at him. He was certain the water would be freezing cold, but the Indian's look was one that could not be denied. Devdan entered the water with slow, ritualistic movements, showing no signs of discomfort. When he followed, he could not suppress a cry as the cold water gripped his body. However, when he got over the initial shivering, he felt a smooth, silk feeling enveloping him. Peace.

"It's healing mineral water," Devdan said, just before dipping his head under. "Thousands of hearts have taken flight in these depths."

At first, this sounded to him like a beautiful, poetic expression. But in the relaxing embrace of the water, he began to think again like a writer. This phrase that Devdan had just uttered was terrific. Hearts were a synecdoche for people—using a part to refer to the whole—the verb "taken flight" was a metaphor for "swum"—replacing one word with a different but similar one—and the noun "depths" was a metonymy for the pond—referring to something by using a characteristic of it. A whole model of the language in a six-word sentence. Thousands of people have swum in this pond.

Thousands of hearts have taken flight in these depths.

When they got out, they got dressed and sat in the shade of a tree. He felt reborn, as if he'd been immersed in the fountain of youth. Devdan pulled out a small flat bottle from his pocket and passed it to him. It looked like whiskey.

"Fire water," he joked.

Devdan laughed. "It's not whiskey, it's a special drink we make with herbs. Take it easy…"

He tasted it. It was sweet, with a complex, fruity flavor, like a port or a sherry. They sat in silence for a while, drinking.

"Do you know what it is you're wearing around your neck?" Devdan suddenly asked.

"It's a Native American fetish, symbolizing harmony," he said.

"It's a spirit that talks to humans, giving them advice on how to live in peace, how to follow some simple rules. Where did you get it?"

"A friend gave it to me," he answered.

They drank another two or three rounds from the bottle, and then Devdan pulled himself up and sat cross-legged. He followed suit.

"Listen, now. I'll tell you the story of Spider Woman," Devdan began.

"I want you to tell me the story of those Code Talkers, during the Second World War," he said, as the relaxed feeling from the dip in the pond started melding with a strange dizziness brought on by the drink.

Devdan gave him a stern warning look and went on with the story, ignoring his request. He spoke about the twin gods of the Navaho, who were looking for the way to the home of their father, the Sun, when at a turn of the road they saw smoke coming out of the ground. They approached it and saw it was coming out of a hole that was the smokestack of an underground chamber, dug into the ground in the middle of nowhere. Looking down they saw an old woman, Spider Woman. When they climbed down, the woman asked them: "Where are you going?" They did not answer.

As he listened to the story, his mind started wandering. He was now feeling, ever more clearly, that he was getting to know himself—not his real self, the one who had come to America; not his assumed one either, the one who had exchanged a Ford for a Mustang; but the self who was beyond names, beyond identities, the self who was light, wind, earth, and water. As Devdan continued telling his story, he saw this self against the light, as if the sun was his cape.

"…Then, Spider Woman said, 'Maybe you're looking for your father, the Sun?'

'Yes,' answered the Twins together, with one voice. 'If only we could find the way to his house…'

'Aah!' said the woman. 'The way to your father's house is long and treacherous. You'll have to go through four dangerous places: the rocks that fall upon and crush travelers, the reeds that cut travelers to pieces, the cacti that tear into them, and the burning hot sand that…'"

Devdan's voice was enchanting. It transported him to strange, yet familiar visions. A different reality, one to which we all belong, in which all of us are the Twins, all are Coyote, all are Spider. He felt a cooling sensation—the cool feeling of leaves, of words, an eternal cool feeling.

"'…but I,' said Spider Woman, 'will give you something that will tame your enemies and save your lives.'"

"She gave them a good-luck charm which was called 'Other Gods' Feather.' It was a ring with three feathers taken from a live eagle. These would protect them…"

He imagined a vase with three flowers, only the buds were human heads: those of Laura, his mother, and his wife. He leaned over each one and inhaled its fragrance. As he smelled each, it would tilt and droop. In the meantime, Devdan was continuing telling the story, until he finished:

"...and the Twins, after overcoming all the obstacles, finally reached their destination and met their father."

He took in Devdan's words and could see the Twins in front of him, as if he was in the story with them. For a moment he felt the urge to get up and start running through the forest, splash in the streams, sing to the sun; but the words flowing out of Devdan's mouth were so powerful that they seemed absolutely true and alive in the telling of the story. And this reality, this eternal truth that exists in storytelling, in the telling of any story, was his only wealth. The only thing that was left in his life. It was "like" happiness—something that was neither absolutely beautiful, nor absolutely ugly, but absolutely true. It was a strong existential vortex, a feeling that everything is everywhere, everything is possible, everything is in the present.

Devdan went on talking about how, for the Navaho, "good" and "bad" are relative values, and how something that might appear to be aggressive (and, therefore, bad) may be transformed into something good if it is brought under control; how the most important value for his people is empathy; and how true empathy is sensitivity towards the world—not only for human beings, but also for the thunder and the lightning, spiders, coyotes...

"All these are people, only they are wearing clothing made from a different fabric..." he said.

Devdan talked for quite a while. When the story was finished, he thanked him. He was now somewhat calmer. The giddy feeling he'd had before had now transformed into a calm awareness. He was still traveling through his consciousness, but not on a wild horse. He was walking. Rational thoughts had begun to weave together, threads to sew together the torn-up images. The logic of the universe was gradually returning. And not only that—he had begun to feel a perfect clarity, as if everything was now comprehensible. If, for a while, he had stood on the edge of the transcendental, he was now landing on the nucleus of reality. A fast replay of the last few days passed in front of his eyes, and in the last frame appeared the questions that had been preoccupying him since the failed meeting in Chicago. He let some time pass and then asked again his question about the Code Talkers.

Devdan answered it this time: "On the one hand, we were a large enough community that could contribute a significant number of soldiers to the U.S., but, on the other, we were too small for our language to have been studied by outsiders, especially German or Japanese anthropologists. Four hundred and twenty of our people were Code Talkers. But it was our language that was considered heroic, not our people. Most of us didn't even have the right to vote… They just created a "Code Talker Day"—the fourteenth of August. And guess who did that—Reagan! The cowboy. Ironic, right?" he said.

"Do you know anything about codes?"

"I know their deepest secrets."

"What?"

"My grandfather was Harry Tsosie. The first code talker to be killed in the war. From friendly fire… He was hit by naval fire, by mistake…"

"I'm sorry."

"Don't be. He's still with us," he said, looking up.

"So what are the deepest secrets of codes?"

"Look for the simplest way."

"If you had a code that was all numerals, what would be the simplest way?"

"We believe in 'nine,' the sacred number."

He took the wallet out of his pocket. The piece of paper with the number Marcelo had written in the day-planner was still there. He passed it to Devdan.

"What do you make of this?" he asked.

"1614180207," the Indian read slowly. "Ten numerals and not one nine… what is its significance for you?"

"It's something which, if I can figure it out, will solve several problems for me."

Devdan looked again at the piece of paper, with intense concentration. He seemed lost in thought, but after a little while, he said, "Go to 'Sky Country.'"

"What do you mean?"

"Let me put it a different way: to the 'World of Numbers.'"

"What's that?"

Devdan looked at him with raised eyebrows. "Is it possible you don't know?" and didn't speak again until they started walking back.

His head was now totally clear. Despite this, inside himself he could feel an echo, an internal song, a fugue, with voices that chased each other, constantly repeating: "I exist, I exist, I exist..." in all of the musical tones. The whole way back it was Devdan's turn to listen to him talk, first about his mother, then about his ex-wife, and finally about his father. He talked leaving out the details, without mentioning countries, places, names, situations, but instead using concepts such as security, rejection, suicide, mourning, then love, surrender, betrayal and, finally, fear, insecurity, panic.

"Aren't there any sounds that make you dizzy, flowers that take your breath away, voices that uplift you, gestures that make you shudder?"

"There used to be," he replied, and went on with his personal, private—if censored—delirium.

When they reached the teepee, before saying goodbye, Devdan looked once more deep into his eyes and told him quietly, "You— are not yourself."

He spent the rest of the day with Laura. After her meeting with Landy, she seemed much calmer. She didn't discuss any details, only: "This man has the ability to enable me to return to what I would like to be."

"And I?" he said, pretending to be hurt. "What do *I* turn you into?"

"You? To return to what I really want to be..." she answered laughing.

That night they had dinner with Carolyn. Landy was busy some-where. Before saying goodnight, the woman gave him a note.

I'll be waiting for you tomorrow morning at eleven,
in corral No. 2. I want to show you a horse.

Their night together was intoxicating. In bed, he saw her eyes shine. He knew that he had finally reached the Fourth World.

The horse

"THE NATURE OF THE HORSE IS SUCH THAT it cannot resist any demand, as long as it can understand it. It has no concept of reality outside its own experience. It cannot assess the forces that are acting around it. It cannot distinguish good from bad. It's in no position to decide easily what it should do and what it shouldn't."

They were leaning on the fence that surrounded the round corral. In the center, a young man was holding the long reins of a palomino and was walking it in a circle. The horse was very young, not quite a yearling yet, Landy had told him. It seemed very nervous, constantly snorting. After several circles, the young man tied the horse on the fence and positioned several objects around the corral: a large piece of wood, a plastic doll, a large stone. He then untied it and resumed walking it around, making sure the objects were right in its path. When the horse's hoof touched the piece of wood, the animal jerked as if struck by lightning. He was startled and took a step back. Landy smiled at him as if he were a frightened little child. This process, with the horse walking in a circle, getting spooked every time it met one of the objects, went on for quite some time. The animal had become agitated, with large drops of sweat running down its sides. At some point, the young man got a bandana and tied it over the horse's eyes. He then walked up to it, bringing the various objects close to its nose one by one, while stroking its neck and whispering calming words in its ears. The animal, at first, was snorting and breathing heavily, but eventually its breathing slowed down and started to become more regular. Afterward, the young man placed the objects again around the corral, untied the bandana from the horse's eyes, and began walking it, again making sure that its path led it over the objects. The horse was now walking calmly, as if on a stroll. When it reached the doll, it bent its head down, sniffed it, gave it a lick, and walked over it.

"In order for the horse to feel safe with strange objects, it must sniff them and touch them. A simple piece of wood in its path may, in its imagination, become a snake, a monster representing great danger, but if you let it touch it, smell it, examine it, that object will never bother it again," Landy said.

That's memory, he thought, *I must feel to remember*.

Half an hour later, they had sat down at a small gazebo and were drinking beer and smoking. It was a beautiful day, with sweet shades of green all around them, under a lustrous sky, the bronze light of the sun fragrant with life. The young man had returned the horse to the stable. They talked a bit longer about animal training until, suddenly, Landy said, "Laura talked to me."

"Yes?"

"About you. She talked to me about you."

"You seem troubled."

"I am."

For a moment he thought that Laura might have told him everything. "She told you something that…"

"She's troubled by many questions about you. From what she's told me, so am I."

"Welcome to the club." Maybe humor would do the trick.

Landy lit another cigarette.

"Laura is very special to me. When I first met her, she was a wild animal, a broken human being, almost destroyed. It took a great struggle and a lot of courage for her to build herself back up to what you see today. I don't want to see her go down again."

"Why are you telling me this?"

Landy turned his eyes from him to the farm and the vista beyond it. He looked like he hadn't gotten much sleep the night before. Without looking at him, he asked him slowly, "What do you want from her?"

"You sound like you're her guardian."

"I may very well be. So?"

What could he answer? Tell the truth? Even if he wanted to, what *was* the truth? What was his truth, with an assumed name in this foreign land? What did he want from Laura? How could he answer this question? As himself, or as Marcelo? What, about himself, was true any more? Maybe one thing only. He was a writer. And in everything he'd written, he had tried to represent not only reality but also the results of his characters' conceptions of reality. He wasn't satisfied with the reproduction of the fragmented face of that which is real, no matter how convincing the representation, but wanted to dig to the deep foundations, the tectonic plates. He wanted to process life with working material that went beyond its subjective façade, not in a simple representational way, but with tools such as fury, pity, empathy, reminiscence. Sometimes he was successful, sometimes not. Mostly not. What he wanted most was the ability to find that sacred, mystical, secret way to retell the world. To channel the clamor of all of those other voices he heard inside his head. Something that Devdan had managed to do in a single morning.

A critic had once told him that one could enjoy a work of art without making reference to any of life's experiences. So, in the end, wasn't what he had done, the new identity he had assumed, his *new self*, by its nature an artistic praxis that excluded all previous experience? Was it not as if one of those voices from inside himself, which whispered its own reality in his head, had come to the surface? And what did that make him? An artist, a creator, or a spectator, a student of his own work?

As an artist, as the director of the adventure he had been living, he could answer Landy's question in concrete ways, in ways that related to the story, the "work in action," in which he was the protagonist. After all, as the subject of his own narrative, he was now evolving in sentences, he was now placing the periods, commas, exclamation and question marks upon himself. However, the work was in progress, so as Marcelo's creator, he could not say anything that would not affect drastically the creation.

On the other hand, as an observer, a spectator of his own "created" self, he was free, free to act as he thought best, to direct the narrative down random, unanticipated paths. Just as the story contains and involves the reader, so the reader, the spectator, creates his own meaning of it, regardless of the intent of the writer-director. So, in the end, he instinctively chose the middle way: prolong the suspense.

"What do I want?" he said. "I don't know. Life has no contracts."

"You can say that again."

"Life has no contr…"

"Do you love her?" Landy interrupted.

"Yes."

"What exactly do you do, Marcelo?"

"What do you mean? What exactly do *you* do?"

"I used to do—now I watch."

"What do you watch?"

"Now only the wall, not the world. I know my wall very intimately now. Every square inch of it," Landy said.

He looked into Landy's eyes, eyes that hadn't seen but seemed to know. He answered, "It's something like that that I'm trying to do too."

"Nah, you're like a colt. You have no idea what's what."

"Well, at least I know about logs and sticks and I'm not spooked when I step on one."

He had figured him out all right. He artfully kept hitting the ball back in the other man's court. He had his reasons.

Landy smiled. "You must have had a good instructor…"

"No, I was myself both the horse and the reins. You, however, were your own instructor."

The objective was met. Transfer. Instead of having a conversation about himself, they would now be talking about Landy.

"Listen, Marcelo. I was born in a small town in Minnesota, the kind of town in which the church is the center of the universe." Landy had no idea that he had almost memorized his biography published ten years before, and which Landy had ultimately renounced, and knew almost every last detail about the musician growing up in Deer River: about his timid father and his overbearing mother; his mentally retarded brother; about Ruth, his first girlfriend and her suicide attempt; even the name of the band in which Landy was lead singer during high school.

"From the time I arrived in Boston after leaving my small town, until I met my wife, the mother of my children, I lived for one thing only: music. Music opened the world up to me. Of course, one can't be both wise and in love… Anyway, before that I was only half a human being, an egotistical little shit."

"Who wrote 'Morning Wind,' and 'Death of Dick Haven?'"

"Don't get confused about things, Marcelo. Talent is one thing and decency another."

"But the lyrics? They have to come from such a deep understanding of the world…"

"I read a lot. Many and varied things. I absorbed everything like a sponge. And there were the 'glorious' moments. Those are moments, however, that you recall without knowing their names— as feelings, not as dates. When you immerse yourself in something you lose perspective on it. You need to let it go so it can come to you. It's what I mean when I say you need to 'take it to bed with you at night.' And in the morning, over coffee, it might re-emerge because it's done its 'work' during the night. So I knew how to recognize those mornings. And that's how those lyrics came to be."

I'm playing him perfectly, he thought.

But Landy was not quite so easy to read. "Anyway, what I was trying to say to you is something else: a woman changes everything," he said, putting out his cigarette. "So, Marcelo, don't think for a moment that I don't know what you're trying to do."

"What am I trying to do?" he answered, his mind back to a time in which he too, in his own way, lived and breathed for those mornings that Landy had been talking about.

"You're trying to get me off track. I am not the subject of this conversation, my friend. You are. You seem like a very confused person; we're talking, and you're sometimes here and sometimes somewhere else. I don't know what you're looking for, but it must be very well hidden. But you're smart. That, I figured out right away—too smart to be what you say you are. Too smart to have come from God knows where, to have driven two thousand miles for a woman you met on the Internet. But… OK, I don't really care what your reasons are. I care about Laura. And she's taking things as they come. I think that she doesn't really care about your past, but only the future that she thinks she can have with you. She might seem to be living in the moment. You may think that she's not expecting anything from you, but that isn't so. She seems to have exiled herself, but her mind is still back in that place she calls her own. And her own place is her ability to love, which was taken away from her. But I need to know. I have to ask you to tell me the truth about yourself."

He paused. He had to stall for time. Across from them a line of broad-leaved trees formed a natural boundary between two cultivated areas. In the background, the hill and the broad Indiana plain. Landy was largely isolated from the outside world. He, however, was even more so.

"I will tell you. But not now, later."

Landy looked him straight in the eyes. He waited a few moments and then said, "OK. We've got time. You can stay here as long as you want. Forever if you want. I expect things from you, Marcelo. Life has been hard for Laura from the time she was old enough to truly understand it. This girl carries all of America inside herself. All of this country's madness is etched on her body and her soul. Every time you kiss her, you don't just kiss a woman. You kiss a map of pain."

He shuddered. Landy could see inside his soul.

They talked for a little while longer, and as they were getting up to go to lunch, he asked him for a favor: to use the telephone. His host smiled and commented, "Words just don't get through to you, eh?" but gave him permission.

The phone was in Landy's house, in a small room with a plain desk. On the wall hung a portrait depicting a prematurely aged Indian, his face marked by countless deep wrinkles. His eyes were almost pleading.

"This is Shin-gos-se-moon, the Great Sail, a chief of the Ottawa tribe. The white man gave him a great gift. Whiskey. He died an alcoholic," Landy said, and closed the door behind him.

He pulled the cable out of the telephone receiver, plugged it into the laptop, and logged on to the web, straight into Marcelo's email. There were two new messages. A spam message advertising pills for "male enhancement" and one from cod-america@aol.com—Doc.

```
Where are you? As you know, I'm sure, the drop
in Chicago went bad. How that happened is imma-
terial. You need to deliver on the second back-
up date. Location: where we'd discussed origi-
nally. Both items. I understand, I open, we're
done. Reply with an OK ASAP.
```

He thought about it for a while before sending a response. About who he should say he was. In the end, he decided he would still be Marcelo, and he responded without making any reference to Chicago, taking the opportunity to try to figure something out.

> Instructions received. I'm at a secure loca-
> tion. I have the video. There's a problem with
> the code. I had to destroy it. Repeat it, along
> with the precise location and date.

Before long he saw the envelope icon of new mail. Doc had replied.

> What video are you talking about? Are you
> crazy? Problem with the code? Asshole, you know
> perfectly well that's the thing I need! Are you
> joking? Get it any way you can! Location and
> date we've agreed upon, before Chicago came up.
> End contact.

So, Doc knew nothing about the video clip. He pulled out Marcelo's piece of paper. 1614180207. This must be the code for the location of the drop. He needed to be there on November 1st. The day before the election. That's where the answers would be found. That's where he'd deliver the box and that's where he'd open it. Did he have any idea about what location this code referred to? Not the slightest.

Digital world

THEY SPENT FOUR QUIET DAYS AT THE FARM. Life was quiet and peaceful there, a refuge from the world. In the afternoons they would hike into the forest. In the evenings they'd listen to Landy's sons practicing, and later they'd all dine together—the sons, their father and Carolyn—and, after a few drinks, Landy would pick up the guitar and play traditional and classic songs: John Lee Hooker, Jimmy Rogers, Pete Seeger, Roy Orbison, Harry Belafonte, Nina Simone, Carolyn Hester. He never again played one of his own songs, despite the persistent requests of his guest. One night, he even got especially agitated, throwing his glass against the wall and screaming, "Shit, lies, all lies, I'm going to delete it all! Right now!" And he was ready to go to the studio and destroy everything before Carolyn intervened and was able to calm him down.

Two of the mornings they got together with Devdan, who led them on long hikes into the heart of the forest and spoke to them about the Indian gods. From everything he heard, he was able to figure out that everything on the earth—the animals, the plants, natural phenomena—were, for the Navaho people, codes—codes that linked their society with the natural world. They weren't strange superstitions, but a perfectly logical and functional belief system. It was the result of rational thought.

One morning, he took them to a flat clear area. There, using five kinds of colored sand he had brought along, he created a painting right before their eyes. It looked like a primitive Pollock, only the technique was purely formalistic. He made two large stylized human figures just as a child might have drawn, using the sand for color and the earth as a canvas. The figure on the right was Mother Earth, on whose body were imprinted the four sacred plants—corn, bean, squash, and tobacco. On the left was Father Sky, wearing the constellations and the galaxy, which Devdan represented with a saw tooth pattern of dots, and also the sun and the moon, circles with lines coming out of their sides. The composition was surrounded by the Rainbow God, but one side, the east, was left open, as an exit.

As soon as he was finished, Devdan sat back and looked at his creation for quite some time, all the while speaking under his breath in totally incomprehensible words. Suddenly he leaned forward, and with his hands wiped away everything he had so painstakingly created. Then he opened the small sack he had brought with him and scooped inside it the now mixed colored sand and dirt.

"Why did you erase it?" he asked Devdan.

"The painting must be destroyed. Just before sunset, I will throw the sand up in the air so that it can scatter and return to Mother Earth. This is our true art. Sacred and unique. Secret. For a long time now, some of our people have broken the tradition by weaving these designs into rugs. They are worthless: reproductions, tradable, safe."

He thought of Landy and his recordings, which Carolyn was going to destroy. Those, at least, would have a longer shelf life: the years that their creator would be alive. And those who broke tradition, the "traitors" in Landy's case, were the entire music industry, which wove and bound in digital format the moment, the elusive. The reproduction was killing the spontaneous. Was it possible that Landy was right? He thought of his own books. How would it have been if they'd never been published? If he'd kept them in a drawer and, like Landy, destroyed them before he died? Was it possible that the only thing worthwhile was the sacred, magical moment of their creation?

As the days went by, things with Laura were getting better and better. The environment seemed to have relaxed her quite a bit. One sign of this was especially moving. She had started letting her hair grow longer. It had already made its way down to the top of the first ideogram. Neither he nor she made any mention of it. They also never discussed the "claimants" and the "interested party," as if that topic had been put in the freezer.

By degrees, Laura was revealing another self—open, sweet, more feminine. She could still be cutting, like a sharp knife, but other times she was affectionate, like a purring cat. Sometimes, after making love, he had caught her looking at him with a different kind of look, the look of a woman opening up inside. For him, for whom love had always been an exile, devastation, this look seemed like a point of light that rendered his loneliness transparent, surmountable.

Because he too, if one didn't count the cancer of Marcelo that ate him up inside, had started to disengage, to soak in the serene daily routine of the farm, to distance himself in stages from the "old reality" and to see—up to a point, naturally—his life with "other eyes." Not that he had become some fundamentally different person. Rather, it was as if he had created a link, a knot connecting his old self and his new, and as if this connection was in the jurisdiction, under the control, of the latter.

He had no news from the outside world; the farm did not even have a TV. When, one day, he asked Landy if there was any way to find out what was going on with the presidential campaign, the look he got from their host was such that he immediately dropped the subject. And when, one afternoon, he asked to use the telephone again, he received a curt, almost insulting, refusal.

In the end, one Sunday, his need for contact with the outside world overwhelmed him. Carolyn had invited him for coffee at the big house, and Landy was out in the fields and had taken Laura with him. When, at some point, Sam came in and told the house-keeper that Landy's sons were looking for her, he realized he was going to be left alone in the house. As soon as he was sure Carolyn was gone, he ran as fast as he could to the building he and Laura were staying in. He grabbed the laptop, returned to Landy's house and ran up to the telephone room. He plugged in the computer and checked Marcelo's e-mail. There was only one message. The sender was candice1970@yahoo.com. The e-mail had been sent on that same day, only forty-five minutes ago. From the first couple of lines he knew who the sender was.

```
Marcelo,
I hope you're OK. I know that these aren't the
best circumstances for us to be in touch after
such a long time. We need to talk. I wouldn't
be doing this if it wasn't something impor-
tant, something that makes me worry about
Jason and myself. In the last few days people
have come to the house three times. They're
looking for you. At first they seemed friend-
ly, but now I'm getting more and more scared.
They're making veiled threats about Jason—
"…Any good mother has to be concerned about
her kid's health" and things like that. What
have you done Marcelo? I need to see you.
You've got to come here. Let me know you got
this. I'm afraid to go to the cops—they might
do something to Jason. I know that this isn't
the best way to communicate with you, but
things are serious. Whatever has happened
between us, Jason is OUR son. I have a new
```

phone number: 407 825 2340. Call me. Please.
Candice

He read it and reread it. He wondered what he should do. Reply as Marcelo? Tell her that Marcelo was dead? And if so, then who was he supposed to be? And where was her husband's body? How did he die? Was it a heart attack or a car accident? And how did he come to be replying to a dead man's e-mails? Suddenly he felt responsible for these strangers—a woman and a child. What would Marcelo do if he were alive? Would he go to her, he wondered? He'd never know the answer to that question. And who was threatening Candice? Was it Jimmy's thugs or Doc's people? The "claimants" or the "interested party?" Since Doc had sent the last message, the obvious answer was the former. Unless the game was much more complex.

In any case, he had to answer Candice. He couldn't make up his mind how to handle it though. His heart told him to tell her the truth, his brain to pretend he was Marcelo, or was it the other way around? Perhaps he was obliged to go see her? Or, perhaps… Perhaps he could bring them here… And Laura? And Landy? He couldn't make up his mind. No matter what, he had to find some way to let her know… Almost impulsively he began typing a reply:

Dear Candice…

At that moment he heard a voice coming from behind him. He jumped.

"You never do learn, do you?"

It was Landy. He was wearing a poncho and a Stetson, with the rim bent up. He looked like he'd emerged straight out of a spaghetti western.

"Faster, faster…" Landy said. "You think you're getting ahead, but it's the speed that's keeping you from getting anywhere."

"It's not what you think. I was only checking my e-mail. There might be something important…"

"Speed. Access. Constant access... Ah, Marcelo! Busy, eh? How come you've been away from your desk for this many days?"

"I'm on leave," he answered smoothly. "Until the elections."

"And after that? What happens then? Are you going back to L.A.?"

"I'm not sure there's anything after that. I don't know if I'll go back."

"The mystery man..."

Coming from Landy, this expression was full of irony.

"Who's talking!" he let slip.

"You've got quite a relationship with words. With minced words."

"There's no such thing as minced words," he said.

"You think?"

The only way out was to turn the conversation away from himself—to gain some time. It was a proven fact that Landy loved this kind of discussion.

"The language is whole. A sentence made up of fragments of words is not possible."

"Let me tell you one," Landy said. "Far-off, most secret, and inviolate Rose."

"Yeats. But here we have infinity, not minced words. There are six complete words."

"Oh, Marcelo, Marcelo, if you're a simple IT company employee, then I'm an uneducated farmer! In Yeats there are six words and half of life's experiences. Let me tell you a story. A while back I fell off a horse and hit my head. When I came to I realized I'd lost my ability to write and play music. Six months later the injury had healed and the music returned."

"What does that have to do with language?"

"It has to do with knowing a language. The music, language, is always there. The ability to use it may disappear and return. So, that's what you make me think of. Someone who fell off a horse and lost the ability to use it. What you're doing on the web is the perfect memory loss." Landy stopped and looked at him searchingly. Suddenly, he said: "Have you ever been to the Holocaust Museum in Washington, DC?"

"No."

"At the entrance, they give you an ID that represents a real Holocaust victim. As you go through the museum, your 'other self' is undergoing all of the suffering of a Jew in Auschwitz. You don't know, however, if you're going to be gassed and incinerated or if you're going to be liberated. You watch films of incredible horror. When you come out you feel that you lived the Holocaust. In reality, however, the whole thing is fake. The museum breeds the death of memory. Absolute amnesia. Wasteland."

"You as..." he started saying, but stopped.

"Me as a Jew you wanted to say? I am nothing. I don't come from anywhere. I don't want to come from anywhere. I was six years old when the country of Israel was founded. I never wanted to have anything to do with either the lobby or the Kissingers it spawned. There were some of us who distanced themselves from the race and were destroyed by remorse. Not me... I was born in the United States of America. I was given the Bible with no instruction manual. I made up my own rules. I crashed and burned, but, in the end, I managed. I figure you know my whole name: Ronel. Ron-el. In Hebrew, 'Ron' means song and 'El,' God. The song of God. When I was eighteen and arrived in Boston, I excised God from my name. I'm just Ron: song."

They fell silent. For a moment he thought that he'd done precisely the same thing. Only he'd excised both his name and surname. He wasn't Jewish, but a descendent of another chosen people, a people who had long ago spread the light of its civilization to most of humanity. Greece did not have a Holocaust; it had four hundred years of Turkish rule. It didn't have a history of exile and wandering. It had something far worse: being stuck in a place so vital that it got swallowed again and again. It didn't have Jews crucifying Christ, it had gods that, instead of having the good grace to stay to be killed and then resurrect, just disappeared. Awkwardly, he turned the computer off, and Landy said, "All right, let's go now, Laura is waiting for you to take you on a picnic."

"Picnic? Where?"

"Wawassee Lake. I told her about the place and she wanted to see it. I'd come along, too, but I'm needed over at the distillery," Landy said and started to walk out, but before going through the door, stopped and turned towards him. "I don't want to ever have to discuss this kind of thing again, right?" he said pointing to the laptop.

He nodded in assent. Like a little child caught red-handed. He clicked the laptop shut and followed.

Phoenix

WAWASSEE LAKE WAS WONDERFUL. Huge, clear blue, calm. They got there in the car at about two in the afternoon, after an hour's drive. At the shore, they found themselves in front of a strange scene: an open-air sermon. The young preacher was speaking from a moveable metal floating dock to a very large audience that was sitting on the sloping shore as in an amphitheater. Behind him, dozens of small boats had congregated, arranging themselves in a semi-circle: a marine fleet of the faithful. Suddenly, a gust of wind pushed up small waves that set the dock swaying. From their vantage point, the preacher seemed to be dancing on the water, while at the same time raising his arms up, as if he was asking something from the heavens.

They stayed for a little while watching the spectacle, but then left to find a more private location. They found a spot with no one else nearby. The only sign of human life was a few boats in the distance that seemed unmoving. Landy had told them there was good fishing in the lake—last year someone had caught a giant sturgeon. Despite it being a bit chilly, they put on their swimsuits and jumped into the water. It was much warmer than they'd anticipated. They swam together for a few strokes, but then Laura left him behind.

She moved beautifully, both in freestyle and backstroke. As she was swimming back towards him, she made a dive. He saw her legs disappear into the water, held closely together in perfect diving form, making the tiniest of splashes, and he was left scanning the surface, waiting for her to reemerge. Several seconds passed, then half a minute and she had still not come up. After a minute had passed, he started getting worried. He didn't want to have to dive himself. Some years ago he'd had to have a laser operation to repair an early stage of cornea separation, and the doctor had explicitly warned him that diving without goggles or a mask could cause the problem to reappear. After a minute and a half, however, he couldn't stand it any longer. He took a deep breath and went under. Below the surface, the lake was perhaps even more beautiful than above. Schools of colorful fish were moving in graceful choreographies, while the fine sand of the bottom was dotted with phosphorous shells that created a calligraphy of curved lines. Despite the fact that the clear water afforded good visibility, Laura was nowhere to be seen. His heart started beating fast. He surfaced and scanned the area where he calculated she'd taken her dive. Nothing. He was getting ready to go under again when he felt arms embracing him from behind. It was she, laughing.

"What happened? I was worried," he said, out of breath.

"I just came up behind you and was watching you the whole time you were looking for me," she said, still laughing. "Did I scare you?"

"Don't do it again," he said, just as she pushed him underwater, not knowing, of course, anything about the problem with his eyes.

As he floated back up towards the surface, he could see her body, headless, suspended in the water. At the surface, her face was waiting for him, bright as never before.

Suddenly, as they looked at each other, somewhere deep inside Laura's eyes he saw something that made him shiver: an expression he recognized as his mother's, an expression that brought back into his mind a hum, the blurred sound of his upbringing. Strange! His first impulse was to tell her about it. But he knew that one must be very careful when dealing with the dead. He hugged her and they walked out onto the beach together.

On the way back, they walked around the perimeter of the lake. They found a kiosk that sold everything. He bought newspapers and they sat down at a café, where he went through them hungrily. Things were not looking too good for Kerry. His running mate, John Edwards, didn't seem to be making up the difference, despite his boyish good looks and populist appeal. In the meantime, there were daily losses suffered by the American forces in Iraq, primarily from suicide bombers. Nowhere could one find pictures of the carnage, however. When he was done and had folded up the newspapers, he wondered why. How come he had this thirst to "know what was happening?" Laura brought him back to reality, telling him that she was getting bored and wanted to find a good place to have the picnic he'd promised her.

They got back in the car and continued driving down a narrow road flanked by tall trees on either side. At a distance, they saw a flat green clearing that looked like a small meadow and decided to head in its direction. Almost precisely in the middle of the clearing, there was a huge plane tree. They parked the car, took out the sandwiches and beers they had bought at the kiosk, and sat down in the shade of the large tree. There was no one else around. They each ate a sandwich and leaned back on the grass. Laura took his hand in hers, and he moved closer and kissed her. In a few seconds, they were rolling on the ground. At one point, Laura got on top and pinned him down. She pulled off her shirt and then leaned over him, unbuttoned his shirt and started kissing his chest.

Laura was in her element when making love. She could see, understand everything, peel back the layers of reality and get to the deepest meaning of things. The circumstances of her life had removed a piece from deep inside her body, but had enhanced the use of the rest. She didn't need to do anything extraordinary; she didn't bring anything especially unique to the arena of sex, but the way she acted when making love, at the same time surrendering and demanding, transformed her. Making love did not break her loneliness, but instead gave it substance. So much so that she could transcend it. Whatever fate had decided for this woman, it hadn't yet said the final word on the matter.

She quickly unfastened his belt and started to pull his zipper down slowly. She had just begun caressing him when they heard a noise coming from behind them, from the direction of the tree—something like a glass dropping, followed by a voice saying something totally incomprehensible. Laura, frightened, got up pulling her shirt on as fast as she could. He jumped up, pulling up his zipper. They turned together in the direction of the voice. From an opening in the trunk of the tree, the small blond head of a boy appeared, only to disappear as soon as the boy spotted them looking at him.

He got up and approached the tree trunk. At its base there was a small opening, obscured by some twigs. Inside was a hollow like a small cave. It was about six feet in diameter, with a small mattress at one end and a homemade table, made out of branches, in the middle. The source of the original noise, a tin cup, had rolled on the ground and was close to the opening. Lying on the mattress, curled up in a fetal position, was a thin blond boy, about ten years old. When he felt their presence, he turned and looked at them. He had an intelligent face, large, constantly moving eyes, and a few freckles on his cheeks. He looked haggard and dirty, as if he hadn't had enough to eat and hadn't washed in quite some time. He was wearing a worn out pair of jeans, an oversized, torn shirt, and running shoes.

"Hi," he said.

The child looked at him with fear in his eyes, but did answer, "Hi," with a voice that sounded too deep for his age.

"What's your name?"

"Phoenix."

"What are you doing here?" Laura asked.

"I live here."

"What about your parents?" she went on.

Phoenix made a sharp gesture with the palm of his hand.

"What?"

"My mom's dead. My father's gone. He's a drunk."

"Don't you have any other relatives?"

"No."

"Where did you live before here?"

"At first with my aunt. She didn't want me."

"And after that?"

"I was adopted by a family in Syracuse."

"How come you're not with them?"

"I ran away a couple of months ago."

"Why?"

"I didn't like it there. They tortured me."

"They beat you up?"

The boy smiled.

"No, no, they tortured me. They wanted to change me."

"Change you into what?"

"Just change me into someone else—someone I'm not."

"Come outside. You can sit with us. We've got food," he said.

Phoenix seemed to hesitate for a few moments, but in the end he got up, patted his clothes and got out of the hollow. He looked strong, but his strength seemed not to come from working out; he moved like a creature that knew how to fend for itself.

"Bad luck," he said, as soon as he was out.

"What do you mean?" Laura asked.

"I killed a spider this morning. I knew it would bring bad luck."

The boy was ravenous. He devoured the two leftover sandwiches in record time. It looked like he hadn't eaten properly in quite a while.

When he finished, he sat looking away from them and refused to speak, as if he regretted having told them as much as he had. After a while, they managed to coax the rest of his story from him. His mom had been killed in a car accident six years ago, going too fast on the freeway after a serious fight with her drunk husband. After that, Phoenix lived with his father for a couple of years—an alcoholic Vietnam vet who survived on odd jobs and petty theft. One day he walked drunk out of their apartment—in a dilapidated low-income housing project on the edge of the town of Syracuse—and never came back. The boy then lived for two years with his father's sister—half-mad—who got rid of him when she got the chance, giving him up for adoption to an elderly childless couple. The Conways, however, were extremely religious. Their efforts to bring the boy on the path to salvation were an abject failure. It didn't take too long for Phoenix to revolt against the discipline and the daily Bible lessons and run away. For the past two months, he had lived in the countryside, finding shelter wherever he could—in derelict cabins, in the fields, in the woods. He knew that the authorities were looking for him but managed to stay away from them. For the last week he'd been living in the hollow of the big old plane tree. "This is the best place," he said, almost proudly.

He wondered why a runaway child, hiding from the authorities, opened up to them and told them everything. Wasn't Phoenix afraid they might try to take him back to his adoptive family? Looking more closely at the boy, however, he could discern such weariness that it was clear the kid had reached the limit.

They talked with Phoenix for quite some time. What made the biggest impression on him was that the boy didn't blame anyone else for his misfortune. "It's not their fault, it's not all the rules they made for me. It's my fault. Something inside of me…" words one wouldn't expect to hear from someone this young. Phoenix, however, was not an ordinary child. This was not an ordinary little runaway, beaten down by the fates. This was a little guy with an attitude. *He too is a fugitive*, he thought.

At one point, Laura asked Phoenix to excuse them for a couple of minutes, took him aside, and told him they should take the boy with them to Landyland. "It's so sad. If we don't do anything, God knows what will happen to the poor kid. I'm certain Landy won't object." He wondered whether it might not be better to return Phoenix to his adoptive family. "But it's clear he doesn't want that. Can't you see how desperate he was to get away from them?" she answered. He noticed her face had lit up. He instinctively realized there were two forces working inside her. The first one was identification. Laura saw in Phoenix's life story something that was very much the same as what she'd had to go through. At the same time, there was something else, the second force, something strongly instinctual. Laura was a thirty-five year old woman, childless, without any family ties. He agreed right away.

When they told the boy, he rejected the idea. He'd just managed to escape the oppressive situation with the Conways, and the last thing he wanted was another oppressive adoptive family. Laura calmly explained the situation—the kid had no idea who Landy was—but when he registered that there were horses, and Indians, and guitars, his attitude changed. He was too proud, however, to accept the offer easily. He whispered something that sounded like "Thanks, but I can't change who I am. I know that I'm going straight to Hell. I've even stolen stuff," in a naive attempt to show them the scale of his transgression. He recounted for them, with a degree of pride, mixed with shame, his exploits of the past few weeks—which included the snatching of an old lady's purse, the "lifting" of the shirt he was currently wearing from a man sleeping on a bench—"it's huge on me, but I like it"—and the artful swiping of a whole picnic basket that a couple swimming in the lake had left unattended on the beach.

He laughed, tousled the boy's hair and said, "You won't need to steal there. You'll have food and shelter." Phoenix made a funny face, slipped back into the bad boy persona, but finally accepted the offer, shrugging his shoulders for effect.

On the drive back, Laura sat in the back seat with Phoenix. He drove all alone in the front, stealing glances through the rearview mirror, watching Laura looking, every now and then, at the child, who was, in turn, looking distractedly at the beautiful landscape they were moving through. He was reminded of himself on similar trips with his father—who would look at him with such a wondrous expression, as if he was trying to figure out what was in the soul of this small creature he'd brought into the world. Something his father had never managed to guess.

The new role

IT WAS NOT SURPRISING THAT, as soon as he got to the farm, the boy went wild about the place. The first thing he did was run to see the horses. One of Landy's young assistants let him get on a pony and led them around the corral a few times. Phoenix, even though he'd never been on a horse before, seemed to be in his element. The boy had no concept of fear. Afterwards, he was shown around the stalls, the barns, the fields, and lastly, up to the teepees. Devdan tousled the boy's hair and uttered another sentence dense with meaning: "The eyes that run everywhere." All that was left was to meet their host so they could obtain his permission for the boy to stay at the farm.

When he saw the three of them, Landy burst out laughing, "You guys are way too fast. You just went on a romantic picnic and here you are, bringing back a ten-year old kid! I know you want to live in the fast lane, Marcelo, but I couldn't have imagined..."

Laura took him aside and explained, briefly, the situation. Landy had no objection. He gave Phoenix a room right next to theirs, and the boy became an official resident of Landyland.

Phoenix brought a whole new dimension to the couple's life, not to mention the life of the whole farm. He was full of life, mischievous, but so charming that everyone forgave him his misdeeds. Everyone, that is, except for Laura, who didn't fall for the boy's charming ways, at least not easily. She was the only one to discipline him, not harshly, but in an entirely unique way, as if she were giving advice to a mature adult. She acted towards him as a mother with modern parenting ideas, or like an experienced older sister who had taken charge of the upbringing of the youngest child of a broken family.

Laura often hinted that he too should get involved in Phoenix's upbringing. "The boy needs a stable male role model," she told him one day, making him smile. Never in his life would he have imagined that he could possibly have taken on this role. It was something that had been broken inside him from early on. It wasn't just the business with his wife's abortion. It was also once before, when he'd gotten close to the point of starting a family. Just the idea of having a child brought terror in his heart. It wasn't because of the necessary change in lifestyle, the added responsibility, and having to really become an adult himself. It was something else, much deeper. Being a "parent" means that from then on your heart will be beating outside your body. And his heart was firmly lodged inside him—deep inside and well towards the back. He could not even imagine himself as a father—because he could not imagine himself as anything, really. But now, as Marcelo, as a Marcelo with a Laura, he had been presented with a little wild Phoenix, a ready-made child that had come out of nowhere. The situation demanded that he play some role.

The boy had assumed that the two of them were married, or at least, a couple living together. Therefore, if Laura had taken on the maternal role, and Landy that of a grandfather—in the mornings he gave him riding lessons and in the evenings he'd show him how to play some simple chords on the guitar—what role was left for him? By all accounts, the role of "father"—a father, however, that possessed neither the charm of the "grandfather," nor the solidity of the "mother." He was an insubstantial father, invisible, erased, with no longitude or latitude. Of course this made him feel bad. How much more so, given the fact that he was pretending to be someone who'd had a child, regardless of whether or not his family was supposed to be broken up. Laura had brought this up right from the start: "How can you act towards him this way? As if you've never been with a child before... No wonder your marriage failed..."

And so, he began to make an effort. At first it was like he was trying to gain the trust of someone of no particular age. Sometimes he acted as if the kid was an adult, in which case Phoenix would soon get bored, and other times as if he was dealing with a five-year-old child, in which case the boy would become resentful. It took a few days for them to attain a balance. This happened when the curious boy, who possessed a natural intelligence, started asking him about his own life. He was very open about it, taking due care, naturally, not to reveal his true identity. He focused his discussion on his own father and their relationship. He talked to the child about his difficulty in getting close to his father, his feeling that he'd come out of nowhere, that he wasn't wanted, let alone loved. When the boy, with the directness that came naturally with his age asked, "So why didn't you run away?" he answered with a question of his own:

"Why didn't you run away from your own father?"

The kid's expression changed. He stayed quiet for a while and then whispered, almost ashamed, "Because he was my dad. He was no good but that's what he was."

From that point on, something changed in their relationship. Phoenix spent less time with his "grandpa" Landy and "mother" Laura and started going on hikes with him and Devdan. When he figured out that the boy was very impressed with Devdan's stories, he decided to introduce him to books. The choice of the first book was rather obvious. He got Phoenix *Huckleberry Finn* from Landy's library. The boy couldn't put it down—he finished it in one day, and from the next day on he went around with a slingshot in his back pocket, like Twain's hero. After all, he too was a Huckleberry Finn who'd run away from his own Aunt Sally. The first stage of the induction to books was, naturally, identifying with the hero. But what came next was truly impressive. The boy, without abandoning his riding lessons and the hikes with Devdan, spent as much time as possible in Landy's library, which was full of treasures of young adults and children's literature. He was happy for the first time in his new role.

Another trait, however, of the boy was the great ease with which he'd tell lies. One afternoon, he accidentally set a storage shed on fire while playing with matches. Phoenix, as soon as he saw the flames spring up, bolted and disappeared, so the workers who got there almost immediately and put out the fire, thought that the cause must have been a short-circuit. He, however, who happened to be reading under a tree about a hundred yards away, had seen everything. Later, he took Phoenix aside and asked him if he'd had anything to do with the fire. The boy strenuously denied any involvement. When he told him he'd seen him, Phoenix turned red with embarrassment, admitted his guilt, but added that he didn't think lying was all that bad. "Lies have saved me from many things," he said and added melodramatically, "OK, now I guess you have to punish me." He then informed the boy that the punishment would be to impose a punishment on *him*.

"But, you didn't do anything wrong, Marcelo, why should *I* punish *you*?"

"Any time you do something bad, *you'll* have to punish *me*," he told the boy, and made him choose one of three penalties he put forth.

Phoenix chose the lightest sentence. The punishment "Marcelo" had to endure was to chop wood and carry it to their building's fireplace. He insisted that the boy watch him while he carried out these tasks. Exhausted, as he was carrying in the last batch of freshly chopped wood, he caught out of the corner of his eye, the kid's face tearing up.

The same process was repeated when, one evening, he caught him smoking, and again, a third time, when he discovered that Phoenix had stolen a ring from Devdan. That was the last significant act of mischief by the boy. When Phoenix had to watch him for hours pulling weeds from a plot overrun with nettles and brambles, he took his hand and declared, "Marcelo, I won't ever do anything wrong again. I swear!"

The presence of the boy, as well as Laura who had become more relaxed and affectionate since they'd come to the farm, along with the conversations and hikes with Landy and Devdan had all contributed to taking his mind off the dark aspects of Marcelo's situation. The "claimants" and the "interested party," however, had not receded from his memory. He often thought of Jimmy, Doc, and—even more often—of the horrible scene he'd walked into at that office in Chicago. The last time he'd had any contact with the situation, indirectly at that, was through the e-mail he'd gotten from Candice. Candice… One morning, he remembered she'd given him her phone number. It was still in the e-mail that was saved in the "Inbox" on his laptop. He retrieved it, went up to Landy's house, and asked for permission to make a personal call. Seeing that he was not carrying the laptop with him, Landy smiled and said OK.

"Are you sure you don't have some secret gadget in your back pocket?" he joked as he opened the door for him.

He dialed the number Candice had given him. The phone rang several times before a female voice answered. The line, at his end, was clear, but the woman seemed not to be able to hear him well.

"Is this Candice?"

"I can't hear you…"

"Yes, may I speak with Candice, please?"

"With… whom?… I can't make out what you're saying…"

This went on for a little while longer, until, finally, the woman at the other end figured out what he wanted.

"You want to talk to Candice? Who may I say is calling?"

"A friend of hers."

"Which friend of hers?"

"It's not important. Is she there?"

"I don't know. I'm upstairs."

"Could you check please?"

"What is it you want her for?"

The "fishing" for information from both sides continued for a couple of minutes, until, suddenly, a male voice came through the receiver.

"Candice isn't here. Don't call again," and the line went dead.

He wondered what had happened. Something wasn't right about that phone call. He got an idea. He called directory assistance and asked for the listing for Candice Dolores Diaz. There was only one listing. The number he got was nowhere close to the one he'd just dialed. He also asked for the address. He jotted down the information and dialed the new number. He got an answering machine: "Candice Diaz is not able to come to the phone right now. Please leave a message at the beep." Hoarse voice, troubled.

So, the e-mail had not been sent by Marcelo's wife. Someone else was the author. Suddenly he cursed silently. Why had the woman on the other end slowed down the conversation so much? Could it be his call was being traced? Had he betrayed his location? It was clear that the situation Marcelo was involved in wasn't finished. For that matter, it could well be that it was just beginning.

Gun, knife, and the dark of night

OVER THE NEXT COUPLE OF DAYS, he tried to call Candice twice. Both times his call was picked up by the answering machine. He thought about leaving a message, but in the end, discarded the idea. Life at the farm with Laura and Phoenix started to absorb him again. For the first time in a very long time, he existed in something that resembled harmony. A forgotten feeling, lost in the distant past. As in a fugue, the voices that chased each other seemed to have reached some accommodation and were cooperating to form a single melody.

Until—one Wednesday morning, they decided to go back to Wawassee Lake to swim, just the three of them. They took with them food, a blanket, their swimsuits, and headed out. Phoenix also borrowed a baseball and some catchers' mitts from Landy's sons. The lake was very crowded, however, and the weather had turned quite chilly, so they went on to the meadow where they had found the boy. Before having lunch, Phoenix wanted to play baseball, which put him in the awkward position of having to confess that he'd never played the game. Phoenix laughed at him, while Laura looked at him shocked and asked how it was possible that he had never played baseball, not even in school. He invented a vague childhood disease, an excuse that did not erase the surprise from the face of the woman, who took on the role of pitcher for Phoenix. Watching them, he felt embarrassed and decided to join the game, with, however, unsurprisingly dismal results.

During the game, going for a spectacular catch, Phoenix slipped and fell, scraping his leg on an old tin can. The cut wasn't deep, and despite a copious amount of blood, the tough little boy wanted to go on with the game. However, the can was old and rusted, and they had to take him in for a tetanus booster shot. They asked at the first gas station and were told that the nearest hospital was in Syracuse. When they got there, the ER attending physician gave the boy the shot, and they started back to Landyland.

Driving through the town, as they crossed a major street, Phoenix told them that the home of his adoptive family was only a block away. The boy asked them to stop across the street from the house, and he parked at a spot from where they could watch it without being observed themselves. In the yard, a woman of about sixty, wearing a green robe with little pink flowers and rollers in her hair, was sitting in a rocking chair, knitting. A man of about the same age, lanky, wearing too-wide pants and galoshes, was washing a white Lincoln with such care that it seemed as if he expected God to strike him dead if he left even a speck of dirt on the car. He wondered how Phoenix had managed even one day in that stifling environment. After a while, the boy said, "Enough, let's go," and they resumed driving towards Landyland.

On the way, Phoenix insisted on tuning the radio to a rap station. He proudly informed them that his favorite artists were Snoop Dogg, a black rapper who'd once had to stand trial for murder, and Flavor Flav, who'd shot his neighbor because he was bugging him.

When they reached the spot with the garage shed where all of the farm's cars were parked, he noticed something rather unusual. A few feet to the right of the building there were tire marks. It looked like someone had made a sharp turn. They left the car in the garage—Sam had given them the key—and they started walking towards the farm. As they approached, they noticed unusual activity. Something strange was going on. From a distance, he saw two Indians moving someone on a stretcher, while a dozen of Landy's assistants were running from place to place calling out to each other. Sam was coming towards them. When he got to them, he looked at him with a cold expression.

"What happened?" he asked Sam.

"They came."

"Who came?"

"Don't you know?" Sam looked at him strangely.

"No," he said.

"We got two injured. Lance, the kid who trains the horses, and Devdan."

"Who did it?"

"Two men. Now you need to come with me right away. Landy wants to see you. He's waiting in your room."

Running towards the house, he reached the stretcher and saw that Lance was in it. The young man's face was ashen, and his leg had blood all over it. He was unconscious.

Landy was standing next to the window, looking down in the direction they'd come from. When he turned around and looked at them, his expression was tense, his nostrils flared, his eyes narrow. He told Laura and the boy to stay in the room and led him to the other end of the hallway, into a small room that looked like it was used for storage. He spoke slowly, almost ritually.

"Who are you, Diaz? You have a lot of explaining to do. This whole mess happened because of your presence."

"I don't understand," he said. "What happened?"

His expression must have shown true confusion. Perhaps it was this that made Landy, instead of becoming more aggressive, to describe what had taken place. The whole thing resembled a court proceeding, where the facts had to be heard before a sentence could be deliberated and pronounced.

Two hours after they had left for the lake, two men showed up at the farm. Sam was the first to see them. They asked to see the owner. Sam, on the basis of standing instructions, told them that they were trespassing and had to leave the place immediately. This was something that had happened a few times before, with crazed fans and a persistent reporter whose life dream was to get an interview with the reclusive musician. The two men, however, would not comply, and Sam became more insistent. At that point, one of them opened his jacket and showed Sam the gun that was sticking out of the inner pocket, demanding that he take them directly to Landy. The people working in the fields just looked on with curiosity when they saw Sam crossing the farm with a couple of strangers following him—they didn't know, of course, that one of them had a gun aimed directly at him the whole time. When they got to the big house, Landy heard Sam calling him downstairs and when he went down into the living room, he found himself in front of the two men shutting the door behind them and repeating the threatening scene with the gun. The one who seemed to be the leader—a red-haired man with round glasses—took him aside and said to him, word for word:

"There's no reason to be afraid, Sir. There is nothing we really want from you; what we're looking for is to speak to Mr. Diaz, and then we'll be on our way."

"I stayed calm—I'm always calm in difficult situations," Landy said, while he, listening carefully, was trying to figure out some explanation that would satisfy Landy without revealing the truth about the situation. At the same time, these events were proving his conjecture true. The e-mail that prompted him to call Candice had been a trap.

The rest of the story was even worse. Landy told the two men that they had no right to be there. "Where is Diaz?" asked the red-haired man, this time with a more menacing tone. "I don't know any Diaz," Landy replied. In the meantime, Carolyn blundered into the scene by opening the door. The red-haired man ordered her to come in and stand next to him. "Your wife?" he asked. Landy nodded "yes." "If you don't want anything bad to happen to her, get him here right now." So, Landy had to tell him that Marcelo was gone but that he would return later. The man didn't believe him and pulled out the gun. At that moment, Lance walked into the living room, having, of course, no idea about what was going on. He was carrying an axe; he'd just finished chopping some wood for the fireplace. Startled, the red-haired man shot him in the leg.

The sound of the shot was audible for some distance outside the house and alarmed all those who heard it. Several of the people working nearby started moving in the direction of Landy's house. The red-haired man told Landy to go to the window and tell them to get inside the buildings; otherwise the lives of everyone would be in danger. He did as he was told, and everyone went away. The red-haired man then sent the second man outside to check the perimeter of the house in order to make sure no one was still around. After that, he continued to make threats and ask for Diaz. At some point he must have believed that Landy was telling him the truth because he said that everyone should sit down and quietly wait for Diaz to return. Time passed slowly, first ten minutes, then fifteen… Landy tried to ask what he wanted him for, but the red-haired man, who was starting to get agitated, told him to shut up or he'd regret opening his mouth to say another word. In the mean-time, Lance was writhing in pain from the wound in his leg.

And then, something unbelievable happened. Devdan suddenly sailed through the window, carrying a knife. The red-haired man, startled again, shot twice but missed. Devdan, moving very fast, got to him, knocked the gun out of his hand and put the knife to his neck. The second man, who had been outside near the door, heard the commotion and hurried back into the room. Devdan told him to drop his gun if he didn't want to see his friend dead. The man pre-tended to put the gun onto the floor but took a shot instead and hit Devdan in the left hand. The red-haired man pulled free and picked up his gun. In the meantime, ten or so of Devdan's friends, who apparently had been hiding behind the house, gathered in front of the door, armed with axes and knives, looking ready to do battle as soon as Landy gave them a sign. "You may get two or three of us, but both of you are going to die," Devdan said. The red-haired man, knowing the game was pretty much up, played his last ace: he took Carolyn hostage and said that all he wanted was to be allowed to go. The Indians followed them all the way to the clearing where the garage was. There, the two men let the woman go, got into their car, and disappeared.

Lance was en route to the hospital in Syracuse, while Devdan was being cared for by his own people, who had pulled out the bullet and begun a traditional Navaho healing ceremony.

When Landy finished recounting what had happened, he stayed quiet for a while. He looked around as if checking for something and then turned towards him.

"And now, Mr. Diaz, you'll tell me why all this took place. Besides, you promised me."

There was nothing else he could do. He tried to sell Landy the same story he'd told Laura, embellishing it with details he made up on the spot. When he finished, Landy had an expression of discontent. It was obvious that he did not believe him.

He bit his lips slightly, brushed his hair back and said slowly, "I'm not interested in what you do, nor in who you are. I know that you're not telling me the truth. I'm guessing that you can't. Under different circumstances I'd help you. But, you've put us in grave danger. I want you to leave. I don't want to find you here tonight." Then he turned his back on him and walked towards the door.

"I only have one question," he said.

Landy stopped.

"Those men, when they were talking to each other... Did you make out any names?"

Landy answered without turning to face him.

"Names? I don't think..." He thought for a moment and continued, "At some point, the other man called the red-haired one Dick, or something like that... No, it was Doc. He called him Doc.

There's nothing else to be said between us," and walked out of the room.

The first thing he did was to find Laura. She was in Phoenix's room. He told the boy to go outside for a little while. Laura had heard what had happened from Sam. He told her what Landy had decided. Laura went pale. Despite her agitation she hugged him. They stayed like that for a while.

"What are we going to do?" he asked her finally.

"I don't know," she answered. "Leave me alone for a little while so I can think, please."

Going outside, he noticed the people of the farm looking at him with curiosity. He walked some ways off, took out his pack, and lit a cigarette. Then, he started walking toward the teepees.

Devdan was lying on a thick wool blanket. His hand wasn't bandaged but packed with various herbal poultices. He bent down and gently touched the man's arm. "Thank you for everything," he said. Devdan did not say anything. He sat for a short while with the injured man silently looking at the top of the teepee that was painted with various Navaho symbols. The smell of camphor and salt was pervasive. At some point, an elderly man pulled back the door flap and glanced inside with a hard look on his face. He stayed a while longer in the silence, and when he finally got up to leave, he saw Devdan motioning to him to come closer, with his uninjured hand.

"I don't know what you've gotten yourself into. But after all the time we've spent together, I've gotten to know what kind of person you are. Your mind is fixated on something. If this something is that set of numbers you told me about, I can tell you what they mean."

You'd said "the World of Numbers." I just have no idea what that means.

"The World of Numbers" is a city. An American city that is made up of numbers. Do you get it now?

He pulled out the small piece of paper he always now carried in his wallet. "1614180207" he read.

"It's a location in the city," Devdan said.

"In the 'City of Numbers?'"

"Yes. An address."

Suddenly he understood. How could he have missed it?

"New York," he almost shouted.

"'Sky Country,' Devdan said and with a motion of his hand let him know he wanted to be alone.

He came closer, took off the necklace with the stones he'd taken from Marcelo's body, leaned over, and placed it around Devdan's neck.

"Thanks, Devdan, for everything," he said again and took off.

Back in Phoenix's room, Laura greeted him with eyes red from crying. He took her in his arms. On the way back from Devdan's place, he had come to a decision about what he wanted to say to her.

"I need to go to New York City to complete some unfinished business. I don't want anyone, and especially you, to be in any greater danger because of me. I have to see things through by myself. Today is Friday, October 29, 2004. By Monday, whatever is going to happen will have happened. There are only a few days left. You can think things through and decide. By Monday night I'll be free, done with this. The story will be finished once and for all, and we'll be free to have a life together. If you still want that, be in New York on Monday evening. When I'm ready, I'll call you. If you don't come to the phone, I'll assume you've decided to stay here, in Landyland. Otherwise, we can leave together, for good— probably by plane, to some other state, maybe even further away, but I don't know for sure where yet. So bring your passport along, just in case. If you come, I'll tell you everything. Everything."

Laura looked at him. Her eyes showed nothing other than pain. He kissed her slowly, pulled together his things, got the laptop and the black box, and while she watched him with tears in her eyes, he bent down and kissed her again. Suddenly, she pulled her lips away and left the room, without looking at him again. He was left by himself for a little while. He opened his suitcase, pulled out the bag with the money and counted out forty thousand dollars. He then opened her suitcase and put the money in the top pocket. He took his things and walked down the stairs. Before long he was heading out of the farm entrance.

End game. Game opening.

A few miles past Syracuse he stopped at a deserted spot. He pulled out paper and a pencil and jotted down everything he had thought about on the way. He was looking for an address in the "City of Numbers," New York City. Manhattan, in particular, where virtually none of the streets and avenues have names but, rather, numbers. From the video, it was clear that he should be looking for a tall building or skyscraper, and the view was consistent with Manhattan. 1614180207. There were ten numbers, quite a few. Most likely, they represented a complete location description, at an intersection of an avenue with a street. So, number of avenue, most likely one digit; number of street, probably two digits; building number, logically a three-digit number; floor number, a two-digit number, if one took into account the video clip that showed an apartment at a fairly significant height; apartment number, the remaining digits.

This reminded him of another one of his books, his third novel. The hero finds an address through the anagram of a phrase he's been given. Here, of course, he was dealing with numbers, but the concept was pretty much the same. He started by looking at the numbers in reverse. After considering several different combinations, he settled on one that seemed the most reasonable to him. If

7 was the avenue number and 20 the number of the street, then 180 was the building address. And since, no matter how tall the building, it wasn't possible that it would have 614 floors, the floor number would be 14 and the apartment number 16. This translated to: apartment sixteen, fourteenth floor of building one hundred and eighty, at the intersection of Twentieth Street and Seventh Avenue.

He looked up and surveyed the landscape. He could see one tree. Only one, alone, in the middle of the prairie. The sky a pool of lavender. The day was descending. It was the heart of the warm earth and the cold light. Of an absolute nakedness. A tree that conversed only with the wind, with the void. Its only language its shade. Centered in itself, with its plant heart beating in the cadence of loneliness. It occupied time with patience and stoicism. He felt jealousy, maybe even resentment. He got out of the car and stood watching it. He watched for quite a while, until the darkness of night spread upon its shade and erased it. Then, he got back in the car and started the engine. To New York City.

PART THREE

NEW YORK

The "City of Numbers"

FRIDAY, OCTOBER 29 2004

THE GEORGE WASHINGTON BRIDGE LOOKED, on that Friday night of October 29, 2004, like a dark net thrown by some contemporary Spider-Woman over the surface of the world, in order to collect a representative sample of both the beauty and the ugliness of this planet. He was entering Manhattan Island, entering the capital city of the world, this crystal arc of postmodern time, with its eight million souls squeezed in its stern, its prow, and its hold. As the Mustang drove through the tunnel of air and he looked at the steel cables that supported it—heavy and proud, oiled with purpose, as if they were tied to a harpoon that some technocratic Ahab was ready to drive into the invisible Moby Dick of the Hudson River—he felt that reality was being transfigured, dissolved, and reconstructed into the string of an imaginary guitar. The string was held taut by a mysterious power, setting a false time, a disguised present, out of which he had to escape once and for all. He was entering a city that was both a comparison and a fact, at once the truth and its parody, a "City of Numbers," as Devdan had said. A city of mathematical emotion, where each building was an algebraic equation and a poem's metrical line as well.

This succession of glass shapes and sparks that he was facing looked like a rational coil, which instead of moving along a corkscrew trajectory, creating a structural DNA strand, an architectural application of the fundamental substance of life, launched straight into the sky like a wedge, revealing at the same time a forgotten, subterranean place where the foundations of night, of numbers, and of knowledge are located. Down there, at the deepest gate, the world's deepest city, at the innermost layer, where memory lodges. He had at last reached the mine.

After all, the canary had managed to stay alive; it had escaped from the cage and had crossed the tunnels one by one. Only the last tunnel was left to cross before it could emerge reborn, victorious, into the fresh air.

From the moment he left the farm, he felt twinges of remorse for all those innocent people he'd gotten embroiled in this adventure, in this affair—which had sprung out of his need to get away, to change, to forget; which became more complex with the disguise, the lie, the flight; and which only God knew where it would end. He felt guilt for young Lance who had been wounded, for Landy whose hospitality he had repaid with that awful incident, for Devdan, lying at this moment in his tent with a wounded hand, and most of all, for Laura, whom he had linked to a gloomy fate that was not even his.

These people had not betrayed him, but had erected a mirror in front of him, in which, behind the borrowed image of Marcelo, he was gradually beginning to see himself. Landy and Devdan had given him a valuable life lesson, Phoenix had touched something that had been repressed deep inside him, and Laura... Laura had offered him something priceless: she had opened a door in his soul, a door that until then he had thought was permanently locked.

Laura. Her eyes. *Eyes, only the eyes of memory...* Laura. Laure, Laura, Lauro: laurel, l'auro: gold; l'aura: a breeze. Laura: the laurel emanating from her body, the gold of her hair, the breeze of her presence.

However it all might turn out, one thing was for sure: he was entering the last chapter of this story, and his life—independently of "claimants" and "interested parties," Marcelo and black boxes—had changed. And that was something he owed entirely to people, living beings, relationships.

Nevertheless, all this had started from a disguise, a role, a lie. A lie, however, constructed from truth. His story in America was a living fiction, a collage of contradictory—real and invented—sub-stories that blew up like fireworks inside a hermetically sealed hiding place, inside a secret, silent box—like the one he was carrying in his tote bag, on the back seat of Marcelo's Mustang as he entered New York City, having smoked a full pack of Marlboros during the trip, and with the sound of old blues playing on the car radio.

Fate had chosen the perfect place to solve the puzzle, to let him finish with this dark comedy, so that he may finally rid himself of the alien shadow. The same fate that had driven Doc to Landyland; made the little blond boy emerge from inside a tree as he was making love to Laura; let Devdan offer him an ageless, timeless key; let Landy whisper to him his latest masterpiece, condemned to be erased; let Laura surf the Internet in a hopeless prayer. But above all, it was that same fate that had sent Marcelo to him as an angel of God in a cloud of dust, in a desolate wilderness in an amnesiac country, which at that very moment was waging an irrational war on the other side of the world.

An adolescent country, ten thousand miles away from his own, the country-foundation that had created everything—philosophy, theater, literature—ten thousand miles away from that provincial flagstone courtyard where he, as a child, had just discovered that clouds moved across the sky.

He tried, for a brief moment, to figure out what, out of all of this, was true. And for a second, he felt that the only real person in this whole story was Marcelo, a dead man.

As he drove over the George Washington Bridge, he could feel the shadows of all the people he had met the last few weeks chasing him. He was a fugitive—a fugitive from his country, a fugitive from himself, a fugitive from Marcelo, a fugitive from the "claimants" and the "interested party," a fugitive from Martin, a fugitive from Landy, a fugitive from Laura, a fugitive from all of them. He was a fugitive at the center of a crazy chase, in a crazy place—a chase in the "Land of Freedom." An American fugue.

Although the undulating crest of the skyscrapers, which he could see in the distance as he reached the end of the bridge, looked like the endings of musical symbols in an imaginary sheet of music, he knew that he was still writing the score. He, himself, was the composer. He was creating in space and time. Only instead of notes he was using words, notions, feelings. He was weaving his own plot. He was composing his American fugue.

Chelsea Hotel

FRIDAY, OCTOBER 29, 2004

HE GOT ON SEVENTH AVENUE AND KEPT ON DRIVING SOUTH. The city, contrary to the well-known saying, was asleep or, at least, in deep torpor. He was heading for the corner of Seventh Avenue and Twentieth Street. A little before getting there, he saw, at the Twenty-Third Street traffic light, a vertical neon sign: Chelsea Hotel. He was startled. If there was one place in New York City that was notorious in his mind, this was it. Destiny was sending him more signs. The hotel had been legendary as the residence of important artists since the beginning of the last century. Mark Twain, Sarah Bernhardt, Arthur Miller, Jackson Pollock, Dylan Thomas, Patty Smith, Leonard Cohen, Sid Vicious—its clientele had been a parade of celebrities. Indeed, the latter had killed his girlfriend in one of the hotel rooms, following a drug orgy. William Burroughs had written *Naked Lunch* at the Chelsea Hotel, Arthur Clark, *2001: A Space Odyssey*, and Bob Dylan, "Sad-Eyed Lady of the Lowlands." And it was there, along the same avenue, three blocks further south, where the place might very well be (if Devdan's reasoning had decoded the Cartesian structure of the great metropolis correctly) that he would at last find the answers to the puzzles of the last few days.

He reached the corner of Seventh Avenue and Twentieth Street and parked the car between an Italian restaurant and a Chinese delicatessen. The moon was almost full and the night starry and bright—the stars looked like a heavenly tiara crowning the city. Facing him, right on the corner of the two streets, he saw a large building, painted in colors ranging from light red to pink, some twenty stories high, with symmetrical openings on the front. There was a "24/7"on the ground floor, a grocery that stayed open day and night. He walked up to the building's entrance, which was located on Twentieth Street. If the building's number was 180, then he had found his destination. The aluminum sign above the entrance displayed three numbers: one, eight, zero. This was 180 twentieth St., and it was right on the intersection of Twentieth Street with Seventh Avenue. He shuddered.

Looking through the revolving glass door, he noticed a plump doorman almost asleep behind his desk. It was after four in the morning, and he didn't try to go inside. Suddenly, he remembered the video clip. He looked at the other side of the street. Some distance down Seventh Avenue, on the right side of the street, there was a tall gray skyscraper with a stair-like top terminating in a conical apex. It was the building he had seen on the laptop's screen. This was the "City of Numbers." Dedvan had been right. He had reached the last tunnel of the mine.

He returned to the Mustang and, looking back at the building from a distance, he thought that it did not look like an office building but more like an apartment building. He started the engine and drove back towards the Chelsea Hotel.

He crossed the hotel's threshold with awe, as if he was entering a church. The lobby was small and eccentrically decorated. The yellow walls were adorned with numerous works of art. On one side of the fireplace was a drawing in a primitive style and, on the other, a sketch depicting something that looked like an abstract vase. Walking up to the desk, he noticed a colorful painting in the style of Chagall: a man with green trousers and a red coat on a vivid blue background. Next to it was an oblong painting featuring a small dachshund with the words "Chelsea Dogs" written along the length of its body. A strange sculpture was hanging from the ceiling: a bent, pink human figure, wearing boots.

The hotel was not too unreasonable, considering its fame—$220.00 a night for a single room. The employee at the reception desk was wearing thick round glasses with a blue horn-rimmed frame that made his blue eyes look huge. He booked a room for four nights just in case. As he went upstairs to his room, he heard the man at the reception desk talking on the phone, continuing the conversation interrupted by his arrival: "I've never watched an English porn film. It's probably full of men with bad teeth and limp dicks."

The hotel room was not made for people who look for business-class hospitality and all its comforts. His room was furnished with a medley of eclectic pieces of varied styles. Next to the art deco desk stood an ultramodern armchair, while on the wall above the bed was a poster of the John Wayne film *The Alamo*, and next to it a reproduction of Vermeer's *A View of Delft*—the same as in his room in Iowa City. An omen? The television had only the local channels. The refrigerator's loud hum accompanied his brief sleep, which was full of dreams. Dreams of being chased, of course.

Ground Zero

SATURDAY, OCTOBER 30, 2004

HE WOKE UP EARLY. The digital clock read 6:34. He turned on the television. On NBC, the national news headlines were being reviewed.

The latest major issue in the presidential campaign: Senator Kerry holds President Bush responsible for the three hundred and eighty tons of ammunition that disappeared from a military warehouse in Iraq.

The Iraqi army of provisional Prime Minister Allawi and the American forces are losing control of the strategically important provincial city of Ramadi.

A Japanese employee of a multi-national company, who had been captured by the terrorist Zarkaoui's forces, is begging his government to withdraw its forces from Iraq—otherwise there will be another beheading.

Senator John Edwards is planning to visit his birthplace in North Carolina, where he will cast an early ballot and afterwards will take part in an event in his honor, at which

Jon Bon Jovi will be present.

He switched to Fox, the channel with a far right-wing perspective. A political analyst was discussing the workings of the George W. Bush administration. He recounted something a senior advisor of the President had told him a couple of years before:

> "People like you belong to the 'reality-based' community,' that is, to those who believe that solutions emerge from your judicious study of discernible reality. That's not the way the world really works anymore. We're an empire now, and when we act, we create our own reality. And while you are busy studying that reality—judiciously, as you will—we'll act again, creating other new realities, which you can study too, and that's how things will sort out. We're history's actors...and you, all of you, will be left to just study what we do."[11]

He was too antsy to sit and watch any more. He turned off the TV and went to the bathroom.

After a quick shower and shave, he discovered something surprising in the hotel's guest amenities book. Notwithstanding the artistic temperament of the décor, which indicated, at least, an eccentric management for the hotel, the room was equipped with high-speed wireless Internet. He immediately got online and surfed the usual set of web pages. There was nothing particularly interesting in Greece and, of course, absolutely no mention of him. The local Iowa City newspaper site had something about an open event of the International Writers' Program. Martin was on the list of participants. In Marcelo's e-mails, there was a sudden torrent of spam with ads about penile enlargement, cheap Viagra and Cialis, and special prices for Prozac. There was, however, one message by someone who signed as "Slopeman." It had been sent two days ago.

```
Presumably, you are now or will soon be in New
York City. Sunday, October 31, 1:00 p.m.,
Brooklyn, No. 322 2nd St., next to Prospect
Park. There is only one day left. You are going
to receive our final offer, which I'm certain
you'll find very interesting, for delivery of
the "item" and the code.
```

There was also an attachment to the message. A photograph. A large black car with a white hood. A man closely shaven, but with a goatee, was smiling in the driver's seat. The "claimants." So, now they were placing their own bid. Strange. Very strange. First of all, as Marcelo, he had never received any e-mail from them. The only e-mails he had received were from Doc and the "interested party." Doc might be aware of his movements, would have known he had gone to Chicago, but his messages revealed he did not know the code would open the box. As best he could figure it out, the "interested party" did not know anything about the apartment. Neither did the "claimants."

His reasoning led him to believe that the code would be somewhere in the apartment depicted in the video clip. He wondered, however, how Marcelo had gotten the address. Who had given him the piece of paper? Since neither group knew the code, was there some third party? In any case, was the code itself to be found in the apartment? Or were there some instructions about the code that he should deliver along with the box? One way or another, now that Marcelo was gone, he was the only one who knew about the place. One might reasonably expect that the information about where the code was hidden in the apartment could be found in the video. But where? Maybe where the camera zooms in? In the book? Could it be that *A Catcher in the Rye* was hiding the secret?

There were, however, other tormenting questions as well. Was

Marcelo ever supposed to learn what was in the box? Would the code be something that made any sense to him? In the end, what was Marcelo's role in this whole story? Was he a simple messenger, a courier who would get only crumbs in comparison with the sums of money that were at stake, or was he something much more? And that was not all. Was Marcelo an agent of this third party he had deduced, or perhaps had he betrayed them and made his own deal with Doc? Why had the meeting with Joshua in Chicago been set up? Why had Joshua been killed?

It was a complex puzzle. He had faced, however, quite a few in his life, in the course of writing fiction, for instance. His mind was trained to analyze and synthesize details. Of course, in his books there was always a second and even a third layer to the plot. But was it not the same here as well? And what about the "blank page syndrome?" he thought for a moment. The writer's block he'd been experiencing, even in Iowa City? Something had changed. In a magical sort of way, it seemed that the block had disappeared. He had a clarity of thought, as if all of the parts of his brain had started working together again. Had he not become involved in this story at such a personal level, he might very well have sat down and started writing a novel. Nevertheless, in this situation it was reality that was urging him.

Naturally, there was only one thing to do. He had to get into apartment sixteen on the fourteenth floor of the building at the corner of Seventh and Twentieth. But he had left out something essential. The e-mail he had just read said that the "claimants" gave him an open invitation to meet at a specific time and place. What did that mean? That they were not afraid their identity would be exposed. Why not? At this point he stopped; the issues were many and conflicting. What was needed was action. Immediate action.

However, there was another e-mail message. From the same address as the one from which they had sent him the video clip: smada@aol.com.

282 • american fugue

The day after tomorrow. Good luck to us.

He replied:

Send a phone number so that I can call you.

but again the e-mail was returned to him. He jotted down the
address "Slopeman" had given him and went down to the lobby. In
a backpack he took with him the black box and Marcelo's papers.
The night receptionist was just leaving, and a plump blond woman
with long fake eyelashes had taken his place.

Outside, people had started their interminable coming and going.
By the time he had crossed the street, he had heard people speaking several different languages, from heavily accented English to
Spanish, Chinese and Russian. Many in the crowd had the telltale
white earphones on, just like the Bono ad for the i-pod. If it weren't
for the shadow cast over him by the e-mails, by his persecutors, if
he had managed to once and for all erase his tracks completely, he
could easily have felt himself immersing in that beneficial
anonymity that is New York's gift to humanity.

An exile from time—that is what he wished to be. But the
metropolis of the empire was still a city decisively poisoned by the
present, and his own "now" was at that moment facing him in the
form of a gigantic bulk on the corner of Seventh and Twentieth. The
angular, commanding building looked down upon him like a deity
from the heavens.

An icy feeling permeated him to the bone; there was a permanent change in temperature. On the way to his destination, he
passed two or three multi-story brick buildings with the characteristic steel staircases in front of them—fire exits. He was anxious,
with an anxiety that was lifted by the light cool breeze, spun around
as if it were a whirlpool of dust and brought back infused with the

aroma of the city.

He was ready to enter the building, but there was something else he had decided to do first. The previous night he had noticed that next door to the 24/7 market, there was a bank. He went in and spoke to one of the cashiers. A little while later he came out with his backpack empty, and with the key to a safety deposit box (where he had stowed away the black box) in the inside breast pocket of his coat. Of course, he'd rented the safety deposit box using the name of Marcelo Diaz.

The doorman had changed here at No. 180 as well. Now it was a young black man with dreadlocks who occupied the chair behind the desk. Before he had time to say anything, the young man asked him:

"May I help you?"

"I am going to apartment sixteen, on the fourteenth floor."

"Fourteenth floor, apartment sixteen. Let me call up, although Adam is seldom here these days."

The young man made the call. He waited some time for an answer before finally hanging up.

"Like I said, it's been over a month since he was here last."

"I would be obliged if you'd let me in the apartment; there's something extremely important I must do there."

"I'm sorry, I can't. It is strictly prohibited by the condominium rules, sir."

"The tenant has authorized me to enter to do some maintenance work on his computer," he improvised, rather lamely. "I have to do it myself. If you want, you can come with me."

"Sir, it is impossible. Please let me have your contact information, and when Mr. Smith returns, I'll notify him."

He persisted for a little while longer, but the doorman would not budge.

He returned to the hotel. He started trying to think of a way around the problem. He had located the building, had figured out the name, Adam Smith, and he knew the apartment number. He had no way to get in. An idea came to him. He logged onto the Internet and typed into a search engine the address and the name Adam Smith. He found hundreds of thousands of references to the famous Scottish economist, thousands more to the same name, and some ten sites about the construction company that had built the building. None of the references, however, combined both the name Adam Smith, and the apartment building address.

He felt exhausted. Everything had started to swirl around in his head. "Interested party," "claimants," "Slopeman," Doc, Adam Smith, the black box, the video clip, the building... He opened a bottle of whiskey from the minibar and lay down. When he woke up, it was already past noon. He went down to the lobby, ordered a cup of coffee, and sipped it while people-watching. He had to clear his mind. He decided that the best thing he could do would be to take a walk in the city. A change of scenery might change his mood. He went out onto Seventh Avenue and started walking down towards Greenwich Village. He had gotten a street map of Manhattan at the hotel, and the city's grid design made it very easy for him to orient himself.

On the corner of Seventh Avenue and Eleventh Street, he noticed an elderly woman who was walking with a kitten in her arms, talking to it, oblivious to anything going on around her. At the intersection with Bleecker Street, he savored the wonderful aromas emanating from a bakery. At a newsstand, he glanced through the papers. They covered the news he had watched in the morning, with editorials reflecting the political leanings of each paper. The tabloid press didn't seem to be paying much attention to politics. One paper had the headline: "Will Scott Peterson Fry?" It referred to the trial of a seemingly charming thirty five-year old man who was on trial for the murder of his wealthy pregnant wife. "Fry" was the way the journalist had chosen to refer to the electric chair. Graffiti covered a nearby wall: "Get US out of NY." Further down, there was a store with children's toys—antiques. In the window, lead figures of the Lone Ranger and Tonto. He turned left on Bleecker Street and from there, via West Broadway, went down Canal Street, into Chinatown where the pedestrian traffic became chaotic. He almost had to shove other passers-by aside to be able to keep walking. The odor of Chinese spices assaulted his nose as he walked by electronics shops, outdoor salesmen, and cheap knick-knack stands, almost tripping on the cracked sidewalks. The thought came to him that he was covering the same ground upon which, four hundred years ago, the secret trails of Devdan's ancestors were marked, before they were erased by the refined wooden shoes of the first Dutch colonists.

When he reached Broadway, he took it all the way down to City Hall Park, from where, to his left, he saw in the distance the Brooklyn Bridge towering above the Hudson River. A few blocks to his right was Ground Zero. A tall fence surrounded the area. Inside, construction work was going on. The fence was covered with big posters showing photographs of the World Trade Center and telling its story that ended with the terrorist attack of September 11. His first impression was that the "empty space" was too small compared with the enormous extent of the devastation. The breeze over the site had a quality that abolished time. The rays of the sun fell almost vertically on the landscape that, three years ago, was shaded by the Towers, as if the destruction had set the light free. The place looked like a vast open-air theater, whose sets had been burned. The adjacent buildings—on some of which damage from the attack was still visible—seemed to resemble huge bleachers that surrounded an arena of death.

Ground Zero. He did not feel animosity, or fear, or even curiosity. Death had slipped through the all-too-familiar television images and had been absorbed. Ground Zero, the "No Place," stripped everything away, just like every other dead site of History. The observer stood alone, in nothingness, which created a feeling of being confronted by a deadly vacuum, a place of death where the bloodstains had been meticulously cleaned up. He imagined a "Museum of September 11th" similar to the Holocaust Museum. At the entrance, you would be given an ID that would correspond to an actual victim. As you moved through the museum, your assumed self would live that terrifying morning. When the plane crashed into the building, you would start running down the stairs. You would not know, however, whether you would be burnt alive or saved. An American Shoah. "There is no business like Shoah business," he remembered discussing with Landy.[12]

Across the street, on the fence of St. Paul's church, were dozens of flags. Most were American, but there were many from other countries as well: French, Italian, Canadian. On the railings of the fence there were hundreds of messages posted. They were written on T-shirts, bits of plastic, pieces of paper, styrofoam. On a scaffold, he saw graffiti that seemed particularly out of place: "The Mets Suck." What was written underneath, however, was infinitely more striking: "Oh, Death, thou comest when I had thee least in mind."[13]

He walked all the way to the Brooklyn Bridge. Something compelled him to walk across it. He was almost at its middle when, suddenly, he stopped and looked down to the river. He shuddered— something from the past, fierce. One of his favorite passages from Henry Miller came to him: *One looks down from the Brooklyn Bridge on a spot of foam or a little lake of gasoline or a broken splinter or an empty scow; the world goes by upside down with pain and light devouring the innards, the sides of flesh bursting, the spears pressing in against the cartilage, the very armature of the body floating off into nothingness.*

He stayed in the area for a little while and then started walking back. This time he took Center Street. At the level of Grant Street, in Soho, he got tired and stopped for a moment. To his right he spotted a Wine Bar. The sign over the entrance said "Lucky Strike." It was a place full of mirrors, very trendy. He found a small table and ordered a steak and wine. When he finished his meal, he ordered another glass. Before long, the glasses had become four.

The table right next to his was occupied by a rather disparate group: a dark-complexioned young man with a buzz cut and Mediterranean characteristics, who spoke with a loud voice, a thirty-something woman, not especially pretty but with an attractive intelligent look, an elegant forty-year-old with gray hair and a three-day-old beard who spoke with a French accent, and a totally bald man, of about the same age, who was dressed in a scrupulously casual way and also spoke with a rather heavy accent—less easy to pin down, possibly Spanish. As he studied this group, his eyes met those of the young man who, obviously pretty tipsy, raised his glass in a toast. "To New York City" he responded, raising his own glass, not being able to come up with anything better in his surprise. The same thing was repeated with the next glass, until the young man invited him to sit with them. He was already fairly drunk himself and accepted the invitation. He introduced himself as Marcelo, of course.

By now everyone in the group was drunk, except for the bald man who was drinking tea. With the strange, surreal focus alcohol tends to produce, he noticed that the milk the man was adding to his tea was creating arabesque designs in the cup that reflected the light of the spotlights above. A memory started to form in his brain but remained fuzzy, just beyond reach; the wine had gone to his head, and he could not bring it to the surface.

The young man was a playwright. One of his plays—he had written three—was running, to critical acclaim, at an off-Broadway theater.

"Yesterday Tony Kushner came," he said proudly. "I don't write from my own experiences," he went on. "What happened to me when I was ten years old would've been enough material for ten plays, had it happened to anybody else. As for me, I just make a single reference to it in each of my plays simply to honor it. All of my material I've borrowed from Greek mythology. A veritable *Courtyard of Miracles*."

The bald man nodded in agreement, raising the cup of tea to his lips. Then the discussion moved on to the subject of love and the woman, whose name was Marie, said, "In the end, we all fall in love with someone it would have been forbidden to love, if we belonged to the opposite sex."

It took him some time to process this, and when he thought he'd figured it out he commented, "So, you're saying that I will fall in love with a lesbian?"

"No, you didn't get it," she answered.

"If you unmask your face—who knows, maybe hidden behind it you'll find something very ordinary, let's say, a blond exotic dancer," stepped in the young man, whose name was Gino, laughing.

The bald man suddenly and forcefully joined the conversation and started to talk about the pleasure principle, the collective subconscious, Jung and psychological theory, while the gray-haired man countered with arguments that proceeded from a more "Christian" approach to love: giving to the other person, etc. Marie leaned close to him and whispered into his ear, "Do you know what Yannis does for a living?" referring to the bald man.

"Who?"

"Yannis. He's Greek."

This disconcerted him at first, but the alcohol immediately acted to ward off his distress.

"He's a professor at Princeton. A brain! He invented a self-destructing DVD, a patent worth millions. It protects copyrighted materials. Think about it. When you play the DVD, in the beginning, a message appears saying: "This DVD will self-destruct in so and so hours." Or there may not even be a message, and then you've got a single use DVD. From the moment you start watching the film, it is being erased; there is no second viewing. You may not know this when you first watch it. And this works not only for the original DVD, but for copies too. You copy, for example, a movie, and the copy, as it is being played for the first time, is automatically being destroyed. The studios would give their eyeteeth for this technology. They're going to make him filthy rich."

"And the other one?" he asked, meaning the gray-haired man.

"Jack? He's from Montreal. A painter. There's an exhibit of his work in Chelsea. Conceptual art."

Then she started telling him about her life. It was an unbelievable story. Her father was sixty-eight years old when she was born. Her mother was forty years younger. When her father had met her mother, he'd made her an offer: that she give him ten years of her life in exchange for his money. He was very rich and his wife lived like a queen. The old man died on the day of his seventy-eighth birthday, and her mother is still trying to spend the fortune. She then moved on to her grandfather, who had been an officer in the German army in the Second World War and had been executed by the Nazis for having taken part in the assassination plot against Hitler in Rastenberg, the famous "Von Stauffenberg Plot." His corpse had been hung from a meat hook. As for her, she suffered from a rare blood disease; each day she had to fight for her life. She was on a waiting list for a transplant—an experimental procedure based on stem-cells or something like that.

He stayed with the odd quartet for another two hours. When he got up to go, he could hardly walk. Just then, the bald man turned to him and said: "You look familiar. Do I know you from somewhere?"

Luckily, before Yannis could make the connection, Jack broke in, "Everyone knows everyone else in New York City," and poured his friend another cup of tea.

He was so drunk that Marie insisted she take him to his hotel, rather excited by the fact that she would escort a businessman from Los Angeles she'd just met, who was staying at the Chelsea Hotel. She seemed to be pretty willing to go upstairs with him, but he said goodnight and kissed her on both cheeks, giving an unambiguous sign that the evening was to end here. Even so, before going, she slipped a piece of paper into his pocket.

Once in his room, he collapsed on the bed and fell asleep right away, even though it was only seven in the evening, without having the time to assimilate in his memory any of the stories about New York he had heard a while ago.

He dreamed that he was walking alone on a totally deserted Seventh Avenue. Suddenly, he heard a sound behind him. Looking back, he saw a horse, the same gray horse that was being trained by Lance on Landy's farm, galloping towards him, right down the center of the street. He started running with all his strength, straight down the street—not turning, for some unfathomable reason, into any of the cross streets. The horse kept running after him down the length of Seventh Avenue and then, even lower down, to the southernmost point of Manhattan. Though he knew that the animal was much faster than he, the distance between them kept getting smaller but the horse never reached him. Fragments from his discussions with Landy floated in his brain: *The slow runner who is ahead always has a head start. So, whoever is chasing us, will never reach us. Unless, of course, we get killed during the race.*

They had by now reached the Brooklyn Bridge. There, under the steel cables, he stopped. The horse also stopped. They looked into each other's eyes. The animal seemed ready to jump on him. Suddenly, with a quick motion, he turned his back on it, climbed onto the railing and was suspended in the air above the waters of the East River. In front of him, he saw something awful. The Statue of Liberty was floating on its base, moving to the East. Suddenly, the statue came alive, blew out the torch, took off its crown and plunged its huge bulk into the river. The point where it lay, directly under the bridge, would be only a short swim. The huge feminine form floated on the water, on her back, with her arms crossed over her chest. Her features started to alter: the youthful, charming face to grow older, her body to shrink, and her tunic to change into a dress. A dress that was very familiar to him. Flowers started to grow on the fabric, spreading to her hair, to her chest, to her hands, everywhere. A sea of flowers covered the prone body. The eyes had started taking an even more frozen expression, the nose had curved, the lips had tightened, and the only thing that remained intact was the cold waxen beauty of the statue.

He turned back, looked once again at the horse, and then allowed himself to freefall into the river, into her watery embrace. She pulled him in and held him close to her. He sensed a familiar perfume, coming back from old times. Motherly.

He woke up shaking. It was still dark. With considerable effort, he managed to fall asleep again. But the dreams were not over. Whatever he had left behind had invaded his sleep and was crying for help.

"New York's not my home"

SUNDAY, OCTOBER 31, 2004

LAURA. Walking on the sidewalk of a small Midwestern town. It could be Hannibal. She is not walking normally. She is leaning twenty degrees to the right, like the Tower of Pisa. She is coming towards him. "Why are you walking like that?" he asks her. "Like what?" she answers, surprised. "You are leaning to the right." "Me? I'm leaning to the right? Are you crazy? Here, look how good my posture is." She walks in a circle around him, still leaning to the right, maybe even more than before. "Stop! Wait a moment. Let me straighten you," he says. He grabs her shoulders. Her body feels like rubber. He pulls her to the left and straightens her. "Walk now." Laura walks another circle, suddenly gets dizzy, and falls down. She lies on the sidewalk, crying. "You want to drive me crazy," she says.

This time he woke up at the crack of dawn. He hadn't even managed to shut the curtains the previous night. His head was splitting. Everything was spinning. He opened a bottle of wine from the minibar. The old familiar trick, from back when he used to drink a lot. He took a good swig of last night's drink. He recovered somewhat. Then he took a quick shower and turned on the television loudly. The news. The headlines.

> A new video message by Osama Bin Laden shakes both campaigns.
> President Bush promises the American people that he will not be challenged nor swayed, while Senator Kerry assures the nation that "we are committed to hunt down and eliminate Osama Bin Laden."
> The rhetoric about assigning blame for the ammunition lost in the Kakaa area intensifies.
> The two candidates continue their final swings through several States.
> Which State will decide the outcome of this presidential election? Is Ohio going to be the Florida of 2004?

After that, the screen was flooded with the commentaries of several spin-doctors. They took on each event, each statement, each action by a campaign, and with amazing eloquence they turned black into white in a couple of seconds. As if the American people could not figure out for themselves what was going on and needed a translation either from the red or the blue side. The polarization of the electorate was unprecedented. Nevertheless, given a certain distance, such as coming from a European perspective, and with a detailed analysis, one could see clearly that the differences amounted to no more than one mouth speaking in two languages, two dialects.s

As he was getting dressed, he felt a piece of paper falling out of his pocket. On it was Marie's name, along with a phone number. He stuck it in his wallet, in the coin pocket.

It was Sunday, October 31. The day he was supposed to meet "Slopeman," the "claimants." He logged onto the Net. There was another message from smada@aol.com.

By now you must be in NYC or, at least, be on
the way. I hope you've had a nice time in the
country with the babe and that she was up to
Jerry's standard! Man, Jerry has made me feel
twenty years younger! Given your history with
women, you need to watch out, right? What the
"reading" is should be clear. And the code for
the door is simple. I programmed your number at
the office. In the fridge there's food that may
interest you.

"With the babe?" He obviously meant Laura. And Jerry must be
his girlfriend or boyfriend? It seemed that Marcelo knew him or
her. The sender also seemed to knew Marcelo very well—maybe
from Los Angeles? "What the 'reading' is should be clear..." This
obviously referred to the book in the last frames of the video clip.
So there was no doubt—"smada" was the tenant of apartment sixteen, Adam Smith.

In spite of his lingering headache, he tried to concentrate. He
read the e-mail more closely and reassured himself: "smada" read
backwards—adams, Adam S., Adam Smith. It was almost certainly a pseudonym. And what about the e-mail's comment about his
office number? Could it be that Adam was a colleague of
Marcelo's? Was it perhaps that, together, they had discovered what
was hidden in the mysterious box? Or maybe Marcelo was simply
Adam's messenger? But how could he be, at the same time, also a
messenger for Doc? Suddenly a light went on in his brain! He
remembered something Marcelo had said in the car: "I'm playing
them all, big guy..." Playing whom? The "interested party," the
"claimants," possibly Adam as well? In the end, the matter seemed
to be even more complicated than he'd thought. A third player had
entered the game forcefully. The mysterious Mr. Smith. He had a
feeling that the "food" in the fridge would provide some useful
information.

He went down to the lobby and had two cups of strong coffee. He was oblivious to everything going on around him. As he recovered from his hangover, he got increasingly preoccupied with how to get into the apartment. Since he could not come up with a better idea, he walked the two blocks to the building again. This time, there was a black middle-aged woman at the desk, who seemed absorbed in a small TV set, watching a soap opera. He played the same role, with the same results, however, as on the day before.

"Mr. Smith is not here," said the woman. "I have no authority to let you in the apartment."

"Do you know how to get in touch with him? I have something important for him. I've been instructed to leave it in the apartment."

The woman's expression changed. A calculating smile slowly formed in her face. He noticed a large opal ring on her right hand. An imitation. It looked out of place on her.

"What is it? A present?"

He knew what to do then. The woman did not seem to be the brightest.

"Yes, a very important present. Where is Mr. Smith?"

"At his job, of course. In Los Angeles."

Los Angeles. Where Marcelo also used to work! His intuition was correct. Smith must have been one of Marcelo's colleagues from work. From MIN, the company that was impossible to track down.

"You wouldn't happen to have his address there?"

"No, Mr. Smith seldom comes here." The woman was looking at him speculatively. Her smile became wider. "What is it exactly that you need? Is the present from..." she asked and winked at him.

"Yes," he answered ambiguously.

"Ah, the blond lady?"

"Yes, the blond lady." He played along.

The woman now had a huge smile.

"You know, we've talked a few times. The poor girl has been very patient. He'd promised her that he'd ask for a divorce this year."

He grasped the situation immediately. Adam was probably married, worked in Los Angeles, and used the apartment as a place to meet the "blond lady." The woman at the desk seemed to be quite a gossip, and he only needed a few smiles and compliments to confirm his guess. Acting as if he knew much more about the illicit couple than her, he managed to confirm that Adam and the blond would meet at the apartment every two or three weeks, usually on weekends. The blond even stayed there some nights alone. "*Man, Jerry has made me feel twenty years younger!*" "Smada" had said in the last e-mail. This was the opening he'd been waiting for. He had to take the chance.

"But that's why I'm here. Jerry herself would have brought the gift, but something very urgent came up, and she'll be gone for a few days, so she asked me to drop it off... You know... To leave it for him in the apartment. Jerry really wanted Adam, Mr. Smith, to see it when he gets to the apartment. It's a surprise. Mr. Smith will be very happy. You'll be doing her a great favor, if you could let me in..."

The woman's face took on a happy expression, reassured that she was really speaking with somebody who knew the situation, but almost immediately her face darkened.

"Sir, only the tenant has the code..."

"Isn't it recorded someplace? If something were to happen and..."

She thought about it for a few moments, then leaned towards him and whispered:

"Every time the code is changed, it is automatically entered into the central security computer. But, you know, getting it from there... it's very difficult because, you understand..."

He opened his wallet and pulled out the corners of three fifty-dollar bills, making sure that she could see them. The woman may not have been very sharp, but understood immediately. Her eyes widened.

"From Jerry. Can you do it?" he said.

She checked all around to make sure they were alone. She leaned even closer to him and continued what she had started saying before, "...because, you must understand... there is monitoring and..."

He showed her three more bills. Fifties, again. The woman took a deep breath.

"Not today. There's a general inspection going on in the building. Fire alarms, elevator inspection, you know... Come tomorrow morning, between nine and ten. Bring only the gift, right? And to be clear with you, I'll have to search you before and after, okay?"

Now he checked all around and, before putting his wallet back in his pocket, slipped out the first three fifties and put them on the desk.

"Agreed. Tomorrow then, between nine and ten, and you'll get the rest," he said, giving her a conspiratorial wink, and turned to leave, while in the blink of an eye, the woman swept the banknotes off the top of the desk.

Back to the hotel. He had a few hours left before he had to leave for Brooklyn. He ordered a cup of coffee in his room, checked the news again. An endless stream of politicians, movie stars, and figures that combined both qualities in their persons, paraded on the screen. Flipping through the channels, he came across a religious network, where a preacher wearing a red cap kept repeating the question "Do you believe that Christ is dead?" Moving on, he checked out a game show, a horror film, and a toothpaste ad. Soon everything blurred into streaks of color on the screen, bunches of flickering pixels. He turned off the television and turned on the radio, a station playing classic rock. Jim Croce: "New York's Not My Home." "Troubadour of the city" he used to be called in his heyday. That is to say, a fugitive, wandering, lost in a place he hated, singing ballads about it.

He lay down on the bed, smoking. The outline of a plan. Gradually, piece by piece, a plan for an exit from the game was forming in his mind, like the last chapter of a novel, where the author is expected to unravel the various twists of the plot in which he has entangled the reader. But, he thought, in a novel, the information is given through the character, not the plot. And the character in this plot was, of course, himself. He was the hero in his own novel.

For a moment, he wondered how things would be when he'd start writing again. He had no answer to this question yet. The thing that was most important to him was to become somebody in the play of his own life. With Marcelo as the point of departure, to become *somebody*. Somebody different, but really himself. A contradiction? Maybe. Himself, but different. An amnesiac who remembers. Remembering in oblivion.

Memories. From the moment he'd set foot on this continent, memories had started to play a fugue of their own in his heart. He knew, better than anybody, that memory is our own exclusive, personal literature. We can rewrite the book, denounce the first draft's lack of maturity, never publish it. But above all, we can start writing a new one. And in his own book, the net of the chapters had gradually started stretching, and the words, the sentences, the paragraphs were now slipping through, dropping one by one into the pit of an old narrative. His literature did not have readers any more, and the only one left had gotten bored. He had grown bored going over the same pages, the same scenes again and again. He had grown tired of remembering.

Memory is what is left when something has happened but has not yet come to a conclusion. But he felt that his own "something" was, at this point, getting closer and closer to the end. He was returning to himself.

Laura again. Laura with Phoenix at the farm. Laura who would, at this moment, be trying to decide whether she would come and meet him in New York. Laura with a past that read like an ancient Greek tragedy. Laura with a past that was worse than an ancient Greek tragedy—because it was a real past: the life of a person, not a mask. Laura, strangely familiar, a sister in diversity, made of the same stuff—proof of a kinship that has no bounds, not geographic, or intellectual, or genetic, none of any kind. A kinship of love? Too easy. No, it was something deeper. A kinship of humanness. Yes. Struggling humanity. Everything that troubled him and everything he wished for.

Laura was, after all, herself. Laura-mind, Laura-soul, Laura-body, Laura-humor, Laura-tenderness, Laura-orgasm. Laura-defenseless child, Laura-wounded adolescent, Laura-fallen apart grown-up. Laura-white, Laura-American, Laura-preacher's daughter. Laura-activist, Laura-without a country, Laura-criminal's daughter. The species Laura. Saint Laura. The human being Laura.

For an instant, his hand reached for the phone. He changed his mind. He smoked two cigarettes. Then he dialed the number of her cell phone. Dead. But of course, it was stupid of him; there was no cell phone reception at the farm. There was only one phone. He knew the number, he had written it down. If he called, Landy would probably pick up, and he would ask for Laura. But not right away; first they would have a talk, the two of them. It wasn't easy for him. However, he dialed the first three numbers. Then, he hung up the phone. He tried again. Five numbers, this time. The third time, he managed to dial the whole number, but he hung up after the first ring.

He stayed in bed for another couple of hours. His thoughts moved from the farm to the box, to the "claimants"—Jimmy and whoever "Slopeman" was—to the "interested party," Doc. His imagination was composing a plan of its own volition. His imagination as creator. As creator of himself in the role of Marcelo. As creator of the "new" Marcelo.

That was what he had done after all. He had created a hero and had unleashed him in the middle of a foreign country, in the middle of a crazy pursuit. And he was letting him improvise. His hero who was not, of course, Marcelo, and also not himself, but rather himself "in the role of Marcelo." He himself "as" Marcelo, he himself "in his place." And the particular "as," the particular "in his place" were immensely powerful. In any case, if one really thought about it, this potential ghost, this "supposition," was basically responsible for the whole of human civilization. As the invented hero, but at the same time as the inventor, he was doubly responsible for the fate of his creation. How much more so when the hero was someone like Marcelo, someone who'd had the luxury of existing in flesh and blood.

If, however, this adventure had been one of his books, at what point in the story would his main character be? He knew from experience that a single tiny mistake is enough to change the fate of a character. How much more so when it is the basic action, the one that sets off the plot. He had no illusions. By now, he was certain. He had made the classic, typical mistake committed by so many heroes of so many stories. He had gotten involved in something that was beyond him. An attractive convention for the reader, but very dangerous for the hero. This admission was frightening. Or, rather, this recognition. A recognition of the true nature of the situation, as in an ancient Greek tragedy.

If he wanted, however, to propel the story forward, it was time to go to the meeting with "Slopeman." That was what his instinct told him, while the author within him, who could see a few pages ahead, was warning him about the danger. Perhaps it was that same inner voice that was quietly whispering all along to call everything off. To disappear. Somewhere outside the U.S.—Mexico, Canada, Venezuela—alone. Money he had enough. He would manage. Get a new start. A Marcelo killed twice. A third Marcelo in the skin of the second.

Sacrilege. You shoot the dead man and then you hang him, too. But, no, that is not enough for you. After that, you burn him. But even the dead have their limits, have rights even. And after all, there was also Laura to consider. So as this internal voice gradually weakened, the compromise with himself became milder, and the destination kept changing. Return to Iowa City. He had thought of that right from the start, back in Hannibal. There was still time; the program was due to end in mid-November. He could probably find some excuse. A personal crisis, falling madly in love, something... But what about the destroyed car? No, no, even if he managed to come up with some excuse, it would be a bitter defeat, a shameful return with his tail between his legs, a sad betrayal even of those memories, the dark possessions from which he struggled to escape. Just like the dead, repressed memory also has its dignity.

The next scenario excluded a return to the small Midwestern town and took him back, to the woods, to her. To Landyland. To love. Why not? Maybe he could work things out with Landy. But was this a real return? Did it justify this whole mess in which he had involved her? At some point, he would have to tell her everything, but what would he be able to tell her then? That he gave up at the last moment? And he had to consider that, if Doc's gang came back, it would be certain that Landy's rifle and Devdan's knife wouldn't be much of a defense.

No. Everything had been decided once and for all there, by the lake in the wilderness, with Marcelo. That was the central decision, the desire. And that desire required a struggle, a journey—it made them necessary. In the beginning, he was running "from," not running "towards" something. He was escaping from his past, but where to? To some other story, somebody else's story. Like an actor in an unfamiliar play, the words of which he did not even know. But the story, this play, had to end somewhere. Otherwise it would be self-destructive. And this, he had known intimately in the past. He knew what self-destruction meant. That was exactly what the life that had brought him to this world had done. It had extinguished itself.

No. Mistake or not, everything had to end here. Besides, there was no book of his where the hero, after overcoming all the conflicts and obstacles in his path, did not finally arrive at a solution. And, furthermore, he happened to be in America—the country of "happy endings." Terror, yes, he did feel that. But by now terror had become a pacing rhythm.

Final *act*, he told himself. *Time for action.* Had he really been Marcelo, he would have said: "*Vámonos.*" But he was not an American citizen of Spanish heritage. He was Greek. And he was not a corporate employee—he was a writer.

A mystery grows in Brooklyn

SUNDAY, OCTOBER 31, 2004

THE SUBWAY LINES—as was to be expected for such a city—were identified by numbers or letters. The one he needed was Line 1, which had a station close to the hotel, on the corner of Seventh Avenue and Twenty-Third Street. If he were to get on the train at that station, he would need to change over to a Line 2 two stops later, at the Fourteenth Street station. Then, ten stops later, he would be at Grand Army Plaza, in Brooklyn, which was only a short distance from Prospect Park, from where Second Street and the address he was looking for was just a five minute walk.

It was rush hour; the subway was packed with people. The train car was a multilingual sardine can, crammed with all sorts of people: Polish immigrants with clean, innocent faces; Chinese students with dragon tattoos; yuppies with unwrinkled suits heading to Wall Street and reading the financial pages of the newspaper; Catholic school children with glassy, unfocused eyes; Puerto Rican women with colorful dresses; Irishmen wearing T-shirts with four-leaf clovers, or the inscription "Saint Patrick Forever;" middle-aged Orthodox Jewish women whispering their prayers with their eyes shut.

An older black woman in a corner was talking to herself in French: "Dieu est clair et Dieu éclaire. Dieu éclaire en deux mots."[14] He thought of Landy. Ron-el Landy. Who renounced the "el": God. An atheist Jew. He knew that Landy had lived in New York, in the Village, for many years. In a city with a larger Jewish population than that of Jerusalem. Landy in the Jewish Mecca, Landy at the Anglo-Saxon synagogue, Landy in Landyland, Landy in America. A Palimpsest. A Russian doll. He looked around the car. A melting pot of nationalities, a tangle of dissimilarities, bound the city together with a thread of lost memory.

He changed trains. Several stations went by: Christopher Street, Franklin Street, Wall Street. Then the train continued without stopping for some time—it seemed they were crossing underneath the East River. Twenty minutes later, it reached Grand Army Plaza.

Outside, the wind was pretty strong. He was surprised by the new surroundings. It was as if he had suddenly been transported from the center of Athens—subterraneously—to the northern green suburbs. Low, two-story brick houses with shingle roofs, peace and quiet, tall well-cared-for trees, the streets covered with fallen leaves. If a word could describe this area, it would be tranquility. Second Street was only ten minutes away on foot, at the corner of Seventh Avenue, Brooklyn's Seventh Avenue. Number 322 was also a beautiful, old two-story house with a small courtyard in front and a few stairs leading to the front door. He climbed the five steps and examined the doorbell. There was a sign: "Ursula Tape - Ted V. Haas." Ursula Tape? Maybe "Slopeman" was a woman? He took a deep breath and rang.

It was indeed a woman who opened the door. Very tall, blond, with Nordic features. About forty-five, very pretty, the kind that had probably made a few heads turn in her life. She was wearing tight, dark blue pants with flared bottoms and a matching jacket.

"Mr. Diaz?"

"Yes."

"Ursula Tape. Please come in."

He entered a small hallway. Straight ahead was a wooden staircase leading to the second floor. The woman took his coat and hung it on the coat rack. They walked into the living room, which opened to the dining room and the kitchen. The furniture was eclectic: antiques tastefully mixed with modern pieces. A few select pictures on the walls, among them a copy of the well-known painting by Goya, featuring the executions. Next to it was an oil painting of a woman wearing a classical short mantle, seemingly addressing a crowd. The Greek word "Ευλογία"[15] was written underneath. A three-dimensional model of a brain was displayed on a bookcase shelf, with different colors representing each of its parts. The whole place looked more like the home of an intellectual couple than the gloomy office of some secret government agency, as he had imagined.

"My husband will be down in a moment. He was typing something up on the computer. You are going to speak with him. Coffee?" asked Ursula curtly.

He nodded "yes," and watched her as she went into the kitchen, noting her aristocratic air, her perfect posture, the ease of her movements.

They sat down at the black oblong dining table. Ursula started asking him about his impressions of New York, playing the role of a good hostess receiving some stranger who is visiting the city for the first time.

"The Guggenheim Museum is hosting a remarkable exhibition of the art of the Aztecs, really a must-see."

He could not make any sense of it. Was it possible he had come to the wrong address?

At least ten minutes went by this way, with Ursula monopolizing the conversation, which mainly centered on the fine arts, when a middle-aged man came down the stairs and into the dining room. He looked like an American version of Omar Sharif, sans moustache. Grey haired, tall, well-built. What immediately drew attention to him were his eyes. Huge, they dominated his face.

"Good afternoon, Mr. Diaz. I'm Ted. Ted Haas, you know me as 'Slopeman.' Would you please come upstairs with me to talk?"

As they were climbing the wooden staircase, he noticed some photographs framed on the walls. Ursula younger—just as he'd guessed, a real beauty—and Ted, younger—looking like a film star—Ted and Ursula in a recent picture with a strikingly handsome young boy, about thirteen years old. It all gave the impression that he had come into the house of a happy upper-middle class family. Ted directed him to a room that was covered wall-to-wall with bookcases. On the right, there was a desk. A large plasma TV stood by the window. Close to it was a large grandfather clock. A man, about fifty years old with sparse black hair, arched eyebrows, and a well-tended beard was sitting in an armchair. He was wearing round glasses, behind which clever-looking eyes sparkled. Before taking the seat that Ted offered him, he took a quick survey of the books on the nearby wall. *Middlemarch* by George Eliot, *Bleak House* by Dickens, the poems of Emily Dickinson, *The Plot Against America* by Roth, a number of books by Leo Strauss (one of the gurus of the American neo-conservative movement), two books by Sayyid Qutb, an Egyptian writer, a radical Islamist. On one of the shelves, a single leather-bound volume: *Education and the Social Order* by Bertrand Russell. He lingered there for a moment.

"You like Russell, Mr. Diaz?" asked Ted with a hint of surprise in his voice.

"Yes."

"Do you know General Russell?"

"Is he an author, too?"

"No, no..." answered his host, laughing, in turn surveying the shelves. "What do you think of Roth?"

"*The Human Stain* was a very good book."

"Don't you think he's somewhat of a misogynist?" asked Ted.

"No misogynist would ever describe Faunia Farley the way Roth did," answered the man with the glasses, in a pure Oxford British accent.

"This is my associate Andreas Mulish, Mr. Diaz."

"Pleased to meet you," he said.

Mulish smiled.

"I didn't expect you to be quite like this," said Ted.

"How did you expect me to be?"

"Mr. Smith had talked to me about somebody more... how shall I put it... more simple."

"I am a simple man, Mr. Haas."

"Mr. Smith seems to have known very well whom he was sending. Now, to the point," said Ted and sat comfortably on the couch, while he took a chair facing the two men. Maintaining his friendly tone, Ted got immediately to the heart of the matter.

"Marcelo, I hate introductions. To cut to the chase, we know what you're up to. We know that you're trying to sell the item to the other side. A fundamental mistake. When two powers want the same thing, that doesn't necessarily mean they are antagonists. One side may be able to protect it better. And we are that side. Naturally, there is always a certain prestige involved. Everyone wants to cross the finish line first. Oh, a few clashes may happen—nothing very serious, some punches thrown, things like that. We know you're playing your own game, independently of Mr. Smith, if that's his real name. Mr. Smith has received such a generous advance that I doubt very much he'll be willing to take any more risks. Naturally, the amount we've agreed on for the delivery is not small, right? But, of course, we know much more than that, Marcelo. We know about your wife, your kid, where they live, what they're doing. We know the company you work for, although it is invisible to almost everyone else. I have to tell you that, in some ways, it is also our company. However, what's most important, Marcelo, is that we know that you don't know what is inside the item."

"Sir, I'm here to listen to an offer. All the rest is of no interest to me."

"Look here, Marcelo," said Ted, taking a paternalistic tone and moving closer to him. "I come from a working family. My father worked his whole life in a factory. My mother did a thousand odd jobs, until, finally, she ended up working at the post office. My parents were Baptists. Now I belong to the Methodist Church. I believe all people are equal before God. I've worked from the age of fifteen, doing any kind of job you can imagine: at a garage, a carwash, an undergarment factory... It took me a while, but I did find my vocation in the end. And I devoted my life to the service of people like my parents. So that they may have better lives as American citizens. With equal opportunities. What I've devoted my life to now is to improve the lives of these people. You know, it is not a matter of Left or Right, nor of secular or religious doctrines, not even—to stretch things a bit—of capitalist or Marxist ideology. Since you seem to like philosophy, you've probably read Hegel? Point and counterpoint equal synthesis. So, how does all this fit with what's happening now? There is, shall we say, a crisis. The crisis needs management. You understand? Our country is going through a crisis, Marcelo. You can see that everywhere. The number one issue today—do you think it's the economy? No, it's security. Security is the prerequisite for a stable economy. Out there, there are forces that recruit uneducated people, turn them into fanatics, and then turn them out prepared to do anything. These people have no country, no philosophy; they only have hatred. That is why we have to be secure, at least inside our country. There are forces in this country that try to take advantage of all those things, use the news headlines to promote their own agenda. No matter how some people may try to use it, the problem is serious. In a secure America, everything is possible. Anything can be accomplished. I'm sure you'll agree with me on that, right?"

"I'm not sure why it's important whether I agree or not," he answered, wondering how the short speech he had just heard was relevant to the matter about which he had come.

"It *is* important, Marcelo. It's important for you to know that not only will you be paid for the service you'll do, but you'll also have done something for the good of your country. You don't know who I am, Marcelo—I don't have a name. I have a family, a position in society, but I don't have a 'name.' If, shall we say, after you leave here, you try to take some action against me, it will have no impact on me whatsoever. On the contrary, it will have an impact on you."

"I have no intention of doing anything like that, sir."

"To get back, then, to what we were talking about before, regarding the box, I'd like to ask you, please, to tell me what you think it contains."

"Something that has to do with... national security?" he said, adapting his answer to what Ted had just said.

"Something that has to do with the welfare of all of us. Something that should be delivered to us, because we know how to handle it."

"And who is this 'we'?"

Mulish, who had been all this time simply listening to the conversation, laughed out loud.

"The man has a sense of humor!"

Ted went on as if the question had not even been asked.

"Now, here's the offer. There won't be another. You should be perfectly clear on that. I assume you do have the item?"

"Of course. Naturally not with me."

"The 'reading material'?"

"I'll have it tomorrow."

"As you know very well, that is the final deadline. Tomorrow, then, Monday, you will deliver to us the item along with the 'reading material,' and you'll have the money deposited in your account immediately."

That is, in Marcelo's account, he thought instantly. He had prepared himself for that eventuality.

"In the e-mail, I had written to you about a final offer," Ted went on. "The difference, now, is that there will be a twenty percent bonus added to the original amount."

He reacted immediately.

"If there's no objection, I'd like to go over the account number again."

"That's fine," Ted said.

He got up and walked to the desk, rifled through a drawer, brought out a piece of paper and gave it to him. *Chase Manhattan Bank*. A couple of letters and ten numbers: LS 4009559660. He was lucky; it wasn't difficult. He grouped the numbers in his mind: 400-955-966-0. He looked at them long enough to memorize them.

"Is the account information correct?" Ted asked.

"Yes," he said, returning the piece of paper.

"Good! The exchange will take place in person, with a representative of ours, Jimmy. I believe you've met him. Jimmy will check the box to make sure that everything is okay and will execute, in your presence, the transfer of money to your account, and to that of Mr. Smith—we have all the information. There is a way—I'm sure you are aware of it—through the Internet, using a laptop. You can witness the transfer and then each one goes his own way. You have our assurance that you will be safe."

"Where will the meeting take place?" he asked, trying to repeat in his mind the account number.

"Times Square. On the corner of Broadway and Seventh Avenue. In front of the Marquee Theater. Six o'clock in the evening. Agreed?"

"Agreed. But my question hasn't been answered. Who are you?"

Mulish spoke. "Marcelo... You seem to be a smart man. Do you really want him to answer you?"

"Yes."

"You've known us right from the beginning as the 'claimants'," Ted said curtly. "And that's as far as we're willing to go."

"I have one more question. Since you are not rivals, as you said, then why did you eliminate Joshua?"

"Ah, you don't know about Joshua?"

"No."

Mulish broke out laughing again and said, "Well, he really does have quite a sense of humor."

Ted motioned to him as if to say: "Don't go any further."

"I think this matter doesn't concern us at the moment. See that you show up at the meeting. And one last thing: If the box happens to end up in the wrong hands... You do understand what's going to happen, right?"

He did not comment on that. He simply said, "I suppose that must be all."

"Yes. You seem to be a reasonable man. I was expecting a delivery boy, but I'm happy that somebody like you has come," said Ted and got up.

Mulish remained seated.

Ted shook his hand and showed him down to the entranceway. As they passed in front of the painting with the word "Ευλογία" the host remarked, "Eulogia: the goddess of eloquence."

Ursula was waiting with his coat in hand. When he came outside, he turned and saw them wishing him a warm goodbye, waving just like any ordinary couple would have done to bid farewell to a guest after a friendly dinner party. When they went inside and the front door shut, he took out a piece of paper and a pen and jotted down the details of the bank account.

He went back to Manhattan with a sense of foreboding. He did not go to the hotel; he wanted to kill some time. He didn't want to think, didn't want to complicate his thoughts any further. He went to a movie theater, to the first one he happened to walk in front of. The movie playing was *i ♡ Huckabees*. A crazy script, supposedly an existential comedy. Starring Dustin Hoffman. It reminded him of *Little Big Man*. The white man and the Indians.

He ate something at the closest pizzeria. Then he went to a bar in the Village and got drunk. Back in the hotel, he took a hot bath, watched some TV—a documentary on Lincoln's assassination—and went to sleep.

The same dream again? Not exactly. Yes, there was the horse chasing him again. Yes, they were going down Seventh Avenue and onto the Brooklyn Bridge. Yes, again, he climbed over the railing of the bridge and was suspended in mid-air. Yes, the Statue of Liberty came to life and plunged into the river. But, no, the statue did not transform itself into the woman who'd brought him into this world, but instead, into a colossal white whale that came swimming and puffing exactly underneath the spot where he was hovering, and with its huge tail slapped the water, which splashed high, all the way to the first skyscrapers. No, the horse did not stop. It went on chasing him—Zeno and his theory took a hike. The moment the horse lifted its front legs and prepared to charge him, he pulled an aluminum cable from the bridge structure. One end extruded a harpoon. He raised it, and with all his might hurled it at the whale. He hit it near its right eye. The huge animal started thrashing, leaping, struggling, and then it stopped and began sinking until it disappeared in the copper-green waters of the East River. He then turned and looked back. The horse was nowhere to be seen. Only a line of people, about ten of them, marching single file across the bridge as if in a parade. They were all there: his wife, his mother, Andreas, his grandmother—strange, he had never met her!—a dark-haired young girl from college, with whom he had once been in love. His own people, familiar people. They were passing before him, looking at him with joy. They blew him kisses. They made jokes. His father was the last one in line. He was different. Older, limping, holding a walking stick in his hand. They looked at each other. His eyes betrayed pain. He was hurting, his whole body shaking. He lifted his walking stick and saluted him, and then with great effort, he followed the others. A harpoon was stuck in his back.

The nightmare had turned into a comedy and then immediately turned back into a nightmare. At the same time, the night turned into day, and the sky of New York was lit up by a warm light. Music from up high: *Paper Moon*.

Books and numbers

MONDAY, NOVEMBER 1, 2004

A MORE RELAXED JOHN KERRY prepares himself for the big day. The Senator from Massachusetts finally abandons the serious persona that he presented throughout almost the whole electoral campaign period.

The television ad war, just for the last week of the campaign, reached a cost of sixty million dollars.

The latest statements of President Bush reflect the first: The world is a dangerous place, and Kerry is not in a position to guarantee the security of the American nation.

Senator Kerry responds: Bush created a dead end in Iraq, did not generate new employment opportunities for the middle class, did not support affordable health care—it is time for a new beginning.

Fears about the inadequacy of the electoral system, a replay of 2000?

America was ready for the next day. He was gambling everything for his own tomorrow. Right after he got up, he did two things. First, he logged onto the Internet and tried to make a purchase using his credit card number, the Greek one. To his great surprise he saw that it was still valid. Nobody in Greece had taken care of what should happen "after." After all, he hardly had anybody left who cared enough to take care of something like this.

He went out carrying the travel bag. It was cold. He stopped at a gift shop and bought something, a cheap trinket, asking for it to be gift-wrapped. He crossed to the other side of the street and reached the building on the Twentieth Street intersection. Through the glass doors, he saw the woman at the desk talking with two of the building's tenants. He waited for them to leave and then walked in. The woman smiled the moment she saw him. He approached and, surreptitiously, gave her the remaining three fifty dollar bills he had indirectly promised her during their previous meeting. In his other hand he was holding the small, nicely wrapped box, deliberately giving her a good look at it.

"Come this way, please," said the woman, directing him behind the desk. She led him to a corridor, which ended at an elevator door—obviously, a service elevator. Before letting him get in, she asked him to lift his arms and patted him from top to bottom, the way security guards do at the airports. Then they stepped into the elevator and the woman pressed the button for the fourteenth floor.

"What's in it?" asked the woman, indicating the box in an attempt to break the awkward silence.

"It's a surprise, a big surprise. Adam will be very pleased. Oh, and Jerry told me on the phone this morning to thank you very much for your help!"

As the elevator was going up, he noticed that the numbers jumped directly to fourteen after passing twelve. Officially, there was no thirteenth floor.

They walked along a rather narrow hallway, covered with wall-to-wall carpeting. When they reached number 16, the woman stopped.

"Look the other way," she said.

He turned his back and heard, after a few moments, the soft sounds made by the punching in of the security code on the door keypad.

"There you are. You've got three minutes."

He went into a small entrance hall. He immediately recognized it from the video clip. Opposite him, on the wall, there was the painting with the river. He turned to the right, to make sure. The same bright living room, with the couch and the television set. The glass wall with the blinds, the buildings across, the picture with the shark, and the folding screen. Everything was clean and in perfect order. He did not lose any time. To the left of the entrance, there was a small kitchen. The woman had stayed at the entrance and was keeping an eye on him, while, at the same time, scanning the hallway. He went straight to the refrigerator. A note pad with a shopping list was stuck on it with a magnet. Turning his back to the entryway, he read it. The list just had what one would expect—so many cartons of milk, so many yogurts, so many bottles of mineral water.

"But what are you doing? Where are you going to put the package?" he heard the woman saying.

"Just a moment, I am leaving a note for Adam," he answered while opening the fridge.

There were two bottles of champagne inside, wine and some cheese. On the bottom rack there was an envelope. Always keeping his back to the entryway, he took the envelope and quickly put it in his coat pocket.

"What's happening? Are you going to leave it in the fridge? What is it? Is it pastries?" the woman kept asking.

"No, I was just checking to see if Adam has everything he needs. You see, there's going to be a little party here. I'm going into the bedroom to leave it on the bed."

"Hurry up," her voice sounded very antsy.

He went out of the kitchen and quickly stepped into the bedroom. There was the desk with the laptop—what he would have given for a chance to turn it on! Next to it, the chessboard with the black knight still in the middle, the small piano and the bookcase. He still had a few seconds of privacy. The woman couldn't see into the bedroom from where she stood. He quickly looked through the books. It wasn't difficult; there weren't many. *Catcher in the Rye* was there, precisely where he had seen it on the video clip, between *Uncle Tom's Cabin* and *The Great Gatsby*. He pulled out the small volume and put it in his other coat pocket. Turning back to the bed, he left the gift-wrapped box on the pillow.

"That was it," he said, returning to the entryway.

The woman looked very anxious. She closed the door quickly and walked fast to the elevator. Downstairs in the lobby of the building, he bid her goodbye, repeating how important her help was and that Adam and Jerry would be grateful to her. The black woman flashed him a bright smile, obviously relieved that her small indiscretion had ended without any problem and, of course, not without reward. She was so relieved that she forgot to search him again, as she had warned him she'd do the day before.

On the way back to the hotel, he stopped at the bank and retrieved the box from the safety deposit. In the hotel lobby, before going up to his room, he was stopped by the receptionist with the round glasses. He had a message, a plain manila envelope. He opened it when he got up to his room.

You've already cost us a great deal. You know what I mean. Also, you've put others in harm's way. In Hannibal we'd settled on one-and-a-half mil in total, including Mr. S., on the basis of the agreement between us. We've lost touch with you, however, my friend, and we don't know any more what your game is. You missed the next alternate date. You understand very well that the final deadline is today. If you haven't gotten in touch with us by twelve noon to arrange a meeting, your family will only be you. Pity, because Candice worships the kid. And now, you understand, of course, we are really in contact with her... Next, it will be your turn. So be careful. You'll go to the booth on Seventh Ave. across from the hotel, and call 212-4... New York is not a good place to die.

The "interested party." Their message brought him face to face with a merciless reality, but for the moment he could not afford to think what he should do about them. He had Ted's meeting to think about; he had the box, and also the book. But he had one box, one book and two recipients. What could he do? The only positive fact was that, at least for now, box and book were in his hands and he had to try to piece them together. One way or another, he did not have much time at his disposal. In his pockets, he had two items that were burning him. First, he took out the book. It was a paperback edition with a gray cover. Somewhere in it must be the code that would unlock the box.

He opened it, expecting to find something inside: a post-it note, something written on one of the pages. He carefully went through the pages from beginning to end. There was nothing in any of the two hundred-some pages of the novel. There was no note, nothing written in the margin—just Salinger's text, untouched. He was looking for ten numbers, as many as were on the combination lock. Could it be that they were the first ten numbers appearing in the book? Yes, why hadn't he thought of that until now? He took a piece of paper and started noting. Already on page two an auspicious beginning—four numbers: "Since 1888, we have been molding boys into splendid, clear-thinking young men." 1888: the first four numbers. Three pages later, another three numbers showed up: "Route 204." He had already had seven! 1888204. He went on turning the pages. From page six on, however, it seemed that Salinger had abandoned numbers. He had to get to page 167, before a "4" appeared in a note by Phoebe, the hero's sister, in her book *Arithmetic Is Fun*: "Phoebe Weatherfield Caulfield 4B-I." He continued looking. Now he had eight numbers. There were only two left to be found. On page 208, "4B-I" was repeated. He now had nine: 188820444. Only one left to go. In the remaining pages, however, there were only letters, letters creating words, phrases, paragraphs, pages, the wonderful pages with which the author closed the book.

He came up with another idea right away: Could it be perhaps the first ten numbers Salinger spelled out? He started going through the text again from the beginning: "first," "first," "second," "two," "two," "two," "four," "one," "one," "two": 1122224112. He tried the number on the lock. It didn't work. Then he looked through the front matter pages, the copyright. The book had been first published in 1951; the specific edition was from 1979. There was the publisher's address: Penguin Books, 625 Madison Avenue, New York, New York 10022, USA, and the dates of additional editions. He was only looking for ten numbers. Could it perhaps be the address? In any case, when he arranged the digits, one after the other, he came up with 62510022—two figures less than he needed.

He had begun to get desperate. If he wasn't able to open the box, he would never manage to figure out what it was that set off this whole story. *Could it be that Adam had a certain surprise in store for me?* he wondered. He took the envelope out of his pocket and opened it. There was a simple eight-and-a half by eleven piece of paper with the following message:

```
My friend,
Now everything is in your hands. I know that
you are burning with curiosity, but we had to
be safe. A deal is a deal. By now, you know what
you should do. I'll check the account on the
evening of the delivery. I hope all goes well.
```

There is no phone number for me any more. I
don't even exist any more. Nor does the company, right? I've left the country with Jerry,
ever since the day I gave the box to you. The
journey of a lifetime—forever, you get my meaning. Beth is looking for me. She was also trying to find you, but my friend, you know nothing about her. You've never laid eyes on her.
You must disappear. Ours is a big country, but
you know with whom you are dealing... My
advice: Do the same. Get out, go to Thailand,
Venezuela, New Zealand. ASAP. On the same day,
if you can manage. Maybe some time, somewhere,
we will meet again.

Adios, amigo.

P.S. Once you've read this, destroy it.

He was still for a moment, looking down at the piece of paper.
He read it three times. His mind was relating, combining, decoding,
as in the good old days when he was setting up plots. The image
began to take shape. Adam and Marcelo had been working for the
same invisible "information technology" company, which could
have been any covert institution: for example, a secret government
agency. Adam finds—let's say accidentally—something.
Something that is of great value to certain people: those whom he
knows as the "claimants" and the "interested party." Something
that implicates one group—let's say the "IP"—which they would
go to any lengths to prevent from leaking out. If the "C's" are the
"IP's" opponents, and they have competing interests, then they
want to have it for opposite reasons. But according to the impression given by Ted, the interests of "C" could be in common with
those of "IP." In any case, one thing is certain. They are not collab-
orating. So Adam negotiates with one or the other side, or more

likely, with both sides. Either way, he makes some sort of agreement for delivery. Maybe with the one offering the most, or with both. Of course, he has received a substantial advance payment from the "claimants." There's no reason to doubt what Ted had said. It cannot be ruled out that he may have received such an advance from the "interested party" as well. The point is that he does not want to put himself in danger. He is clearly much higher placed in the invisible "company" than Marcelo; the apartment in downtown Manhattan indicates pretty deep pockets.

So Adam picks Marcelo, who, during the brief time they spent on the road, had given him the impression of being a simple lower level employee—someone who just happened to be at the right place at the right time, or maybe the exact opposite. Adam, covering his back, suggests to the deceased to take on the role of messenger—naturally for a cut of the proceeds. Marcelo, abandoned by wife and kid, going through a personal crisis, seemingly stuck at a dead end, accepts. Adam apparently gives him some money from the start and entrusts him with the delivery. The original date of delivery is, maybe not by accident, November first, the eve of the election. And the place: New York City. Evidently, Adam's agreement with "C" and "IP" was reached much earlier. For some reason, however, Adam does not agree to deliver the box right away, maybe because he's still trying to bargain or to gain time. Time to organize his escape, his disappearance. Meanwhile, he secures a hefty advance.

The point is that Marcelo has the box in his possession at least a month before the delivery date. He figures that this is a chance for him to rebuild his life. He has some weeks at his disposal, had already started exchanging e-mails with Laura—this woman had touched something in him. He decides to quit the company and, until the time comes to carry out the delivery, go and find her. He imagines, maybe, a new life of leisure together with her. He is a rather heavy drinker, somewhat of an adventurer, not a first class mind—an ideal person to undertake the dirty work Adam wants done. Marcelo, however, does not know what it is that he has to deliver. Adam—an assumed name, of course—has locked the "item" in a safe box and has hidden the combination in a book. The people to whom he is going to make the delivery know that they are going to receive the "item," safely sealed, along with the combination that unlocks the box. Of course, they have been told by Adam exactly where in the book it is hidden; otherwise, there is no sense in the delivery of the box along with the "reading material," as Ted had put it.

Marcelo is entrusted with the delivery of the box along with the book, without ever being told the code, without ever having seen the contents, although he has the box in his hands for quite some time. It appears, therefore, that the messenger decided, at some point, to play his own game. They have located him—both sides have demonstrated they have a very high level of access to information. Marcelo possibly senses that much more money is involved than what he's originally been promised, so he tries to set up his own deal. Of course, he is taking a major risk, which becomes apparent from the pursuit by Jimmy and his henchmen on the road to Chicago, and by the events in Landyland, and especially, by the trap at the meeting with Joshua.

But who eliminated Joshua—obviously one of Doc's men? At first, he thought it was "C." But today, in Brooklyn, they did not touch a hair on his head. According to what Ted had given him to understand, "C" and "IP" might want to possess the same thing, but they would never get into a direct interaction. Consequently, what could Joshua's role have been? Did he too want to profit from this affair? Why did he have to be eliminated? After all, "IP" had also shown they wouldn't hesitate to use violence. They'd been ready to kill Marcelo in Chicago, probably in Landyland as well. Could they really get rid of him right in the center of New York City? For the time being, he was kept safe by the box that nobody could open. But after?

Getting back to Adam, if everything he'd come up with in his analysis was true, Marcelo's "puppeteer" had not realized that his messenger was also playing his own game, trying, it seems, to increase his cut. The proof of that was the letter he'd found in the refrigerator. Adam had probably also secured a double advance up front, since he too seemed to have been playing both sides. So he had been able to vanish and was now waiting for the rest of the money to appear in his account as a bonus.

He lit a cigarette. Yes, the whole affair seemed—on the surface at least—plausible. Complicated, yes, maybe more convoluted than any plot he had ever come up with, but he felt that the scenario he had just created had a sound basis. Marcelo had probably scented gold, but did not know the nature of the treasure with which he'd been entrusted. He, however, was not Marcelo. He did not have Marcelo's mind; he had only taken on his identity, his mask. And what was after him, in fact, was not "C" nor "IP." It was something else entirely, something of another order of magnitude. It was that "Εγώ," the different one, the one written with an omicron, the "Εγό." In order to escape its cage, however, he needed to find a solution to the puzzle.

He took the book in his hands again. He was looking for numbers. Numbers. Figures. Devdan. The "World of Numbers." The "City of Numbers": New York. Where houses, buildings, streets, avenues are all figures. Where the whole city is an algorithmic allegory. However, what he was holding in his hands was a book. A book is not a number. It is a reality, often even more real than life—and that, he knew quite well, better than most. A book is a whole world. Nowadays, however, the whole world, the whole planet is codified, identified—starting from GPS down to the DNA molecule. Everything is now products. Products secured by the use of codes. Numbers that explain, classify, identify. We think that we choose, but it is others who choose on our behalf. Landy had said it all. The book, however? How does a book enter this chain? How is it described numerically? How is the book that captured the essence of postwar America codified?

Suddenly, he started smiling, then giggling nervously, and finally he burst into roaring laughter. Obviously, the simplest answer! Columbus's egg. He turned Salinger's book to the back cover. At the bottom was the code number, which, according to law, is obligatory for every book published—the ISBN code, the International Standard Book Number. The number that allows editors, libraries and bookstores to identify each book. Without it, it is as if a book does not exist. He read ISBN 0 -14 00-1248-6. That is 0140012486. He counted the figures. There were ten.

He applied the numbers, one by one, hastily, to the combination lock. His eagerness was such that after the number "four" he turned three of the little wheels to zero instead of two. The lock did not open. He tried again, forcing himself to calm and slow down. An imperceptible "click," and the steel bolt that fit inside the lengthy notch popped out. He raised the box's cover. The interior was filled with a styrofoam coating. But there was, in the middle, a crack through which the slim black back of a plastic object was visible. He put his hand in and pulled it out. It was a DVD case. He opened it. Inside there was a disc. It had no label or any other identifying mark on its surface.

He immediately turned on the computer and put in the DVD. Nothing. The disc was locked, the computer was asking for a code. He thought suddenly, *Could it be the same one—the ISBN?* He typed in the ten-digit code that opened the box, and almost instantly saw the Power DVD icon appearing on the screen. Almost shaking with excitement, he moved the cursor to PLAY and clicked.

Secrets, lies, and DVD

MONDAY, NOVEMBER 1, 2004

THE IMAGE WAS DARK, the room poorly lit. In the middle was a simple, long and narrow desk with a designer's studio lamp. The camera was placed somewhere high up, probably in the ceiling. It was fixed in position, clearly hidden. The single angle offered a "diving" shot, straight down from high up. Two men were sitting facing each other. The one on the right appeared in profile: he seemed to be about fifty, fifty-five, with angular features, short gray hair and a small mustache. He had seen him before. He remembered where and when: on television, the day of the debate, when he was channel surfing in Hannibal. It was the president of the multinational corporation who had been talking about consensus on NBC. The other was rather portly, a little older, bald, wearing glasses, with only a small part of his round face showing. Nothing else was shown in the frame. No other feature of the room appeared. The video began at some point in the middle of their conversation. The sound was of better quality than the picture. The angular man was talking:

"We've got unbelievable material. It can bury both of them. No mercy. There is, for example, the file on 'Brown Brothers' and 'Harriman.'"

"How far back does it go?"

"Way back, all the way to old Prescott Bush,[16] back to his investments in Germany. The 'Union Bank Corporation' is also in the game. We have all the details, my friend. Contacts with Reinhardt Gehlen, recorded tapes, everything..."

"And McCloy?"

"Bingo! There's a film dating from the time of the Berlin Olympic Games. He's sitting at the same stand with Adolf. There is also an interview of the time he was on the Warren Commission investigating the murder of JFK. He talks about everything, the editing of the film, everything. And texts by General Russell—the whole secret correspondence with Taft."

" William?"

"What are you talking about? With his father, Alfonso. And the whole Rockefeller affair. 'Lead better,' every-thing."

"Skull and Bones..."

"Skull and Bones."

"But the Senator is Skull and Bones, too."

"American democracy is Skull and Bones. Well, any dim-witted journalist can find most of this stuff just by googling. Everyone can write whatever he wants. But the evidence that I'm talking to you about is for once first-hand, alive, undeniable. Of course, this stuff is what hap-pened then. Okay, it's great for the historians, but it's only the hors-d'oeuvre."

"Right, it's ancient history. We are here and now."

"Skull and Bones of the twenty-first century. No cere-monies, no mysticisms. All that stuff is passé. This is the digital age. And, let me tell you, we've done first class work here."

"So, what exactly is the main course?"

"All the conversations about the company. A documentary of the agreement. The Vice-President overwhelmed with joy. His smiley-face is right up close. And it's a very good quality DVD. Top technology. And you know, he lays everything out in the open, about 'Halliburton,' everything. It's not some crazy kids writing about conspiracies on websites. No bloggers. It's solid evidence. Image and text. What really went on. Full disclosure—they let it all hang out. And the cherry on the cake, bribery of a journalist."

"Who, Tony?"

"Yes, Tony. The fat one from CNN."

"What have we got on the other side?"

"A blockbuster! Signing a secret agreement with the channels. The 'hero's' baby-doll with a toothpaste ad smile on her face. The signature laid out on the table. Just imagine it becoming public. We've got them both by their balls."

"Both parties... Just like that!"

"Both."

"Have you talked with them?"

"With both. They've signed their offers. 'Top Secret.' Look."

The guy pulls out two documents and waves them towards the other man. He then leaves them on the table. The camera zooms on the signatures. The two best known.

"$120,000,000 each..."

"What's in it for us?"

"What's in it? We have total control, right in our

hands. We choose the new one. We have chosen."

"The 'pilot'?"

"The 'pilot,' again. They offered a better deal. Reconstruction: we get the whole business. And the oil wells in the north. A letter has been sent to him from upstairs. It only contained a number: 322."

"Ah, Skull and Bones. We're talking to him in his own language, no?"

"Skull and Bones, yes. A skull has been sent to the 'hero'. Geronimo's skull."

"They gave it?"

"It's the greatest consolation prize that a member could ever receive. 'We respect the old traditions, we create the new ones.'"

"An Apache skull..."

"An Apache skull."

"How's it going to be done? With Ohio this time?"

"If the results go the other way, with Ohio. It's simple. The terminals are ready."

"And the 'hero'?"

"He'll quietly go home. The agreement specifies that next time it'll be the black one who'll be up. They'll ensure a sponsorship for our company starting from '08... neat business. One for you and one for me. He has already been advised."

"The black one? Well, I'll be damned... And not the 'first spouse?'"

"The black one. It's more 'PC' that way."

"What's in it for me personally?"

"Apart from your delight about all this, you're going to get an open-ended contract. Satellite communications for the entire U.S."

"That's perfect."

"Hey, big guy, is that yours?"

"What?"

"A pen down there to your right."

The portly man bends down to pick up the pen. His face turns towards the camera. A media mogul. Known to everybody. He looks at the pen.

"No, that's not mine, I have mine here somewhere."

The video clip ended at that point. There was also a folder. Scans of the signed agreements. That was all. He played the clip another three times. He had guessed wrong. The contents of the box did not incriminate one side or the other, the "claimants" *or* the "interested party." It incriminated both of them! And even more importantly, the "umbrella"—the whole system.

He lit a cigarette and sat there, smoking, looking at Vermeer's painting. Then he took out the map of New York City and marked the exact location of Times Square. He looked for some familiar place close to the square, and then for another one, further north.

Eleven years of silence

IN THE PHONE BOOTH ACROSS THE STREET, he dialed the number. Before he could say a word, he heard a hoarse male voice.

"Listen carefully. This afternoon, you'll go to..."

He immediately interrupted him.

"I'll tell you when and where."

"You got that wrong. You're not in a position..."

"Six thirty at Rockefeller Center. In front of the statue of Prometheus. I will have both the box and the code. See to it that you have the rest."

He hung up. After what he'd seen on the DVD, his mind had shifted to high gear. He had to hurry up. As if he had to deliver an article on deadline. However, there was still one piece missing from the puzzle. Unexpectedly—in the way those glorious moments appeared, like when he felt his writing suddenly dictated by some unknown power—an idea came to him. This time it really was *the* idea. He took out his wallet, found the piece of paper he was looking for, made a phone call, then another one, and arranged for a meeting in half an hour. He might have gotten very drunk that evening, but the relevant information had made such an impression on him that he remembered it.

Back from the meeting, with another two DVDs in the pocket of his coat, he walked towards Sixth Avenue. On the corner with Twenty-Second Street there was a huge department store. After spending at least half an hour on the floor with home goods, he finally managed to find a black box that was almost identical in appearance and size with the box he'd inherited from Marcelo. He also found Styrofoam lining, but they did not have anything like the ten-wheel combination lock, so they referred him to a specialized store three blocks away.

The closest bookstore, Barnes & Nobles, was five minutes away. It may well have been that *The Catcher in the Rye* was the Bible of American literature, but, probably precisely because of that, there were hundreds of re-printings. He was lucky, however. The specific Penguin Books edition of 1979 was still in stock. He checked the ISBN and bought the book.

He still wasn't ready, however. He found a men's clothing store and bought a pair of black corduroy pants, a thin light blue sweater, a black leather jacket, a pair of brown low boots, two white shirts, underwear and socks, and went back to his hotel room.

He turned on the laptop, went into the e-mail program and erased all the correspondence between Marcelo and Laura, along with all the e-mails he himself had received. Everything. Then he opened Marcelo's box, substituted the original disc with one of the two DVDs he had brought back, and locked it. He put the new Styrofoam lining in the box he had just bought, created an incision and placed the other DVD from his coat pocket in it. When he was done, he locked this second box with the new lock, setting the combination to the ISBN of *The Catcher in the Rye*.

He undressed and packed all of Marcelo's clothes and things in the suitcase. He left out only the clothes he had bought at the boutique, along with the dead man's passport and the envelope with the fifty eight thousand dollars that had been left from the initial one hundred and ten thousand. He placed the laptop on top of the suit-case together with two hundred dollar bills and a piece of paper on which he wrote:

> Please deliver to Mrs. Candice Diaz, wife of Marcelo Diaz. The money is for the shipping expenses.

Lower down, he wrote the address and phone number in Florida, the one he had gotten from directory assistance when he was staying at the farm. Finally, he sat at the desk and wrote a let-ter. Three pages long. That was for Candice, too.

When he was done, he put the two black boxes into his back-pack, the original and the new one that he'd assembled, along with the two books, the one from Adam's apartment and the one he had bought at the bookstore, and placed Marcelo's passport in the inner pocket of the leather jacket. He put the original DVD in a manila envelope, sealed it, and wrote an address on the cover. His hand was not steady. He was almost trembling. He was still afraid.

He went to the bathroom, filled the bathtub with hot water, got in and soaked for an hour. The green bathroom tiles were making him dizzy. A gloomy scenario of all the things that were about to happen passed before his eyes. He slid down the tub until his head was under the water and stayed submerged as long as he could bear it. For that brief time, he felt protected, hidden, as if in a warm mother's nest. He then dried off and studied himself in the mirror. For a long time, until his eyes hurt. There was no excuse any more. When you've got nothing, you've got nothing to lose.

He picked up the phone. He moved his right hand to the keypad. He pressed the first three numbers, 0-1-1, then the code for Greece, 3-0, then the one for Athens, 2-1-0... Then he stopped. After a while a loud beeping sound came from the receiver. He did not hang up. He surveyed the room. Chelsea Hotel. New York City. USA. His eyes rested successively on Marcelo's closed suitcase, the laptop and the backpack. Some time went by. He put the receiver down and lifted it up again. This time he dialed the whole number. After four sharp rings, he heard an aged male voice. For the first time in years.

"Yes?"

The connection was good, but the voice sounded far away, as if coming from the bottom of a well.

"It's me," he said.

He heard a sound, as if the phone had fallen out of the hands of the person on the other side. They talked for an hour and a half, which of course, was not enough to make up for eleven years of silence.

He looked at the clock in the room. It was ten to five. He dressed in the clothes he had bought and checked his new self in the mirror. Then he put on his leather jacket and backpack, went down to the reception desk, paid, faxed the three pages he had written to Candice's fax number, and exited onto the street, abandoning his whole past as Marcelo in the room of the Chelsea Hotel.

It was cold outside. Seventh Avenue was full of people. Behind him, someone had written on the wall with spray paint: "If you want to make a symbolic gesture, don't burn the flag. Wash it." He disappeared into the crowd.

The emperor of ice-cream

TIMES SQUARE: the din of thousands of people, lights. News headlines endlessly chasing each other on the illuminated board. "Tomorrow America elects its president." "A day of celebration for democracy." There was a man fifteen feet across from him, outside the Virgin Megastore. A homeless person. He was sitting on a blue bench, bent over. Blue jeans, a torn sweater fished out of the garbage. Boots with soles detached. He was holding a paper bag. Their eyes met. He felt something strange, as if the beggar was X-raying him. But he didn't have time for this kind of thing, even though he'd come early. He started to cross the street to the other side, toward the Marquee Theater. Then he changed his mind, walked a little ways up to the ABC building, turned and stood in front of Planet Hollywood. He took out a cigarette, took some nervous puffs and put it out. Out of the corner of his eye, he saw the beggar approaching.

"Hey, Mister!" he heard him call out.

He turned. The man was standing a couple of feet away and had taken the posture of an actor—his hands bent in front—and to his great surprise, started reciting:

Call the roller of big cigars,
The muscular one, and bid him whip
In kitchen cups concupiscent curds.
Let the wenches dawdle in such dress
As they are used to wear, and let the boys
Bring flowers in last month's newspapers.
Let be be finale of seem.
The only emperor is the emperor of ice cream.
Take from the dresser of deal,
Lacking the three glass knobs, that sheet
On which she embroidered fantails once
And spread it so as to cover her face.
If her horny feet protrude, they come
To show how cold she is, and dumb.
Let the lamp affix its beam.
The only emperor is the emperor of ice-cream.

The crowd went on by or stood indifferently before the dirty homeless man reciting poetry. He stood, too stunned to move, watching him.

"Wallace Stevens, 'The Emperor of Ice Cream'" he said, without thinking.

"Bravo! Mister, most people think that I just pull the stuff out of my head! Luther is my name. From Cleveland. I know more poems by heart than any professor of English literature."

He took out his wallet. He was in a hurry. But Luther, happy to have found at last someone who appreciated his art, started to chatter.

"They call me 'the Poet.' Look at this," he said and took a book out of his bag. "William Harmon: *The 100 Best Poems of the English Language*. I found it in the street. Twelve years ago. I've read it so many times, that now I know it by heart. In America, sir, in order to survive, you must have some sort of capital. Otherwise, you are a slave. My own capital is this book. I know it by heart.

Keats, Matthew Arnold, Whitman—everything by heart!"

He had no more time for talking. He pulled a fifty dollar bill out of his wallet and gave it to Luther. Before the beggar could recover from the surprise of the biggest "donation" he'd ever gotten in his life, he had crossed the street and started walking towards the Marquee Theater. He checked the time and lit one more cigarette.

His heart was beating faster. All around, throngs of people. As he took his last drag, he saw across from him a familiar silhouette, a short man with a chubby face, holding a blue briefcase. Jimmy. He checked all around. The guy seemed to have come alone. Jimmy came close to him and said rapidly, "Quickly, we have to get it over with in five minutes."

He opened the backpack, took out the black box and the book and handed them over. Jimmy opened the book to the first page, wrote down the number on a piece of paper, and handed it back. Then he entered the code into the locked box with quick movements. It opened and he took out the DVD.

"I check it, and we're finished," he said.

"Here?"

"The safest place."

Jimmy pulled out of his briefcase the smallest laptop he had ever seen in his life. He inserted the disc and turned his back to the wall of the Marquee Theater. He stayed there for three or four minutes. Lots of people passed in front of them, in waves. The latest news was running on the bright signboards. He was perspiring slightly. With his peripheral vision he saw Luther standing on the corner of the street. *Watching them, perhaps?* he thought, at the same moment that Jimmy turned towards him.

"Everything's okay. Now watch."

He bent down, closer to the tiny screen. Jimmy was entering a code on the web site of Chase Manhattan.

"Is it the one?"

He looked at the account number: LS 4009559660 and the name of the account holder: Marcelo Diaz.

"Yes," he answered.

Jimmy entered a six-figure amount. The same procedure was repeated with the account in Adam Smith's name. Double the amount.

"Okay?" Jimmy asked.

"Okay," he said.

Jimmy shut down the computer, put it back in his briefcase, and turned to go.

He was ready to go. He had decided beforehand, however, to ask: "I only have one question: What exactly was Joshua?"

Jimmy looked back at him searchingly.

"A bad employee," he answered with a half-smile.

An ambulance went by, siren wailing, horn blaring repeatedly. The cars pulled over to let it pass.

"Don't you want this?" he asked, indicating the box.

"No," said Jimmy and, giving him a friendly pat on the shoulder, walked away in the direction of the traffic light.

Point one: Times Square. The first part seemed to have ended without incident. He watched Jimmy walking away and disappearing in the crowd. Then he looked towards the spot where Luther had been. The beggar was not there. He took the black box in his hands and examined it for a few moments. All of a sudden he felt as if he had never seen it before. Without giving it any more thought, he threw it into a trash bin that stood in front of the theater's box office. Then he crossed to the other side of the street.

He walked east, towards Sixth Avenue—the Avenue of the Americas—and turned north. He tried to freeze all the myriad thoughts that fought to take over his brain—he had to stay focused. The only thing before him was Point Two: Rockefeller Center. When he reached it, he stopped, as if he didn't know where to go next. The complex John Rockefeller had bought in the 1920s was huge: it spanned the area between four streets and two avenues. He turned right on Forty-Eighth Street and started walking towards Rockefeller Plaza.

In front of the gilded statue of Prometheus, in the area below street level, the traditional winter season ice-skating rink had been set up. At this hour, it was full of people who were skating on the artificial ice. On the right, there was the recently set up "Republic Square," the communication center from which NBC was broadcasting news about the election. He walked up to the statue. There were only five or six Japanese tourists there, photographing everything. He looked at his watch. He was nine minutes early. He started to light another cigarette, but changed his mind. He walked towards the ice-skating rink, stayed there for a while, watching the skaters, returned to the statue, waited there for two or three minutes. Nobody. Finally, he decided to walk towards "Republic Square." Under a large white tent there was an exhibit with voting booths from various eras. Large screens were replaying historic moments of previous electoral campaigns. Also on display were a genuine copy of the Declaration of Independence, with the signatures of the Founding Fathers and other mementos of the history of the "Great Republic."

He did not stay there for long. Five minutes later, he walked out and went back to the statue. He sat down right in front of it and waited. Five or ten minutes went by. At twenty minutes to seven he heard a nasal voice behind him.

"Marcelo, I suppose?"

He turned around. The speaker was a tall, red-haired man with round glasses, wearing sweat pants and a sweatshirt with large pockets.

"Yes. You must be Doc?"

"Let's say I am. Actually, I should punch in your face, but we got much more important business to conduct."

He made a move to open the backpack. Doc grabbed his hand.

"Not here. We will go to the station, to the restrooms."

"But what about our agreement?"

"Don't overdo it," said Doc bluntly. "Follow me."

They walked together towards Forty-Eighth Street. When they

reached Park Avenue, they turned left. They continued on to Grand Central Station. Doc was checking him out from the corner of his eye. Neither spoke.

Inside the station, there was complete chaos. They took the stairs down and went straight to the men's restroom. Just outside the entrance, Doc turned towards him:

"You go in first. You leave it. I get in, I check it out, I come out, you get paid, and that's that."

They went into the restroom. Doc directed him to the last stall. He went inside, still carrying the backpack. He left the locked box and the book behind the toilet tank, waited for a couple of moments and walked out. Doc was standing right outside and went in at once after him. He went to the sink and washed his hands. Then he stood in a corner and waited. A few minutes later Doc came out of the stall. He also went to the sink and washed his hands. Then he approached him.

"Everything checks out," Doc said lowering his voice. "The package is waiting for you," and passed to him, in a flash, an even smaller computer, no bigger than a personal CD player.

He looked at the screen. Another six figure number at the web site of the same bank, in the same account of Marcelo Diaz.

"Click on NEXT," said Doc.

He clicked on it and saw the same site, only the account with Adam Smith's name. Adam was indeed playing both sides... Here too it was double the amount.

"Okay," he said and returned the device.

Doc put it in the pocket of his sweatshirt.

"And now, stay here for another five minutes, and then leave and forget you met me," he said, and left without a second glance behind him.

He stood for a little while in front of the mirror, looking at his image. Then he checked his watch and left two or three minutes later. Outside the station he felt dizzy. He stopped to catch his breath. Suddenly, he heard a voice behind him.

"Hey, Mister!" It was Luther.

"What is it, are you following me?" he said, annoyed.

"Busy, busy, huh?"

"Come on, man, I already gave to you before. Aren't you happy?"

"Oh, no. I'm very happy... But since you enjoyed Stevens so much, I thought you might like Shakespeare even better," said the beggar and started reciting:

That time of year thou mayst in me behold,
When yellow leaves, or none, or few do hang...

He interrupted. "That's enough, I don't have the time," he said, afraid he'd have to listen to the whole sonnet recited. He pulled a bill out of his wallet and pressed it into the beggar's hand. Luther was now richer by a hundred dollars in total. His eyes dropped for a moment to his open palm. Before he even realized it, his benefactor had vanished in the crowd and had taken off, almost running, to the north.

I know

AFTER HE GOT RID OF THE BEGGAR, he wondered for a moment what kind of omen this could be. A homeless man, who begs by reciting poetry. The hundred dollars he gave him were less than one eighth of a thousandth of what had been transferred in total to Marcelo's account—by "C" and "IP." It seems that out of the total of 3.3 million, one-third went to the courier, who had clearly managed to substantially increase his compensation. This money, as he'd explained to Marcelo's widow, could be collected by her. Candice and her child would be able to live a comfortable life, provided they disappeared ASAP, as he warned her in the fax he had sent, in which he gave Marcelo's account number and an e-mail address to contact him. He told Candice to let him know the address to which he should return her husband's passport, which he still needed for a time, for the final journey.

He went out on the street and hailed the first available taxi he came across. He gave the address: 229 West 43rd Street. In less than ten minutes, he was in front of the building that housed the *New York Times*. To the right of the main entrance, there were mailboxes where correspondence for the newspaper could be dropped off. He took out the manila envelope he had prepared at the hotel and dropped it in one of these. On the yellow paper he had written with a thick marker:

November 1, 2004
To be delivered at once to:
Editor-in-chief
The New York Times
CONFIDENTIAL MATERIAL
Extremely Urgent!

Inside was the original DVD from Marcelo's black box.

Mission accomplished. He took a deep breath. He had a few hours left until his plan could be brought to fruition. Only from now on, the outcome he sought depended exclusively on another person.

He found the nearest phone booth and called Laura on her cell. Silently he prayed to get a connection, which would mean that Laura was in New York. His prayer was granted.

"Yes?" he heard her voice.

He almost yelped in delight. Words started flowing out of his mouth uncontrollably. He told her he was done with that unfinished business once and for all. Now he was free, and he wanted to see her right away.

"I have a proposal for you, but before..."

"Tell me what the proposal is first," interrupted Laura.

"I'm done with that business, but now I have to leave the country. I'd like us to go to Greece together. I have plane tickets for Athens. The plane is leaving at 1:30 a.m. from JFK."

"Greece? Why?"

"I'll tell you when I see you."

"How many tickets do you have?"

"Two, one for you and one for me."

"We are not two," she answered and started explaining what she meant. She told him everything in detail, with the result that every few minutes, he had to drop another coin into the payphone slot.

On Saturday, she had gone with Phoenix to meet his adoptive parents in Syracuse. When she had first told him they needed to do that, Phoenix had reacted very badly. He was almost ready to run away again—from the farm, this time—but when she explained to him the reason, she managed to convince him. In the beginning, she found herself in the center of a psychodrama: the couple had been very distraught by his disappearance. When she heard what they had done in order to find him: all the resources they had mobilized, she was quite surprised that the kid had managed to hide for so long. The Conways, in the end, turned out to be good, simple people. A quiet, childless, religious, provincial couple that had really come to love the young boy. It took her five hours to convince them that the best thing for Phoenix would be for him to stay with her. She had dressed in the best clothes she could find at the farm. She had tried to give the impression of a stable, single woman with a boundless reserve of energy and love she would devote to raising the child. Indeed, at some point, Mrs. Conway started crying. Phoenix, through all this, sat in a corner and did not talk. The only thing he said right at the beginning, was "I won't come back here for anything in the world." In the end, the Conway family was convinced. The forty thousand dollars he had given her seemed to have also played a role in the acceptance of her proposal. The solution they came up with was simple. Considering that the adoption could not be easily undone, the Conway family would assign Laura custody of the boy. The reason would be "inability to provide proper care for the child due to the advanced age of the adoptive parents." A court hearing would be conducted as a formality, given the consent of all parties, and in a few months, Phoenix would be in Laura's custody officially, in full compliance with the law.

It was eleven at night when they left in the car lent to them by Landy, although he'd talked to her for a while, trying to convince her to stay at the farm. All of Phoenix's belongings were in the trunk of the car, and Laura had the boy's papers in her purse, along with all the contact information for the Conways' lawyer.

"Since you have his papers," he said, "there's no problem. If you accept my proposal, we'll get a ticket for him at the counter."

"If? What do you mean by if? I'm here, no? I'm coming with you."

"First there is something I have to tell you. Where are you now?"

"Somewhere in the Village."

"Get a cab and come to Central Park. To the entrance across from the Plaza Hotel. We need to be somewhere where there are a lot of people."

"What's going on?"

"It's something very important, and you need to know it before you decide to come with me."

There was a brief silence at the other end of the line, and then Laura said, "There's no need. I already know."

"What do you know?"

"What you want to tell me."

"You can't possibly…"

"I know that you are not Marcelo."

The phone almost fell out of his hand.

"How… do you know?"

"It doesn't matter. Let's talk, okay. But don't worry; I want to come with you. Who you really are is another matter."

He had not yet recovered from the surprise.

"I have to explain to you, though… Before we go, you must know the whole truth… In Central Park… Come as soon as you can."

After they both hung up, he remained frozen for several seconds. He was astounded.

The window, the aisle, and the emergency exit

HE WAS ABLE TO HAIL A CAB RIGHT AWAY, and in a very short time was at the entrance to the park. He checked the time on the big digital clock in a store window: 7:59 p.m.

At the entrance to Central Park there were, strangely enough, not many people: and a few tourists and a peddler who had set up a handcart with New York City souvenirs. He looked around. Laura, naturally, was not there yet.

He would be seeing her soon. Since, ultimately, Laura had known all along, then everything that had happened took on an entirely different significance. Laura, who never said anything to him about it, Laura who stayed with him, Laura who tolerated his theatrical performance, but more than anything else, Laura who, knowing the truth, had come to New York and was ready to leave with him for Greece. And Laura would also bring Phoenix along with her. The child they had found together, the child who had "dropped from the sky," or rather, who "sprang from the tree," one day when they were making love in an open meadow.

He stepped down the stairs and entered the park. Inside it was mayhem. Throngs of people, all races and all religions thrown together. White yuppies with running shoes and trained bodies, blacks with the polished skull of the twenty-first century in place of the afro of a bygone era, orthodox Jews with black hats, Muslim women with headscarves—the multi-colored merry-go-round of civilizations in a daily performance.

America, he thought. *A monstrous farce, a festival of the mad and the wise, a crusade with no Holy Land. America with its elections, its scandals, its empire, its liberty, its corruption, its morals. America with the colonists, with New England, the Indians, Devdan, the Civil War, with the murderer in Hannibal, with Hollywood, Howard Stern, Bush, Kerry, the "interested party," the "claimants," Landy. America with its obsessions, with its Ground Zero. America murdered from high up in the sky. America—a wounded wild animal. Laura's America.*

Laura's—who knew. Laura's—who must have known the truth right from the beginning. He remembered their first encounter, the first time he saw her. She was holding a gun in her hand. Her distress on the invasion of her house by a stranger was surely much greater than what she had felt when she realized that this stranger, who introduced himself as Marcelo, was not the man she was expecting. "No photos" she had written in her e-mail. Yes. Maybe, however, Marcelo had sent her some of himself anyway. Perhaps she realized it sometime later; perhaps she knew it from the start. And possibly she went on watching him closely, studying him, getting to know him, falling in love with him, not as Marcelo, but as himself.

He had come to America to forget. He had not managed to do it by himself. He'd had to take somebody else's place. This was a serious infraction, but there was no other way. During the time he stayed there, he lived through things he could never in his life have dreamed of. It was not a journey of forgetting. It was one of rebirth. Orpheus went down into Hades under the condition that he could never look behind him. He, however, had turned and looked. And he had seen the past, as a landscape bathed in sunlight where souls no longer grieve. All those who have wandered were tired, and their sufferings by now had ceased. The great machine of life, however, went on, unforgiving and eternal. The wheels continued to move according to their own rhythm, and this time they were bringing him back, with a woman he loved, a child, and the memories of an unbelievable adventure, which, perhaps, was not over yet. Nevertheless, he himself had also applied a bit of the oil greasing the spring that moved his destiny.

At one point in his life, he knew within himself what precisely his role would be on this earth. He felt certain that it would be realized. At some point he came out and announced it. And somebody killed it for him. Now, this consciousness was awakened again, and when some day he would die, he would not die of death—he would die having lived.

In Greece, however, he was already dead. How should he account for his sudden "resurrection?" His mind started putting together various scenarios. He was on the third one, when he felt tired. He took out his pack and told himself that this would be the last one.

For a moment, he thought of Marie, the woman he had met that drunken evening. He remembered her surprise a few hours before, when, on the phone, she heard him asking for Yannis's telephone number, her friend from Princeton, who had invented and held the patent of the self-destructing DVD. Then, the surprise of Yannis himself, when he heard him speak in Greek. He had asked him for two blank DVDs. Five thousand dollars was a tidy profit for a quarter of an hour's work. Yannis (without, of course, looking at the contents) had copied Marcelo's original disc onto them and applied the ten-figure pass-code. This was a unique patent that had not yet been used commercially. The first time each disk would be played on a device would also be the last one, without the user knowing this. The "claimants" and "interested party" now had in their hands only burned clean little round discs of no value and with no recoverable content.

The game was savage. He was still wondering how he had found himself caught up in it. A ruthless game in a ruthless country. A country that does not forgive. A country melting-pot, that sucks in everything and runs like crazy without knowing where. The entire country a gigantic experiment, a gigantic mistake.

The beginning of the century was finding America stretched to its limits. Maybe the real American had not arrived yet. When he would come some day, he would be an amalgam of all races, all religions, all political systems. A palimpsest with no memory, no roots. And this would mean one of two things: either the end, or the beginning of the end. It would be something that he wouldn't want to witness. In any case, Marcelo's mission had ended. His own was only starting. Marcelo was an American, and in the life of an American there is no second act. He, however, was Greek, which meant a life in three acts and catharsis in the end.

In front of him on a bench, he saw a newspaper. "Tomorrow: Democracy's Big Day." But for now, the night had just thrown its veil over the city—the biggest night of his life.

He was not yet forty years old and his mother was dead. She had taken her own life. *Her* life. His father was alive. He was sick, very sick, but still alive. His father was certainly guilty, but how long would he be able to keep being angry with him? For how much longer would he continue his revenge? They would be on speaking terms again. And this was something that during the last ten years had never even entered his mind. This is what he had come to understand. That the wound was not an attack against himself—it *was* himself. If he erased it, by succeeding in his revenge, he would not be himself any more. They would speak again. As for his wife, she had left him. *She* had left him. They had gone through the pages of one another, page by page, through to the last one. The book had been read; it had been finished; it had been pulped.

He would come back from the void, filling it up with something. Back, back, to the same, to the different. With another vision. With other eyes. Yes. Something is on its way. Another way to see.

To see or not to see. This, finally, is the question. He imagined the two phrases in print. Life is nothing more than a torn cloth that enfolds us, from first cry to death rattle. It was his job to look through himself and to express this spirit as honestly as he could. Yes, when he was back, he would write. He would write again. But not thrillers. He had at this point his fill of adventure. That vehicle was not necessary to him any more—he would remove it from circulation.

He was a writer. That is, the window, and the aisle, and the emergency exit.

That which comes after

THE WEATHER WAS RELATIVELY GOOD. Some people were having a picnic in front of the statues of Simon Bolivar and José de San Martin. There was a huge moon that illuminated everything. He felt its rays washing over him. To his right, some young people were throwing a frisbee around a colonial style rustic little wooden house. To the left, in a large playground, dozens of little kids were playing on the swings, teeter-totters and slides, while others were jumping around and chasing each other around a fountain. Sounds of joy filled the area. He climbed a small mound from where he could see the entrance, but also the area immediately below. There was a strange smell in the air, a smell of civilization mixed with nature, of the invented and the primeval. And a distant murmur, which seemed to be coming down from the tall oak trees.

It was now eight twenty. The sun had set some time ago. Night had driven away the day, and the park was a map: a map of the moment, the city, cities, the whole world. Suddenly, something flashed in his mind. The light of Greece came to his mind—black and brilliant at the same time—a stone-paved street, the Caldera of Santorini, an orange tree, a little church, the smell of burnt fir tree, a blue ribbon tied to a small bucket, a flagstone-paved courtyard, two people, the conflict, the fear, the forgiveness. He drew the last puff. The smoke thinned out, traveled in a spiral shooting tendrils that followed the sky's tracks and climbed high as a memory.

As he was about to stomp on the cigarette butt, his eye fell on a tall bush next to the fountain. The way it was illuminated by the moon, it resembled a face looking straight up to the sky. He started walking towards it without knowing why. The image of an older man with an oval face, arched eyebrows, drooping eyelids, a thin mustache, and ever so slightly powdered cheeks was coming to mind. Just then, a squirrel ran out in front of him. As he approached, the squirrel paused at that same spot, motionless, as if hypnotized, unexpectedly fearless. He was only five or six feet away from it when, from behind the bush, he heard a child's voice:

"Hey. Come here! Come here!"

The squirrel lowered its front legs and ran away very fast to the north. At the same moment, about fifty yards away straight ahead of him, a little blond head appeared from behind the bush. His face had strong features, big playful eyes, and freckles on his cheeks. He wore new, well-ironed clothes.

The child stopped and stood looking at him. He did the same. Before either one could say a word, a woman's voice called out, "Phoenix!"

The woman came out from behind the bush. She was dressed in simple jeans and a white sweater. It was Laura. Her hair had started to grow longer.

Everything was finally coming to an end. This chapter was closing. In a few hours they would be in an airplane that would bring them back. He had made it. Yes, America, the country of the "happy ending."

He started walking towards them. He was among the trees, surrounded by people, with the seconds, the minutes swirling around him like the autumn leaves that were falling from the trees in waves, leaving their trunks naked, as a slight breeze caressed the landscape. Everything looked transparent, as if an invisible rain shower had washed it clean.

And, suddenly, he felt it. First it was a sharp pain in the back, and at once a terrible jolt of the spinal cord. A hot wave traveled instantly through his whole body. At the same time, everything around him started growing dark. Within less than a second, he felt another piercing pain, this time in his neck, even more acute. Without thinking, he turned around. He could not make out anything, anybody. Sounds started to be muffled, and his mouth filled with liquid. The trees around him looked as if they were bending, as if they were holding their branches up with difficulty in a sky that was being split from within. Everything fluttered, darkness spreading like mist. The air was carrying the city's smells: human, foreign, unbearable. He felt himself falling. It was a slow fall, almost pleasurable. Mixed sounds journeyed through space and danced in his ears. Among them, a child's voice. Phoenix's. Lying on the ground he saw the faces of strangers over him. He tried to bring into focus the images made luminous by the moon. His eyes did not respond. He felt a hand touching him. Then a face coming close. A blond head. Hers. Laura bent down and took him in her arms, while all around, unfamiliar voices seemed to be chasing one another. Her lips were close to his. He smelled something vaguely familiar, but the perfume started to dissolve like smoke.

As the faces around him were starting to melt and the darkness grew denser, he saw himself pushing open a way through the shadows and approaching a line of people, who in single file, were walking across a bridge as if in a parade, and one after another were dropping into the water. They were all relatives of his. When the last of them, the one with the harpoon in his back, fell, the scene was lit up for a moment. Everything slowed down, as if the earth was condemned to stop. In the far distance, at the limit of his sight, a meadow appeared, just like those he had crossed when he traveled across America. Only it was a little darker, a little warmer, a little dryer. In the center, a heap of crops was burning. From high up, in the cloudy sky, the image of his mother began to fade away, and

Laura's face returned in light on shadow, shadow on light. When the flames shot up, with great effort, he moved his face closer to her and whispered his name to her.

His real name.

He fell back and Laura bent over him. He saw the pupil of her eye growing larger and in it, as if in a Flemish mirror, he saw Marcelo's face, crowned with a marigold garland, smiling at him. For a moment, everything was revealed. Lying on the green grass of Central Park, with a bullet in his back and another in his throat, he learned finally and for all time who he was. "Why? Why now?" he heard himself whispering through a crack of his soul. A whisper full of dust, that turned against him like a whirlwind of incomprehension. From someplace far away, he heard an answer that floated around him and disintegrated in the exhausted air. Everything darkened, as at last, his memory departed. His heart fluttered softly and stopped, surrendering its beat to the night.

The last image in his mind was the ideogram on her neck fading away, until all sound retreated, the light withdrew, the sense of taste dissolved and began—following the laws of a world impossible for us to know—that which comes after.

Afterword

LATE, ON THAT SAME NIGHT OF MONDAY, November 1, 2004, at the *New York Times* headquarters, an extraordinary meeting took place that lasted four hours. The five top staff-members of the paper took part in it. The result was that the controversial DVD was locked in a special safe-deposit box in the newspaper's vault, with the prospect of being opened again after twenty years. The newspaper, until this day, has published nothing related to its contents.

On the next day, Tuesday, November 2, 2004, George W. Bush won the American presidential elections.

Notes

1. Vieu(x) (French) = old

2. This city can swallow you up.

3. You are a clever guy. You're going to have problems

4. Walter Lippmann (1889-1974): Famous columnist of the Herald Tribune

5. The opening sentence of Salman Rushdie's Satanic Verses.

6. By the Greek poet Andreas Kalvos: "Tenth Ode." Motherland's Altar, ί', 48-49

7. The Weathermen were a group of the Radical Left made up of splintered-off members and leaders of the Students for a Democratic Society (SDS), which formed on the campus on the University of Michigan in the 1960s. The group referred to itself as a revolutionary organization of women and men whose purpose was to carry out a series of attacks that would achieve

the overthrow of the government of the United States. During the period 1969-1976, its members carried out a series of bombings and organized a number of violent riots. (Author's note)

8. Fuck it!

9. Edward Hopper (1882-1967): The most famous realist American painter of the inter-war period. (Author's note)

10. City in the Garden

11. The actual quote, from an un-named senior advisor to the President, first appeared in an article by Ron Suskind: "Faith, Certainty, and the Presidency of George W. Bush." *New York Times*, Magazine Supplement, Oct. 17, 2004.

12. The Jewish term for the Holocaust. "There is no business like Shoah business" is a phrase coined by the Jewish historian Yaffa Eliach. (Author's note)

13. A verse from *Everyman*, a British morality play of the end of the 15th century. (Author's note)

14. "God is clear and God enlightens. God enlightens in two words" is a wordplay based on the pronunciation of the words "est clair" (i.e., "is clear") that is identical with that of "éclaire" (i.e., "enlightens").

15. The word "Ευλογία" in Greek means both "blessing" and "speaking well."

16. References in the dialogue on the video include the following:

- Prescott Bush: Father of George H. Bush and grandfather of President George W. Bush.

- Reinhardt Gehlen (1902-1979): The most important Nazi to work for the USA. When the defeat of Germany became apparent, Gehlen, then director of German military intelligence, offered to help the USA. Later, he helped in the development of American strategy during the Cold War.

- John J. McCloy (1895-1989): Secretary of War in 1941, later President of the World Bank. President of the Ford Foundation and of Chase Manhattan Bank.

- William Huntington Russell: Founder of the Skull and Bones Order along with Alfonso Taft.

- William Taft (1857-1930): Twenty-fourth President of the USA (1909-1913).

- Alfonso Taft: One of the two founders of the secret organization Skull and Bones (1832). Father of President William Taft.

- Skull and Bones is a secret society at Yale University. Among its members were President Bush and Senator Kerry. It is believed by some to "govern" America.

- 322: The secret number of Skull and Bones.

About the Author

ALEXIS STAMATIS IS THE AUTHOR OF FOURTEEN BOOKS: eight novels and novellas as well as six collections of poetry. Among his fourteen books are his most well-known novels: *The Seventh Elephant* (1998), *Bar Flaubert* (2000), *Ash Mother* (2005), and *Villa Combray* (2008). Stamatis's work appears in many leading Greek magazines and newspapers; recent reviews and interviews with the author regarding the new novel, American Fugue, appear in venues such as *Vogue* (Greece), the literary magazine *Diavazo*, and *Athens Voice*. Reviews of Stamatis's translated novels have appeared in distinguished publications such as *The Guardian* (U.K.) and *Le Monde* (France). Stamatis received his education in Greece and the U.K., at the Greek National University, the National Technical University of Athens (Architecture), the Architectural Association School of Architecture (Graduate School) in London, and the Polytechnic of Central London, for a post graduate diploma in Film and TV Studies. Stamatis is one of the best of a new generation of Greek writers; *American Fugue* is an exciting example of this international quality, with a Greek protagonist who visits America, travels across the country, and has a strange and compelling adventure.

About the Translators

DIANE THIEL IS THE AUTHOR OF SEVEN BOOKS OF POETRY, nonfiction and and creative writing pedagogy including *Echolocations* (Nicholas Roerich Prize,) *The White Horse: A Colombian Journey*, *Resistance Fantasies*, *Crossroads: Creative Writing Exercises in Four Genres*, and *Winding Roads: Exercises in Writing Creative Nonfiction*. Thiel's translation of Stamatis's American Fugue received a 2007 NEA International Literature Award in conjunction with co-translator Constantine Hadjilambrinos and Etruscan Press. Thiel's work appears in many journals including *Poetry*, *Best American Poetry 1999*, *The Sewanee Review*, and is re-printed in over 40 major anthologies. She received her undergraduate and graduate degrees from Brown University. A recipient of numerous awards, including the Robert Frost and Robinson Jeffers Awards, and a recent Fulbright Scholar, she is Associate Professor at the University of New Mexico. For more information, please visit her webpage: www.dianethiel.net

CONSTANTINE HADJILAMBRINOS, A GREEK NATIVE, received his PhD in Public Policy from the University of Delaware in 1993, and his articles on energy and environmental policy have appeared widely. His co-translation (with his wife, Diane Thiel) of Alexis Stamatis's *American Fugue* into English received a 2007 NEA International Literature Award, in conjunction with Etruscan Press. He is Associate Professor of Public Administration and Political Science at the University of New Mexico.

BOOKS FROM ETRUSCAN PRESS

Drift Ice | Jennifer Atkinson

The Widening | Carol Moldaw

Parallel Lives | Michael Lind

God Bless: A Political/Poetic Discourse | H. L. Hix

Chromatic | H. L. Hix (National Book Award finalist)

The Confessions of Doc Williams & Other Poems | William Heyen

Art into Life | Frederick R. Karl

Shadows of Houses | H. L. Hix

The White Horse: A Colombian Journey | Diane Thiel

Wild and Whirling Words: A Poetic Conversation | H. L. Hix

Shoah Train | William Heyen (National Book Award finalist)

Crow Man | Tom Bailey

As Easy As Lying: Essay s on Poetry | H. L. Hix

Cinder | Bruce Bond

Free Concert: New and Selected Poems | Milton Kessler

September 11, 2001: American Writers Respond | William Heyen

etruscan press

www.etruscanpress.org

Etruscan Press books may be ordered from:

Consortium Book Sales and Distribution
800-283-3572
www.cbsd.com

Small Press Distribution
800-869-7553
www.spdbooks.com

Disability and Spirituality

Recovering Wholeness

William C. Gaventa

BAYLOR UNIVERSITY PRESS

Cover design by Rebecca Lown
Cover art: Rachel Gadsden, detail from *Station 12: Christ Dies on the Cross*, Stations of the Cross Commission for St. Joseph's Cathedral Abu Dhabi.

Library of Congress Cataloging-in-Publication Data

Names: Gaventa, William C., author.
Title: Disability and spirituality : recovering wholeness / William Gaventa.
Description: Waco, Texas : Baylor University Press, [2018] I Series: Studies in religion, theology, and disability / series editors, Sarah J. Melcher and Amos Yong I Includes bibliographical references and index.
Identifiers: LCCN 2017034337 (print) I LCCN 2017047921 (ebook) I ISBN 9781481308007 (web PDF) I ISBN 9781481307994 (ebook: Mobi/Kindle) I ISBN 9781481302791 (pbk. : alk. paper)
Subjects: LCSH: People with disabilities—Religious life. I People with disabilities—Religious aspects.
Classification: LCC BV4910 (ebook) I LCC BV4910 .G38 2018 (print) I DDC 248.8/64—dc23